By J. J. McAvoy

Aphrodite *and* the Duke

Aphrodite *and* the Duke

A Novel

J. J. McAvoy

Dell | New York

A Dell Trade Paperback Original

Copyright © 2022 by J. J. McAvoy

Published in the United States by Dell, an imprint of Random House, a division of Penguin Random House LLC, New York.

DELL is a registered trademark and the D colophon is a trademark of Penguin Random House LLC.

LIBRARY OF CONGRESS CATALOGING-IN-PUBLICATION DATA
Names: McAvoy, J. J., author.
Title: Aphrodite and the duke: a novel / J.J. McAvoy.
Description: New York: Dell Books, [2022]
Identifiers: LCCN 2022003007 (print) | LCCN 2022003008 (ebook) |
ISBN 9780593500040 (trade paperback; acid-free paper) |
ISBN 9780593500057(ebook)
Subjects: LCGFT: Romance fiction. | Novels.
Classification: LCC PR9199.4.M386 A86 2022 (print) |
LCC PR9199.4.M386 (ebook) | DDC 813/.6—dc23/eng/20220208
LC record available at https://lccn.loc.gov/2022003007
LC ebook record available at https://lccn.loc.gov/2022003008

Printed in the United States of America on acid-free paper

randomhousebooks.com

2 4 6 8 9 7 5 3 1

Book design by Virginia Norey

Dedicated to
the women like me
who wanted more stories like this

Beloved Reader,

This is a Regency romance involving nobility and high society, in which there are Black people. This is fiction, and anything is possible here. I truly hope you enjoy it.

Sincerely,
Your Author

PART ONE

I

Aphrodite

My name is Aphrodite Du Bell.

Yes, truly. Aphrodite, as in the goddess of love and beauty. A name wholly magnificent, yet, to my mind, utterly cruel to give a child, for who could live up to such a grandiose mantle? Was it not daring all the world to measure a young lady's beauty not against her peers but against a goddess? If she did not meet the measure, she would be left to ridicule and mockery. Should she be blessed with extraordinary beauty, she would be cursed with the expectation of magnificence. Failing to meet that expectation would *also* herald ridicule and mockery. It is an unforgiving name, and I believed it was fated to bring forth some great tragedy, just as in the myths.

For all the stars in the sky, I could not fathom why Father and Mother had given me this burden. Even upon asking them, they had no remorse for their actions and thought themselves quite clever. So much so, they proceeded to name my three younger sisters after goddesses as well, though they were more fortunate than I with their names—Hathor, Devana, and Abena. If you were not as scholarly as my father— who had taught much to my mother in terms of Egyptian, Slavic, and West African mythology—you might be utterly unaware that those were the names of deities. So my sisters' burdens did not equal my own. And my two brothers, named after heroes, Damon and Hector, made off quite easily as well, though they were men, and such were their lives.

We were the six children of Lord Charles Du Bell, the Marquess of Monthermer, and Lady Deanna. To all the world that mattered, we were among the most prominent families, fortunate with title, wealth, wit, beauty, and of course, a loving home, which was Belclere Castle. With the exception of my elder brother, not one ill word could have been uttered about any one of us . . . until certain events came about in my life. After years of running away I was now in a carriage on my way back to London society.

"The man is a fiend, a wolf among men just like his father was," my dear brother Damon complained.

"Careful, my dear, you shall wake her," his soft-spoken new wife, Silva, said in reply, believing I had somehow managed to fall asleep. I could feel the pressure of their gaze upon me.

"We have only just succeeded in convincing her to return," my brother whispered. Damon had many talents, but holding his tongue was never one of them. "Now sister's letter says that beast will also return to London this season."

They were speaking of *him*. Rather than betray any inner workings of my mind or heart, I kept my eyes closed.

"It is to be expected. Does he not have a sister due to come out as well?" Silva asked.

It *was* to be expected. As our sister Hathor and his sister, Verity, had now come of age, at eighteen.

"I may have forgotten, but surely our mother did not. She should have instructed Hathor to wait another year to spare us the reopening of this wound."

How unfair that would have been to Hathor.

"Do you believe she did not know? The duke is a widower now," Silva said.

"After the disgrace and humiliation he delivered to my family? He does not deserve even the poorest of women, let alone my sister. I will never allow it."

"It is not you who would be called to allow it but your father. And should your mother wish it, your father will allow it."

The sound that came from his chest was one of evident frustration. Again, his wife was right.

"If my mother arranged this on purpose . . ." He sighed heavily. "I am at a loss as to the state of her mind. How could she possibly forgive him?"

"Is she not his godmother?"

"Is my sister not her daughter?" he retorted angrily.

"Calm, my dear."

Once more, they were silent and undoubtedly examining me to see if I had awakened. But I had become proficient in the art of feigning sleep. It was all in the breathing.

"He may be her godson, and his mother may have been her very best friend, but surely none of that can overcome the love of a mother for her daughter." He spoke resolutely, so it was only natural that his wife agreed.

"Then, by your reasoning, it cannot have been done on purpose, so you can spare your jaw any further tension," Silva replied. The soft laughter between them nearly made me break my act, as I wished to smile alongside them.

My brother Damon, though kind and sweet to his family, had had the reputation of a rake in society before he wed the young Miss Silva Farbridge, the only daughter of a baron. It came as a surprise to everyone, even my mother, who had an eye for these things. The many women he'd had dalliances with were rumored to be very handsome indeed. Miss Silva Farbridge, however, was thought to be quite plain. She, a lady he had seemingly overlooked, and he, a lord that all were sure she did not like, until a few weeks ago when they became beside themselves in love. I was unaware of what had brought this love to fruition, and the two of them held that secret close. The only explanation they offered anyone was simply that their previous encounters had been misunderstandings. No one asked anything more, and they were quickly married, though I was desperately curious.

"Your sister is a great beauty. I am sure there will be callers in line at the door for her hand as well as Hathor's," Silva said.

"Yes, it is good for her to return to London. My only fear is that she shall be led astray upon seeing him, and be hurt once more."

"It has been four years. You believe she still thinks of him?"

"I do not know. Odite never lets any of us in on her true thoughts. The only thing we are all sure of is that she loved him. I can only pray that she has fully removed him from her heart."

There was no doubt in my mind that my brother would do anything for me. Not just him, but my father, my mother, and my other siblings as well. They all loved and cared for me so very much and I wished not to worry them, but my thoughts would either shock them or cause them unease.

Often, I felt as though I were a rare and precious bird, trapped within a cage of gold, on exhibition for the world. It was my duty to appease my viewers, and truly, I did my best, but there were times when it was all so arduous. I wished to be free. And the only time in my memory I had felt such freedom was in my youth . . . with him, Evander.

Since my mother was his godmother, we were afforded many opportunities to speak with each other growing up. He frequented our home freely, though our encounters always took place under the watchful eyes of my governess or lady's maids. Evander had the keen ability to see through all my acts. When my sisters had all but driven me mad, and I said nothing, allowing them their way, he knew I cursed them in my mind, and would walk by and say the curse for me to hear. When I wished to eat more at the table than what was becoming of a young lady, he would secretly have a dessert saved and left for me in my rooms. Books that had been withheld from ladies or amended for decency, he would lend me in the full version.

And when I was sixteen, he made me this one promise: *When we are married, you will be free to be however you wish to be. I swear it.*

I had stared at him in awe and wished to marry him right then. But my family would not allow it. My mother said I was still far too young, despite knowing others my age who had married. We were of two great and noble houses, so all things had to be done in order and with the utmost care. She believed I must wait until the opportune time. I did not think it would be a whole two years later. But once my mother was determined, there was no winning against her. I was mightily cross with her.

But finally, on the day of my coming out, as everyone else fluttered about nervous at being before the queen, I was calm. It was said that I looked like royalty and had been trained as such all my life. The truth of the matter was that my thoughts and emotions were elsewhere—on a future that I had assumed would begin with him. Several gentlemen called upon me the day after, but I gave no heed to any of them as I waited only for him.

I waited in my very best dress.

I waited until the sun went down, and my mother forced

me to bed. The very next day, I waited again. For five days, I waited, confident that whatever held him would soon end, and he would appear before me. Until the sixth day came, and we got word of a wedding.

His wedding.

Taken aback and confused, I did not speak or eat that entire day. It was only when it had long been dark that agony ripped through me. I should have gone into the garden. I should have held my hands over my mouth. But all of me hurt so deeply and thoroughly that when I sobbed, it was as if I were dying. The sound of my grief woke the whole house. My mother stayed with me, which was wise, for I soon collapsed.

We returned to our country estate immediately to avoid the talk of the ton. I wished to never return to London, for it was the place where my dreams had died. When my family went down for the season, I always remained at Belclere Castle. Until now.

I wanted to refuse their demand that I return, but then my brother reminded me that my sister Hathor would have her special day ruined, as the talk would be unbearable.

I believed it would be unbearable either way. My return would cause a stir. My absence would also cause a stir, but at least in my absence, I could pretend to be ignorant of it. However, that would be selfish. And I had been selfish for four years, allowing my mother and sisters to face the ton without me.

All agreed it was time for me to move on, even me. But on to what?

I opened my eyes to the greenery of the world outside.

"And here I thought you intended to sleep the whole way," my brother said.

"Forgive me, brother. Have I missed anything of interest?"

When my gaze fell to him, there was a soft yet woeful smile on his face, as if I were a wounded animal that needed the lightest care.

"Of course not. I only jest. Though I do wonder how you manage to sleep with this jostling," he replied just as the carriage shook violently. "Gently!" he called out to our driver.

"Beg your pardon, my lord. The road is not good this season," he replied.

"Then why on earth did he take this road?" Damon frowned, looking at his wife, who just gave him a slight glance, but it was enough for him to hold his tongue.

"London fashion has changed since you were here last, Aphrodite. We must go to the modiste together to get you new dresses," Silva said. I was not sure if it was the musings of my imagination, but she always seemed to become more rigid when she spoke to me. Perhaps she was still not accustomed to being part of our family.

"We are sisters now. You may call me Odite or Dite if you prefer," I replied. "And yes, I will accompany you to the modiste, though I do not believe I will be in want of any dresses. I am sure my mother is more than prepared."

"Hmm." Damon chuckled, nodding in agreement before looking at his wife. "Knowing our mother, the modiste is already in our home, awaiting our arrival."

"I fear Mother will not be pleased with how big I have gotten," I said.

"Forgive me, but big where?" Silva laughed, her brown eyes looking me over.

"Her imagination." Damon laughed along with her. "Sister, you must not aim to fit Mother's standards of beauty. They do not exist in this world. You now embody the dream of almost all young ladies everywhere."

"He is right." Silva let out a deep breath. "If you are self-deprecating, what hope is there for the rest of us mere mortals?"

"You both hold me in too high regard," I said. I did not seek to be self-deprecating, nor did I believe there was anything wrong with me. But my brother was correct—our mother's standards were not achievable. She remained more unnerved by my aging than I did. The slightest growth or change in my appearance would not escape her eye.

"Odite, you are a Du Bell. High regard is the standard to which you are meant to be held." Damon nodded as if his words were gospel. To him, I was sure they were. "Worry not, sister. Truly, I believe this season shall be one you will not forget. So long as you allow yourself to enjoy it."

"Of course." It was all I could bring myself to say in return, as I shifted my gaze to the trees and blue sky above. Then, without notice, the whole carriage shook with such force we were jostled out of place.

"By heavens! Driver!" Damon called out, grabbing hold of his wife.

"Forgive me, my lord. There is an accident ahead!" the driver called back.

"Oh dear," Silva said as my brother checked out the window. "Is anyone hurt? Should we stop?"

"Drive on!" My brother's voice roared like thunder and his fist clenched in rage, leaving us both perplexed at the change in his demeanor.

"Are you well?" I asked him.

"Quite," he grumbled and kept his head high. "Do not look out the window. Women should not gaze upon such unsightly events."

"Unsightly?" Silva giggled and moved to see. "What could possibly—"

"Silva," he reprimanded, and she stilled. The carriage filled with silence, allowing us to hear the conversation outside.

"Your Grace, are you well?" one voice questioned.

"Yes."

My breath caught at the sound of that voice. It could not be.

"Verity, are you injured?"

That was as sure a confirmation as any. My brother's gaze shifted to me, and I understood why he had shouted at the driver.

Remain calm, I directed myself, lifting my head high and following Damon's direction to not look out the window.

But the fact that our paths had already crossed when we had not even entered London yet was unsettling. Even worse was how my ears strained to hear his voice as we moved farther away from him.

Plato said love was a grave mental disease, and I feared returning to London would make me realize I was still quite ill.

2

Aphrodite

"Odite!" my younger brother called as he ran toward me.

Immediately, my arms opened and braced for the impact of his small body, though it was not as small as I remembered.

"Oh, Hector." I laughed, squeezing him tightly. "Look at you. From where did this height come?"

"From his father, of course," replied the deep and jubilant voice of my papa. He joined us in the foyer, with a book in one of his hands, as always.

"Papa." I smiled and let go of my brother to embrace my father, hugging him tightly as if *I* were the child of twelve rather than Hector.

"We have missed you, my dearest," he replied and kissed the side of my head before stepping back to look me over. A smile spread across his white face. "A vision. More and more, you take after your mother. One would think I had nothing to do with the creation of you."

"Then one would not know me, Papa, for are we not alike in mind?"

"That we are. Thus, I have this," he replied, lifting the book so I could see. "It was very well received last winter, and I could think of no one else who would truly appreciate it."

It was in German, but the title roughly translated to *Chil-*

dren's and Household Tales, by the Brothers Grimm. What a strange name. It was true I dearly loved to read, no matter the language, but the books that enticed me would not be given to a daughter by her father, nor would they have the word *children's* anywhere upon the cover. Nevertheless, his joy in giving me the gift increased my joy in receiving it.

"Thank you, Papa. I shall begin this very night—"

"You shall not!" her voice bellowed and caused both my father and me to stand ready.

Upon turning, I was met with the fiercest of women, dressed in the richest of purples and all other finery, her skin a deep and warm brown like mine and Damon's. Her dark, curly hair was pinned up and away from her face.

"My love—"

"Again, with the books?" my mother interrupted him to say.

"They are mere children's tales." He sought to brush off the matter.

"Tales in which she shall be engrossed all night, leaving her looking as if she were daft or addlepated come sunrise."

"Mama! I have only just arrived and have yet to read even a single page. Must you be so severe?" I exclaimed.

"Yes. As your mother, it is my duty, for tomorrow is far too important." She stepped closer to me, cupping my cheek. "Welcome my dear. There is so much to prepare."

"I was under the impression that the preparation was for Hathor?" My father sought only to save me and was rewarded with a harsh glare from my mother, which made him pull Hector in front of himself as though the boy were his shield.

As I grew older, I learned that the relationship between my parents was anything but conventional. Most husbands I had observed sought to avoid arguments with their wives. Father seemed to revel in battling with Mother, though he had yet to land a victory in their nearly thirty years of marriage. I could not fathom why it brought him such joy to annoy and tease her. But it did.

"The preparations for Hathor have long since concluded. Now I must focus my attention on this one." She lifted my chin with the edge of her finger, examining my face. "You have indulged in cakes."

"I have not!" I lied.

"She shall ruin me!" My sister Hathor stood at the very center of the stairs, her shoulders slouched, messy brown curls now beautifully styled and full of blue ribbons. "Mama, Papa, send her back. This is meant to be my season! Who is going to call upon me when she is here, looking as she does? If this is her after a long journey, imagine the uproar she will cause well rested."

"She shall be the most handsome in the ton, and you shall be utterly forgotten." Abena, my youngest sister, giggled as she skipped down the stairs, hand in hand with our other sister Devana, whose blonde curls bounced freely on her way to me.

Of us all, Devana was the only one with white skin, blue eyes, and golden hair, taking after Father as completely as Damon and I had taken after our mother. Hector, Hathor, and Abena were different degrees between them, though Hathor's eyes were more the color of honey.

"What have I told you?" our mother replied, turning to my sister. "Beauty is magnified when surrounded by beauty. Now come here and welcome your sister."

Hathor glowered, marching down as if she were going to meet an archenemy and not her sister. "Odite," she said to me.

"Hathor," I replied in turn.

We stared each other down.

"Would it have been such a burden for you to eat more cake?" She pouted.

"Even if I were to become as round as a pig, I doubt that would hinder the loveliness of my appearance," I jested.

She spun around to shriek. "Send her back at once!"

I laughed and hugged her, kissing her cheek. "I have missed you, sister, and from your numerous missives, I am well aware you have missed me, too. Even if you should not admit it."

"I know not what you mean. I merely sought to keep you informed of the ton should you be bored."

"Should anyone wonder, let it be known that Devana is my favorite sibling!" spoke Damon at the door. Devana was two years older than Hector and was at Damon's arm already. "For she seems to be the only one who has noticed I am here."

"Aphrodite, who is this strange fellow yapping at my door?" my father questioned, his eyes squinted, causing us all to laugh.

"Good afternoon to you, my lord." Damon sighed heavily as he handed his coat to the butler. "It is only I, Damon Du Bell, Earl of Montagu, your first son and heir."

Our father glanced down at Hector, who still stood before him as a shield. "Did you know of this?"

Hector laughed and nodded. "Yes, Father."

"Strange. Very strange," my father said with humor.

Damon did not say another word to our father, for it would only add to his antics. Instead, he approached our mother, hugging her. When he stepped back, Silva advanced only to curtsy. "Your ladyship."

"Come now. Such formalities are not needed among family." Our mother gently placed her hand on Silva's cheek. "You both are welcome."

"Yes, yes, everyone is welcome. You are welcome. She is welcome. Now, *Mama*, my dresses have yet to arrive. What am I to do? Can we not fetch the modiste?" Hathor interrupted.

"Calm yourself. Not only have the dresses arrived, but the modiste will also be coming soon for any last-minute adjustments you or your sister may need for tomorrow."

"Did I not foretell it?" Damon muttered to Silva.

"Mama, it has been a long journey. I am weary," I said to her.

"Then you shall retire to your rooms where water shall be fetched for you so you may become *unweary* before the modiste arrives. Go on."

I felt the urge to revert to Hathor's dramatics and protest but marched obediently up the stairs. Knowing the conversation in my absence would most likely be about me . . . and Evander.

No, I chided myself, *I should become accustomed to calling him* the duke.

Damon would surely tell them about the brief almost-encounter, and they would take even greater care to not speak his name around me. Entering my rooms, I did what I always did when in privacy: I removed my hat and shoes before throwing myself upon my bed and closing my eyes.

Though I wished I had not, for when I did, I heard his voice. It was merely five words yet they repeated in my mind, unleashing the wisps of feelings I thought sure to have been buried.

Shifting to sit up against the pillows, I opened the book my father had given me, preferring anything else to captivate my thoughts. But the story I turned to seemed as though it were there to mock me; the title of the tale I translated read, "The Golden Bird."

"I knew it!"

Startled, I closed the book and hugged it to my chest, staring into the brown eyes of my mother.

"Mama!"

"I shall have the book," she demanded, hand outstretched.

"Mama." I frowned. "I had read but a sentence."

"And you shall be free to read more at the end of the season. And even to your heart's content once married." She beckoned for the book.

"Was it not you who said wives do not have time to read, for they must tend their household?" I asked, giving her the book.

"So you *are* able to hear me. Very good. Now listen, for I have much more to say." She handed the book to the maid who had come with my water.

When did she *not* have much to say?

"You will marry this season," she said.

"Mama, I beg you to focus only on Hathor," I replied.

"Your request is denied," she stated with no compassion whatsoever. "I will give you two options. Either you shall come to find yourself concerned with a new gentleman, or I shall engage you to Evander."

My eyes widened. "Mama? That is— he is— I— he does not want me. And I do not want him!" I added the second part quickly so as not to sound so desperate and foolish.

She sat on the bed beside me, her face close to mine. "You must tell me the truth. For if you wish I will move heaven and earth to see it done. He is a widower. Are you sure you no longer wish to wed him?"

I knew for certain that I did not wish to wed a man who did not wish to wed me. And Evander—*the duke* did not wish to wed me as he had clearly shown all the world.

"I am no longer so naïve as to want such things. Truly. I do not want him."

Her gaze was unnerving.

"Very well." She rose from her place. "Then we will see you married to the very best of the ton."

"Mama, must it be him or anyone—"

"It must!" She huffed. "If you are no longer so naïve, you should also recognize that your position impacts the rest of your sisters. There is already talk, and do you know what the talk is of? They say the ladies of Du Bell are blessed with beauty but cursed in love, for no one wants them. Should you not marry this season, it shall be harder for Hathor."

"Hathor is beautiful and sharp-witted. She will surely—"

"And if Hathor marries before you, my dear, it will hang over you like a dark cloud. Then the talk will not be of the ladies of Du Bell but of you alone, Aphrodite, and it will be you whom they slight. You are already twenty-two. I will not have it."

I hung my head. "Is marriage really all we can aspire to?"

"Yes." She lifted my head once more. "And a good marriage is a joy. I shall not let you waste away, you are far too precious to me."

I wished to ask: What if I did not have a good marriage like her and Papa? What would become of me then? Would I not simply waste away in another grand house? Instead, I nodded. "Yes, Mama."

"Good. Now make haste and prepare. The modiste has already arrived and is with your sister." She nodded to the maid to help me before leaving just as swiftly as she had entered.

"My lady, I will help you with your coat," the maid, Eleanor, said, and I stood, allowing her to do so.

With my arms outstretched, I wondered if I fluttered my

arms hard enough, would I truly become a bird, and if so, how high could I fly before hitting the roof of my cage?

Damon

"I have made the situation quite clear," my mother proudly said as she entered my father's study.

"Well done, my love. But what is the situation?" My father glanced up from the books upon his desk.

My mother's head tilted to the side, a gesture she was prone to when feeling aggravated or disregarded. "The one regarding our eldest daughter," she replied.

We both waited quietly for her explanation, which was surely coming.

"I explained to Aphrodite that she must marry this season."

"I am not opposed, but what did she say on the matter? Did you tell her of Lord Wyndham's son?" my father asked.

"Lord Wyndham?" I said, folding my paper to look at him. "Is his son not already wed?"

"His first son, yes, but his second is still unwed and apparently caught a glimpse of your sister last summer while she was visiting your aunt and uncle in Drust. They say he is madly in love." He chuckled, leaning back in his chair.

"Father, his second son has neither title nor estate."

"Ah . . ." My father lifted his finger and smiled, a gesture he was prone to when he thought himself privy to knowledge the rest of us lacked. "It has come to my attention that Lord Wyndham's eldest son is quite sickly and very well may not make it to the end of the season. *He* has no heirs."

"Still, Odite can do much better than an earl."

"You turn up your nose at an earl *as an earl*, my boy."

"Yes, but only for a time. I will one day inherit the title of marquess from you."

"So, what of a duke!" My mother cut in loudly, clearly not pleased with being overshadowed. "Evander is—"

"Mother, no," I said.

"Do not interrupt her," commanded my father, forcing my lips to seal. "As you were saying, my love, what of the duke?"

"Yes, as you know, he is now a widower. It is my dearest wish for them to reunite," she said.

"While I do always strive to accommodate your dearest wishes, once more I must ask: What are Aphrodite's thoughts on this matter?" my father asked.

My mother stood straighter, toying with her shawl, a gesture I also knew. "She is . . . confused. But I am sure that upon seeing each other, the clouds in her mind will clear, and she will understand what I have always known—that the two of them are meant for each other."

"I see," my father said. "And has the duke spoken to you or her? For he has given me no word or indication."

Again, she toyed. "No, but surely he will."

"Hmm," was Father's reply. "Very well. I shall wait."

"Good."

"Not good. May I remind you both that blackguard jilted her and left her open to the ridicule of the whole ton." I would sooner applaud her betrothal to Lord Wyndham's second, *untitled* son than sit by and see her with that detestable man. "I beg of you, Mother, do not be biased in his favor due to your past friendship with his mother."

"Do you think that you are more concerned for your sister's well-being than I am, her own mother?" she retorted.

At that moment, my answer would have been yes. However, I could not say as much. My father might hurl a book at the back of my head. "All I mean, Mother, is the talk of him is not pleasant. They say he drove his wife mad and had her confined, their child is being raised without any care or compassion. To my understanding, he is more like his father than his mother. Cruel. Such a man is not worthy of my sister."

"I do not believe a word of that." She was truly unrelenting. "I all but raised that boy alongside you, Damon. I know him as well as I know you."

"Mother—"

"When all the ton spoke of your *affairs* and proclaimed you would never be serious, I laughed, for I knew your time would come, and so it did. Now when they look upon you, they see what I saw first, an upstanding—though a bit severe—earl with a respectable wife. I was correct about you. I am correct about him. I shall not be deterred. And that is that. So if you will excuse me, I must tend to my preparations," she declared and left the room just as she had entered, head high.

"Is it not unreasonable for her to bring my past into this?" I asked, looking to my father, who had already returned his attention to his books.

"Your first mistake was to argue at all." He moved the paper closer to examine the page. "One would think, being a married man yourself now, that you would have learned that already."

I frowned. "Father, it is not my desire to argue. I am merely concerned and am lost as to why you are not. Is Aphrodite not your favorite?"

"A father has no favorites among his children."

"What a load of bollocks."

He chuckled and glanced at me. "But should there be such a ranking of my children, I would have you know that you are at the bottom."

"However shall I survive?" I mocked, resting back into my

chair. "Father, honestly, I fear Mother might push too far. Aphrodite is still fragile."

"You said you all came upon the duke on the road?"

"Yes, of all times, can you imagine? What are the odds of his wheel getting caught in a rut at the same time we are passing?"

"The roads have been poor due to the heavy rains this year, so accidents are bound to happen. It is unfortunate your sister came across him so soon. How did she react?"

"She did not see him, though she stiffened like a young fawn lost in the wilderness at the mere sound of his voice. It was clear to all who had eyes that she sought to gather her wits."

"So, your mother is correct then. She may still feel for him?"

"Father, it was never her feelings that were in question. The question has always been his feelings, and he has expressed them quite clearly. If it is a matter of making her a duchess, Evander Eagleman is not the only duke in the land. You need not support him."

"I support only this family," he said sternly. "Status or title is less important than the happiness and safety of all my children, Damon, as you know. I will not allow your sister to fall into distress again, least of all with the duke, but there is little reason to pick a fight now as it is the nature of women to dream and flutter, especially about marriage. There is no need for us to speak until we must. And we must only when one of your sisters has been given an offer. It may very well be that your mother's efforts will be in vain, or Aphrodite could become enamored of another gentleman. It is our duty as men of the house to watch over them as shepherds do sheep."

"And should a wolf arrive in disguise as we are waiting?"

"If you had read the *progymnasmata* by the twelfth-century Greek rhetorician Nikephoros Basilakes as I instructed you,

you would know the answer to that question," he replied, rising to his feet. He rummaged through a stack of books behind him, selected one, and held it out. "Fill your mind with this instead of the silly talk of women."

If there was a problem, my father had a book for it.

I never thought myself foolish or dimwitted until I spoke with my father. The breadth of his knowledge seemed ever-expanding.

"How is it you are so keenly able to cut me to size but are powerless against Mother?"

"A few more weeks of marriage, and you, too, Damon, will understand. That I promise."

I feared such a time, for if my father in all his wisdom never stood a chance, what would be my fate?

"I shall go find my wife," I said and rose to leave.

"Do take care to read Basilakes's words this time. And do not fold my pages!"

"Yes, sir," I replied, all but giving up my efforts to speak to either of my parents.

How odd they were.

3

Aphrodite

"You look beautiful. You need not worry," I said to Hathor as we sat in the carriage on our way to the palace. I could see she was distraught, nervously adjusting the feathers in her hair. I wished I had known how to give her confidence, but, as I had been told so often, there was no more superior praise for a woman than the reassurance of one's beauty.

"I cannot compare to you," she muttered, staring down at her hands.

"Must you measure yourself against me?"

"Everyone else does." She swallowed and looked back up to me with tears in her eyes that she did not let fall. "And when it was your time, you were flawless. It's all anyone could talk about. Even I remembered the sight of you and was astonished. I have practiced my walk and curtsy a thousand times, and still, it pales in comparison. How did you do it?"

To tell her I had put no effort in it at all and lacked any genuine care for the whole charade, or that I could not even remember much of it, would only crush her spirit.

"I believe all you must do is trust yourself and remain calm. It is but a few seconds," I replied.

"Yes, of course. Why did I not think of it that way?" She

huffed and looked out the window as we passed through the gates.

No further conversation was my best option to not aggravate her more. Instead, I studied my other sisters, Devana and Abena, who gaped out the side window in amazement at the fuss being made and those in attendance.

"Hathor, I do not think you should be worried. So far, all the other girls look as queer as Dick's hatband," Abena said.

"Abena!" Hathor gasped in horror at her language.

"Where on earth did you learn that?" I asked, trying not to giggle.

Abena shrugged and turned back to us. "I heard one of the maids say it."

"Well, are you a maid? Never repeat it, especially in the company of others. It is beneath us as ladies and unseemly to hear," Hathor declared, causing Abena to glare at her.

"So, what do you call someone who is ugly or not right-looking?" Abena shot back.

Hathor paused as she tried to think. "Plain?"

"People call Silva plain, but I do not think she is ugly," Abena replied.

"Oh . . . will you stop thinking so much? Say nothing then. Why can you not be more like Devana? See how quiet she is."

Abena crossed her arms. "You do not like being compared to Odite, so why do you compare me to Devana?"

"Will you—"

"Enough," I said gently. "Hathor, you will become flushed, and your face will strain if you continue."

She gasped, placing her hands on her face, pressing hard as if to stop any emotions from showing. A lady's face on her debut must be serene and elegant but also innocent *and* enticing. It was a standard I thought impossible for anyone to meet, yet I was told I had. I could only assume the secret was to simply not care at all.

"We've stopped!" Devana's low and soft voice exclaimed. She shifted from the window, allowing the footmen to open the door for us. When Abena began to move, I shook my head, holding her back.

"Hathor goes first," I informed her and then looked to my sister. "It is your day. Mother says it is best to take a moment to stand alone before the carriage."

She nodded, inhaled deeply, and stepped out with the help of a maid waiting to adjust her white gown while the three of us waited behind. Only when our mother arrived at her side did we step out ourselves.

I could not help myself. I searched through the sea of people and carriages before me. My actions must have been more obvious than I presumed, for my brother appeared beside me.

"Whom are you looking for?"

"No one," I lied and faced him. "I was looking at all the gowns."

His eyebrow rose. "They all look so similar."

"Such is the eye of a man." Silva giggled and took his arm. "One would wonder why we ladies try so hard."

I believed it was for the eyes of the other women who judged us. For the ton, the faster all of us married, the better. It displeased me that beauty and family status were how a woman was ranked. But simply because I detested it did not mean I was ignorant of the fact that Abena was right. Hathor was far more beautiful than nearly every other lady here. There seemed to be a force, an air around our whole family as we entered the court. Some looks were curious, others awe-stricken, and a few jealous, but all made way for us. Oh, to be a Du Bell.

As I walked I was noticed more now than I had been on my own day.

It made me wish I possessed Plato's Ring of Gyges as he described in *Republic*. The ring would afford me the power to become invisible at will. What talk would I truly hear then? What secrets would I uncover? Although Plato would argue that I was not honorable by choosing to use the ring and, therefore, nearly as bad as any evildoer I might discover.

Stop thinking of books, Aphrodite, I thought, reprimanding myself.

"Look, that is the Duke of Everely," a lady whispered. They had taken their fill of us and now sought a new target.

I did my best not to turn, but I could not help myself. In a deep blue jacket, Evander's skin was an ever sun-kissed and warm brown, a trimmed beard upon his perfectly squared jaw, his shoulders broad, giving every viewer an account of his good height, his brown eyes focused on his younger sister . . . Oh no. Oh dear. My breath caught. He was even more handsome than I remembered.

He had changed, but for the better. The longer I looked upon him, the harder my heart began to beat. Then, without notice, as if he could hear the drum in my chest, he glanced up, and our eyes met. All the world seemed to have stopped, even my own heart. I felt . . . I felt something whenever I looked at him and I was unable to bear it. I spun away as quickly as I could without falling over, but nearly knocked into my father.

"Odite?"

"Yes?"

He looked me over and then offered his arm, as my mother and Hathor had gone to the waiting room.

"We must go to our places."

"Of course," I replied and held tightly to his arm.

Whatever was left of the duke in my heart, I would rid myself of it as he had rid himself of me. I would show him that I had no desire for his attentions, nor was I some pitiable creature. Just as I would surely hear of his wedding this season, he would hear of mine. He would see me content *without him*.

"Papa," I said softly as we stood in the receiving hall.

"Yes, my dear?" he whispered, eyeing the door.

"Would you be pleased if I married this season?"

He looked at me, pausing for a moment before squeezing my hand. "It is not what pleases me, my dear, but what pleases you. Fear not. Even if you wish never to marry, I shall support you."

"Mama would have your head for telling me that."

"Let it then be between just us, though, should you not marry, you would forever have to face your mother."

"Are you supporting me or threatening me?"

He chuckled, and a broad smile appeared on his lips, which made me smile as well.

The queen's arrival was announced. Immediately, I released my father's arm, bowed my head, and curtsied before slowly rising back up. When I lifted my head, the queen was looking right at me, her figure domineering under heavy silks and jewels, her wig high. Everyone else followed her gaze—thus, everyone's eyes were upon me. Not a word was said, and she looked away just as she looked at me . . . at her leisure.

"Begin," she declared.

And so it began.

The scrutiny.

"Lady Clementina Rowley, presented by her mother, Her Grace, the Duchess of Imbert." The doors opened to reveal a rather tall young lady, perhaps taller than any man there, with a particularly long neck. Her very short mother was behind her. She was not unseemly, though her walk . . . wobbled. I glanced at the queen, who had a disagreeable expression upon her face. I immediately felt for the girl. The queen could and *would* be vicious.

When Lady Clementina Rowley reached the queen and curtsied, the queen sat up and asked, "My poor girl, were you stretched as a child?"

A few snickers engulfed the room, and I looked away from the brutality of that moment. I found myself staring at the one person I did not want to see—Evander. His brown eyes stared back at me, and I at him, and he at me, and so on. I could not read his expression. Every so often, he would look away, and then I would look away. The ladies came and went in between, and then once more, I found myself looking when he was not. Finally, tired of this ridiculous game, I focused on the door.

"Lady Verity Eagleman, presented by Her Grace, the Dowager Duchess of Everely."

Evander's sister had blossomed. I remembered her from when she was just a little girl, quite sneaky and devious, always seeking to play in the garden. Her features were soft, her face heart-shaped, and her skin the same as her brother's. Her walk, while graceful and gentle, unlike the dowager, was . . . not right. Even worse, she had somehow managed to wear the same color as the queen herself.

I stole a glance at Evander, unable to stop myself, and I could read the horror on his face. I quickly turned my head to the queen, for if there was anything she hated, it was to be outdone, especially within her own walls.

Verity curtsied slow and low. The queen's face did not reveal much.

I wished to save Verity somehow. Should I faint? Cause a commotion?

"Queer as Dick's hatband!" Abena shouted.

All eyes shifted to us. My father looked at me in panic and moved to grab Abena when all of a sudden, a laugh echoed through the hall. It was the queen. She threw her head back, placing her hand over her stomach, then stopped and waved off Verity and the dowager.

"Next!" she declared.

I squeezed my sister's shoulders and whispered down to her, "Mama will have your head."

She shrugged. Abena was fearless, and it made me proud.

Finally, it was Hathor's turn.

"Lady Hathor Du Bell, presented by her mother, the Right Honorable Marchioness of Monthermer." This time, when the doors opened, all was correct.

The manner in which they both were dressed, the speed they both walked, and the grace they held as they curtsied low were perfect. I so wished for the queen to say a few words of praise for Hathor. She badly needed it.

The queen peered over them, then lifted her head and nodded. For most, that would be more than enough, but likely not for Hathor.

And though it took a great deal of time, all finally came to an end, and we were free to return to our homes until the ball. The walk back to the carriages was filled with talk, and I did my best to ignore it but found myself unable to.

"Pray tell how a girl can be so demure, yet her mother looks like a tragic opera singer." The ladies in front of me laughed, unaware I was behind them.

"You mean *Her Grace*, the Dowager Duchess of Everely?" Her companion laughed. "It is clear as day she is a fake."

"A fake?"

"You didn't know? She is not the duke's birth mother. The first Duchess of Everely died in childbirth with the Lady Verity, and not even two months later, his father married that woman. She became their stepmother and even had a child soon after."

I was close enough that when they began to whisper, I could also hear.

"It's said he had kept her as his *ladybird* for many years, and her first son, who is older than the current duke, is actually his illegitimate elder brother."

"No!"

"Yes! They say the moment he wed her, she remodeled the whole estate, but because she came from such a low standing, she was at a loss for what to do and made a mess of the finances. When the former duke passed, his heir, the current duke, had her removed from the estate in Everely and given a smaller apartment here. He then sent his younger brother— the legitimate one—away to school."

"Rightfully so. Such a woman, clawing her way into the aristocracy, is distasteful. Look at the mockery she made of their name today. The queen will surely remember."

"In all honesty, the whole family is quite rotten. Noble birth or not. Did you hear that the duke jilted the famed beauty Aphrodite Du Bell?"

"I have heard her name spoken but do not know her."

"She is the one whom the queen looked upon for so long at the side of the room today, the one with the renowned curtsy."

"That was her? I noticed the lady as soon as she entered. She is quite exquisite."

"The most desired of the ton . . . even despite her age now. Well, desired by everyone but the Duke of Everely. He preferred a simple bowl of soup to her luxurious feast. So much so, apparently, he drank his fill before they were even wed, ignoring the poor, *poor goddess*."

They laughed, and I swallowed the lump in my throat.

"If it's simple he wants, maybe I shall send my daughter his way."

They giggled.

"He would sooner take her over the goddess. Sometimes too much beauty is a curse. Men want fun, not a living painting. Though I do hear that he is quite the rake now that his wife has died, indulging in all types of things."

I noticed one of them had dropped her handkerchief, so I picked it up.

"I beg your pardon, madam," I called out. When they turned to me, their eyes widened. I lifted the handkerchief to them. "Did either of you happen to drop this?"

"Oh yes, my dear, thank you," said the elder of the ladies.

"Not at all." I smiled at them and walked on to our carriage. Luckily, ours was the only one yet to have come. I did not realize how fast I had been walking but preferred it so I could breathe and kick the ground before me slightly.

To hell with you fat-witted dirty-dish old wenches! I screamed in my mind and kicked once more. *No good, jingle-brained—*

"Aphrodite!"

I jumped at the sound of my mother's voice. "Mama!"

"Did you forget you had family, or did you seek to fly? What on earth had you walking so quickly and away from us? I called to you, and yet you kept walking."

"I'm sorry, Mama . . . I was lost in thought."

"These thoughts of yours." She huffed, shook her head, and

turned back to look for my sisters. "Hathor, hurry. We must return so you may all prepare for the ball."

"What is the point? The queen said not a word to me!" Hathor cried as she entered, yanking the feathers out of her hair.

"Consider yourself lucky, for the words she did speak brought the other young ladies to tears," my mother replied.

"You are not riding with Father?" I asked Mother.

"Do you seek to calm her down alone?"

I did not.

"Abena, here," she ordered our youngest sister, who was trying to stow away in the other carriage.

"Mama, would you not—"

"Here," she repeated.

Devana laughed at her as she was able to ride with our father.

Abena marched to the carriage, was helped inside, and the door closed. My mother reached to grab her ear, but Abena hugged me. "Mama, people can still see."

"So you are aware, and yet you spoke out of turn before the queen, and not only did you speak, it was language unbecoming of a lady!"

"But the queen laughed," Abena tried to argue.

"You shall wash the pots!"

"Mama!" She gasped in horror.

"If you wish to speak as maids do, you shall work as maids do. May that remind you of who you are."

Abena looked at me and shrugged, trying not to laugh. I had been mistaken. It was not Abena's head Mother would have but apparently her poor hands.

"Do you all not see that I am distraught?" Hathor wept dramatically.

"Hathor, how many times must I tell you that you are perfectly fine?" Mother said.

"I did not want to be *perfectly fine*. I wanted to be the season's incomparable."

"Then you should have stolen Aphrodite's face," Abena teased, and Hathor nearly lunged at her. "All eyes were upon her, even the queen's."

"You!"

"Enough!" Our mother started rubbing her temples. "I beg of you all, enough. Hathor, gather your wits. The day is not yet done. Instead of your theatrics, regroup and prepare for the real battle, for that begins tonight. And you"—her gaze shifted to me—"remember my words."

I nodded. "Do not fret, Mama. I understand."

I would find someone, and then talk of me would finally change.

4

Aphrodite

I could not recall the last time I had been to a ball, and it dawned on me as I stood amid this one that in my absence from society the world had passed me by. I did not know any of the steps to these new dances. I watched my sister accept dance after dance while I was forced to reject those who came to me. My mother was not pleased, as she had not been aware I was so lacking, and I was not pleased, for it forced me to recall the words of the women earlier in the day, when they had called me a living painting. Dressed finely, I only stood or sat under the appraising gaze of those present. And the gaze I felt most of all was that of the duke. For he was here, and I watched him dance with no one other than his sister. That did not deter the many other young ladies who sought to speak with him and have his company. Once I knew where he was, I did not look in that direction, and was thankful he had managed to greet my mother while I was not beside her.

"If you are unable to dance, sing. If you are unable to sing, then play," my mother muttered beside me and nodded to the other room where the pianoforte was left for many ladies to demonstrate their talents. They had all but gathered in a line. It seems rather silly but this night was meant to parade the new young ladies of the ton *and* all they had to offer in front of eligible men.

"I think not," I replied to her. "For it would—"

"Do we fail to impress you, Lady *Aphrodite*?"

Upon hearing my name and the music stop, I came face-to-face with . . . the queen. I immediately dropped low into a curtsy, bowing my head.

"Forgive me, Your Majesty. I did not see you."

"Do rise. I must have my answer."

I did as she commanded, rising slowly, then lifting my head. She stood before me in a rich crimson gown and a white wig, a cane in one hand.

"I could never be unimpressed by such splendor," I replied as now all of the world—well, this small universe—focused on me.

"And yet I have not witnessed you take even one dance, nor heard you sing, nor seen the faintest look of amusement or joy upon your face. Why is that?"

I wished to tell her it was merely the condition of my face. However, that would not do. All knew that the queen had become truly harsh, unlike her formerly kind self. My uncle had mused that she had taken her frustration with the king's condition out on society.

"Well?" she demanded.

I curtsied once more, but not as low, and remained in position. "Forgive me, Your Majesty, for you have caught me, and I cannot escape."

"So, you admit to being tired of us?"

"No, never. I confess to being terribly unlearned," I replied. "I truly wish to dance, but as you may know, I have been far from society and know not the new steps, and sought not to make a fool of myself."

"Lady Monthermer, I was under the impression your daughters were the most erudite of society."

"It seems I must apply more effort, Your Majesty." My mother laughed, but I was sure she was not amused, and I feared what she would say to me later.

"So it seems," said the queen, and I thought that would be the end of my torment. However, instead of going to a new victim, she turned and ordered, "The Lady Aphrodite wishes to dance. Thus, we shall accommodate her. Perform something from the former seasons."

I did *not* wish that. My mother pinched me to keep me from speaking my mind, not that I ever would have.

"Thank you, Your Highness," I said, lifting my head. "But I lack a partner . . ."

No sooner had I said the words than did men suddenly approach. A white-faced, brown-haired gentleman with green eyes, whom I knew to be Lord Wyndham's son, was the quickest, but I could not recall his first name. "Lady Aphrodite, it would be my honor to have your first dance," he said, outstretching his hand to me.

Under the queen's and Mama's gazes, I could not deny him. "Of course." I allowed him to take me onto the floor. Only when I was in place did a piece of music I knew begin to play.

The image of a bird again came to mind as we danced. They had rattled my cage, and I had to perform and do so most elegantly.

"You do not remember me?" my partner questioned as we turned.

"I beg your pardon?"

He smiled kindly, his hand raised and hovering before me. "We met last summer at Drust, while you were in your uncle's care."

I thought back to my time in Drust, which I'd enjoyed. I

did not recognize his face. "My apologies. It seems I do not recall."

"At Paravel Square. You had dropped your handkerchief, and I returned it to you."

I still did not remember, so all I could say in return was "Thank you."

He chuckled, and we turned to the left. "I am not surprised, as you were most engrossed in a book. I believe it was some work of Shakespeare."

That sounded like me. "Ah, yes." I nodded.

"You have a particular talent."

"Particular?"

He nodded. "Never have I witnessed anyone maneuver through a market square, nose deep in a book, and not even misstep. It was as if you were clairvoyant, knowing a puddle was before you and, thus, walking around it, or others would merely stop to allow you to make your way. It was truly a sight of wonder."

I laughed. "Sir, I assure you, I have fallen a great many more times than I wish to admit. I was merely lucky that day."

"Please, call me Tristian," he requested as the dance came to an end.

From the corner of my eye, I saw that my mother and the queen were still watching me.

"Another?" Tristian questioned.

I smiled and nodded as I was trained to do. This dance had us change partners. The first time I switched, I paid no mind. But the second, I found myself on the arm of the man I sought most to avoid, and I felt a spark at the touch of our hands. Once more, my heart jumped. He stared down at me and only at me.

I could not breathe.

He opened his mouth to speak, but the dance called for us to change partners once more, and I was back to Tristian. I found myself glancing over to where *he* now danced with his sister. Was he about to say something? What was that feeling upon touching him? Was it my imagination again? And what in God's name was the matter with my damned heart!

Be calm! I scolded my heart, and just as it began to listen once more, we changed partners again, and I was before *him*.

"Aphrodite," he whispered.

I was utterly speechless; it had been so long since I had heard my name upon his lips. His voice made all of me quiver.

Partners changed, then I was back with Tristian, and it was only then that I could breathe. I prayed for the end of the dance to come as quickly as possible.

My mind was blank.

I wished to think.

But my thoughts were gone.

My body moved as we reached the conclusion of the dance, but I was empty. I heard the applause, marking the end, saving me. I curtsied to Tristian and began to walk back to my mama, pleased the queen had moved on.

"You were magnificent." Silva smiled at me.

I parted my lips to speak but found myself winded. I must have danced more than I thought. "Mama, I think I shall go into the garden."

"But the ball—"

I had already started walking. It was rude of me, but I could not be denied. All of a sudden, I felt an arm take mine. When I looked, I saw it was Silva.

She smiled gently at me. "It is improper for you to be without a chaperone."

"We are the same age," I replied.

"I am wed," she reminded me.

Ah, of course. Briefly, I had forgotten what separated us. I nodded, allowing her to join me as we stepped into the cool evening air. Closing my eyes, I breathed it in, wishing the breeze to carry me away as well.

"It is beautiful," she spoke, drawing my attention.

I opened my eyes to see the garden lit with strange lights. With not a soul among the grass, nor near the water where the swans rested, it was a sight.

"I much prefer it out here."

"You do not like the ball?" I asked.

She sighed as we walked. "I . . . I am enjoying the ball, but not so much the talk within it."

"Ah." I nodded. "Yes, the ball is the epicenter of gossip. Was anything of note said?"

"Is that the point of such conversation or is it merely to ridicule one another?" she snapped, lifting her dress as we walked upon the grass, her face in a deep frown. She must have noticed her tone and my silence, for she looked to me. "I apologize. I meant—"

"You are right. Many take much joy in the ridicule of another. I wish to say I am better than they are, but I have done the same in my mind."

"Truly? You seem impervious to it all."

That again. "So I have been told. I do not know if it is a blessing or a curse that my face portrays nothing. I assure you, if you knew my thoughts, you would wish to escape me as well."

Silva giggled. "Never. I've come to like your company. Though I must admit, it is intimidating to be beside you for long."

"So I have also been told, numerous times," I replied, lifting my skirt to avoid some muddy water. "What was the talk that made you wish to escape?"

"Nothing that has not already been said . . . of me." She frowned. "They all think me . . . ill-suited to your brother."

I rolled my eyes. "Anyone but their own daughters is ill-suited to a lord of wealth and prominence. No matter what my brother may be like, I think you are excellent."

"Truly?" She looked at me, surprised.

"Yes. Why are you astonished? Did my face give you another impression?" It was my face, yet it seemed I had little control over it.

"No." She shook her head. "Well, I am unsure. I just assumed everyone was anticipating greater for him."

In all honesty, my mother was glad any woman with sense and a half-decent background had subdued him before he got himself entrenched in trouble like Ev— *the duke*.

"My parents are very honest people, which is where Abena gets it from. If they did not like or approve of you, there would be no need to assume. You are great enough for my brother, maybe even greater, for you are more level-headed," I replied, and she donned a large smile.

"Thank you— Ah!" She gasped as she stepped on the edge of her hem in the mud. "Oh no!"

"Remain calm. It is not so bad. My mother is always prepared for such matters. There should be something in the carriage. Come," I said, already taking her hand to lead.

"I see the carriage," she said as she let go of my hand. "Go back inside. I'll be right there."

"Are you sure?"

"Yes, it's all right. I do not wish your mother to say I took you away."

There were very few times I could be alone, and I wished to

enjoy it. It was a small pleasure and reminded me of how I would sneak off to walk through the woods on our family's estate. Should my father or mother ever know, I would be strung up by my ears. But it seemed ridiculous to me that a woman was not even allowed to walk on her own. We were not children, despite how they all seemed to treat us. If only I had a good book, I would find an excellent tree to sit underneath, maybe with treats.

Oh, how small and simple my desires were.

"Ahh . . . Ahh . . ." I heard someone cry out from within the bushes.

Was someone injured?

Just as I was about to call out to whomever it was, I saw them.

Well, I could not really *see* them, nor did I think they could see me.

There among the bushes were a woman and a man doing what was beyond anything I had secretly read in books. Her dress bunched around her waist, her breasts exposed to the air, and he, like some beast, was above her. I had half a mind to think he was hurting her, but her face did not look like that of a woman in pain. She was . . . joyful. It was lewd, it was sinful, it was against all morality and propriety, yet I could not look away. I watched as he kissed her neck, and then sucked on her breast as a babe would. How perverse! Like animals, they grunted and groaned.

Look away! I shouted to myself.

I did not. The more I watched, the warmer I felt. My breath . . . heavy. My body . . . strange. What was the matter with me? Was whatever had possessed the two of them now infecting me? The woman's face—never had I seen such an expression before.

I touched my neck, and it burned. What was I feeling?

I was mesmerized and had just leaned in to examine more closely when I felt large arms around me, yanking me back. It happened so quickly that I did not have time to scream. Before I knew it, I was farther away, and when I turned to find my attacker, I was met with the angry eyes of Evander.

"What on earth are you doing?" I gasped trying to stand upright.

"It is I who should be asking you such a question!" he said angrily. "Aphrodite, have you gone mad?"

"I beg your pardon!" I cried out. "I am perfectly sane!"

"The sane do not watch others . . . in such a manner," he replied. "Look at yourself."

I glanced down at my body, but I did not see anything amiss. "What?"

"Can you not see you are aroused?"

"As from slumber?" I asked.

"Dear God, help me." He put his hand on his head, taking a deep breath as he stepped away. Then he moved back, still upset. "I know you to be an inquisitive one, Aphrodite, but this is no way to learn!"

"I do not know what you are talking about, but you will stop speaking to me like this!"

He stared at me for a long time, inhaling through his nose. "Forgive me."

I nodded. "Now explain."

"I shall not!" he said. "Rather, you explain what you were doing."

"I do not need to explain anything to you. I merely came out for fresh air."

"Well, it was not air that you took in."

"Then what was I taking in?"

"One day, you shall learn from your husband, not from rogues among the shrubbery!"

"Why must I wait for a husband to teach me?"

"Because you are a lady of noble birth, Aphrodite."

"And you are a gentleman of noble birth. Why are you permitted to understand these things before having a wife?"

"Who told you I understood them before having a wife?"

"Do not take me for a fool, Evander! I may not know much, but I know that if there had been no encounters with a woman, you would not have ended up with a wife! For you surely know that despite your many promises to me, there were no . . . interactions!"

He paused as my breath rose and fell. We stared at each other.

"Or maybe you are right, for I truly do not understand. Maybe the answer is you simply did not wish to have me. And that is fine, for I no longer wish to have anything from you, either, Your Grace." I curtsied to him before turning to leave.

"Aphrodite, wait—"

"Aphrodite?"

I froze when I saw Silva. "Is everything well?"

"Quite," I said, quickly taking her arm and rushing to get away.

"Aphrodite, what happened?" she whispered. "Did he—"

"Nothing, I swear. Please don't say a word to anyone!" I begged.

She frowned, examining me.

"Please."

"Very well. Thankfully, I did not return inside without you. The footman informed me you had not left the garden. Did anyone else see you?"

"No." I shook my head, though I did not know for sure.

"Calm yourself. Eyes will be on us," she directed.

"I look uncalm?"

"You do not look yourself."

I did not know what that meant. But I tried to push away everything that occurred within that garden.

Everything.

5

Aphrodite

I managed to gather my wits until we returned home.

I survived the lecture from my mother, who now added dancing lessons to the things I would have to learn "most urgently." I could only do as I always did and agree, wishing for the stillness of night to allow me time to reflect. I wished to think rationally, but as I lay upon my bed now, I could not escape the vision of that couple in the bushes. He kissed her as if he were trying to devour her flesh—and how eagerly she sought to be devoured. Did it not hurt? The way he grasped her like a beast would—grunting and breathless. As I remembered more, I felt a sort of pain that was not pain. I remembered the way he took her nipple into his mouth, and the thought caused my own to tighten.

It was maddening.

Can you not see you are aroused? His voice shot through my mind, and it made me tremble. I had not realized that we'd had our first conversation in years, and he'd spent it mocking me and insulting my intelligence. I leapt out of bed and grabbed my robe and the candle from beside it.

How dare he laugh at me!

I crept into the library and did not stop until I grabbed a

Latin dictionary and settled in at my father's desk. The moment I sat down to open the book, the door flew open.

"Aphrodite?"

"Papa!"

He frowned. "What are you doing? It is late. Are you not weary from the day's events?"

"No, actually. I am still quite stirred up from all the festivities and thought to calm myself with some reading."

"I do wish your brother was similarly afflicted." He came over to see which books I'd taken. Even though his desk was covered, he was always aware of any changes. "You wished to read dictionaries? Well, that is one way to lull oneself to sleep!"

"Er, I came across a word I did not understand and wished to search for the meaning."

"Really?" he asked excitedly. For if there was anything my father loved, other than my mother, it was to teach. "What word? Is it rooted in Latin or Greek? I see you have taken the Latin, but you can never be too sure."

Oh, lawks! "It was—"

"Why are you not in bed?" my mama snapped from the door. "More books! Aphrodite, we are expected at the park in the morning."

"Of course! Good night!" I grabbed my candle and rushed past them.

"What of your definition?" my father called after me.

I did not reply but hurried up the stairs and back to my room, shutting the door behind me. I took a breath of relief for managing my escape before putting my candle down and throwing myself upon my bed. This was all foolish. I was foolish. And Evander, the duke . . . ugh!

I placed the pillow over my head, trying my best not to think. Willing sleep to come but each time my eyes shut, I saw that couple upon the grass. And soon, the image of them in my mind changed. It morphed into . . . into Evander and me.

"Aphrodite." His voice was in my ear.

"Aphrodite." His breath was upon my skin.

I curled into a ball, hugging myself, waiting for it to pass. But it did not. I lay there, tortured by the things I had seen, until the sun began to rise, filling my room with light. Never had I been so exhausted.

"Good morning, my lady," my maid, Eleanor, said as she opened the curtains. "Which dress do you wish to wear for promenading in the park? The family shall be having breakfast there."

I tossed my head to the side, not ready for the full light of day. "Tell my mama I do not feel up to the park today."

"Good morning, Odite!" Abena dashed into the room and jumped onto my bed, giggling.

"Can you spare some of your energy, sister?" I inquired.

"How?" she asked.

"Abena!" shrieked Hathor, causing Abena to jump down and hide under my bed. Not a second later, Hathor entered and scanned the room as she held a ripped ribbon, her hair still within her nightcap. When she did not spot our sister, her honeyed eyes snapped to mine. "Where is she?"

"Good morning to you, too, Hathor," I replied.

"Good morning. Where is the wild one?"

"I know not."

She narrowed her eyes on me and then screamed, "Abena! Where are you! You tore my ribbon! I had it made specifically for today!" Not seeing Abena, she rushed out of the room, still screeching just as Devana entered, holding the doorknob.

"Morning." Her soft voice was most welcome.

"Morning," I replied and lifted my arms, allowing her to crawl into bed with me.

She lay down, and I brushed her golden curls from her face. "Did you sleep well?"

She nodded.

"I did not." Abena sprung up from behind the bed, and the moment she did, Hathor jumped right back into the room.

"I knew you came in here!"

Abena made a dash for it, nearly throwing Hathor to the ground. "You are older. You are supposed to forgive me!"

"You are supposed to be remorseful! And not touch my things!" Hathor called out as she chased after her.

"My lady, your dress?" Eleanor, who was quite used to our morning chaos, asked.

"May I choose?" Devana requested.

"Please."

Devana giggled and got off the bed to look at the dresses along with my coats.

"Green!" She pointed and turned to me. She nearly always chose green since it was her favorite color.

"Green it is then," I replied, sitting up before my mama entered to admonish me for something. Eleanor brought me a basin, and when I had cleaned my face, I looked into the mirror, staring at my brown eyes.

"Odite, you have flowers!" Abena ran back to report. "I think they came from a suitor."

"I knew it," Hathor grumbled, pushing Abena out of the way so she could walk into my dressing room and throw herself upon the longue. "Are you happy now? All the gifts this morning are for you. You even have the queen's favor."

"Favor?" I asked as I toweled my face. "What favor?"

Hathor scoffed. "Do not pretend to be ignorant. That makes it worse. Last night she spoke to you, of all the ladies there. She directed the rest of the evening to accommodate you. *You!*" She huffed and crossed her arms. "I swear, one would think you were her daughter."

"You exaggerate, but if you wish to stay here and complain, allowing me time to ready myself instead of you, that is fine by me."

Her eyes widened and she took off running again, calling to her maid, "I need my hair done first!"

Part of me missed the quiet mornings I had primarily to myself in Monthermer. Though as I watched Abena and Devana look over my dresses, I also considered how nice it was to be near them again.

"Abena, Devana, you must hurry and get ready, or Mother will have pots for you," I said.

Their eyes widened, and they took off.

"These are for you, my lady. Your mother asked that we bring them up." Two maids held an arrangement each—one was of white tulips with red stripes, while the other was a large bouquet of roses.

I walked to the tulips, lifting them from her hands with a smile. "These are so beautiful. Who sent them?"

"His Grace, Lord Evander Eagleman, the fourth Duke of Everely." My mama entered with a grin. "And the roses are from the Honorable Tristian Yves, Lord Wyndham's son. It seems you have made your choice."

"Mama, may I not simply admire a flower?" I said, quickly handing them back to the maid.

"You may. I am merely noting which flower you chose." She was not *merely* doing anything. "It seems Evander remembers the way to gain your attention—to present that which is unordinary."

"You make me sound rather odd."

"You are odd, child." She huffed, looking at me. "I blame your father and his books."

"You always blame Father when we do not behave to your liking."

"Then behave to my liking! Today at the park, you will promenade with Evander."

"I will not!"

"Why? He has clearly shown interest."

"I do not trust his interest. He showed *his interest* before and look what trouble it caused." I selected a rose. "I shall wear one of these today."

I moved to sit before my dresser.

She sighed and, as she left, said, "You're stubborn against your own happiness."

Is my happiness dependent only on Evander? I would hope not, I thought, twisting the rose between my fingers. I was determined not to allow myself to fall to any further chaos caused by him.

Just because he was now a widower did not mean I would take him. And just because he sent me flowers did not mean he was serious. I did not know his mind. But I did need to speak to him—if only to confirm he would not speak about the previous night. Should anyone know I was alone with him or that I had seen anything "inappropriate for a lady," it would be my ruin.

"My lady, would you like me to add the flower to your hair?" my lady's maid asked.

"If you wish," I said, giving it to her.

I thought at the very least my mother would seek to maintain the pretense of an unarranged meeting in the park. That this was merely a family outing in which we came across the duke. However, upon arriving it was clear, as he waited where our servants had already set our tents, that the only purpose was for Evander and me to speak.

My mother not so discreetly lagged farther and farther behind, giving us as much space as propriety allowed. Her machinations seemed wasted as the duke and I walked in silence. I thought I had never minded silence, but his vexed me.

"May I count on you to keep our previous encounter a secret?"

"What previous encounter?" he questioned.

"Exactly." I nodded.

"Ah, you mean when I saw you spying in the gardens last night."

I paused, staring up at him in anger. "Why are you teasing me?"

"Forgive me," was all he said, looking down at me gently.

We began walking once more.

"I am unsure of how to speak to you," he said quietly.

"The appropriate manner is with courtesy and respect in adherence to social rules."

"And yet you do not call me Your Grace, nor offer a curtsy."

I stopped and gave him a dramatic curtsy. "Forgive me, Your Grace."

He frowned and tilted his head at me. I walked on.

"Do you find me so distasteful now that you cannot treat me as we once were?"

"And what were we?"

"Friends."

I scoffed and shook my head. "We were not. We were children, and then you were the person I assumed I would marry. None of those things applies any longer. You are just a duke, and I am just a lady."

"I will not accept that."

"What does that mean?" I was suddenly aware of how close he was to me, and my heart, the traitorous beast, began to beat faster.

"I will not accept that nothing lies between us but platitudes."

"And because you will not accept it, I must agree?" I snapped. "Why is it that *I* have always to follow *your* determinations?"

"I did not mean—"

"I did not choose to walk with you, yet here I am. *I* wish there to be only platitudes between you and me, but *you* disagree. And because you are the man, it will be as *you* wish."

"I do not mean to anger you, Aphrodite."

"And yet you do." My heart twisted once more. "What do you want from me, Your Grace?"

"A second chance." He stepped close. "Aphrodite, I wish for another chance for us."

"Do you know you never explained to me what went wrong the first time?" I asked him, staring into his brown eyes, waiting, hoping he'd oblige.

"Forgive me," he whispered. "I beg of you."

"Clarify then, and do not beg."

He hung his head, closing his eyes. "I cannot."

I wished to hit him. To scream in his face and push him over.

"Your Grace, know this: One day I may be able to forgive

you, but by then I will surely be married to someone else, and it will no longer matter. Until then, please leave me be."

I turned and left his company, walking in the direction of my mother.

She grabbed my arm. "What has happened? What have you said?"

"Mama, if you love me, you will not force me into such a position again," I replied and pulled my arm out of her grasp.

6

Aphrodite

"And one, two, three. One, two, three. That is right, my lady, and now turn," said my instructor from the piano as I moved about the drawing room under my mother's gaze, for if there was anything she would not allow, it was for me to miss a single step. She had always believed that instructors and governesses were far too easy on me when she was not present. "Very good—"

"Not good at all," my mother interrupted the woman. "Perhaps for another lady, but not for you. Again, from the beginning! I will not have us disgraced before the queen once more."

"Mama, it has been hours," I begged.

"Do you believe me harsh, my dear girl? Let this serve as a lesson, then, for all the time you wasted in Belclere sulking. There is no way to outrun your responsibilities, only delay them."

I exhaled and truly wished to stomp my feet on the floor and wail as Abena did when she was tasked with pots to clean.

"Where is your mind, my dear?" my mother asked as I began to move to the music. "And why is your face still so stern? Do you dislike your partner?"

"I have no partner, Mama. I'm trapped alone in this dance."

"I have been told that books inspire imagination. Since you

are so besotted by reading, use your imagination and create a partner."

I knew whom my mind would imagine, and I dared not torture myself any further. The man was already in my dreams. He did not need to conquer my waking hours, as well.

"Aphrodite—"

"Your ladyship," a maid called, entering the drawing room.

"Yes?" My mother looked at her.

"A gentleman has come for the Lady Aphrodite."

"Who?" Both my mother and I asked in unison.

"A Mr. Tristian Yves."

My mother's shoulders fell.

This was my chance to end my musical misery. "I shall see him."

"And your steps?" my mother questioned.

"Can be taught another time? Is not the purpose of learning such steps for me to charm a suitor? Well, one has called."

She did not frown, but she did not seem pleased, either. Instead, she looked at my instructor, dismissing her.

"I do hope you know what you are doing," she said, picking at me as she moved to sit at the other end of the room where her needlework rested in wait.

"I am doing precisely as you requested. Finding a husband."

Neither she nor I could say more as the gentleman entered with another bouquet of roses in one hand and a wrapped gift in the other.

"Your ladyship." He nodded to my mother.

"Mr. Yves, your timing is most interesting," she said to his confusion as his brows came together.

"She means most welcome," I interrupted with a smile. "For you save me from many more dancing lectures."

"It has always been my wish to be a hero."

"Well done." I nodded and looked at his full hands. "And these . . ."

"Gifts!" he said as if he had only just remembered them. "For you. I do hope you accept them."

"Thank you." I took the bouquet, smelling the flowers before I gave them to the maid. He handed me his second gift. The moment it touched my hands, I was instantly aware it was a book. "May I open it now?"

"Yes, please."

I carefully undid the white string and peeled back the brown paper to reveal a rather expensive-looking edition of Shakespeare's sonnets, which truly made me smile.

"I know you are fond of reading," he said to me quickly.

"I am!" I said happily—until I opened it and saw that it had been marred with black ink.

"I wished not to shock you with anything unbecoming, so my mother had the book edited for content inappropriate for a lady," he said, proudly. I now wished to throw the book at his face—such a fine book.

"How thoughtful of you," my mother replied.

I thought she might have been mocking, as I wished to mock this stupidity, but she seemed earnest.

"Do you like it?"

"Yes," I lied with a smile. "Would you like to stay for tea?"

"It would be my pleasure."

I nodded and turned to the maid, who quickly went to fetch it. I waved him to the chairs. "Please."

"Thank you," he replied.

In truth, I could not wait for him to leave. But under my mother's eyes, I could not refuse his company now.

"I did not have the chance to inquire earlier, but you said you were in Drust last summer? Do you like it there?"

"It is far too uncivilized for my liking, so overrun by nature. I only go when forced," he answered with pomposity.

I very much liked Drust *and* its nature. "Pray tell, what forced you to visit such uncivilization?"

"My family owns a bank in the area, and sometimes I am called to check up on the running of things," he said as the maid returned with our tea and nibbles.

"Oh, so you are a banker?" I offered him a cup of tea.

"Yes. My family owns property in several counties, and it allows me to travel throughout the country."

Finally, something we shared in common. "I can say I am quite well-traveled, or at least more traveled than many my age, with my uncle and aunt."

"Is it not horrible?" He chuckled, and my shoulders fell slightly. "The long journeys, terrible roads, and I have yet to find an inn up to snuff."

"Yes." I nodded through the boredom.

And one, two, three. And one, two, three. The music played on in my mind, and I imagined myself dancing in the trees in Drust or the flower fields of Belclere. The sky bright and the air clean. I imagined myself running and laughing far too loudly. I thought of the horse I wished to ride as fast as its legs would allow. The cakes I could eat as I watched the sky. I thought of many things, and the duke—Evander—was there. It was not fair, for all the things I loved now and had loved as a child, he was in those memories alongside me.

"Forgive me. I am rambling on, but I must admit I have never been at such ease speaking to a lady before," Tristian said.

There was a twinge of guilt within me. "Thank you, and thank you for coming to see me. It is getting quite late."

"Yes, of course," he replied. "If you do not mind, may I call upon you again?"

I nodded. "Of course."

"Good day to you, Lady Aphrodite."

"And you, Mr. Yves."

He took a step back and nearly tripped over the foot of the table. He laughed awkwardly before turning to my mother. "Your ladyship."

"Do tell your mother I said hello."

"Certainly. She would very much like to speak with you— I mean meet you whenever you would like," he stammered.

My mother merely nodded, and it took some time for him to gather himself to leave. When he was gone, I exhaled deeply.

"You do not like him," my mother said, now at my side.

"What do you mean? He is a fine—"

"You do not like him. And he is clearly smitten with you. Entertaining him will give him hope. Can you be responsible for that?" she questioned, looking into my eyes. "For if you allow him to come down this road and are not prepared to give him an answer to his liking at the end, you would be very cruel, my dear."

"Mama, it is only the second time I have spoken to him." Surely, he did not plan to propose to me so quickly.

"In his mind, it is the thousandth time, for that is the nature of loving someone. They conquer your every thought, so while you may have met only once or twice, to him, it feels like many times before."

I knew not what to say, as that sounded like madness, and yet I knew the feeling.

"Careful, my dear. The pride of a man is far too dangerous to trifle with."

"I seek not to trifle with nor be cruel to anyone. I am merely doing as you instructed. I do not understand how a lady is meant to be amenable but not too amenable, for she may either look desperate or offend the pride of men. If I was to refuse to entertain his company at all, I would be branded a snob."

"My dear, you are going through what we all must and you will find your way, I swear it," she replied, cupping my cheek but offering very little answer, as always. Our whole lives, we were merely told to trust. To ask no question or seek any explanations.

"You have yet to tell me what was discussed between you and Evander."

"Mama, why are you so set on Evander?"

She cupped both sides of my face. "Because you are!"

"I am not—"

"You have fooled no one, Aphrodite. All day, you sit like an angel among men, unfazed, unbothered, as if you are not part of this world. And then he appears in front of you, and you become mortal. You show your anger, your pain, your joy, your fear, and, most dearly, your heart."

"Mama, he betrayed me—"

"He did." She nodded. "I racked my mind for nearly four years as to why. I do not have the answer, and it made me angry just as it did you. I was ready to let him and the whole business go. But fate has afforded you a second chance, and I do not wish to see either of you waste it because of pride."

"And I do not wish to be hurt again, Mama. Please excuse me," I said and left the room, rushing up the stairs to my own.

I had decided to marry as she asked, and if it was to be to someone like Tristian, then fine. Who cared if he did not like nature as I did? Who cared if he thought me unable to handle the works of Shakespeare? How would my life be any different? I already did things I did not like to do.

"Odite!" Abena burst into my room.

"I am unwell, Abena. I wish to rest."

"Papa said to give you this."

I looked to see she held a dictionary in her hand. Sitting up, I opened the book, and sure enough, it was edited.

This would always be the condition of my life.

Under Papa, then under a husband.

"Are you crying?" Abena poked her head underneath mine.

I smiled. "Yes, with joy, Papa truly knows how to brighten one's day, does he not?"

"I'll tell him." She smiled wide and took off running again. Of all my sisters, I was jealous of her the most, for she had the greatest freedom and did not even know it. Oh, how that freedom was wasted on children.

7

Aphrodite

The season was grueling. Every other day, there was breakfast or a ball or a gathering or an opening by one of the
numerous prestigious families hoping to secure their daughters a well-to-do husband. And though our itinerary was full,
my mother had taken note of the fact that there were fewer
invitations for us this year, seemingly on account of Damon
now being married. She believed that other families were
worried that Hathor and I would steal all the attention of the
night. What was her remedy? To host a ball herself. Thus, our
house was now in splendid chaos.

"What color are you wearing tonight, Odite?" Hathor asked,
rushing inside my room as I tried to read.

"I have not decided—"

"Will you please decide so *I* may decide?"

I rolled my eyes. "Very well, I believe I will wear white."

"I shall wear pink!" she said and ran out.

I shook my head and turned the page again, only for there
to be a knock at the door. I sighed and looked up to see Devana.
"Yes?"

"Can I have your ribbon?" she asked politely.

"Let me guess, the green one?"

She smiled and nodded.

"Go on."

"Thank you!" she replied, going through my drawer and taking it before leaving. Once more, the door shut, only for there to be *another* knock.

I kicked my foot and then composed myself. "Yes?"

"My lady, you have letters," Eleanor said as she entered.

I outstretched my hand for them. The first was from my aunt, the second from Tristian, and the third . . . from Evander. I was tempted to open his first, but I took Tristian's. As always, they had been inspected, as I could see the envelopes were opened.

Tristian had written, *I find myself unable to wait, for I fear I may lose my chance, and seek to request the honor of your first dance this evening. —Tristian Yves.*

I set the letter down and opened my aunt's, which was mostly about her life at Drust and how she missed me now that I was gone, but I couldn't concentrate on it. It all felt like a distraction before reading *his*. I could wait no longer.

> *I deserve your anger and reprimands, for I know that I have disappointed and hurt you. It truly was not my intent. And there is nothing I seek more than to fix what I have broken between us. Aphrodite, I will not fail you this time, I swear it. Forgive me just this once, spare me just this once . . . never will I hurt you again. It will be like it was, laughter between us, not bitterness. They say we cannot go back, but they say, too, that love is the greatest of all forces, and I am inclined to believe in love. Take my hand tonight and allow me your first dance. Allow it to be our first of many.*

> *—Yours, Evander.*

"Do you wish to wear the family pearls or diamonds to-night?" my mother asked.

I had not realized she had entered. Of course, she most likely knew the contents of the letter I now held to my chest. Her ability to appear when I least wished her to was astounding—or very well calculated on her part.

"I believe pearls will do just fine, Mama," I muttered, rising from my bed.

"Can I wear the diamonds, Mama?" Hathor ran in to ask.

"You may not!" she said.

"Mama, can you not be so obviously biased in her favor! I am your daughter, too," Hathor said.

If Hathor kept Mama occupied, perhaps I could make my escape.

"Aphrodite, where are you going?" my mother called after me.

"For a walk around town!" I said, rushing down the stairs.

"But you need to prepare!" She followed after me.

"The ball is not for several hours. Mama, I could walk to the other end of the town and back and still have time."

"Then help your sisters!"

I spun around and looked over her shoulder. "Hathor, do you need my help?"

She crossed her arms. "I am quite capable of looking well enough without you. It is not as if you ever know much to do anyway."

"Yes, thank heaven for natural beauty," I said, knowing how she would reply. She inhaled like a pufferfish, her arms dropping, and I, along with my mother, braced for impact.

"Let her go, Mama! Hopefully, she falls into a pigsty and never returns!"

"Hathor!" my mother yelled at her.

"And then her ghost would forever haunt you," Abena said, her head appearing at the top of the steps. "Everyone would say, 'Oh, such a shame about poor Odite.' All your days, they would talk of her. And I would tell them you cursed her."

"You little bug!" Hathor went after her.

"Girls! You will cease this moment!"

I glanced over to the library door where my father was watching. He looked at me and shook his head. I winked, moving to the door.

"Chaperone," he mouthed to me, and just then, fortunately, Silva stepped out of the drawing room.

I rushed over and linked arms with her. "May I steal you away?"

Before she could answer, I took her with me out the door as another maid joined, rushing with our purses.

"Where on earth do you wish to go?" Silva said as they started to walk.

"The moon? Is such a thing possible?" I asked.

"No, not at all." She laughed.

"Forgive me for pulling you away like this. I needed peace and, in the process, may have disturbed yours." I nodded to other ladies as they passed us by.

"No matter. A walk always does the body and mind good."

"I believe so, too, though I prefer a walk through nature and not the town," I said.

There were so many people it was impossible to truly relax.

"I find it amusing."

"Find what amusing?" I questioned.

She looked at me. "You wish to escape your family, yet I rather enjoy them."

"I enjoy them as well, just not all the time and especially not when I wish to be alone. I never get the chance to be alone. I have always had my brother, then, of course, my governess, then my sisters came, and I found myself never *not* under watch."

"Such is the nature for all young ladies, even I."

"Yes, but was your home not less chaotic as an only child?"

"And endlessly boring!" She sighed and glanced over at me. "I am already plain, so belonging to a plain house is overdoing it. Do you not think so?"

I giggled. "No."

"You truly do not know how blessed you are to live in such a household," she said as we turned and crossed the street, "where everyone loves and cares for and teases one another. Even your mama and papa."

"Are not husbands and wives meant to care for each other?"

"What is meant to happen and what actually transpires is often not the same. It is rare for true love matches to exist and survive the tenure of marriage. My parents, though I love them dearly, cannot wait to be separated from each other."

"I am sorry."

"No, do not be," she mused, "it is a system that works for them. They have their own rooms and appointments, times at which they both eat, and it changes only when we have company."

That sounded terribly depressing. I wished not to pry, but I thought that surely such an arrangement was not the case for Silva and my brother.

"Ladies."

One word.

It took just one word, and I was able to discern whose voice it was. So when I lifted my head and saw Evander alongside his sister, my heart fell.

"Your Grace," Silva spoke to him first.

"Lady Montagu." He nodded to her and then refocused on me. "Lady Aphrodite. How are you both this morning?"

I still did not speak, so Silva did. "Quite well, Your Grace. If you will excuse us—"

"Thank heavens I ran into you both," Verity exclaimed suddenly. "I have been utterly at a loss about what to do."

"Are you well?" I asked her.

"I am not." She frowned. "I have no dress for this evening's ball, and my brother is as clueless as a bird about how to help me. If you both can spare the time, will you accompany me to the modiste?"

"My dear, I do not believe any modiste will be able to fashion a dress for you in mere hours. Do you not have a dress among your things?" Silva questioned.

"I fear I have worn all my finest ones already. And I do not wish to appear before her ladyship in a less than fine gown. Of all the ladies in the ton, she would notice." She smiled sweetly.

I glanced at her brother to see his focus entirely on me. It took a mere moment before my heart began to quicken.

"I will do my best not to take much of your time." Her face fell, and her eyes softened. "It is times like this when I wish I had Mama or an elder sister."

"Does the dowager . . ." I tightly squeezed Silva's arm to stop her from speaking.

Despite our close connection with the duke, I did not know much of the Dowager Duchess of Everely, except that she was greatly disliked, especially by three people—Evander, his sister, and my mother.

"The best course of action would be to add finery, lace, or silks to an already existing dress," I said to her. "That is something even a household seamstress may accomplish on such short notice. Madam Marjorie's shop has the best."

"Oh, that is not but a short walk from here. Will you join me?" she pressed.

"Of course." I nodded to her, and she smiled wide. So I looked at her brother. "Your Grace, we shall return her in one piece. You need not accompany us, for I know men have no desire to be part of such things."

"Very true. However, I shall accompany you anyway as I fear you underestimate the monetary damage my dear sister can do in a single shop."

"I know nothing about that!" Verity lifted her head high and took hold of Silva's arm, pulling her away from me, which then forced Evander and me to walk together.

Hathor had informed me that she was able to speak with Verity while at the park and found her a bit devious . . . I did not understand at the time. But now I surely did.

"Are you not ashamed to use your sister as a method to speak to me?" I asked.

"You are the one who spoke first." He was right.

So I was silent, and he spoke again.

"I must admit, however, that I do enjoy when she plots in my favor."

"So, you are aware of what she is doing?" I looked at him.

"Was she not obvious?"

"Very."

He laughed. "Yes, but what were you expecting I should do? I wished her success, and she succeeded. Consequently, I am able to speak with you again."

"Devious." I stared at the back of his sister. "You and her both."

"Me? I have done nothing."

"By doing nothing, you allowed *her* to do what you wished. Devious," I shot back.

His eyes danced with amusement. "Very well, I shall plead guilty."

"Good. Now let us not speak."

"If you saw through my sister's act, you could have rejected her offer."

I frowned. "She still might need help with dresses. And as she said, she does not have another lady's company she relies on."

"Ah, so you're here out of pity."

"Do not say it like that," I replied sharply. "I merely . . . I merely . . ."

"Wished to speak with me as well?"

"You think highly of yourself, Your Grace."

"I am quite tired of thinking lowly of myself," he muttered, and when I looked at him, he said nothing more for a moment. Then he whispered, "Did you read my letter?"

"What letter?" I pretended to be ignorant as I held my head high.

"The one open in your hand."

My head dropped immediately, and I looked to my hands where I still clenched his letter.

He chuckled.

And I glared. "Are you laughing at me?"

He nodded. "Yes, for you have become an even worse liar."

"Some of us cannot be as proficient as you, imp." The words came right out of me before I had thought to stop them. My eyes widened, and I dared not look at him!

"You have become a worse liar and a better curser, I see," he muttered.

"Forgive me." I brushed my hair behind my ear. "That was—"

"I remember when you were all but twelve. Your sister

ripped your favorite book, and your mother told you to forgive her. So you did as you were told, then marched deep into the gardens at Belclere until you got to a strong tree where you proceeded to call your sister a ninny, maggot pie, and fart from hell."

I bit my lips to keep from laughing.

"You nearly broke your toe kicking the tree," he said as he gave in to his laughter.

"Stop!" I begged.

"There were older marks on the tree, and I realized then that you had a cursing tree, and you used it often."

"I know nothing about that," I said with a smile. "A lady never uses foul language."

"Unless the lady's name is Aphrodite. Then she uses it all the time, just unbeknownst to her victims."

"I am no longer speaking to you," I said, like a child. As we reached the dressmaker, I walked inside, knowing he would not follow. But when I recognized one of the patrons inside, I turned right back around and stood beside him.

"What is the matter?" He tried to look.

"Do not!" I muttered.

"What is it, Aphrodite?"

"It's her," I whispered.

"Who?"

"Her!" Our faces were far too close, so I jumped back. He seemed not to be affected by proximity like I was. "Her . . . from the shrubbery . . . in the garden of the ball."

"Truly." He gaped. "Which one?"

"What are you doing?"

"Looking for her."

"Why? I saw . . . I saw . . . you know what I saw."

"Exactly. She should be more afeared of seeing you than the other way around. Though I doubt she knows you exist."

I frowned. "You do not think she saw me?"

"Despite how long and intensely you were observing?" he teased. My eyes narrowed to a point on his face. "No. I do not believe she saw you. I believe she was far too taken away to notice any of the world around her."

"Really?" I glanced back as the young lady was looking around the shop with her mama. She looked to be even younger than I in the light of day.

"Are you sure it is her?"

"I have seen her face too many times in my dreams to be mistaken."

"Is that so?"

The gaze of his brown eyes shifted. And it felt as if he were pulling me in, and I could not look away.

"Yes," I finally managed to answer.

He inhaled through his nose and glanced away from my face, looking to the sky. "I swear. Aphrodite . . ."

"You swear what?"

He swallowed hard but said nothing.

"Do not become reticent. Speak your thoughts."

"I cannot."

"Why not?"

"Because my thoughts are beastly," he replied, finally looking at me. "And I fear you are not afraid of beasts."

"Is that not a good thing?" I whispered. "To not be afraid."

"No, for it makes the beasts even more hungry," he whispered back. "It takes them to the point of starvation until they can no longer remain gentlemanly and find themselves in the shrubbery."

A warmth spread over me . . . as it had at night while I remembered what I saw in the gardens. My breathing felt heavier. "Does it hurt . . . being taken to the shrubbery?"

He glanced down, flexing his fist. "Aphrodite, I beg of you, let us speak of something else . . ."

"Does it hurt?" I repeated my question.

He said nothing, again inhaling through his nose before looking at me. "The first time for a lady, it may, depending on her partner. Truthfully, it always depends on her partner whether it is a painful or pleasurable experience."

My heart quickened, and my chest tightened. "The one in there had a pleasurable experience?"

"I did not see well enough, but I would assume so."

Finally. Answers.

"Aroused?" I stepped closer to ask.

"Yes."

"Yes, what?" I asked, not understanding.

"You asked me if I was aroused, did you not?" he asked, head tilted to the side as he looked into my eyes. "Or do you still think it merely means to arise from slumber?"

"How can I know any other meaning when no one tells me?" I questioned. "So tell me."

"It is hard to explain . . . for it is a feeling."

"What is this feeling?"

"Like heat." He stepped closer. "Like fire spreading throughout your body, desire pulsating upon the skin, and an ache in the pit of your stomach."

"To what end?"

"The shrubbery." He inhaled and looked as though he would eat me like a beast, and I felt my breathing become much slower. "Or if you are skilled enough to release on your own."

"My . . . my . . . own?"

"Lady Aphrodite?"

I spun around to see Mrs. Frinton-Smith, an older woman, whose great-great-grandfather was once a famed peer, I believe, and her father the third son of a viscount, but her husband was a rich merchant who owned several shops down the lane.

"Mrs. Frinton-Smith, good morning. How are you?" I asked, watching as her blue eyes skimmed over Evander. Oh no, here began the start of a new rumor.

"I'm lovely, my dear. What brings you in today?" she asked as if she were the shopkeeper.

"Lord Everely's sister is seeking a modification to a dress for my family's ball tonight. My sister-in-law, who is just there, watching by the window, and I came to help when I found myself a bit heated and remained outside. My maid is just there as well," I said to give myself as much cover as possible.

"How kind of you to wait with her, Your Grace," Mrs. Frinton-Smith said to Evander.

He nodded to her. "It is more for my sister's sake. I would rather be at the club with the other gentlemen."

Her eyes widened, and I wished to hit him upon the head. Now she would think he did not wish to be in my company.

"Well, I am sure they will not keep you much longer." She smiled at him. "Lady Aphrodite, I would like to introduce you to my niece, Miss Edwina Charmant, who came down for the season. She is most excited about your ball. Edwina!" she called into the shop, and out came Edwina, the woman from the garden!

"Hello," was all I could muster, my mind a blank.

"Hello, my lady. You truly are a beauty. I am very excited about your ball," she said.

"My dear niece is quite taken with our great ton," Mrs. Frinton-Smith said. "She's still a bit green, so I do hope you will take care of her tonight . . . should you not be too busy." Her eyes shifted to Evander. She should have kept her gossiping eyes on her niece, for I was worried about our garden.

"Of course." I nodded.

"Aphrodite, we are finished," Silva said, coming out with Verity.

"Well, we will not hold you, as everyone must prepare." Mrs. Frinton-Smith and her niece took their leave.

When I saw the driver of their carriage and the look that he and Edwina shared, I was sure he had been her partner in the shrubbery.

I had never known a scandalous tale before anyone else. I was not really sure what to make of this information, but I was worried for her. She was young and this match was also wholly inappropriate. More so for her than him. He would be a rogue . . . but she would be ruined.

"Should something be said or done?" I whispered watching them go.

"About?"

"Her," I said forcefully before looking to him. "No matter how . . . pleasant the experience, she is still but a young lady. What if she is being taken advantage of and knows not the risks?"

"All young women know of the risks—"

"We do not. For love blinds us and makes even the wisest of us fools," I snapped angrily at him.

He frowned. "And so, what shall you do? Rid the world of love?"

"Aphrodite, we should return," Silva called out to me as she suddenly took my arm before I could reply.

"Yes, we should." I held on tight, aflutter with emotions. "Goodbye, Your Grace—"

"Lady Aphrodite," Evander called to me, "I do pray that you accept the request of my letter."

I stared at his face for a long moment before turning to leave.

I needed to think.

8

Aphrodite

*L*ike *fire spreading throughout your body, desire pulsating upon the skin, and an ache in the pit of your stomach.* His words repeated in my mind as always but this time with inescapable intensity. I now also had a more profound ability to understand them, but it was not enough for me. Some of his words I still did not understand. I felt that, should we be alone, or as alone as we could be, he would answer truthfully. He would protest just slightly, but he would do so in the end, and that was far more than I received from any other person. The prospect of not being treated like a child who was kept ignorant of the world was breathtakingly freeing.

I was eager to see him again.

"Have you chosen who shall receive your first dance?" Hathor asked as she entered my room once again unannounced, dressed not in pink but red.

"You have changed your color for the evening," I replied.

"Yes, more catching to the eye," she said. "I need all the advantage I may get."

I smiled, toying with the feather in my hands, as my maid finished my hair. "What are you seeking to get, sister?"

"A husband, of course."

"And yet you have rejected all the callers who have come to see you."

"I refuse to accept anything less than a duke." She lifted a vial of scent from my table, sniffing it.

I scoffed. "Then your choices are a duke or a prince. Your standard may be a bit high, for I do not see many princes around."

"Then I shall have a duke." She shrugged, placing the scent upon her neck. "Why, are you saying it is impossible for me to be a duchess?"

"No, by all means, you would surely be the greatest of our time."

She grinned at my words. "I believe so as well."

"And pray tell, how many dukes are here this season?"

"Three, if you must know, well two, seeing how you are blinded by one of them."

I tore my gaze from her and glanced back into the mirror to check my hair. "I know not what you mean."

"Oh, please. All the ton is abuzz with talk of you. Apparently, Mrs. Frinton-Smith saw you and the Duke of Everely speaking rather intensely in front of Madam Marjorie's shop."

How did gossip fly so quickly?

"Oh, and?"

"They said you looked rather smitten, and he uninterested . . . again. Odite, they are saying that you will chase after him and fail once more."

I placed the feather down and waved off my maid as I rose. "They do not know what they are speaking of."

"Of course not, but you fuel their fire by entertaining his company." She followed after me. "It is *he* who wishes to court you, but because of his past actions, the gossips think you seem desperate for his attention."

"Are you worried for me?" I put on my pearls. "Would you not rather I am mocked than praised?"

"I am not cruel." She sighed. "I simply do not wish to always be in your shadow. That does not mean I want you to be mocked. You are the eldest, so if you are the subject of ridicule, so am I."

"So this lecture is partially out of concern for your fate?" I asked as the maid handed me earrings.

"Yes, partially," she admitted and then came to stand in front of me. "But the other part is true. I do not wish to see you so utterly disappointed again. Mama says the best type of gentleman is a reliable man like Papa, who will always be there when you need him."

"Mama is fond of Evander."

Her shoulders dropped. "Oh dear, you have returned to calling him by his name."

I rolled my eyes. "Hathor, please. It's not so remarkable to call a childhood friend by their Christian name."

"Mama might be biased in his favor," she said sternly. "But everyone in the family is against him."

"I hardly think you can speak for everyone else. Besides, Papa seems uninterested."

"Papa is always interested. He likes to see the full play unfold before adding commentary. You know that."

"That is true. Do you remember when we went to see—"

"No, you shall not derail me!" She held her hands up as though she were Mother, and so I smacked them down.

"If you wish to be a duchess, you should remember your manners."

"Sorry," she said, realizing her actions. "But promise me you will not let yourself be swept away."

"Hathor, I am fine. I have not been swept anywhere. Now, are you ready?"

"Ready for what?"

"The ball. I am finished. We may go."

"Odite, we cannot possibly go down now."

"Why not?"

"There are not enough people. It will spoil my entrance." She paused and looked me over. "On second thought, if you wish to go, you may, as then they will have all drunk their fill of you by the time I make my arrival."

"The way in which your mind works is unmatched." I rolled my eyes and lifted the edge of my dress as I turned to leave, but she did not follow behind me. "Do you seek to wait in my room?"

"Yours has the best view of the entrance, so I shall be able to see who has arrived."

"Hathor, no! Out!"

"Oh, please! I swear I will not do anything else. The only other rooms with this view are Mama and Papa's and Damon's. I cannot wait in a married person's room."

"Fine," I said. "But if you touch—"

"I shall sit here and take my leave only to come down to the ball."

She was, as always, ridiculous.

As I entered the hall, I heard music playing and the soft chatter of the voices from below.

"You look pretty." A harsh whisper came from above me.

When I looked, I saw the faces of Hector, Devana, and Abena peering at me through the gaps in the railing, their maid and governess behind them to keep watch. I was sure that was as far as they would be allowed to come down.

"Are you sure?" I whispered up to them and spun so they could see my full dress. "Does it look nice?"

Each of them nodded, and Hector even gave a wink.

I smiled. "If it is boring, I shall sneak up and spend time with you."

"Can you not bring us down?" Abena questioned. "We would surely make it unboring."

"Mama said if she saw you that you would sleep with the dogs," Hector told her.

"But we do not have dogs," she argued.

"We had a dog, and he died. He is buried in the yard," he lied to her, and her eyes widened.

"We had a dog?"

Not wishing to spoil Hector's fun, I nodded. "And it seems Mama wishes to bury you with it if you come down."

"That is unreasonable," she said.

"Papa says Mama is not reasonable," Devana replied gently, and I truly wished to laugh at the three of them.

"Aphrodite, do not linger!"

At the sound of our mother's voice, they all ran back up the stairs quickly. I descended, and when I reached her level, she stepped back to appraise me. She adjusted bits of the gown's neckline, pushed my shoulders back, and then nodded to herself.

"Where is your sister?" she questioned.

"Waiting to make a grand entrance."

"The girl can be sharp." My mother grinned. "Why are you not waiting with her?"

"Because my presence is so grand that whether I entered first or last, I would gain attention," I said in jest.

"Very right."

"Mama"—I laughed, taking her arm as we walked toward the ball—"I was not serious."

"Well, you ought to be. Tonight is very important."

"How so?"

"You shall publicly choose whom you wish to dance with."

I sighed heavily. "Do you not get tired?"

"Of?"

"Everything, especially trying to arrange a wedding based on the slightest of interactions."

"One day, when you become a mother, you will tell me of all the things you'd rather do, and you will do them. Until such day, I shall plan. Now, whom shall you choose?"

I said nothing as we had reached the hall. I released her arm as the butlers opened the door for us, and upon entering, I found myself wondering exactly how many more people Hathor was waiting for, as the hall was already near full.

"This is more than I expected." I laughed, looking at the wonder of our transformed hall. It was decorated in the finest vinery, which even hung from above, there were also the richest foods, and even a sculpture made from desserts in the shape of a bird. Farthest from the door was a stage on which singers were preparing to perform.

"Do not stare in wonder, my dear. It is our home," my mother said. As we walked through, the guests nodded to us, to which my mother offered a polite nod in return.

"It is hard not to, Mama, when you do the wondrous." I smiled as we reached my father, who was glancing up at the garden above our heads.

"Would it not have been less trouble to have us host this *in* the garden, my love?" my father asked.

"And risk rain ruining my event? I think not."

"I see." He nodded and then paused. "Where is Hathor? Still preparing?"

"At this point, she may as well just stay in her room," Damon said as he reached us.

Silva was behind him in the most beautiful red silk. Hathor's color. But then again, Silva was married, so hopefully Hathor wouldn't be upset.

"But she was ready when I saw her," Silva added when Damon gave her a drink from one of the servers.

"Hathor is the least of my worries," my mother said, looking around the ballroom.

"If she is the least, does that make me the greatest?" I asked.

She did not answer, causing my father and Damon to chuckle.

I looked upon the guests who had already arrived. Suddenly the doors opened, allowing entrance to a new guest, and my mother cursed under her breath for the first time that I'd ever heard.

"That whore."

I was so taken aback that I stared at her in amazement. Only when she took a step forward and my father grabbed her arm, stilling her, did I get over my shock.

"Do not make a scene, my love," my father whispered.

"How dare she come here?" my mother said with a hiss.

I finally turned to see Verity, but it was not Verity my mother had an issue with.

It was the woman beside her. Dressed in jewels with a grand wig and her dress of heavy silks stood the Dowager Duchess of Everely. I looked to see if Evander was with them, but he was not.

"Remain calm," my father said to my mother as the dowager and Verity made their way to us.

My mother lifted her head, breathing through her nose. On the other side of her, I watched as Damon took Silva's hand and stepped farther away from our mother. Should I have moved, too?

"Lady Monthermer, how splendid your home is," the dowager said.

My mother stared at her for a long moment . . . too long.

"Thank you, Your Grace," my father spoke for her. "It was chaos, but my wife has managed to pull it off once again."

"Yes—"

"Verity," my mother cut her off, "how beautiful you are. Every time I see you, it is as though I receive a vision of your mother."

"Thank you, your ladyship," Verity replied. "Though I do not know if I live up to the grace of my mother."

"Yes, the duchess was very well received by all. In fact, even the queen considered her to be the crown jewel of the season. She would never have been held as a mockery to the nobility at court." My mother smiled and looked over to the dowager, who was now glaring at my mother.

My father squeezed her hand.

My mother said to Verity, "You have her grace. Do not worry. Such things are what we are *born* with."

"If only those with such high birth lived longer," the dowager said, and now I truly felt as though I should move back.

I looked at Verity to see if she wished to escape, but instead it seemed she was rather amused, eagerly waiting for my mother's next jab. And my father could not grip strong enough to stop her.

"Yes, if only. But it is better to have a short and noble life, forever held in high esteem and beloved, than to be shameless, pretending to be something one can never be. And marring such beautiful silks and jewels with a stench that cannot be removed, thus decreasing their value altogether. As I told your mother, Luella, once, if you put a pig in a dress, it is still nothing but a pig in a dress."

My father's eyes shot to me, willing me to say something.

"Mama," I said, placing my hand on her arm. "I fear now upon seeing Verity's dress that mine might not be up to par. Should I change?"

"No, my dear, both you and Verity look splendid. As I said, it is a thing of birth," she replied, and my father again looked at me. Luckily, she switched her attention to Verity. "Come, my dear, I wish to introduce you to friends of mine. I fear for the company around you at times."

"That would be most welcome, for sometimes I find myself afraid, as well," Verity replied and shot her stepmother a glance before walking away with my mother.

The dowager stood there, trembling in rage before she gave a quick nod to my father and walked in the opposite direction.

"Dear God," Damon said as he rushed back over, laughing as he looked us over. "Never has there been a sharper blade than the tongue of a woman."

Father exhaled looking to me. "That was the best you could do?"

"You have been married to her for over thirty years. Was that all *you* could do?" I pressed back. "Reason dictates the more experienced party take charge."

"And society dictates a man does not interfere with the battles of women," he replied. "Next time, drag her away."

"Impossible," Damon and I both said, then looked at each other and laughed.

"May I ask?" Silva questioned, now in our little circle as well. "Is it wise to make an enemy of the dowager?"

"It is not," my father replied. "But they have been in this battle since before any of you were born. So only the second coming of Christ can end it now."

"Lord Monthermer!" one of my father's friends called.

"Finally, sane company. Excuse me," he said and left us.

"So, let me understand," Silva whispered. "Your mother *abhors* the dowager to this degree due to her friendship with the former Duchess of Everely?"

"We Du Bells are a stubborn and loyal breed," my brother explained to her. "We do not easily forgive anyone who hurts our own. And in the case of Lady Luella Farraday, the former Duchess of Everely, my mother forgives not at all. She truly considered her a sister."

"Is it wrong that I feel slightly for the dowager?" she asked. We could both see the dowager in the crowd, spoken to by few but shunned by many more.

They were not as harsh as my mother, of course, greeting her politely and then moving on.

"Believe me when I say, from my memories of past events, she deserves it and much more," my brother replied. "The cruelty she may seem to be a victim of is no more than the cruelty she offered, especially to the former duke's children."

"What do you mean?" I asked. "What cruelty?"

He looked me over, opened his mouth, and then stopped. "Nothing, sister."

That was not *nothing*. "But—"

"Look who has arrived," he said, and my heart started beating quickly.

I turned, thinking it was him, but it was just Tristian. And when he saw me and started to move toward me, I put my drink down to walk away.

"Where are you going?" Damon called after me.

"I shall return in a moment." Though I did not know where I could hide in a ball, not when everyone kept slowing me down to speak or introduce me to someone else. All the while, I could feel Tristian coming toward me.

The only refuge was outside, so I rushed to the servants' door and raced downstairs to make my escape to the only place I thought I could breathe freely.

"My lady?"

I turned to see the whole kitchen pausing their work to stare at me.

"Is there anything we can help you with . . . ?" asked the maid standing before me.

"Um . . . no . . . I mean . . ." I did not want to return upstairs, but it was not correct for me to be among the servants. Then again, I was a lady of the house. Surely, I was free to stay wherever I liked.

"I know this is quite odd." I laughed, but they just stared at me. "But may I stay down here for a moment?"

They all gave one another knowing looks.

"Of course, my lady," the butler said, pulling out a stool for me to sit on. He dusted it as best he could with his hands.

"Thank you," I said and sat down.

They returned to their work, but it was now very quiet. I was obviously impeding them. And it made me wonder what in the world I was doing.

Why had I come down here?

Why was I staying down here?

Evander, my heart answered.

Sighing, I reached for one of the pastries on the table.

"Aphrodite!"

I jumped off the stool, my hand dropping as I turned to meet the face of my brother.

"What on earth are you doing down here?"

I stared. "Sitting?"

He frowned and came over, taking my hand. "We are going back up. You cannot sit with the servants. You are bothering them."

"I am not," I lied and turned back to see if anyone would vouch for me. They all looked away. My presence was more disturbing than I'd thought.

"This is very immature."

"I was merely sitting—"

"You were hiding." He gave me a look. "You do not want to accept Tristian's first dance?"

"Does everyone know the contents of my letters?" I frowned.

"Aphrodite, you are my most sensible sister."

"Liar," I muttered. "That is Devana."

He smiled and nodded, and I smacked his arm. "Nevertheless, you have a great deal more sense than other young ladies. Please do not let Evander steal it from you again."

"I am not—"

"Yes, you are." He frowned. "You ran, because you are waiting for him. And that in itself is the problem. No gentleman, duke or not, should keep a lady such as yourself waiting. A true gentleman who requests the first dance comes on time to secure that dance. Who is here?"

I said nothing.

"You do not have to accept Tristian, but you still owe him better than to hide."

"Yes, brother," I replied.

"Good. Now let us return," Damon said, offering me his arm.

I accepted it, taking his words to heart as we walked back

toward the ball. Evander had been so adamant that I forgive him, that I give him my first dance, but he was not yet here. Even as I returned, I could see his sister with my mother. How had she arrived before him? Were they not coming from the same place?

Gentlemen were supposed to be reliable.

"Lady Aphrodite," Tristian said, appearing before me. "As always, you are the sun in the room."

I smiled as Damon released my arm and slowly stepped to the side. "Thank you, sir."

"It would be my honor if I could have your first dance."

His offer hurt, and the disappointment hurt. Once again, Evander had given me hope, only to fail.

"Of course," I said, giving him my hand.

As if fate wished to mock me, that was the moment Evander entered the room. I looked away and allowed Tristian to lead me to the center of the dance floor.

9

Damon

H is eyes were upon her like a starving man before a feast. All of him disheveled and distraught. When he took a step toward her, I was already before him, blocking his path.

"You are too late," I said.

"Move."

"I will not. And you will mind yourself, for you are in my home," I reminded him. "You have no right to come here and cause a scene when you are the one who failed to show."

"I was . . ." He stopped and looked down, breathing in through his nose. "I must speak with her. I must explain."

"I said no," I replied and grabbed his arm. He hissed in pain and I felt the dampness of his coat, lifting my hand to see blood. "What in God's name?" I leaned closer to see the blood now spilling down his hand. "You are injured. We shall call for a—"

"Say nothing!" he snapped and stepped back. He glanced once more at my sister before taking his leave.

"Is everything all right?" Silva asked as she came to my side. "Why are you bleeding?"

"It is not mine," I whispered, hiding my hand. "Remain here."

"Damon."

"Later," I said before rushing out the door.

The fool cannot possibly be thinking of riding home alone in the dark while injured. I watched him lift himself onto his horse and take off into the night.

Shit. Shit! *Do not get involved . . . I ought not to get involved.* Really. Damn that man!

"Sir, I will need to borrow your horse! Forgive me," I said to the first gentleman I saw dismount. I did not even wait for his reply.

Kicking the horse, I went as fast as I could, feeling the wind push against me. It was dark but not so much that I was unable to make way.

It took all of ten minutes before I caught up with the madman, which was proof enough there was something amiss, for he had always been the better rider between us. His figure hunched, and his horse slowed before he slumped from the animal's back.

"Evander!" I hollered, coming up on his left side, gripping him before he fell. "Are you a fool?"

"Leave me be!" he hollered, trying to steady himself.

"I will not. Should you die, my mother would blame me." Not to mention Aphrodite.

He chuckled, lifting his head as he struggled for air. "I am her favorite between us."

"Oh, shut up!" I snapped, rolling my eyes. "Can you still ride? We need to get you home and seen quickly, or I can go back—"

"So you still do care, *bro*—"

"Do not," I cut him off. "I am merely acting as a Good Samaritan for a mentally challenged man."

"You believe me to be mentally challenged?"

"Clearly, for there are only two of us here, and I am not the one short of breath and bleeding," I snapped. "Can you still ride if I am here guiding?"

He nodded.

"Good. Go, but slowly," I ordered.

He was a year older than I. We had grown up together, and throughout all that time, he was always the responsible one, the noble one, the most capable one. Much the same as Hathor felt toward Aphrodite, I had felt toward him—part sibling, part rival. But he no longer matched the man I competed against in everything, the one who spoke six languages fluently, who was an expert marksman, skilled horseman, and even scholarly enough to speak with my father. Once upon a time, I truly believed he was made differently than the rest of us.

But now . . . now he was pitiful.

It took us twenty minutes to reach his home, and by the end of it, he was nearly unconscious.

"Call a doctor!" I hollered to the hands coming to fetch our horses, and jumped down.

"No . . . it's fine," he said, nearly falling. I caught him and pulled him down.

"Did I not tell you to shut up?" I held his arm around my neck, looking back to the men in the yard. "Fetch a doctor!"

"Yes, my lord!" they answered.

"Can you make it to the stairs?" He did not respond. "Evander!"

He still did not answer.

Shit.

"Where is the parlor?" I screamed at the maid, causing her to jump.

"Here, my lord." She directed me, and I took him to the divan.

"Fetch water and a cloth and . . . brandy!" I pulled off his necktie and his coat, trying to find the source of his wound, only to discover more blood. "Dear God."

He groaned in pain as I removed his coat.

I finally got to his shirt and saw the makeshift bandage over his shoulder, which had become soaked in blood.

"The things you asked for, my lord!" The maid came in.

I rose, but I knew not what to do beyond this.

"The doctor, my lord!" another servant called.

"Oh, thank God! Bring him in!" I said, moving to the door as a young gentleman not even my age rushed inside. "This is the doctor you found? A young boy?"

"I assure you I am not . . . my lord. And you will find no better than me at this hour. The patient?" he asked and did not wait for me to direct him before going to Evander's side. "What happened to him?"

"I am unsure," I said. "I saw him bleeding and brought him home."

He checked the dressing and Evander's shoulder before releasing the bandage, as the blood flowed heavily.

"Well?" I asked, leaning closer.

"He has been stabbed."

"What?" *Stabbed?*

"And from the look of this, he sought to bandage himself. He's truly blessed. He should have long since bled out."

What in the hell had he gotten himself into? "But he can be saved."

"He will need to rest his shoulder as well as overcome this fever to recover," the doctor replied, reaching into his bag. "I am more concerned about the fever. What prevented him from getting help?"

As if Evander had heard him, he breathed his answer heavily, "Aphrodite."

"What?" the doctor questioned.

"Ignore him. It is his madness." I shook my head, picking up the bottle of brandy the maid had brought and taking a large drink of it. I stepped back, allowing the doctor to work, and I had to admit, he seemed proficient and managed to stop the bleeding.

It felt as though ages passed before he finally stopped and wiped his brow. "He will need medicine and to be monitored through the night, simply for his fever to break. I will remain if you do not mind."

I did not. I much preferred it, actually. However, I knew Evander rarely allowed people into his sphere. Should he awake with a strange man in his home, who knew what he would do.

"Of course. I will remain as well."

"Do you not need to return to your ball?" he questioned.

"You are aware of who I am?"

"I was not aware until he said the name Aphrodite. There is only one person within all of London who has such a name. And from your clothes and closeness to the duke, I merely assumed. His Grace, though, is wearing a footman's coat."

I had not even noticed until he lifted the coat for me to observe. Evander's clothes were always much more refined.

"He was determined to get wherever he was going." The doctor frowned, standing. "Very foolish. He could have died. It is good you followed after him."

I glanced over at the man now resting. I was unsure of how he had been injured, only that despite his wound, he sought first to go to my sister, even if it was to kill him.

Damn him. For now, I was a villain in his story, having all but told Aphrodite that he was a disappointment for showing up late. Had I not gone to fetch her, she might have come back up only when he had arrived, and his sacrifice would not have been in vain.

No. I shook my head. It was best Aphrodite did not get dragged into his chaos.

"My lord . . . my lord?"

"Yes? I mean, pardon me." I shook my head. "I have not even gotten your name."

"It is Dr. Theodore Darrington. I would shake your hand, but . . ." He lifted his blood-stained hand to me.

"I understand. There is a basin of water, and brandy." I lifted the bottle. "I do not know what else to offer—"

"It is fine. I will wait until the patient is well. He will need something to sleep," he said and moved to the basin to clean his hands.

"I am fine," the stubborn fool called, trying to rise, forcing the doctor and me both to his side.

"You are not fine, Your Grace—"

"Wallace!" Evander called out, and immediately, the butler appeared. "Show the doctor out and see him paid handsomely."

"Evander," I snapped.

"Your Grace, you are not—"

"I trust I can rely on your discretion," he said exhaustedly to the doctor.

The doctor stared down at him and sighed before glancing at me. "His fever needs to be checked in the course of the night. If it is not down, have him take this." He handed me a vial.

"Thank you," I replied.

"Your Grace, please heed my word and rest for the next few days. And call upon me again so I may observe your wound."

Evander nodded, and the doctor gathered his things to leave.

"Must you be so stubborn?" I asked.

"I trust only my people," Evander muttered and lay back on the divan, swallowing slowly. "Do not allow strangers into my home again."

"Next time, I shall merely leave you to die," I scoffed and took a drink of brandy. "What happened?"

He did not answer, because he was Evander and seemed to care only about one thing. "How am I to make this up to her? I had just gotten her to speak with me, and not in anger."

"When?" Then I remembered the recent gossip. "Ah, the dress shop. What makes you so confident she would have accepted you had you not been delayed?"

He did not answer, which was troubling. Instead, he said, "She would have accepted me because she loves me still."

I laughed, pulling up a chair. "If only we could bottle your ego, for it is stronger than all of the brandy in the world."

"You mock us unfairly," he muttered.

"I mock only you, and you give me no other choice," I stated and drank once more.

"Can you not just support me as you once did?" He groaned, shifting to his other side.

"With blind loyalty? Never. Evander, please let my sister go. I do not want her involved in whatever this is. Women need reliability."

He chuckled and opened one eye. "Never would I have thought you to say something like that."

"Yes, some of us grew up," I scoffed, looking at the bottle in my hand. "You have a sister, and a younger brother who could come into control of your estates should something happen to you. Surely, you would not like to hand such a victory to your stepmother."

"That woman and her children are my curses," he sneered. "Am I mistaken, or was she at your home?"

"You are not mistaken."

"Your mother did not kill her?"

"She did in every way but physically. My mother called her a pig, as well as being ill-bred and tarnishing the very clothes she wore. She left the *dowager* standing there in front of all the ton, dumbstruck."

Evander laughed outright. "I did not think I could regret missing tonight any more than I already did. Your mother has always been my heroine."

"At a great cost to the rest of us, I might add," I shot back bitterly. "I often wonder what sort of friendship inspired such deep loyalty that it superseded your mother's passing and moved on to her children."

"The irony of you asking that when here you are, my loyal friend."

"I am most definitely no longer your friend!" I declared, pointing to him. "As I said, I am merely a—"

"A Good Samaritan? Yes, I heard you. In fact, your voice is still very much ringing in my head. You certainly can yell."

"I see you truly will survive, for you have returned to being a nuisance."

"We will be brothers again, so it is best you get acquainted with the feeling once more." He grinned and closed his eyes.

"I hope my sister shatters your heart."

"She does every day when I awake and see that she is not

my wife." That was the last thing he said before succumbing to his exhaustion.

Love's greatest fool.

Aphrodite

"Where is Damon? Is he not yet awake?" Father asked as he came to the breakfast table and walked to the head chair.

"Not so loud, my love," my mother whined, waving him to sit down.

He looked at her and grinned.

"Mama, were you foxed?" Abena asked as she reached for the bread.

"How many times must I teach you to watch your mouth, child?" my mother snapped at her. "But no, I am not. Ladies do not become foxed. Because it is unbecoming to drink to excess."

My father snorted, and when my mother's glare shifted, he focused on his newspaper.

"Your ladyship," the maid said, giving her a drink that was only needed for when one drank in excess.

"Thank you," my mother replied and then drank all of it . . . at one time. My father watched, rather amused.

"I am glad you enjoyed your ball, my love," he said to her when she was finished. "So much so you did not even realize you drank to excess."

"So you were foxed!" Abena exclaimed.

"Pots!" Mother snapped at Abena.

"Mama, it is breakfast." Abena pouted then looked at our father, who was hiding behind the paper.

"You may have all the breakfast you want when you learn proper breakfast conversation," my mother said.

"Papa—" Abena began when we saw Damon finally enter the outside hall.

"Damon?" Silva began to rise but then paused, looking to my mother. To leave as she desired would have been rude.

"Mother, Father, excuse me," Damon said when he entered the room. "I will change and come right down."

"You mean to tell me you have not been here?" my mother questioned and then looked to Silva, who had told us he retired earlier in the evening. "All night?"

"I was needed elsewhere. Excuse me," he said and turned to leave.

"I shall go tend to him," Silva said, rising.

I watched as Abena filled her plate with as much food as she could carry. "And I shall go to the pots!" She ran off.

My mother usually would have called her on her actions, but her mind was elsewhere. Sneaky little squirrel.

"He was out all night," my mother said to my father, who was reading the paper.

"Apparently, he was needed elsewhere," my father replied.

"The only one who could have needed him at such an hour is his wife, and she was here," she muttered angrily lifting her hands to rub her temples. "My ball was a success, yet all you children seek to give me panic."

"What did I do?" Hathor exclaimed. "It was Odite who stood melancholy all night despite all her suitors asking for dances, which you made her quite proficient in. And Damon vanished. I was splendid."

"Do not let me cast my eye on you, child, for if I do, you will see that I caught all the times when you dropped your handkerchief or fainted upon the Dukes of Brunhild and Alfonce as if you were not born with strong enough lungs to contain air," my mother replied.

Hathor looked away to drink her juice, and Hector and Devana giggled.

"And you." My mother finally reached me. "You and I shall speak later."

"Mama, are you not tired?" I asked her for the second time in two days. "Why not take the day and rest your nerves?"

"I assure you, you do not wish to deal with her well rested," my father chimed in.

"Later," my mother repeated.

Heavenly Father, spare me from my mortal mother.

10

Aphrodite

It was later.

And I waited by the piano for what was to come, preparing to tune out her voice. Though I was sure it would not work completely, it had to lessen the blow of whatever it was she wished to speak to me about.

As soon as the doors opened, my hands were on the keys.

"Ah, so now you wish to practice," she said.

"Of course, Mama, for how else could I be considered accomplished?"

"Quite right." She nodded. "And how accomplished you shall be as the Countess of Wyndham."

"I beg your pardon?"

"Well, his brother is still alive at this present moment, but it is now certain he will not survive. Thus, Mr. Yves will become the Earl of Wyndham after his father."

"Mama, this concerns me not—"

"Oh, but it does concern you, my dear, as Tristian asked your father for your hand last night."

I arose so quickly that I nearly kicked over the piano stool. "He did not."

"He very much did, and your father very much approved."

"Why?"

"Why would he not?" she said, leaving me utterly baffled.

"A gentleman of standing, with title and wealth, who has a reputation of being gentle and amiable, asked for your hand. Why would any father reject that for his daughter? If you accept, you shall be wed by the end of the season. Well done."

"Not well done! For I do not accept, as I do not wish to wed him!"

"Then you must tell him so. He will ask in three days' time at the queen's garden party, where his mother and father both shall be present. In fact, all of the ton will be present. So, it shall either be a grand celebration or a massive embarrassment."

My mouth opened in horror. I had to stop this.

"I need to write to him at once and tell him before—"

"He has left London to visit his brother," she cut me off. "By the time you get a letter to his family home, he will be on his way back for the garden party. You may send it to his home here, but there is no certainty he will have seen it before meeting you."

I fell back down upon the stool. "Mama, he is kind. I do not wish to embarrass him."

"Then you should not have taken his hand last night. Did I not tell you each time you accepted him that you gave him hope?"

"I danced with others as well."

"But you gave him your first dance as he requested and then spoke mostly with him," she reminded me. I opened my mouth to explain, but she held up her hand, stopping me. "Whether you were interested during your conversations matters not. To all those who witnessed you, it seemed as though you were a couple. So here we now are. You will be either his betrothed or the lady who led him to disappointment."

"That is unfair!" I protested. "It is all unfair! And I have had enough of it. You wish for Evander. Everyone in the house wishes for Tristian. I am pulled in every different direction. I did not wish to give him my first dance last night. However, Damon came to get me—"

"Did your brother tell you to dance with him?" she replied. "Aphrodite, your choices may be limited but do not act as if you have not had them. You merely keep wishing to run because you are afraid. You had no business being with the servants. Should a gentleman ask you to dance, you are free to refuse!"

"Am I? Am I free? I think not. Freedom would have been to not be at the ball. Freedom would have been to leave me be in Belclere!"

"Your family was not in Belclere! And the freedom you seek is not afforded to anyone. Not men, not women, not servants, not even the king! Everyone has responsibilities. You cannot just sit in a castle, eating cakes and reading books all day. What do you think affords you such a life? Is it not your father? Is it not generations of women who married and men who toiled to create this world? You whine and complain about such a grand life, where your biggest worry is marrying a future earl. The servants in this house make harder choices than you do every day."

I hung my head, gripping my hands tightly, seeking to calm myself. She came to me, placing her hands upon mine.

"You are truly blessed, my dear, but you must grow up. And you must make a choice. Either you will accept him, or you will stand firm and reject him, knowing it will hurt him, but it is your future that matters." She kissed the side of my head. "Think wisely on what it is you want—who it is you want."

When she turned to leave, I sat back down and rested my forehead upon the top of the piano.

"Has she gone?"

I turned to see Abena's curly hair poking out from the side of the chair.

"How long have you been there?"

She brought her hand away from around her mouth, covered with a mess of sweets. "The whole time!"

"Abena!" I gasped as she rose and skipped toward me. "I thought you went to do the pots?"

She made a face. "I hate the pots."

"Is that not the point of punishment?"

"Why am I always the one being punished?" She sighed, and I moved, allowing her to sit beside me. "All I do is talk."

"Ladies are not to talk much or often or truthfully. So I am told," I replied.

"Then why do we have mouths?"

"Well, in your case, it seems it's for sweets." I laughed and used my handkerchief to clean her face.

"If it was just for sweets, I would be . . . mute?" She tilted her head to the side. "Those are people who cannot speak, right?"

I nodded. "Yes."

"Right, so if my mouth was just for sweets, I would be mute."

"Very good argument, and I concur. But as we are mere ladies, nobody will listen to our arguments, even if they are logical, because they think us illogical beings." For wanting everything men had. How nonsensical.

"I do not understand." She shook her head.

"Neither do I," I replied, placing my hands upon the keys.

"So what are you to do?"

"About?" I questioned as I played.

"Mr. Yves. You dislike him."

"I do not. I just do not wish to marry him."

"Is that not because you dislike him?" she pressed.

"Well, Abena, it is complicated."

"Why?"

"Because it is."

"I do not understand." She frowned again. "If you do not like someone, do not marry them. If you like them, marry them." She lifted her hands in front of herself like scales. "You do not like Tristian, so do not marry him. You like Evander. Marry him."

My head whipped to her. "Who said I like Evander?"

"You?"

"When did I say that?"

"When you were sleeping, you kept saying *Evander, Evander, Evander*—"

I clasped my hand over her mouth. "I do believe food suits your mouth much better!"

She broke out into a fit of giggles, poking my side, so she could hop away. She spun in the room. "You like him. You like him."

"I shall tell Mama how her Preston pearl necklace broke."

She froze, eyes wide, and I smiled at her. "Big sister."

"Yes, little sister?"

"I am sorry."

I tried my hardest not to laugh. "Good. Careful, for I know a lot more and keep your secrets."

"That is why you are my favorite." She grinned from ear to ear. "If it was my choice, I would want you never to marry."

"You wish me to be a spinster?"

"Can we not all stay as we are? When you are married, you shall leave. Then Hathor will leave. Then Devana, too. I am the last. It shall just be me . . . and Mama."

I giggled when she shuddered. "Damon and Hector will remain."

"They are boys. You all are my sisters. Who will play with me?"

"You mean whom will you fight with?"

"That too."

I outstretched my arms, and she came and hugged me. "It is sad to think of us leaving here, but we all must grow, and we all must start our own families. Like Mama and Papa. And should I get married, you will have to come to visit me often, for you are my favorite, as well."

"Then I pick Evander," she said.

"What?"

"Everely House is closer to Belclere than Mr. Yves's home, right?" She looked back up at me. "I looked on Papa's maps."

"What if I do not choose either Evander or Tristian?"

"But you like him," she repeated.

"Simply because I . . . may like him does not mean I will marry him."

She sat up. "That makes no sense."

"Well, when someone hurts you, even if you like them, you have to stay away."

"Can you not just forgive them?"

Her logic was so pure and simple that it made me feel foolish.

"It is complicated, little sister."

"I never want to grow up," she replied. "Everything is always *complicated*."

"I concur. Stay this age forever."

"I am going to go play. Do you want to come?" she asked.

I shook my head. "I am a grown-up now, and I must figure out my complications."

"Good luck!" She ran off, not at all caring. Then again, that was what made her fun—not having to care. It was a simple matter of forgiving.

Forgiving.

I did not wish to marry Tristian.

But I also knew I would not be happy marrying Evander, not when there was so much I did not know or understand. He wanted forgiveness—he said so in a letter—but he had to earn it.

The words of Epictetus echoed within my mind. *The greater the difficulty, the more glory in surmounting it. Skillful pilots gain their reputation from storms and tempests.*

If that was the case, then this would be a storm, and I sought to pilot. I walked to the desk, where I lifted a paper and took the pen from the well.

Dear . . . I paused as I did not know the correct way to address him, so I remained proper, taking out a new piece of paper.

To His Grace, the Duke of Everely,

I write to inform you I received your letter but could not grant your wish, as you were otherwise engaged and arrived far too late. It has come to my attention that I shall be given an offer of marriage in three days' time, to which my answer shall be very clear—unless another offer were to come, along with further explanations on events as they transpired in the past. Should such an offer not be made by then, let it never be made in the future.

Sincerely,
A

I looked over the letter. If Evander was serious, he had to prove it to me. If he wished for my forgiveness, he had to show me.

I grabbed the bell pull in the room and rang it.

The door opened soon after. "Yes, my lady?"

"Make sure this reaches the Duke of Everely's home directly," I said, handing it to her. "You may take the day off, but it must go there now. I shall inform my mother."

"Yes, my lady." She reached for it, and when she did, I leaned closer.

"Eleanor, make no stops and do not speak to anyone else till you reach his household."

"I understand, my lady."

"Good." I gave her the letter and exhaled.

Verity

"You are not welcome here," I said to the horrid woman who stood before me.

Her eyes were a pitch of darkness, hate, and cruelty. "Verity, in times of crisis, ladies must stand as one," she replied and stepped closer to me. "It has come to my attention your brother is ill."

"How strange, for I live here with him and have seen no such illness," I lied with a smile. "I thank you for your concern, Datura, but you may go."

"I will not!" She huffed, lifting her head as if she were born a queen and not a butcher's daughter. "If there is an issue with your brother, it is vital that I know, as it affects the family and of course—"

"And, of course, who is the duke?" I questioned, arms crossed. "Are you still praying for my brother to die so Gabrien may inherit the title?"

"You speak of the silliest things, girl." She giggled, though her eyes were clearly peering over my shoulder. "Whether the two of you like it or not, I am still your stepmother, and as such, part of this family, deserving of the truth."

The truth was that she deserved whatever spot in hell she had earned.

"And I am providing such truth. My brother is well, merely resting, and you are disturbing his rest."

"Evander resting midday in midweek?" She smiled. "You are a poorer liar than I gave you credit for, Verity."

"You will watch your tone when speaking to my sister, Datura!"

At his voice, I turned to see him dressed and descending the stairs as if nothing were at all amiss.

What are you doing? I mouthed to him.

He ignored me. Slowly, I turned back around and smiled pleasantly.

"Did I not warn you never to come to my door unannounced?" he stated coldly, staring down at her. "Do we not suffer enough of you in society? Must we now return to suffering in private?"

Datura frowned, her evil eyes scanning the length of him. "I merely wished to see if you are well."

"Quite well, in fact," he lied, "or as well as one can be in your company. Is that all, or have you burned through your allowance?"

"If I did, would you increase it?"

"Not even if doing so would stop the sun falling out of the sky," Evander sneered. "You have what my father allowed and nothing more. Now remove yourself from my home, or I shall have you removed."

"Very well. I shall see you both at the queen's garden party then—"

"You shall not."

She paused. "I beg your pardon?"

"Invitations to the queen's garden party were sent to the nobility and the nobility only."

"I am Dowager—"

"You are . . . forgive me, for I cannot use the language I wish to before my sister. Let me say instead. You may have married my father, you may cover yourself in any number of jewels you desire, but that will not cover the situation of your birth—as the queen knows. Her invitation was clear. It was addressed to the fourth Duke of Everely and the Lady Verity. Spare us any further disgrace to our family name if you *please*, and stay the hell away. Now I have told you as my godmother has told you."

The rage upon Datura's face was no match for his words. She clenched her fist and then, like a dragon, she swallowed the fire in her, turned, and departed.

"Brother, you must return to bed."

"One moment longer," he said, watching until her carriage was gone. Only then did he reenter the house. Within a second, he collapsed onto the floor.

"Evander!" I screamed, grabbing hold of him. He was hot to the touch. "Help!"

"I have him, my lady," our butler said, with a footman standing nearby.

"Take him to his rooms. Have you found that doctor?" I followed them up the stairs.

"No," my brother grumbled even as they carried him. "I will receive no treatment except from Dr. Cunningham!"

"Dr. Cunningham is in *Everely*. It shall take him days from there, and by such time, you will be overcome with fever!"

"I . . . I . . . trust no one . . . else." He gasped as they put him upon the bed. "The doctor may have been the one to tell her."

"I highly doubt that she would have used the doctor to gather information and not to kill you," I replied. He groaned, rolling onto one side. "Hurry, take off his clothes! Why did you dress so much?"

"She . . . would . . . suspect."

"Your fever has gotten worse. I already instructed them to call the doctor again as you have been sick all morning. If he should be a spy, let him at least heal you first," I said, turning to leave as they began to undress Evander.

Just as I stepped out, a very young-looking man with short, curly hair came up the stairs with a bag, accompanied by the maid.

"My lady, this is Dr. Darrington. He first saw His Grace," the maid said.

He bowed his head to me. "My lady."

"You are a doctor?"

"Yes," he replied, already at the door. I tried to follow but was stopped. "If it is to your liking, you may have male staff present, but I do not see fit for you to be in here."

"It is my home and brother."

"You are keeping me, my lady." He closed the door in my face.

11

Aphrodite

The term was *déjà vu*, taken from the French, meaning *already seen*. I had already seen these events before. Nearly four years ago, to be exact. For some reason, I truly believed he would call upon me at the soonest opportunity after he received my letter. But three days later there was still no reply.

I was foolish.

And now, I was terribly afraid of what would become of me once I had rejected Tristian's offer. As we entered the garden party, I found myself unable to smile or even to take in the queen's wondrous decorations.

"Are you truly so aggrieved at the prospect?"

I lifted my head to see my father had now stepped from my mother's side to my own while she sought to help Hathor.

"Tristian is a very good man. You shall live a good life. And I doubt he shall worry you much. Must you reject him?"

"Yes, Papa," I whispered, and I took his arm to hold on tightly. "I do not feel for him in any manner."

He sighed and patted my hand. "Sometimes I fear your mother and I set the wrong standard and focused far too heavily on feelings instead of practicality."

"And what is practical?"

"Knowing when it is one's time and realizing that time is brief. For a while, you may be the most handsome and sought after. But your competition rises with your age. Do you not see all the fine young ladies here?" he questioned and nodded to the women already dancing with gentlemen. "They are younger and, dare I say, slightly more . . . amiable."

At that precise moment, a young lady pretended to trip to be caught by her partner. It was very obvious, but the gentleman looked altogether pleased with himself. I could not help but giggle.

"Yes, very amiable indeed," I replied.

"Which is why, should you reject Tristian, I fear you will reach a height you cannot descend from."

"Which is?"

"Unattainable." He pointed up to the sky. "Beauty like the sun, you exist and illuminate the world but are a distant sphere, hard to look upon fully, thus noticed but ignored. Is that what you wish?"

"Do you wish me to enter a loveless marriage merely out of fear of being unattainable or left behind?"

"I do not." He frowned and shook his head. "But I do not wish you to miss your chance—overlooking fertile ground where love may grow for a desolate country that has never supported a blossom. I merely enjoyed your mother's company when I first met her."

"Were you not besotted during your match?" I looked at him somewhat confused, for that was the story they had told us.

"No." He grinned and looked down. "Do not tell your mother that, for she is convinced she had me wrapped around her finger like ribbon."

I was convinced that was still the case. "So, what did you feel?"

"Comfort and ease." He nodded assuredly. "Comfortable with the knowledge she would make a fine wife, as she came from a fine family. Ease in conversation with her, for as you know, I tend to ramble on."

"Just a tad."

He smiled. "Yes, and always of the most boring things such as books and history. And yet your mother listened, even though she did not have the same passions. And she did not just pretend but truly listened and never once faulted me if I bored her. In turn, I learned to ramble less, and to seek out subjects that she might enjoy. For marriage is accommodating of each other."

"I hear you, Papa. Truly. But I cannot accept him."

"Well, the hour is now upon you to tell him," he said as we caught sight of Tristian and his family, a smile appearing on his face.

It left me feeling quite ill. "I wish Mama had let me stay home."

"And disappoint your other admirers? The world would come to an end first."

"What other admirers?"

He nodded to the right of me, where I saw the queen sitting upon her throne with her ladies and dogs, watching me rather intensely.

I glanced away quickly. "I am always at a loss as to why she stares at me so."

"Is it not admiration?"

"For what reason would a queen admire me? I have done not a thing and have said only a few words before her."

"Who can know the mind of the monarchy," he said, letting go of my hand. "Our duty is to be respectful and loyal. Thus, we shall greet her, and you will go to your fate."

I did not wish to let go of him, but he had to go stand beside Mama as we followed the line to greet the queen.

"She will surely comment on me today," Hathor whispered, fixing her gloves. "I have worn her favorite color and refined my curtsy. Mama said it was the most splendid she had ever seen."

"Let it please happen as you wish," I whispered back, for I would have much preferred her to have the attention.

"Lady Monthermer," the queen stated when we rose from our curtsies. "I have asked all the young ladies here a question. I wish to ask your daughters as well."

"It would be their honor." My mother smiled and then glanced at us with a look of pure warning.

"My question is simple. How do you like my garden?"

The simplicity of the question startled me.

"It is the most splendid, Your Majesty," Hathor spoke up first. "A beauty only you can maintain, for not only does it house the most glorious flowers but birds and swans and other creatures of the earth in perfect harmony."

How lyrical.

I did not think it to be an inadequate answer, but the queen merely nodded and then shifted her gaze to me.

"Well, Lady Aphrodite," she spoke my name with the same soft and drawn stretch of the letters as always. "Do you not like the garden?"

"I do not see myself fit to judge Her Majesty's garden," I said.

The queen narrowed her eyes, and I felt ready to change my response when she spoke again. "Lady Monthermer."

"Yes, Your Majesty?"

"Do not allow this one to go to waste. I have not seen one of her makings in many years," she said, causing mouths to flutter behind us, my mother to smile as though she had been crowned herself, and Hathor's shoulders to drop.

"Yes, Your Majesty." My mother curtsied, as we all did.

The queen waved us off, turning her attention to the next party.

"My darling girl." Mother all but beamed. "How blessed you are to be given such favor."

"Yes, Mama, and I'm beginning to wonder if she did not steal all the blessing with birth," Hathor said before she marched away.

"Do not pay her any mind. One day, she will realize how lucky she is for her elevated standing as well," my mother said.

"Once more, this was all a great deal of fuss for such a simple answer." The truth of the matter was that I did not know what to say, as I had not truly looked upon the gardens.

"Lady Monthermer."

We both stopped and saw Tristian before us, and my heart stirred in the most uncomfortable of ways. "May I be allowed to speak to the Lady Aphrodite more privately?"

I turned to my mother, eyes wide, begging her not to leave me, hoping she would allow me more time to brace myself.

"Yes, of course. I will stand by a short distance," she replied and released me. Upon turning her back to him, she whispered, "Be gentle."

"Lady Aphrodite . . . a walk?" He held his hand out toward the path.

I only nodded, allowing him to lead.

"The queen thinks highly of you. In fact, everyone thinks so highly of you that it makes me all the more nervous—"

"Please say no more!" I stopped, unable to stand this any longer. He turned to me, and I instinctively did my best to smile, but how did smiling help at this moment? "Mr. Yves, you are a man of great reputation and kindness. And I know what you are about to ask, but I must request you do not, for I cannot give the answer you seek."

"Have I offended you?"

"Not in the least."

"Do you find me distasteful?"

"Of course not."

"Forgive me. I am confused." He frowned, now stepping back. "Is it because of my current lack of title, if so—"

"I care not of titles!" I exclaimed. "You are a good man, a kind man, but I feel no special way toward you. Forgive me if I led you to believe otherwise. I sought to try at least a little, but I could not . . . I could not . . ."

"Forget about the duke?" he asked.

I hung my head. "Forgive me."

"I am aware you and he had . . . a history, but I was sure by now you would see him as most unreliable."

"I do."

"And still you wait for him?"

"I wait for no one," I stated angrily. "I simply do not wish for you to be with someone who cannot match your feelings."

"And that cannot change over time? For I can wait," he said.

"I do not believe so. And as one who has waited in the past, I can tell you it is a painful experience."

He looked down, nodding to himself. "Forgive me. I must go."

"Yes, I understand," I whispered, allowing him to leave me among the hedges.

"Well, you have successfully ruined a very good match."

I glanced to see Damon now beside me. "When did you arrive?"

"Just in time to hear that man's heart shatter upon the

earth. Mother could not watch and asked for me to stand guard."

"Even she felt for him, and he was not her choice?"

"It is hard not to feel for the innocent."

I glowered, turning to him. "Am I not the innocent?"

"You are, but not more than he."

"You are becoming less fun to talk to, Damon," I snapped, marching around him. "All of you, casting me in roles I do not wish, demanding I act when I have no desire, directing me here and there. Making me into a cold heart!"

"That is not what—"

"Is it truly wrong to want something else? If it was easy to simply want what was practical or logical, what others expected, do you not think I would? What moves me is what moves me! Whom I like is whom I like! Whether that person is reliable or not . . . it is whom I like."

"Of whom are we speaking exactly?" he questioned.

I paused, taking in the air. "No one."

"Are you certain?"

"Please do not lecture me any more, you have already made yourself clear. You were correct the night of the ball. He is—"

"I was not completely right."

"What?"

"I still do not think him worthy or suitable for you, but that night, he went through hell to arrive for you, only he was just too late."

"I do not understand." But then I did not want to find another reason to keep excusing him. "It doesn't matter, for even if he did try that night, he still failed to show today."

"What do you mean?"

"I wrote him a letter telling . . . telling him to come to me. He did not respond—"

"For the love of God." He sighed, hanging his head. "I do not know if you are both fated or cursed! Or why I must now be in the middle of it!"

"In the middle of what?"

He stared at me, jaw clenched and expression tight.

"Damon?"

"Bloody . . ." he stopped himself. "He did not arrive on time to the ball because he was injured."

"What? How?"

"I do not know, but it was quite serious, which was why I followed him back to his home and did not return till morning. And because he is a stubborn mule, he did not take medicine as the doctor prescribed and got worse."

"He is—"

"He is better now. However, I do not believe he is aware of the letter yet, Odite." He chuckled and shook his head. "Do you now see the ill fate in this?"

"I need to see him."

"What?"

I grabbed his arm and started to run, and, as if my actions angered the heavens, the skies darkened and rain fell.

"Odite, we need to—"

"I am sick of the confusion and the misunderstandings! I shall see him at once!" I hollered, pulling Damon to run with me.

The whole of the queen's garden party scattered as they sought protection from the rain. I saw my father calling to us, but I would not be stopped, running to where Damon's carriage would be.

"Odite—"

"Keep pace!" I shouted at him.

I would have an answer today. Let the world flood for all I cared. It would not stop me.

Verity

"You should have gone to the queen's lunch," he said as I helped him down the stairs.

"From the looks of it, I was right not to," I replied as rain drenched the world outside. "Then again, I would have very much enjoyed the looks of those fussy ladies, shrieking to get to dry ground and weeping about their poor, *poor* dresses."

"I must say, you have become far too cynical for your age." He chuckled as we reached the bottom stairs.

"When is an appropriate age to be cynical?"

"For a lady? When you are old. Thirty at least."

"That does not seem so old to me. Truthfully, I think such an age the best suited to marriage."

He stopped and looked at me aghast. "Please do not worry me. Seeing you well married should be the least complicated of my tasks, I beg of you."

I felt the urge to roll my eyes but stopped as soon as Wallace appeared. "Your Grace, your letters have accumulated—"

"Can he not have a short break? He has only just become well again."

"Do not mind her. Where are they?"

"Your study, sir."

"Very well," he said as we walked there. "You should rest. I am not so feeble as to need my sister to watch me read letters," he said, moving to his desk, shuffling through his correspondence.

"Fine, I will go check on lunch and bring your medicine," I replied, going to the door.

I had only just stepped into the hall when his voice roared out like thunder, and all of me jumped at the sound.

"Wallace, my horse!"

I turned to see what in the world had gotten into him. He was no longer at his desk but running toward me and then past me so quickly he nearly knocked me over.

"Evander!" I screamed. "What is it?"

He did not seem to notice me, so I grabbed the hem of my dress and ran after him.

"Evander!" I called again, but he was already rushing down the stairs.

By the time I made it to the door, he was upon a horse, the rain beating down on him and all the world. The man did not even wear a greatcoat!

"Are you mad?" I hollered from the door. "Do you not see it is raining? Evander! You have just recovered!"

He merely took off through the gates as fast as the horse would take him, and his figure grew distant in the fog and rain.

It was behavior like this that made me sure that should I ever marry it would not be until he was either wed or dead.

Aphrodite

"Let it be known that you forced me to abandon my wife to become your servant!" Damon yelled at me from outside, his voice fighting against the rain.

"Can it not be fixed?" My head was outside the window to see as they—my brother and the driver—tried to adjust the carriage that had caught in a road rut, the wheel now out of place.

"Of course, it can be fixed, Aphrodite. Merely not in these conditions!" Damon tossed up his hands so as to remind me that we were on the side of the road. "Why on earth you could not wait is beyond my comprehension!"

"Will you please stop yelling at me—"

"I will not! For I am wet, cold, and covered in mud!" He now waved his hands at the dirt that had covered his bottom half and the rest of his body. "Aphrodite—what in heavens are you doing?"

I got out of the carriage, my feet nearly slipping as they sank into the mud. "I shall take one of the horses then."

"You will do no such thing!"

"It is either that or walk!"

"My dear sister, can we please go home? He shall be there tomorrow—"

"If I go home, Mama will talk to me, then Papa, then you, or Hathor, and even Abena! And you all shall confuse my thoughts. I must go now," I said, though I had no clue as to how to undo the horse. "Will you please help me with this?"

"I will not!"

"Must you be difficult right now, Damon?"

"Me, difficult? At present, Aphrodite, you have made yourself the queen of all things difficult!"

I glared at him a moment, the water from my hair dripping into my eyes. Tired of his complaining, I lifted my dress and turned to walk.

"Aphrodite!"

"If you do not seek to understand the urgency of my situation, that is fine. You may wait here. I truly would have come without you!"

"Aphrodite?"

I turned, as that was not my brother's voice. Like a figure out of a myth, he appeared upon a dark horse—drenched as I was drenched, with no greatcoat—at the other end of the road, breathing harshly.

"Brilliant. The other difficult one has appeared," Damon muttered.

I ignored him and looked to Evander.

"Where are you going?" I knew why I was attempting this madness, but what could have caused him to go into the rain as he was?

"To see you," he replied, his eyes never shifting from mine.

"Why?"

"I have only now opened your letter." He stepped closer. "Tell me you did not accept him." It sounded as though he were hurt. "Aphrodite, I beg of you, please tell me you did not," he whispered.

"I did not. Would I be here if I had?"

He released his breath. "Thank God."

"Why are you thanking God I did not accept him?" I asked, clasping my cold hands together. "For I am not accepting you, either."

"I do not understand. Then why are you here?"

"To demand the truth." And now that I had said it, I was not going to back down. "You asked me for forgiveness, for a second chance. I will give neither until you tell me the truth from the beginning—all of it. I cannot make any decisions until then."

"Aphrodite, I—"

"If you still refuse to explain, then that is it. You will find neither forgiveness nor a second chance. I swear it in all things."

I bit my lips to keep the tears back. "This will be the last time we speak."

"Aphrodite, I wish to tell you, but I am afraid—"

"Is that fear greater than losing me forever?"

"It is not," he whispered. "Nothing in this world is worse than losing you forever. I shall tell you all of it. And in so doing, I pray you to see that I have loved you all of my life. When I learned what love was, I understood it to be you."

Four years.

I had been waiting for this moment for four years, and it felt like I could finally breathe, that the stone had lifted off my back and I could rise again. I could genuinely smile again.

"I—"

"Is there any possibility that this discussion can happen indoors? Preferably by a fire," my brother said, now at my side, holding the reins of a horse from the carriage. "Do you seek us all to catch a chill?"

I wished I had left him behind!

12

Aphrodite

I could barely remember this home, since I had come only once with my brother and Mama when I was a child. I did recall that it was a lovely place, even more refined than our own, so I did not touch anything, in case I was punished, and sat by the fire where I was told. My brother had gone to play with the other boy. My mother was upstairs with the lady of the house, and I was bored. Then I was hungry. So, believing my mama had forgotten me, I stuck my head out the door to see if I could find help. The hunger had gotten so bad that I was near tears when an older boy appeared and said, "Are you all right?"

I saw that boy—now a man—before me, changed into new clothes as I was, thanks to his sister, looking at me with the same timid and worried expression as he had done all those years ago.

"Are you all right?" he asked just then.

"I was four when you first asked me that question in this very home," I replied, hugging the shawl around me more tightly.

"You remember?" The corner of his mouth turned up. "That was the first time we met each other. I had met your brother before but not you."

"I was scared my mama had forgotten me. And Damon was playing . . ."

"And you had gotten hungry. So, I brought you to the kitchen, and I was not sure what to offer, but you had already found the servant's pork pie." He chuckled, and it made me smile. "I turned around, and you were eating with your hands."

"And, of course, that was when my mama reappeared." I laughed, as I could remember her shrieking my name in horror. "She forced me to spend extra time at table lessons once we returned home."

"You do not recall what happened before that?" he asked.

I paused. "No."

"You became ill. The cook was getting rid of the pie, it had gone bad. You became sick, and my mother . . ." He paused, swallowing. And I remembered she had died later that same year. He was only ten years old. "Our mothers were terrified, and the doctor was called. The cook, Damon, and I were reprimanded severely for not watching out for you. My mother was even more beside herself than yours for days, even after you had gotten better."

"Well, that might explain why I cannot stand to look upon pork pie. Even now."

"Yes, I know."

We found ourselves staring at each other. It was only when the door opened that I turned away to see my brother had entered, wearing clothing that I could only assume belonged to Evander. His gaze shifted between us, and then, without a word, he walked over to tend the fire.

"I have sent word to Mother and Father. We shall stay the night here," he said, tossing another log onto the flame.

"We will?" Papa would not like that, while Mama, I was sure, would be grinning happily somewhere by her own fire.

"The rains have not eased, and your carriage needs repair," Evander said. "It is best to go in the morning."

"It is also good for her to retire early," Damon interjected, now poking the fire, making it obvious that he was my chaperone. Slowly, he moved to the other side of the room to gaze out of the window, giving us distance. "Do not mind me. Speak as you must."

"I think it is best for you to sit by the fire," Evander said, noticing I still shivered.

Feeling the chill once more, I moved to sit. He no longer looked at me but at the flames beside me. It was three full minutes, at least, before he spoke again.

"You know about my mother?" he finally asked.

I nodded. All of the ton spoke of her, the great Lady Luella Farraday, beloved by everyone except her husband, the duke.

"Your father had . . ." I stopped, not desiring to harm him with the words.

"My father had a kept woman," he said. "A Miss Datura Topwells. He would not marry her, as he sought a wife of noble birth, but he kept her, nonetheless. He had a son with her, Fitzwilliam. All of this was kept from those who knew him, even my mother. It was only when she gave birth to me that she discovered the truth. That was when my father allowed Miss Topwells into Everely. It was more than my mother could bear, but she could not leave, for my sake. My father had his heir and would see me raised as such under him . . . beside his other son."

"He grew up alongside you?" I frowned, not remembering ever meeting this brother. "I knew of him, but I have never seen him."

"Yes, and my father at least had the sense to avoid parading Fitzwilliam or his mother around. But they were very much in our lives."

I did not know it could be worse and I did not want to.

"I shall not bore you with more. Instead, I shall explain how this forced me to break my promises four years ago."

I was fearful of this truth, but I desired it more than anything else.

"As Fitzwilliam grew up with all the finery that comes with being a duke's son, he grew more frustrated by the two things he was not given—status and recognition. This worsened when my father passed, and I inherited everything. He was enraged. He believed it was his right, not mine. We had never maintained a good relationship, but any pretense died along with my father. He demanded part of the estate, which I refused, and sought to have him and his mother removed from Everely. I also sent our younger brother to Eton. For years, I had waited for that moment, so I did not hesitate. To avoid having her living in poverty—she was still the mother of my younger brother and the former wife of a duke—I gave them funds. I even bought apartments in London for Datura but made it clear that I sought to never look upon their faces again. And that they were not welcome to return. Fitzwilliam swore revenge. I scoffed, paying him no mind, for what could he do? Then he took you from me."

"Took me?" I frowned. "I beg your pardon. No one has taken me."

"Forgive me. My words were clumsy," Evander said quickly. "I meant he caused me to lose my chance at marrying you."

"How could he do such a thing? Was it not because of some baron's daughter—"

"It was not that!" he snapped, and I jumped slightly.

From the corner of my eye, I saw Damon shift.

Evander stepped back and looked at the fire. "Forgive me,

but that talk . . . that lie, it haunts me. It was not I who took that girl. I do not know if Fitzwilliam did so on purpose to ruin me or if it was just a series of events that worked to his favor and my detriment."

"I do not understand how his actions could affect you so."

"Fitzwilliam pretended to be me." Evander turned back to the fire, a glow cast upon his eyes. "We grew up together, so everything about the estate, down to my signature, he knew. Father had even made him a ring with our family seal. It is not as though all the world knows what I look like. He took Emma, telling her that she would be his duchess, and when she was caught with child, she told her family the Duke of Everely was responsible. Her father came to me the week before your coming out, demanding I wed her. I refused and told him it was the most wicked of slanders. But the girl had letters, and he swore he would take me to court and thus, ruin my good name."

"So, you just married her, you fool?" Damon gasped, now entirely away from the window.

"Of course not! I beseeched the girl to tell the truth!" he exclaimed. "But she was terrified and refused, as doing so would leave her even further ruined. I told them that I would go to court and prove this to be a fraud. Her father was enraged and demanded a duel."

"I beg you, say you did not." Damon sighed heavily.

"I did no such thing." He frowned. "I did not fire. I tried to reason with him, swore to him that I had not taken advantage of his daughter. But the foolish man shot at me anyway."

"Were you injured?" I sat up from my chair.

He smiled half-heartedly. "No, the gun backfired, and he wounded himself. The witness can attest to this. I have it in writing as well. I refused the duel, and he injured himself. After the man died the next morning, I realized the fate that was left to the girl and her mother. Neither would admit the truth, especially as they had lost all protection."

"So, you married her," I whispered.

"The whole affair at that point had gotten too rotten, Aphrodite," he said, shaking his head. "Should it have come to light, my name would've been ruined and, thus, my sister's, maybe even your own."

"You could have fought it!" Damon retorted.

"How long would that have taken?" Evander questioned in return. "How would it have looked? As her belly grew and she was forced onto the streets. Her father had more debts than any man should—it was a disgrace."

"Why did you not just tell us the truth? Could we not have helped you?" I asked. "Do you truly believe us so concerned with reputations that we would shun you?"

"It is because your family cared so much that I was concerned," he said. "It was not as if it were my only issue. My brother was—*is* still out there, still trying to use my name. However, I have fortified myself much better, having changed everything down to my signature. I even sought to slightly alter our seal. I have men searching for him to hold him accountable for his crimes, but he continues to elude justice."

"He's the one who stabbed you?"

"Stabbed?" I glanced between them. "You were stabbed?"

He nodded.

"This brother is mad," I said.

"Back then, it was too much for me. I gave in to the easiest road, marrying the girl in hopes of getting her to write the letter of confession."

"Did she?"

He nodded. "When she became ill, she sought to make peace, though I will not use it."

"Why in the hell not?"

"Because the daughter she bore is innocent," he said without hesitation. "And she has no knowledge of any other family. I swore to her mother I would protect Emeline."

"Then what was the point of asking for the letter?" I questioned.

"Protection against the woman's mother, who knows the truth but said nothing and pushed her daughter to do the same." He stared into my eyes. "There was nothing I wished more than to marry you. I could not allow you to join that chaos."

"How is it any less chaotic now?" Damon grumbled, coming to sit with us, rubbing his temples as Mama often did. "Your wife is dead, but your brother is still out there and violent—"

"I have enough evidence against him now, and he has no means to protect himself. It is only a matter of catching him. I should not have gone out alone that day to stop him. I—I was simply so eager for this all to be done for good that I let down my guard. I make a mistake only once, which is why I cannot let you go again." The last part he said directly to me.

And something stirred in me.

"I wish to rest," I muttered, rising from the chair.

"Of course, you may use the same room you used earlier to change. Should I call the maid?" He was already moving to the door.

"Thank you," I said as I walked out to find the maid already waiting.

"Aphrodite?"

"Yes?" I paused at the bottom of the stairs to look at him.

"Please do not speak of this to my sister. She does not know the full truth."

I nodded and said nothing more to him.

"Do you need assistance with anything, my lady?" the maid asked once we reached my room.

"No. Thank you."

"Good night, my lady."

When the door closed, I collapsed onto the bed, putting my hand over my face as I bit back the tears.

This feeling in my heart—it was a relief.

Relief in finally knowing . . . it was not me.

It was not that he did not want or love me.

I was not the fool.

13

Evander

I could not sleep, the knowledge that she was so close and yet so far haunted me. I saw her face each time I closed my eyes and remembered how badly I desired her. To keep my mind from such thoughts, I did what I always did—I rose to clear my head in the night air. As if . . . as if we were blessed, there she was in the hall. Her brown, curly hair cascaded down her back, and she was wearing a long, dark robe with her arms hugged around herself. She tiptoed down the first few stairs, searching carefully.

"Aphrodite?"

At the sound of her name, she spun around so quickly she nearly lost her footing. Instantly, I caught her wrist, managing to steady her, her body pressed against my own. If ever I had willed my heart not to burst, it was at that moment. Her eyes held the warmth and curiosity of the whole earth. Her face was so close to mine that I could feel her breath upon my lips.

"Are you all right?" I asked, and she nodded, still looking upon my face. She inhaled, and I felt her breasts upon my chest, and it made me want to hold her tighter. I had to remind myself that I was not a beast but a man, and she was a lady. Also, I feared she might feel my desire upon her, so I moved to the step below.

"Thank you," she said.

"Of course," I replied, feeling my hands still stinging from the touch of her. "Were you in need of something?"

"No, I . . ." She trailed off as her stomach exposed her, growling loudly. Her eyes widened, and she quickly wrapped her arms around her midsection.

I grinned. "You are hungry?"

"I have not eaten since breakfast."

"Well, we cannot have that." I was about to reach out to her, but we were already breaking all rules of decorum. "Come, we shall see what is left in the kitchen."

"I do hope it is not pork pie again."

And I laughed. "Yes, this feels as if it was déjà vu."

"I thought I could remember where the kitchen is, but I cannot," she said, following after me.

"It has been many years. Do not blame yourself," I said, checking to make sure no one else was in the hall before we moved forward.

"I do not seek to blame myself. Only it made me wonder why our families did not spend time together here."

"After my mother passed, my father refused to open this house."

"Why?" she asked as we entered the kitchen.

I did not wish everything I told of my life to be negative, but I feared she could sniff out any lie or deflection. "My mother died here," I said, looking to see what food was left. "There is only bread, milk, and apples. Will that do? If not, I can call for the cook."

"It is far too late to call for a cook. That is fine."

I turned to her, holding what I had found. "But it is cold milk. You only ever drink yours warm."

"You remember?"

I grinned, nodding, as I remembered everything about her. Or, at least, everything up to four years ago.

"I prefer warm, but those in need of charity should not be so particular, as my papa says." She searched and found another glass and plates, setting the table in the center. "Will you eat with me?"

"For as long as you will allow," I responded, sitting across from her.

And as she poured me a cup of the milk before her own and ripped the bread then cut the apples, sharing them between us, I could not help but wonder . . . would this have been our lives? Had we married four years ago, would we be like this? Could we be like this in the future?

I certainly hoped so.

"The intensity of your gaze is making me nervous," she murmured, nibbling a tiny bit of bread.

"Forgive me." I glanced down, eating quietly.

"And now the lack of your gaze is making me sad."

"Then tell me what to do."

"I do not know." She sighed, her shoulders dropping. "Evander, I do not know what to say about anything. You confuse me."

"Good."

"Good?" She gasped. "How is that good?"

"It means I am in not only your mind but also your heart."

"Even if it is in a muddled manner?" she pressed.

"Is it muddled only because you fear giving in?" I watched her face to see how she would react.

"Giving in to what?"

"Your feelings, of course."

"It has been four years. My feelings could have changed."

"Then why did you reject *Tristian Yves*?"

"Because I . . . he is a good man and deserves a lady who loves him, and I do not," she said. Though she stated she did not love him, her speaking highly of him bothered me.

"That is not the only reason, or you would not have come to me in the rain as you did."

She took a much bigger bite of her bread, and I fought not to laugh. When we were younger, people often said Aphrodite was the hardest to understand, that she did not communicate well enough, simply because she chose to be silent instead of revealing her innermost thoughts. And yet, to me, her silence was always as clear as a freshwater spring.

"It has been four years. There is a chance I could have changed from the girl you knew."

"Is your favorite color still blue?" I asked. "And not any blue, but the color of the sky on the clearest of days? Do you still detest champagne but love port, of all things? Do you still consider cake suitable for dinner? Do you still curse people in your mind when you are angry? Is your favorite book still by Samuel Richardson, but no one knows as you were forbidden to read it, and I snuck it to you? Do they believe you are the biggest fan of Shakespeare?"

"I am a fan of Shakespeare," she said quickly.

"You like only the *Merchant of Venice* and his sonnets. The others you do not mind, but you find it frustrating that no theaters seem to do them justice."

"Because they do not, with the exception of *Macbeth*!" she complained, biting into her apple angrily. "I believe the theater is greatly lacking, especially with Sarah Siddons now retired."

I bit back a grin as she eased into the manner I once recalled. "So what you are telling me is that you are still the girl I remember."

She paused, realizing she had revealed herself. "Fine, I have not changed that much. But what of you?"

"I fear I have changed greatly." I had become cold without her, without her family, whom I had only ever considered my own.

"How so?"

"After all that has occurred, I find that I am far less trusting." Outside of her family and Verity, I believed the world to be the cruelest place filled with only opportunistic people.

"Well, you were not very trusting and open before."

"I was to you, was I not?"

"No." She huffed, ripping the small piece of her bread angrily. "You and I spoke often, but you never told me about your family or how you felt. I know you, but I do not know you. Back then, I told myself not to push, as I would be . . . married to you and find out later."

"I—"

We heard movement outside the door, and immediately, she dropped under the table, hiding, for if anyone saw her with me at this hour, dressed as we were, it would ruin her. I moved to block the door.

"Who is there?"

It took a second before Wallace arrived stoic-faced and holding a candle, staring at me in confusion. "Your Grace? What are you doing here? I was sure I heard—"

"I was hungry."

"I can have the cook—"

"No need. I am finished and about to return to bed. You may go."

Suddenly, there was a soft sneeze behind me, and I wished to close my eyes and hang my head.

"I see, Your Grace, pardon me. Good night." He nodded and took his leave.

Aphrodite rose quickly, rushing to me. "He heard me? What if he—"

"He will say nothing," I assured her. Had it been anyone else, I would be worried about gossip spreading among the servants by daybreak. "Though we must get you back to your rooms, as I do not know when the other servants awaken."

She nodded. "Or my brother."

Now *that* was even more concerning. "Stay behind me."

She hurried behind my back, and I did my best not to smile as a memory of her playing with her siblings popped into my head—she always was the best at hiding.

I felt childish hurrying and sneaking through the halls of my own home . . . but at the same time, it was good fun, and I had not had that in so long that reaching her door was actually wretched.

"Thank you!" she whispered and dashed inside, but before it shut fully, I saw her face through the narrowest sliver of the door. "Good night."

"Good night, though parting is such sweet sorrow," I whispered back.

I stood there for a moment, trying to contain my delight. If not for the fact that I worried I would be seen, I might have camped outside her door.

Foolish. I was, but she made me so. And I did not realize when it had happened. At first, she was merely my friend's sister, my godmother's daughter. It was only when her mother had written to inform me that she had spoken to my father of a betrothal between Aphrodite and me that I realized I loved her. She was but sixteen at the time, and I was still at Cambridge. It was as if someone had brought light into a dark room. I was so delighted. And it occurred to me then why I had been so dissatisfied with all the other . . . encounters I'd had before. Why all of those *encounters* left me feeling more hollow than the last. It was because someone else had taken root in me. So, I wrote to my godmother in return, telling her that I would be pleased to do so but only if Aphrodite was just as eager. I did not know she felt for me more than a brother until I returned. Though she was too shy to have admitted it.

And it felt as though I had finally gotten lucky. My father would accept it. He cared only about himself, our family name, and line. As long as she was part of the nobility, she would do. When he died a year later, I was even overjoyed, for I thought Aphrodite would be spared seeing the ugliness of my family. I would rid myself of them, and we would all start anew. I wished to marry her just then; however, her mother insisted we waited until she was eighteen at least. I agreed for it was only a year away at that point. I would have agreed to anything to have her.

"Um . . . please . . ."

I heard it just as I walked past my sister's door, her whimpering and sobbing.

Not this again.

"So dark . . ."

I knocked gently, but she did not hear.

"Verity?" I whispered, entering.

She froze stiff upon her bed. Sweat dotted her forehead, and she gripped the sheet.

"Verity!" I called, grabbing her, trying to wake her.

She sat up, gasping for air. "Uh . . ."

"It is okay," I said to her as she looked to the left and the right. "You are okay."

The terror in her eyes was evident, and at that moment, she hugged me, holding on to me tighter. This was the reason I would never forgive them. Not my father, not Datura, not Fitzwilliam. None of them. Ever.

Aphrodite

"Are you sure you cannot stay a moment longer? You have not even eaten breakfast," Verity asked as I stood at the door. My father had sent a new carriage before first light and demanded we return.

"My papa is expecting us." I smiled, looking upon her gently, and she hugged me. "I have behaved most irregularly as it is. I cannot possibly stay longer. It is not proper."

She sighed heavily as we parted. "Very well, we will just have to wait to have breakfast together when you are married to my brother."

My eyes widened, and I tried to find the words to speak. "I—I have yet to accept . . . I mean your brother has not asked or . . ."

"I was not allowed to listen to your conversations, but seeing your reaction, as well as the fact that our brothers are now speaking"—she nodded to where Damon and Evander stood at the carriage—"I am positive you shall be my sister at long last."

"I—" The amused look upon her face reminded me of her brother. "A lady ought not to be smug," I finally managed, at which she curtsied to me.

"Yes, Your Grace."

"Verity!"

She giggled, spun around, and skipped off, completely unaware of the nerves she had left me in. For could it be that easy? I once thought that, and everything had come to a painful halt. What if that were to occur once more? What if it were, as my brother said, ill-fated?

"Odite, are you ready?" Damon called out.

I nodded, hugging myself gently as if to keep all the emotions from spilling out. I was so happy and at ease with Evander in the kitchen. Every time he looked at me, it felt as though he were touching my soul. When I reached the carriage, he outstretched his hand, as did my brother, to help me inside. I took Evander's hand, and our eyes locked for a moment.

"I shall call on you to speak to your parents," he stated before my brother could even sit down. "Will you permit me to see you?"

"Yes," I whispered.

The corner of his mouth turned upward. He nodded and stepped backward, and the driver, with no sense of my desires at all, moved immediately, forcing me to turn to look at him.

"Temper your expectations, sister."

The look upon my brother's face troubled me. "I expect nothing—"

"You do. So remember, nothing is set until it is set. Even now, knowing the truth."

I did not respond, as I knew not how to. Instead, I found myself just thinking and waiting, as always. Waiting to see Mama and Papa so I could tell them all I had learned, thinking of what the information now meant for me—for *us*. But most of all, wondering why it had happened to him. How long he had suffered and withstood it all alone. How misunderstood he had been.

I was so distracted that the trip back home was nearly instant. I expected everyone only now to be rising for breakfast.

The house was still, except for my mother, who stood in the foyer, awaiting us. Upon seeing me, she smiled.

"Well?" She rushed to me. "Did Evander propose?"

"Is that not too soon, Mother—"

"No! It is much overdue," she snapped, interrupting my brother and taking my hands. "My dear girl, tell me everything. What happened? What did he say—"

"It matters not," my father interrupted as he walked down the stairs.

My father rarely grew angry with me. Even when I was wrong, he left discipline to my mother. So I was not used to the severity on his face.

"Your behavior, Aphrodite, was unacceptable. Return to your room."

"Papa, hear me first. This has all been one great misunderstanding—"

"Your room," he replied sternly.

"Yes, sir," I muttered.

"And while you are in there, make other arrangements for your future," Father said as soon as I passed the stairs. "No matter the reason, I shall not accept the duke."

"Papa!"

"Charles!" My mother gasped.

"Papa, you do not know what—"

"I need not. Now go," he ordered like a king.

Grabbing my skirts, I made my way up the stairs to my rooms, and as I went, the first thing I saw was my sisters, along with Hector, peering over the rails.

"Where—"

"Leave me be!" I replied, rushing past them.

"You cannot just demand we leave you," Hathor called out, following after me. "Where were you all night? Papa and

Mama would not say, but Papa was very upset after receiving Damon's letter. At first, I thought it was Mr. Yves who made you run. Then I realized that made no sense, and now Mama said something of Evander? Is that where you were? You could—"

At my door, I spun back to her. "Hathor, go find someone else to question."

"Quite difficult when you are the only one with the answers—"

I shut the door in her face. I did not have time to worry about her. I had to figure out what to do, especially if Evander were to come, when my father had just dug his heels into the dirt. I paced, sat, then rose to pace once more before, finally, I could not help but go to the window to watch for his arrival.

Knock. Knock.

"Hathor, will you please leave me be!" I hollered, but the door opened to my annoyance.

"It is not Hathor but me," Silva said upon entering, and my shoulders relaxed. "I came to see how you are."

"You are very kind. Much too kind after I stole my brother from you again."

She chuckled, walking to me. "When I married Damon, he warned me to expect that there would be days when he might be more occupied with his siblings than with me."

"Truly?" I asked, shifting so she could sit beside me.

She nodded. "He said that he did not know how but he always found himself in one predicament or another due to the five of you. And he is often powerless to stop it."

"He is right." I winced. "Forgive us."

"I think his dedication to his family is commendable. It shows he is soft-hearted even if he would not admit it."

"That he is."

Damon was very stubborn and believed himself always correct, but he listened and allowed others to say their piece.

"They've finished discussing."

"They have? So, Papa knows the truth now?"

She nodded and frowned. "Yes, but he has not changed his mind. Your mother was most aggrieved to hear about Evander's troubles and then became furious as your father declared, *even still*, he would not accept him."

"But why?" My heart sank.

"I do not know," she said and placed her hand over mine. "Let's not be discouraged. Mother will fight that battle for you as long as you want it fought. Do you?"

"Whether I do or don't, she would still fight."

"But do you?" she repeated.

My thoughts were a scattered mess. I knew the truth. I wanted to not have to sneak around. I wanted us to stay in that kitchen, discussing whatever we wished with no mind to the servants. I wanted . . . to know so much more of him.

"Yes. Even after all this time, I very much do."

"Then—"

"Aphrodite!"

I nearly jumped from my seat, hearing my mother's voice at the door. She came in hard-faced, nostrils flared, and her eyes narrowed on me, her demeanor shocking to Silva.

"Yes, Mama?"

"You shall bathe. The maids will bring you your finest gowns to choose from, and shall do your hair. Then we shall go to the park for a walk. After that, we are going to the Milbourne Ball. Furthermore, tomorrow, we shall have another breakfast in the park. All of these events shall be in the company of the Duke of Everely. Prepare yourself, for you shall be very busy!"

And with that, she began shouting orders into the hallway. "Eleanor! Bernice! Ingrid! Call them all!" she ordered with the force and fury of a queen, and within a mere second, my room was filled with her army. "If your father wishes to be stubborn, I shall be even more so. Twenty-two years I have waited for this moment, and he refuses? Ha! Let us see how he shall manage it when all of the ton sees you and Evander together every day and asks him when there shall be a wedding!"

I glanced at Silva out of the corner of my eye. I could see her trying not to laugh. My mother had been fully galvanized.

"Well, let us begin. Now!" She clapped her hands to the maids, and I was pulled away . . . and I was happy to be.

14

Evander

"I recall prescribing you rest," the doctor muttered as he roughly tended to the wound on my shoulder. "You are fortunate that your shoulder will heal, but how well is still up to you, Your Grace."

I looked down at my hand where I could still feel her touch. "I shall take your prescribed rest later."

"Then it is useless." He pressed hard near my shoulder.

I gritted my teeth, glancing up at him. "You're harming me, Dr. Darrington."

"You are harming yourself. You must not exert any more strain," he demanded as he handed me a vial. "Take this for another two nights. I will check on you again in three days. You should be well enough by then."

"Do you always take this much care with patients?"

"Yes," he said earnestly. I noticed that Dr. Darrington, despite his young age, was serious and skilled in his work. He had even been as discreet as he had promised. There was no talk of my illness or injuries, according to Verity.

"Thank you," I said to him seriously.

"It is my job." He cleaned his hands before packing away all his tools into his black leather bag.

I glanced at the vial and then at him for a moment. I did not wish to discuss this with anyone, but I thought of Verity and could not allow myself *not* to ask.

"Is there medicine for someone who . . ."

"Yes?" He waited, lifting his head to me.

"Who has horrible nightmares?"

"How bad?"

"Sometimes the afflicted cannot move, and other times, they sweat and scream. It varies."

He frowned. "If such is the case, I should first prescribe you another medicine—"

"It is not me," I said, and he stared at me for a long time before nodding.

"Then I need to speak to the patient—"

"I can tell you what occurs, but the person does not like to talk about it. Another doctor prescribed something to help with sleep, but it does not always work."

He closed his bag, lifting it before turning to me. "Your Grace, I cannot blindly prescribe medicine based on *your* assessment of the issue. I need to speak with the patient and see for myself."

"Could you do something if you did?"

"I do not know. But I doubt it."

"You do not give much comfort or confidence, Doctor," I said.

"Nightmares are rooted in other issues. That being said, medicine can ease a person's fear and anxiety as they deal with whatever it is."

That was the problem. Verity never wanted to talk about all the things she'd dealt with while I was away. I do not know why I'd believed our father would watch over her. He had not cared for our mother. He cared only that I was his heir. What was Verity to him? I should have known that.

"Your Grace—"

Knock. Knock.

"Enter." I turned to find my sister had come in with a maid, holding a tray of soup and bread.

She looked between us, confused. "Are you finished? Is he better?"

"Much."

"Some. Not much," Dr. Darrington replied sternly. "If that is all, I must go check on my other patients."

"You do not wish to eat? I had the maid—"

"No, thank you, my lady. Good day." He nodded at me then Verity before walking out of the room.

"I do not know if I like him." Verity frowned, glaring at the door. "He is not very amiable. Comes in, demanding to see you, then waltzes out swiftly."

"He is a working man, Verity," I replied, putting on my coat and going to the mirror. "If he spent time conversing with everyone, he would never see his patients."

"We are not everyone. You are a *duke*. One would think he would be more . . ."

"Amiable?" I repeated her word as I tied my tie.

"Oh, forget about the doctor. What happened with Aphrodite?" She smiled, skipping next to me.

"What do you mean?" I replied as she leaned in, her grin wide and eyebrows raised. Such a nosy one. "Nothing happened."

"Everything happened! She came here. You both spoke, correct? She stayed. And now you are getting dressed to see her."

"How do you know I am going to see her?"

"Because you are happy."

I glanced down at her, and she lifted her head in defiance,

daring me to disagree. I sighed and nodded. "It is still . . . unclear."

"Go clarify then."

"That is what I am seeking to do, but someone is distracting me." I reached up, poking her forehead to push her away.

"Fine, I will knit or read or do something boring as all ladies are supposed to do while you go out and have fun in the world. All after I spent the last four days nursing you back to health. It is almost as if I did not come out this season at all."

Dear God. Could she apply any more guilt?

"I will not take you to their home. It is serious, Verity. But there is a ball tonight, and I shall accompany you."

"I am tired of balls."

"You have yet to reach your peak, and you are bored? Is that not the point of coming out? What else is there to look forward to?"

"Yes, of course. What else could there possibly be for a lady than a ball." She sighed and started to leave.

"Why do I sense you are mocking me?" I called out to her, but she was already gone. I did not wish to be distracted. At least not at this moment. I still had too much to do today.

The first on my list was Aphrodite's father.

Aphrodite

I paced back and forth in the drawing room, doing my best not to pick at my nails. It was now midday, and he had yet to come.

"You could at least pretend not to be so eager. If not for

your own sake, then for my drawing." Hathor frowned, lifting a horrid sketch she'd created of me.

"Is that supposed to be me? Is your talent not the arts?"

"It would be if you ceased to move about the room like a deranged ghost," she replied, tearing the paper to start over. "If he comes, he comes. If he does not, you have only yourself to blame for trusting him."

"Hathor!" I snapped.

"What?" She huffed. "I am wholeheartedly on Father's side of this war."

"You do not know his circumstances."

She turned and faced me. "Then tell me."

I opened my mouth but then turned away from her. "Where do you wish me to be for this painting?"

"Are we not sisters? Why will you not share with me?"

"Why must I share with you?"

"So I may pick a side with a clear conscience! Mama is in his favor. Papa is not. And Damon seems to be neutral. I must know so I can—"

"Break the tie?" I smiled. "No need, sister, for I have already done so."

"So, you have accepted him?" she asked.

"Hurry, or I will not sit for your painting—"

"He is here," Devana said from near the window. She was so quiet that I had all but forgotten she was in the room. "The Duke of Everely is here."

Both Hathor and I rushed to the window. And sure enough, it was he, dressed in a deep green jacket and cream-colored vest. All of him finely trimmed, and in his hand, a small stack of old books.

"How scheming he is, using books to soften Papa," Hathor

muttered, her face so close to the window she nearly pressed against it.

"The correct word you are seeking is *clever*," I shot back, and almost as if he had heard me, he glanced up at the window. I looked away quickly.

Hathor giggled. "Yes, because by doing that, he will surely not think you were staring eagerly."

"I shall hit you." I glared at her.

"That is not the behavior of a duchess." She stuck her tongue out at me and went back to the door.

"Where are you going?"

"To see him enter and Father's expression," she replied, and I felt the urge to follow, but I stayed, not wishing to expose myself any further. Instead, Devana went to peer out the door along with her.

"He is now inside," she whispered and glanced back to me once again, smiling. "Now Mama is hugging him!"

"Yes, but Papa's face is strained," Hathor added. "I do believe he is not pleased."

I stood, wringing my hands, and then I sat once more.

"Papa is taking him to his study," Devana's gentle voice whispered, but then suddenly, both of them closed the door and turned back, rushing to their places.

That could mean only one thing.

"What have I told you all about eavesdropping?" my mother said as soon as she came in.

"Not to," Devana responded.

"Then why were you?"

"Mama, we heard not a word, so it was more like spying," Hathor said as she shifted to paint me once more.

"That also is unbecoming of a lady." She huffed, and her brown eyes narrowed on them before they shifted to me. I stayed where I was, and she came to sit beside me, taking my hand. "My dear girl, you have suffered long."

"She is not yet there, and might not ever be, if Papa has the last word," Hathor interrupted.

My mother's head whipped back to her. "At your age, do you not think it is fitting to mature?"

"No, for such maturity would be wasted, as Odite is the center of topics," she grumbled. "She is now most likely going to get two offers this spring. And me? Did anyone notice it was meant to be my season?"

"How could we forget when you remind us daily." My mother sighed. "And I promise you, my dear, once I am finished with your sister, you shall have my full and undivided attention, so do prepare yourself. Your time is coming."

Hathor got up, abandoning her art. "I shall believe it when I see it. For now, I will go prepare for the ball."

"Directly to your room, Hathor, for if you dare eavesdrop or spy, you shall join Abena," my mother warned.

"Yes, yes. I know, the pots—"

"No more pots. She has gotten used to it, so she is now in the kitchen peeling onions!"

"Mama, that is cruel!" Hathor gasped. "Her hands will smell for days!"

"Yes, good thing she has nowhere to be. In your case, who will dance with a lady who smells like onions?" Our mother lifted her eyebrows.

Hathor's eyes widened, and then she smiled. "Straight to my room, of course. Devana, come. You shall be my witness, for she believes you more than any of us."

Devana took her hand, and both of them left the room. My mother shook her head before glancing back at me.

"You are mighty, Mama." I smiled at her.

"You all trained me well." She chuckled, squeezing my hands. "Worry not of your father. I shall wear him down."

"Why is he so against it?" If Father did not support any engagement between Evander and me, it would break my heart, for how could I choose between my father and anyone else? "I thought he liked Evander."

"He did—he does," she assured, leaning closer. "He merely . . . worries."

"About what?"

"Everything, but especially for you." She cupped my cheek. "Everyone knows you are his favorite."

"Papa says he has no favorites."

"A *Papa* must say that, for it would cause mutiny amongst his children if he did not."

"Well, if I am the favorite and I wish there to be an engagement, why not give me what I desire?"

"I love your father very much, and I believe him a cut above all men. In the end, he is still a man. And consequently, he believes himself able to see things we women do not." She scoffed.

"What does Father think he sees?"

She opened her mouth and then closed it once again, shaking her head. "Do not worry. Everything will be well."

I disliked when she did that—when she stopped herself from telling me the truth. I knew she did it to spare me, but not knowing what they were thinking or were concerned about only made me feel like a child. Like everyone was permitted to have these discussions except me, even when the topic was of my fate.

"Due to the horrid rains, we cannot go to the park as I planned. But there is still the ball this evening. You shall be a vision, and Evander will be speechless."

"Does that mean even though he is here, I cannot see him?"

"It is best not to provoke your father further," she replied, fixing the curls over my shoulder. "And what a shame after all that time to prepare you for the afternoon."

I did not say more, and eventually, she left me to sit by the window. It felt like ages had gone by before Evander finally stepped out of my home, and the moment he did, he glanced up. I did not look away from him this time, so I could see his faint smile. What did that mean? Was it good or bad? How did the discussion with my father go? I did not know. He merely smiled and walked away.

I rose from the bench and rushed to the door, stepping into the hall just as my father came out of his study.

"Tell your mother that I am going to the club to see Sir Larson," he stated as the butler met him at the door with letters.

"Papa—"

"Tell her not to worry. I shall make it back before the ball."

"Papa!" I said firmly, causing him to look at me.

"Not now, my dear. I must go." The expression on his face left no room for disagreement, so I nodded, watching him leave.

I very much disliked all of this.

This was my life.

And since they would not allow me to participate in the conversation, I would have to take control of the situation . . . or at the very least try. I did not want to lose any more chances. I no longer wished to wait for . . . for others to decide what they believed was best for me.

Tonight, I would not just be silent and wait, I would act.

15

Evander

There was no place I detested more than a ball—actually, that was not true. I loathed being in the presence of my late father, Datura, and her offspring more, but balls were a close second, as they were filled with mothers desperately searching to find a match for their daughters. They paraded their daughters before me, and their daughters were all too willing, thinking me senseless enough to fall for their charms and antics of fainting on cue, fortuitously bumping into me, or dropping their fan or napkin before me. Even the fathers partook in the sport, though not so heavy-handedly. Their method was to categorize this whole ordeal as a business prospect. *Take my daughter, and in exchange, you shall get this much dowry or access to this bank, or inherit this much land.* It was all quite revolting, that they could sell off their daughters or believe me so avaricious and craven as to accept such offers. Balls were nothing but a façade created for the sole purpose of marrying and marrying well.

But such was society, and society had to go on. Thus, the balls had to go on, and I needed to do my part. This was complicated because I was here to seek a match for my sister. I glanced over at her as she hummed to herself, watching everyone else dance.

"You do not wish to accept a partner?" I asked, for she had refused two already.

"I do not like anyone here," she whispered.

"How do you know when you have not spoken to anyone?" I questioned.

"The same way you know there is no other person for you but Aphrodite," she teased, smiling at me slightly. "Just like you, I will know instantly when I have met my match."

That was not true, though she did not know, nor could she ever, that I had spent time searching—well, not so much searching but exploring females—before Godmother came with her letter.

"At this rate, you will not find anyone this season. Is that your wish?" I whispered. "If you do find one who catches your eye, I shall do my best to make it possible for you, Verity, should they be appropriate, of course."

"I did not come here for my season but yours," she replied, lifting her wine to her lips.

"Mine?"

"Surely you have seen all my efforts?" She leaned in closer. "I heard that Aphrodite was returning this season and, thus, pressed you to come immediately. Otherwise I am sure you might have delayed longer."

I stared at her, not altogether surprised, as I had seen her antics before. "How on earth did you hear talk from London while we were in Everely?"

She grinned and did not reply.

Devious indeed.

"Do remember to save this skill when you begin entrapping your husband."

"I shall." She huffed, not at all denying the effort to entrap a husband, as I thought she would. "Though I must confess I have given no thought to such as my biggest worry is for you."

"Me? In what way?"

"Whether you will be able to let me go." She lifted her head. "It has always been just you and me. And as I brace myself to share you with someone else, you will need to do the same. But I do not believe you easily capable of such. It might break your heart should I move far away, somewhere not under your protection."

The words alone broke my heart. She was right, and I did not wish to ever have her not at my side. And that brought to mind my conversation with Aphrodite's father. I could see he was torn, which eased my frustration or even sadness. Just as balls had to go on, fathers had to part with their daughters.

"And now I shall stop speaking, as your match has arrived." She giggled, stepping away from me.

Immediately, I turned to the door to watch Aphrodite as I always watched her, like the divine. How was it possible that every color was meant only for her? That anything that looked ridiculous on another became magnificent on her. She was the crown jewel of the ton—the most perfect of all jewels. It was her face that, in public, never frowned nor smiled but remained in a constant state of serenity. It was her walk that looked fit for the clouds of heaven. Every time she entered a room, all eyes turned to her because she looked as though she did not belong in this world.

When her beautiful brown eyes met mine, I smiled, knowing how different her outward expressions were from her inner thoughts and desired behavior.

On the outside, Aphrodite was innocent, docile, and softspoken, but on the inside, she was persistent, curious to a fault, and sometimes unforgiving, unless she was forced to forgive.

She was a wonder of things, but the world saw only a fraction of it.

And the greediest part of me wished to keep it as such, so only I could see the real her. However, I suspected once she gained the wisdom she desired there would be a new dawn of her. I desired to be in that twilight. So, before her family had even fully settled, I found myself walking toward her, and I was not the only one. *Tristian*. However, I was before her first, and her eyes were on me alone.

"May I have your first dance, my lady?" I asked, offering my hand.

"Yes," she replied, placing her hand in mine. As I led her to the floor, the looks from all in attendance were far more intense than even I would have imagined.

"The talk will be severe," I stated.

"Just as Mama planned." She moved before me as we waited for the music to begin and others took their places.

"How so?"

"She believes the talk will push Papa to . . ." She did not finish her statement. The music began, and so did our dance.

"Push your *papa* to do what?" I inquired as I walked around her back.

"Agree to whatever it is that brought you to our door this morning," she muttered as she moved in the other direction.

"And had you been sitting at the window?"

"I always sit at the window," she answered, her face before mine, lifting her hand.

I lifted my hand as well. "So finely dressed?"

"Yes."

"How fortunate are those who receive such a sight."

"Yes, I believe so, which is why I stay at the window."

I could not contain my grin, which only caused talk around

us to continue further. "I shall be cognizant of that fact when we are married, and order thicker draperies."

She nearly missed her footing. "I have not yet been proposed to, but if I was, I think I might reject an offer from any man who would drape windows during the day to trap me in darkness."

"Draperies? Did I say draperies?" I stared in horror. "Never. Heaven forbid, for I would build you the largest window to be admired from."

"If I *was* married to you," she corrected. "But I am not."

"When you *are*, you may demand anything of me," I pressed, turning behind her again.

"That would require a proposal."

"One seeks to offer," I whispered when she stood in front of me. "But I have been given a condition."

"A condition?"

I nodded. "Your father is not pleased with my situation and will not approve until Fitzwilliam has been found."

"What?" she asked a little too loudly, as the music faded and our dance ended. She noticed quickly and adjusted her forlorn expression.

I offered my hand to lead her from the floor. "It is my full intention to propose to you," I whispered, taking her farther away from the eager ears. "For nothing in this world would make me happier than to have you as my wife."

"But all that stands between us is my father?" She frowned.

"Not your father." I did not wish her to blame him. "It is Fitzwilliam. Your father worries that with such a vicious person threatening me, you may be injured in some way."

"Have you not been seeking to apprehend him all these years?"

"Yes, but—"

"Then it is a possibility that it could take you even more years?"

"I hope it will not—"

"But it could. What if after his attack on you he flees the country?" she pressed.

"I doubt he would." The only way he'd managed to hide this successfully was thanks to Datura, I was sure. The woman still had spies around Everely. In fact, I was of the mind that he had confessed to his attack on me, so she had come to see herself.

"'I hope.' 'I doubt,'" Aphrodite repeated sadly, holding her hands and hanging her head. "How does one cast their future on such things?"

Fear crept into me at her words. "Aphrodite, I swear to you, I will accomplish this and then—"

"And then propose?" She glanced up. "Do you not think I have waited long enough?"

"Of course, but—"

"I am tired of being forced to wait for the life I want, Evander. I will talk to my father."

Eyes wide, I stepped in her path, stopping her. "You cannot."

"Why not?"

"Because he has already spoken on the matter, so all you will do is anger him. He has given me a task, and I will complete it and gain your hand."

"My hand is already yours, Evander. It has always been yours. Why must my father—"

"He is your guardian."

"I am of age. More so now." The determination in her eyes made my heart stir. But I couldn't ruin my chance this time by being impatient.

"You may be of age, Aphrodite, but you are still under your father's care. Will you make me a thief, or worse, a rogue with no respect for the order of things? He could shun us both. Your dowry, are you going to forsake that? Surely, I would take care of you always, but even still, your father may refuse to see you again. Approval isn't just a formality, it is peace, and I could not bear knowing I had broken it in your home."

"My father would never. You know he is a kind man."

"Nevertheless, it is not proper to take advantage of his kindness and love of you."

Her shoulders dropped. She inhaled deeply, staring at my hand. "I understand your concerns. Truly. Have you thought of mine?"

"Yes."

"Do you see everyone's eyes on us?"

I did not have to look to know.

"The first time they all laughed at me, mocked me. I could not even breathe in high society. And now we have come full circle. Any delay will further insult me and misunderstand you. Whatever you face, I shall face with you if you let me."

I could not have been more madly in love with her. "I will come back in the morning to speak to your father again and propose."

"I shall wait . . . as always."

I wished I could kiss her lips at this moment. Instead, I kissed the back of her hand.

Soon, so very soon, she would be mine.

Aphrodite

My father would not speak to me on the way home, nor did he speak to any of us once we had arrived. Instead, he went to his study immediately. I finally retired to bed, but I could not sleep, as my heart was still racing. While at the ball, I was strengthened by Evander's presence. But was I pushing him too far? Was I too stubborn? Should I have simply accepted what he and my father had agreed to?

I spent all night tossing, turning, and thinking. It felt like I had only blinked when I began to see the light of the sun enter my room. Father always awoke at first light when he had something on his mind, as the house was quiet and allowed him time to read. I knew this since I'd often joined him when I was younger. I rose from my bed, and I took my robe before peeking out of the room. Seeing no one there, I quietly headed down the stairs. Doing so reminded me of being in Evander's home, sneaking to the kitchen together. Sitting across from Evander, I had dared to dream that we could be like that without having to hide.

It was that dream that gave me courage as I reached my father's study door. I inhaled through my nose, held my head high, and knocked.

"Yes?" I heard his voice.

I entered to see him standing by his book stacks, already dressed for the day. Upon seeing me, he frowned.

"How did you know I planned on sneaking out early today?" he asked.

"I didn't. But you always rise early when you are anxious," I answered, closing the door behind me.

"Why do I have the sense you are about to make me more so?" he muttered, looking back at his book.

"I am." I smiled. "Evander will come today to propose to me."

"I talked to Evander yesterday."

"But you did not speak to me."

"Because there is nothing to discuss, my dear," he replied, going to his desk to pick up his bag.

"On the contrary, Papa. It is my life."

"Hence why I am doing all that I must to ensure it is a good and safe one. You are caught in your emotions and cannot see," he replied sternly.

"I'd rather be blind than emotionless," I argued.

He chuckled, shaking his head. "Aphrodite, we shall talk about this later—"

"We will not. You will ignore and hide from me."

"You are being ridiculous. I am not hiding from you. I am sparing these conversations as they will go nowhere. I will not change my mind—"

"Then I will marry without your permission, and my wedding will be the happiest and saddest day of my life."

He froze, shocked. "You . . . you are threatening me?"

I shook my head. "I am not, Papa. I am telling you the truth. I am telling you what I want."

"And what you want is not easily done."

"But it can be. Evander—"

"Evander's family is full of complications. Some of which you do not know or understand!"

I stepped forward. "All my life, you, Mama, and my governess have told me I am to stand by my husband. Even if his life is full of complications. Did you not mean it?"

"I see all these years I have spent seeking to educate you were a waste. The book I gave to you, the story of 'The Golden Bird,' did you not learn about the misfortunes one goes through when one does not take advice from the wise?"

"I did learn," I replied, and, seeing the same book on his desk, I walked to it and lifted it to show him. "From this and all the books you've given me. All tales, Papa, have struggles. Just as you could not protect me the first time my heart broke, you cannot protect me this time. I do not know what shall happen, but I trust I can succeed in an even happier life. I only beseech you not to be another struggle for me to surpass. Be on my side. Even if it looks unwise, Papa, be on my side and trust me."

He took the book from me and placed it down. "Now I fear I educated you too well, for you are far too good in your argument."

I grinned, daring to hope. "So you will give him your blessing?"

He frowned. "Can you not let him work for it more? After how shattered you were, do you not think it wise to make him grovel? At least till the end of the season?"

I shook my head. "Do you not think he has suffered enough? Cannot one thing be easy for him?"

"He has a dukedom full of wealth and power by birth," he said, and I was sure I had won.

"And you were given your title, full of your own wealth and power, with a loving wife and children, a peaceful home— well, sometimes," I countered. And he laughed, stepping in and hugging me.

"My dear girl, you have squeezed my heart since you were born."

I hugged him in return. "I shall still do so, just not as close, once you accept him."

"Oh, very well!" He huffed and sighed, letting go of me. "But say not a word to him. I shall see him grovel before me at least once more!"

"Papa!"

How blessed was I?

16

Aphrodite

There was a white-and-red tulip waiting by the window seat for me. Surely he had not placed it there himself. I knew that for sure. But still, seeing it, undisturbed and waiting for me, only further excited me. My mother sat quietly as if she did not notice it at all. Lifting the tulip, I inspected it closely, touching its petals. The first time I had received one from him, I was so curious I later sought the meaning of this beautifully strange flower in a botany book. The red expressed deep love and the white symbolized forgiveness.

"Why is he here again?" Hathor questioned, drawing my attention as she entered with our sisters. I glanced out the window to see Evander speaking with one of the doormen at the gate, who allowed him to enter.

"Obviously, he is here for Odite," Abena replied, all my sisters now crowding around me by the window.

Evander glanced toward me, and the corner of his lip turned upward. He even winked. Devana and Abena giggled.

"Coming here a second day is a bit aggressive, is it not?" Hathor huffed, taking a seat.

"I think you are just jealous." Abena stuck her tongue out, and Hathor glared down at her. "Odite is going to be a duchess, and you shall be a spinster—"

Hathor grabbed the window pillow and threw it at Abena's head.

"Hathor!" my mother snapped at her. "Have you lost your mind?"

"Not at all, Mama. I merely found aim."

"Lose it once more! You are a young lady, or have you forgotten?" my mother replied and looked at Abena, who was holding the pillow as if she saw fit to throw it again. "And you. What have I told you about picking a fight with your sister?"

"Not to."

"Then why do you continue, my dear?"

Abena shrugged. "I did not know speaking the truth was picking a fight!"

"I will crush you, little bug!" Hathor snapped, rising to fight Abena despite our mother's warnings. Before the war could ensue, my father entered the room.

"Well?" my mother asked before I could.

My father took a deep breath, and then shook his head. "I thought long and hard on it, but I cannot accept him."

It was as if he had slapped me. I could only stare, stunned. Had all my words been for naught? Did he not already promise me?

"He has left," Hathor said to me.

And I spun around to see him exit the gate without a single glance back at me.

"Papa," I gasped, now turning my body to him. "What—"

"What have you done?" my mother screamed at the top of her lungs. "Charles! What have you done? Call him back this instant, or I shall never speak to you again! How could you? I—"

I stopped listening as I felt everything fall to ruin once

more. I could not believe he would do this to me. Before I could say a word, there was a hard pinch on my arm. I turned to see Hathor smirking at me.

"He is in the garden, waiting," she whispered.

I did not understand until I saw my father's amused expression as my mother paced in front of him, ranting angrily. When he caught my eye, he winked.

Oh . . . they were terrible.

"Well, are you going or not?" Hathor asked.

"I shall get you for this," I whispered to her. As my mother went on, I made my escape, turning left in the hall before going down the stairs and out the double doors into the gardens. And there he was, standing beside the row of juniper trees.

"You have colluded with my father?"

He turned to me, grinning. "Forgive me. It was his request, and I saw fit not to go against him in anything and risk my chance. Were you dismayed?"

"Not at all," I lied, placing my hands behind my back as I walked to him. "I saw through your little game immediately."

"I see." He looked me over carefully. "Then I shall not withhold this part any longer."

I stepped closer, and he opened his mouth, but not a word came out. Instead, he just laughed gently.

"What is it?"

"Everything," he replied, lifting his head to meet mine. "I stand before you, Aphrodite, full of *everything*, from nerves to hopes, to the greatest of happiness, and most of all, the deepest of love. I have long loved you to a degree and passion that nearly drives me mad. The sight of you is like the sun, and the last four years without you left me in a dark abyss. I thought I would never escape it, and then you rose again in my life. And now I know that as birds need the sky and fish the water, I need you. I could not know any other honor than to be called your husband—if you shall have me? If you will be my wife?"

I inhaled as if I had been underwater for the longest time and could only now fill my lungs with air. My eyes stung from the tears, the grin spread across my face, and I wished to speak, but the lump in my throat would not let me. I could only nod.

"Truly?" the silly man asked.

"Yes," the word squeaked out. "Yes, I shall be your wife."

He exhaled and laughed. Taking my hands into his, he brought them to his lips and kissed both knuckles. "Then let us finally wed."

"Yes." Now that was the only word I knew to say.

We stared at each other, our faces so close that we surely would have kissed had it not been for the small giggle I heard behind me.

I turned to see Devana putting her hand over Abena's mouth. But Abena pulled away and said, "So, is this really happening now?"

"Abena!" I said sharply, glaring at her. But Evander laughed and lifted our entwined hands.

"Yes, it is truly happening. Do I have your blessing?" Evander asked her.

"Yes!" Devana nodded happily.

"If you wanted our blessing, should you not have asked earlier?" Abena questioned with her arms crossed.

"Abena!" I scolded.

"You are very much right, my lady." Evander humored her. "How can I atone for the delay?"

I looked at him. "Evander, you do not need—"

"You shall let her visit," Abena said sternly. "Or I can come to visit . . . a lot."

"Of course! All of you are always welcome at Everely, and we shall never be far. We shall visit as often as your sister wishes."

Abena observed him, then nodded. She looked at me then ran back into the house. Devana watched her go and then focused on me. "Sorry to interrupt, but can we save Papa now?"

"Save Papa from what?"

"Mama. She is still angry."

My eyes widened. "He has not told her yet that he was merely joking?"

She shook her head of blonde curls.

"Your father is very peculiar." Evander laughed. "Shall we rescue him?"

"Please." I nodded, fully aware that we were still holding hands, because his touch was like a warm fire. It did not burn, but it did make me feel sort of strange. Though we were now engaged, to be holding hands like this was still a bit forward, which was why some of the servants who saw us nearly had their eyes pop out of their heads while others grinned and a few looked away quickly. I was sure by high tea the talk would have spread.

However, I could not focus on anything but my mama as she angrily ordered around the servants.

"Have all of my things moved to another room! I shall not speak to him! I do not even wish to see him, seeing as how he does not care in the slightest about my—".

"Godmother," Evander called out.

"Not now, Evander. I am very ang—" Her words drifted as she spun around. Then her brown eyes glanced down at our hands and back to our faces. She did not even ask. She spun once more to the door where my father stood beside Hathor.

"What were you saying, my love? I do not care about what?" my father asked, trying to contain his laughter.

"You. Oh! Later!" she snapped at him, and then her attention was once more on us. "Tell me you are engaged."

"Yes, Mama!" I said with a smile. "We are."

"Finally!" she squealed. Honestly and truly, like a child to the point that I could not help but laugh at her. She rushed up to us and placed one hand on each of our arms. "Worry for nothing. I shall take care of it all! You shall be married by the end of the week!"

"The week?" Not just I, but my father, Hathor, even Damon, who had only just entered with Silva, all asked in chorus.

"Yes." My mother looked at us all in confusion. "I cannot possibly move any faster than that. You will need a new dress and—"

"Is not a week too soon?" I asked her.

"No," she said instantly.

"It is, Mama," Hathor said. "People will talk of some sort of scandal should they wed so quickly."

"I do not care," she said and then asked Evander, "Do you care?"

"Not at all. I would wed her today if I could."

"Neither of you may care, but you will need a special license," my father reminded them. "I know it has been a while, my dear, but the banns should be read out on three successive Sundays."

"Then we shall get such a special license." My mother huffed.

"Mama, truly, it can wait—"

She looked at me sternly. "I shall let nothing stop this wedding *again* because it has been a very long time coming for me. Therefore, it shall be done in a week. Understood, my dear?"

How embarrassing. "Yes, Mama."

"Then it is decided! Come, sweet child! We must prepare and call the modiste at once!" She all but tore me from Evander and pulled me up the stairs. I glanced back down at him, as I had not said goodbye and, truthfully, did not wish to. "Come. Come. He shall have you soon enough. We must get this correct! Hathor! Come help your sister."

"With what?" Hathor called from behind me. "I am not the modiste!"

"Hathor!" My mother's voice was stern.

I could hear grumbling as she marched up behind us. I focused on Evander for as long as I could.

Evander

"And so you have won," Damon said, handing me a glass of brandy.

"I am still afraid to hope." I smirked, looking down at the liquid. "I think I will not believe it until after I hear her announced as my wife before all the world."

"You believe something may occur to rip you apart once more?" he asked.

It was not that I believed it, but I feared being too content.

"When your life is disrupted, you begin to think that it is never going be whole again, that any good moment will be subsequently met with bad. As if it were punishment for daring to be happy."

"You are not instilling much confidence, and I truly wish for my sister's happiness," he said.

"As do I." I nodded. "Be assured I will do all in my power to ensure it."

"Good. Now, how the hell did you convince my father? He was ready to go to battle over this. He would not even listen to my mother."

I shrugged, as I honestly did not know. "I doubt it was anything I said or did. I believe it was your sister."

"Ah, now it makes sense." He chuckled, shaking his head.

"How so?"

"When my father wishes to be a mountain, he is a mountain. Not even my mother would dare try him. However, Aphrodite is like a breeze. She simply goes right through him. It is the talent of the favored."

"So, you have no idea how she does it, either?" I chuckled at him.

"None. But I shall enjoy watching you and gaining further clarity, for I believe you might be less successful at denying her than even Father."

"You may be right." There was nothing that I could think of now to deny her.

"Allow me to ask you then," he replied seriously, so I gave him my full attention. "What shall you do with the girl you are raising? Is my sister to raise her? Have you spoken on it?"

That was one of the things her father had mentioned to me as a reason for his hesitance to our union. And I had thought of it.

"Emeline is under my care. She has a nanny and will soon get a governess. If Aphrodite does not wish to concern herself, she does not have to. The child shall have a woman's care either way."

"Your sister was raised in the arms of nannies and governesses. Do you believe that is wise? Does the child not long for a mother?"

I drank before answering. "I have done more for Emeline

and her mother than anyone else in this world. It may be cold of me—may I be forgiven for it—but I wish not to think too much about it. And I dare not anger or disturb your sister with her."

He nodded. "I understand. I just remind you because . . . I remember Verity."

I stared at him, shocked at the connection. "Aphrodite would never harm Emeline. You know this."

"I know it. I merely meant how your father did not concern himself. I wish your home peace, Evander. But just as that girl's real father is against you, I wish you not to cause the one in your home to turn bitter as well, by turning your attention to your future with Aphrodite."

When did he become so insightful? "I do my best to show her kindness and care."

"Then pardon me for intruding so far into your personal business."

Before I could answer, there was a knock at the door.

"Enter."

Aphrodite arrived, looking between us both curiously. "Dinner is ready. Mama said to call you both."

"Perfect timing," he said and walked to the door.

"Is everything all right?" she asked when her brother was gone.

I wanted to say yes, but Damon's damn words were now in my mind.

"Oh no, you are hesitating. What did he say?"

I chuckled at her expression. "Damon merely reminded me that I must be more honest with you."

"How so?"

I placed the glass down, stepping to her. "I have told you the whole story. But I do not believe I was clear. You are aware that I raise the daughter of my former wife as my own."

She nodded. "Yes, you said so."

"Aphrodite, I truly do my best to tend to the girl as if she were mine. In reality, she and the world believe me to be her Papa. I told your brother that I expect you to do nothing else but treat her cordially."

"Do you believe I will not?" She frowned.

I reached to touch her shoulder but noticed a maid walking by, peering in, and stopped myself. "I believe it is hard to raise a child who is not your own, speaking from personal experience. I only wish you to let me know how you would like to handle the matter. I will not be disappointed either way. I know you are kind. I merely seek to make sure you enter our marriage well aware."

"Thank you, but I do not know what exactly would be needed of me. I am ready to face it with you," Odite replied.

"And I you." Once more, I lifted her hand and kissed the back of it. "Now let us go to dinner before your maids break their necks looking in."

She sighed, shaking her head. "I see why Mama wishes this wedding to be done so quickly now."

"Does that displease you?"

"Of course not, though part of me worries my mother may have forced your hand a bit," she replied.

"Never. I am eternally in her debt. My mother left me with two mighty benefactors in this world."

"Two?" She tilted her head to the side.

"I have been sent to call you both," Damon said from the door, arms crossed, frowning. "And I am displeased doing so, as I do not wish to see the *fire* in your eyes."

Aphrodite glanced around the room. "Fire? But there is no fire to glow in our eyes?"

I bit my lip to hide my amusement, as she did not realize it was not a real fire he spoke of but desire. Oh, thank God it would be only a week, for there was wickedness inside of me, a beast that hungrily anticipated removing all of the innocence from her.

It shined so profoundly that her brother saw it and was clearly uncomfortable. I did my best once more to tame it.

Father in heaven, may this week be the shortest in the history of mankind.

17

Aphrodite

I always knew my mother was a force to be reckoned with, but I did not know she was a miracle worker. Everyone had told her repeatedly that it would not be possible to do what she asked in a week's time. The modiste told her she did not have the fabric to make the dress, and the baker told her he did not have enough time to make the cake. The cook complained that he did not have enough hands to create the feast, the decorator said there was no time to prepare the house, and, most of all, the ton said they would not be able to attend on such short notice. And yet everything was ready, and the last person had sent notice they would be in attendance at the reception—that person being the queen!

I lay on my bed, staring at the dress that hung in anticipation of my wedding in the morning. It was a beautiful white, with accents of gold and silver. The more I stared at it, the more mesmerized I was with its detail.

Knock. Knock.

"Come in," I said, still unable to look away from the dress.

"Are you sleeping?" Hathor asked.

"No," I muttered. I tore my gaze away from the gown to see Hathor in her nightdress, her hair in her cap. "What is it?"

She closed the door and came to my bed, lying down beside

me. She shifted a few times before she was comfortable and looked at me. "This is your last night here."

I frowned at that. "It is not. I promise I shall be back—"

"But it is your last night here as Lady Aphrodite Du Bell. Next time you come, you shall be Her Grace, the Duchess of Everely. You shall be a married woman, and I will not be allowed to come into your room like this. Even if the duke does not come with you."

"Are you saying you shall miss coming into my room like this?"

"I am saying I shall miss . . ." She thought for a moment. "I shall miss being on the same side of the line with you. You shall cross over and be a wife and know of . . . whatever it is wives know. And I shall still be a child."

"Do you really believe Mama is going to let you off? The moment I am away, you will have what you have always dreamed of—the attention of all the ton." For the good or the bad sometimes. "You will join me on the other side as a married woman before too long."

"Ummm. Very true," she muttered and shifted to lie on her back, looking up at the ceiling. "But then what will we fight about?"

I laughed and turned onto my back as well. "I do not know, but we are sisters, so I am sure we can find something."

"Promise me you will be careful, Odite."

"Of?"

"Everything. You shall be the mistress of your own home. You will have a husband to tend to. Mama says that is not easy, even if she makes it look so. Then there is the whole estate to manage. Mama says it is of paramount importance to understand the lay of the house and make sure the servants respect and, most importantly, like you. They already had a mistress before, so they may be biased against you. It is good that Mama has given you Eleanor for assistance. She is very diligent, but one maid on your side is not enough. A house cannot run without the servants."

"I know," I said, smiling at the worry in her voice.

"Then, on top of that, there are, of course, tenants on the land. All the farmers and there are even a few mills in the duke's authority. As the new mistress, you will need to get them all to like you in turn. Mama says this is hard because they can believe us toffee-nosed. The first few weeks—no, the first year is important as you see them through a good or bad harvest."

"I know." Everything Mama had told her, she had already told me, as she had been preparing me to be the Duchess of Everely for . . . for as long as I could remember. She did not teach me how to run *any* estate. She taught me how to run Everely. She did not teach me how to manage *any* tenants. She taught me how to manage the tenants of Everely. Maybe that was why she wished for me to be eighteen to marry before being left to care for such a grand estate. But truthfully, looking back on my instructions and lessons, it was quite dangerous of her, because what if I didn't marry Evander?

"And the most concerning of all of this," Hathor said, shifting to look at me in the darkness, "is his family."

"What do you know of his family?" As she should have known nothing. The circle to which Evander had told the truth was comprised solely of Father, Mother, Damon—and by connection Silva—and me.

"He has a daughter already." She frowned heavily. "Have you thought of how you shall manage her?"

I shook my head. "I have not."

"You must now think of these things, Odite." One would

have thought she was the elder of the two of us. "Of course, it is unbecoming of you to be cruel. The child bears no fault. But no matter what your name is or how handsome you are, you are a human with feelings. Seeing the child will hurt your heart, will it not?"

I had honestly put no thought into it. "I shall be all right, I am sure."

"You do realize that baseless confidence of yours is your most infuriating feature? Everything does not always work out simply because you are sure."

"Yes, I am aware." I was marrying four years later than I'd planned into a much more complicated family than I'd thought. "I am sorry if it is infuriating, but I do not know what else to say."

"They shall eat you alive." She sighed heavily. "Especially that stepmother of his, the dowager duchess. Mama was greatly displeased that she had to invite her to the reception. She believes the woman to be deeply cruel-hearted and full of evil intent. And I agree with Mama, for anyone who did as she did and tortured the former real duchess, Lady Luella, is wholeheartedly despicable. Do not trust her at any cost, for she is like the snake in the Garden of Eden."

"Is there anything else?" I tried not to laugh at her.

"Yes, you—"

Knock. Knock.

"Come in," Hathor answered even though it was my room. When the door opened, we saw the faces of Devana and Abena.

I sat up. "What are you both doing?"

"Can we stay with you?" Devana asked while Abena was already halfway onto the bed.

"Of course." I laughed, shifting to allow Abena to situate herself in between Hathor and me.

Devana closed the door and also came to lie between Hathor and me.

"What are you two talking about?" Abena asked.

"How to lose you in the forest," Hathor muttered.

"I already know how to do that. I would just leave food for her." I laughed, making the rest of them, except for Abena, giggle.

"Or tell Mama she's the one who ruined her favorite shoes. She would run for sure into the forest then," Devana said.

Even in the darkness, I could see Abena pout.

"Why are you all picking on me?" she asked.

I hugged her tightly. "Because you are the littlest, and I'm mad at you for teasing Evander today."

Hathor chuckled. "I cannot believe you mocked the duke."

Abena gasped. "I did not."

"Yes, you did," Devana confirmed.

"All I said was that if he kept looking at Odite so hard, he would trip and fall on his face. And no one wants a face full of dirt for a wedding."

"That is teasing," we all told her.

She crossed her arms as we laughed at her. "Everyone always says I am teasing when I'm just talking," she grumbled.

I understood how she felt.

"Talk less then," Hathor suggested.

"I do not want to. I like talking."

"We know," all of us said in unison once more, which had us laughing and giggling. With the four of us in bed together, I nearly fell off the side but did not mind. Hathor was right. This was the last time we could be like this . . . the Du Bell girls. We would soon have our own homes, with our own families, and we would be mamas. It was so surreal to think that, but I was on my way.

We talked and talked, and I felt as if I had only just closed my eyes before I heard a terrifying voice.

"What is this?"

"Umm . . ."

"No," Abena whimpered, turning away from the light, kicking me in the side.

"Ah!" I rolled.

"Hathor, Devana, Abena, get up now!" My mother's voice was like a crack of thunder. "I sent her to bed early so that she might be lively this morning, and you all were in here playing!"

"Mama, I am fine—"

"Hush, you!" She pointed to me and smacked Abena's backside. "And you, get up, little miss."

"Mama, I am tired—"

"Then go to your room." She leaned over and spoke directly into her ear. *"Now!"*

Abena sat up, holding her ears. "Mama!"

"Go. Your sister has much to prepare. I will not let you lot distract me today of all days."

Grumbling, Abena hopped off the bed. Now my mother's eyes were on me.

I smiled at her. "Good morning."

She shook her head. "You should have kicked them out. Look at you, you're so tired."

I rubbed my eyes. "Mama, it was our last time together. I am fine. I am . . ." I did not have the words for what I was at this moment, because it was morning. It was my wedding day, and I looked at the dress waiting for me.

"And the wedding day nerves have arrived," she said. "See

why you needed rest? Nerves have a way of taking even more of your energy, and today you need all of it. Come now. A fresh bath shall help."

I trusted myself to her because today was my wedding, and though I had said I was fine, a small part was very much not fine. I turned to my mother.

"Everything will be as I wished today?" I asked her.

"Yes," she replied without hesitation.

"How are you sure? Last—"

She held the sides of my face. "Because I willed it so. Today will be everything you dreamed of, and tonight . . ." She paused, dropping her hands from my face. "Tonight, you shall be a wife."

"What does that mean exactly?" Would it be like the shrubbery? Would it hurt? "Mama—"

"I will explain before you leave with him tonight. Now come, let us make you a bride worthy of your name."

Nerves. They came suddenly and engulfed my very being. All I wanted—all I needed—was for the day to go as it should.

Please.

Evander

When I awoke in the morning, I stayed in bed for another ten minutes. I had not slept more than three or four hours because I was too anxious. I even prayed. Truly, I did.

Entering the church early, I stood there and prayed again.

It was only my sister and me, and she said not a word, sitting in the pew quietly. Damon arrived with Silva half an hour later, which was still an hour earlier than when our wedding was scheduled. I looked at the anger on his face.

"Is everything all right?" I asked him, quickly rising.

"You are the most infuriating of men!" he snapped at me. His wife grabbed his arm, pulling him back.

"What—"

"Forgive him!" Silva said to me. "There was talk that you had left London early this morning. It reached the house. Everyone was worried, and he went to your home, and they said you had left already but did not clarify where you had gone, so he panicked."

"I did not panic," Damon lied and then looked at me. "Why are you here so early?"

"I couldn't wait," I replied honestly.

"I cannot even be angry at him when he is so earnest," Damon grumbled to his wife.

"I shall go back and let everyone know to remain calm," she said.

"I will go with you," Verity added, getting up and taking her arm.

I watched them both go before looking at Damon as he walked to where I was, taking a seat in the pew, dusting off his hat. "I am exhausted, and it is still morning."

"Did Aphrodite believe I had left as well?" I asked.

"Could you blame her if she did?"

I could not. "My household, here at least, knows to be discreet. That is why they may not have spoken even though it was clear I was heading to the church. Forgive them. Forgive me. I should have said something."

Though I did not know how I could have told them that I could not bring myself to wait in my home any longer out of fear that I would convince myself it was all a dream.

"Everyone is on a razor's edge. No need for apologies," he replied.

"Hmm." I nodded, leaning back and breathing in through my nose.

There was nothing to say. There was nothing more to do, so we sat there, waiting until everyone finally arrived, marked by the sound of the door opening and the muttering of her younger sisters. All dressed in spring colors, Hathor gave me a careful once over. Devana only smiled gently, but Abena waved to me, and I waved back at her. Hector, her younger brother, held out his hand to me.

Damon chuckled behind me, but I took him seriously and shook it.

"Take care of my sister," Hector said.

"Always." I nodded to him.

"I was waiting to say that after the wedding," Damon muttered.

"Never wait to say the things you wish to say. I learned that a long while ago," I replied, moving to my spot as the clergymen entered.

I nodded to them both. They looked quite bored but nodded back. And that was actually comforting. For them, this was any ordinary day. When my sister and Silva arrived with Aphrodite's mother, who came in with a large smile on her face, I knew we had made it.

Then, not even five minutes later, the music began, and the door opened for the final time. Aphrodite walked in on the arm of her father, holding a bouquet of red tulips, and stole my soul. I could not look away from her.

My heart began to race so loudly, and my mind was so focused that I missed her father's voice when he reached me with her. It was only when she glanced at him that I looked as well. He just chuckled and kissed his daughter's cheek before stepping off to the side.

The priest spoke on and on with blessed words, but she and I cared only about one part, a few lines of words.

"Lord Evander Eagleman, do you take Lady Aphrodite Du Bell to be your lawfully wedded wife? To have and to hold from this day forward, for better, for worse, for richer, for poorer, in sickness and in health, to love and to cherish, till death do you part, according to God's holy ordinance?"

"I do," I said.

She was asked the same question for me.

Her eyes shined as she whispered, "I do."

"Then, by the power vested in me, I pronounce that your wedding vows are sealed, and you may henceforth be known to all as husband and wife. You may now kiss your bride."

Finally, I thought. With one hand on the back of her neck and the other on her waist, I brought her to me. Kissing her . . . it was a dream long in the making.

Finally.

PART TWO

18

Aphrodite

My lips still tingled. It had been a while now since we had kissed at the church, and yet the feeling of his lips on mine was all I could concentrate on. After the wedding, we could not speak to each other, at least not freely, as we were expected to tend to the guests who had come to see with their own two eyes that we were, in fact, husband and wife.

Husband and wife.

I glanced up at him as he stood by my side, my thumb playing with the gold band on my finger. He was my husband now. I could stand by him publicly, we could hold hands and talk and laugh with no one judging us to see how close or far apart we were.

I must have stared at him for too long because he glanced down at me, his eyebrow raised. But before he could say anything, I looked back out into the crowd of people who were now in my home—my parents' home—to celebrate us. Except for Datura, Evander's stepmother. When she approached, Evander stiffened beside me, and his fist began to clench, so I did what was now allowed. I placed my hand on him, and when he felt it, he released his fist and took my hand.

"Welcome into the family, my dear," Datura said with a kind smile. "Much overdue, but all things happen for a reason."

"Yes, and be very sure I will *never* forget the reason," Evander whispered down to her.

Datura ignored him. "My dear girl, should you have any questions about Everely, I am here to help in any way I can."

"Thank you," I said. When I noticed Evander about to speak once more, I added, "However, I do not doubt that by the time I would have sent word, any issues would be resolved."

"Oh dear, you do not possibly believe that I will be remaining in London, do you?" she asked.

"Where else would you be if not in London, Datura?" Evander asked.

"Home, of course," she stated, and the level of sweetness she applied to her words made me feel wary. "Everely is my home."

"I made it clear—"

"Yes, yes, I know. You shall not have me at the estate. No matter, I have managed to secure my own property not far away. I was born in Everely, so I shall remain there till I die. Besides, I would like to see your brother Gabrien often, and he does not prefer London."

Evander's nose flared. I hoped the conversation looked cordial, with her smiles and his efforts to remain calm. But being beside them both, I could feel . . . their hate.

"I wish to bid congratulations to Lady *Everely*, but it seems my presence is not noticed."

I noticed then the queen, yes, the queen, approaching, dressed in her favorite red, now before us, holding her sleek gold cane. Immediately, I curtsied low. Immediately Datura vanished from before us.

"Your Majesty," I said, as did Evander beside me, before slowly rising to look at her.

She tilted her head to the side, and I remained calm, not

speaking another word until she addressed me. However, she shifted her eyes to Evander.

"Your mother was not a crier," she said suddenly, and the words made me anxious for him. "No matter whom or what she faced, not a single tear would slip from her pretty eyes. I believe today, though, she would be weeping with joy to see how fortunate you are, Duke."

"Yes, I believe so, too, Your Majesty."

"I trust you will be wiser than the former duke and keep the rabble-rousers out," she muttered before she addressed me. "Congratulations, Lady Everely, though I worry your real work is only just beginning, for the previous holders of this great title left much to be desired. Do remind them all of our difference."

I curtsied to her once more. "Yes, Your Majesty."

She turned around, with a small personal sphere of ladies in waiting accompanying her. Only when I heard her cane on the ground, clicking as she moved away, did I rise, though a bit confused. Remind them all of what exactly? I had said yes because what could I say to the queen but *thank you* and *yes*.

"I do wonder if this was the best time for such advice," Evander whispered. He smiled as he looked at me. "I wish for Everely to be your refuge, to do whatever it is you please without worry."

There it was again, that rush, that feeling down my throat, spreading throughout my body, making a mess of all my thoughts and emotions. I wished to smile to the end of time for how happy I was, then laugh and dance. I wished to sing and then also desired time to freeze so I might remain only in this moment. When he reached up and brushed a curl away from my face, I wished to kiss his hand or, better yet, have him kiss me again as he had in the church.

It was all so very splendid.

"May I steal my daughter one last time from you?"

I turned to see my mama smiling at us, though her brown eyes shined with . . . tears. My mama never showed tears.

"Yes, of course," Evander replied, releasing my hand. My mother interlocked her arm with mine and led me away.

"Mama, are you crying?" I asked.

"Of course not. Married ladies do not cry in public. It is childish." She huffed and lifted her head high. "And you are not a child any longer."

"Married or not, I am always your child, Mama."

Evander

The reason her mother had taken her was quite obvious, even if it was tradition. Yet I could not help but wonder what she had told her, because when Aphrodite returned, her face was . . . perplexed and slightly alarmed. She looked truly lost. So much so she barely said a word for the rest of the evening. Only when the last guest had gone and we stood before our carriage in front of her family along with Verity, who took it upon herself to decide to stay with them for the remainder of the season, did she speak.

"Abena?" she said to the youngest sister, opening her arms. Typically, Abena could not hold her tongue, yet today, she'd stood beside her father, her eyes red and a frown on her lips. "Will you not wish me well?"

The little girl looked down. "Bye."

"That was wishing me off but not well. I demand a hug," Aphrodite said. Still, Abena refused.

So, Hathor and Devana grabbed both of her arms and yanked her forward. All three sisters were now thrown against my wife. I stepped forward to catch her should she fall, as she nearly stumbled back at the force. She stood firm, and they all hugged tightly.

"You must write to us!" Hathor declared.

"Married women do not have much time to write, Hathor," her mother called.

"I shall find the time," Aphrodite said with a laugh.

"We can visit later?" Devana questioned.

"And married women do not have time to entertain their little sisters," her mother added, shaking her head.

"I shall find the time," Aphrodite replied.

When Hathor and Devana released her, there was only Abena still hugging tightly. Aphrodite bent down to pinch her cheeks.

They hugged her once more before her brother Hector stepped forward and embraced her.

"Father says the most important thing is to be happy," he said, "so be happy."

"I promise it."

He glanced over to me, glaring, and I had to say, for a boy of such young age, he held a very mean gaze. "Make her happy."

"It shall be my life's work." I watched her say goodbye to her mother and father. I had been so focused on little Abena that I had not noticed the other red face here—Lord Monthermer. He swallowed and nodded over and over to himself, widening his eyes and holding back his own tears before he hugged her. I did not know what he whispered into her ear, but I knew it made her smile. They both even shared a small laugh before she took a step back. I looked at my sister.

"You shall not weep and hug me?" I asked.

"Why? I shall see you in three weeks, a month at most," she said with not a care.

"Do not cause them any trouble, Verity," I warned, giving her a stern look. Truthfully, I was worried about her condition and others knowing, but she said she was taking the medicine prescribed to her by Dr. Cunningham.

"Thank you for keeping her," I said to my godmother, who nodded, seemingly choking on her own emotion as well.

"You both should get on," her father said.

"Right," I replied, waiting for Aphrodite. When she returned to me, I helped her inside the carriage before going in myself.

From inside, she glanced once more at her family, waving to them as they waved back. It was only when they were too far to see her in the dark that her eyes also glazed over with tears. When one escaped, I reached over and wiped it away with my thumb. Startled by my touch, her eyes finally met mine.

"Forgive me, I am not sad . . . I am only . . ."

"Sad," I answered when she did not seem to have the words.

"I am happy. It is just . . . both."

"I understand," I whispered. "When they return to Belclere Castle, we will invite them to visit, or we may go to them if you prefer."

"Thank you." She smiled.

How was it possible for one woman's smile to take such command over all my thoughts, all my life?

"Are we going to Everely now?" she asked.

"We shall go. But not immediately to the estate. I hope to spend some time showing you a bit of the other towns along the way, as I know you enjoy your freedom."

"That sounds lovely . . . and tonight?" She asked softly.

"Tonight, we will remain at my—our—home here," I answered. I wondered once more what she had been told to expect of her wedding night.

The ride back to the house was silent, and the closer we came to reaching our destination, the more anxious I found myself becoming. It was as though the beast in me was at the table, pounding his fist, demanding to eat, and there before me was a lamb feast. I hungered for her, ached for her, and now that I had her, I feared that hunger was so severe I would forget myself and, most importantly, forget how delicate she was in this matter.

"Welcome home, Your Grace," the footman said as he opened the carriage door. When I reached back for her, she stepped out, looking to the house as though she had never seen it before.

"Your Grace," the footman said to her, and she stared at him for a moment longer before nodding.

"Come," I whispered, leading her inside to where the maid was already waiting. "Your maid has gone ahead to Everely, so I arranged to have someone attend to you for the night here."

"Thank you," she said.

"This way, Your Grace," the maid said, leading her to the stairs. When I did not follow her up, Aphrodite paused and glanced down at me.

"Are you not coming?"

"I shall. I need to confirm some matters for our trip in the morning. I will not be long," I lied, for everything had already been confirmed. There was nothing left to do, but I wished to give her a moment.

Walking into my study, I sat down and closed my eyes. I desired brandy but did not touch it, since I needed all my wits about me. The waiting was torturous.

After what I hoped was a sufficient amount of time I finally got up and walked to the door. Upon opening it, I saw the very same maid that I had sent with Aphrodite now coming back down.

"You left your mistress?" I asked her.

"She dismissed me for the evening, Your Grace."

I glanced up the stairs. "She is ready for bed then." I was not asking her but telling myself.

"Yes, Your Grace."

I walked up slowly, anxious once more. When I reached the door, I was unsure whether or not to knock but erred on the side of caution.

"You may enter."

I was not sure what I had expected, but it was not to see her on the lounge chair, reading, in the very same dress, the only difference being that her curly hair was now down, and she was barefoot. She stood up, placing her book down.

"You have not changed?" I asked her.

"Am I meant to?"

"Are you not uncomfortable?"

She shook her head. "I am not."

What was I to say?

"Very well." I merely nodded, going to my side table and removing the cravat around my neck. We remained in silence, and it was very . . . tense. I knew not how to break the tension.

"Am I supposed to be undressed?"

"Supposed to be?"

She nodded. "Mama said that . . . you . . . you may . . ."

"I may what?"

"Wish to do it yourself?" she rushed out.

I tried not to grin too much. "I am not opposed to doing so, but I do not believe it is standard practice."

"So, what am I to do?" She sighed heavily, her shoulders slumped.

At that, I did laugh. "What do you wish to do?"

"I do not know. That is why I am asking!"

I dropped the cravat behind me and leaned against the side table, crossing my arms. "What did your *mama* tell you?"

"Nothing that made sense," she grumbled.

"How so?"

"Must I live through it twice?"

"Humor me, I beg of you, for I have been curious as to why you looked so afraid when you returned."

"Mama . . . said . . . it hurts . . . and I would bleed." She squeezed her hands. "And it does not make sense to me because I saw the girl in the shrubbery, and she did not look to be hurt or bleeding."

I clamped down on my lip, looking at my boots.

"You are laughing at me."

"I am not!"

"No, but you wish to."

I lifted my eyes and looked at her, nodding. "Slightly."

"Do not. It is unfair. I cannot help that I am ignorant of these things!" she snapped. "Any time I sought answers, I was told my husband would explain, and I would learn of such matters when I was married. Well, here I am, married, and here you are, my husband. So explain."

"Very well." I took a seat beside her. "Your mama is right. It may hurt and you might bleed slightly, but only the first time. The woman we saw among the shrubbery was most likely well past that stage."

"So tonight shall hurt?"

"Only for a moment, and then, hopefully, it will be a pleasurable experience for us both." I cupped her cheek before I leaned forward and kissed the side of her face. "I will always take care of you—trust me."

"I do," she said with a smile.

I nodded and rose, taking her with me and bringing her before me in the mirror. It was only then that I brushed her hair to the side and kissed her neck. When she closed her eyes, I reached for the top of her dress and slowly pulled down the sleeves. Right before it was to fall, she grabbed on to it under her breast, her eyes meeting mine again in the mirror.

"Trust me," I repeated.

She nodded, allowing me to help her out of the dress. Then I undid the lacing of her undergarments, one by one until she stood before me as Venus. She nervously took in a breath of air, not meeting my gaze in the mirror any longer.

"I thank God for allowing me such a sight," I whispered into her ear. "I swear I shall worship you for the rest of my life."

Standing in front of her, I lifted her head, wrapped my arm around her body, and kissed her lips.

19

Aphrodite

This kiss was different from the one in the church. Very different, as his tongue was in my mouth and his arms now tightly around me. The feeling of his hands directly upon my skin burned. I felt as though I could barely breathe, as if he were stealing all the air out of my lungs. When our lips broke apart, I nearly stumbled forward, resting my body on his and breathing heavily. He licked his lips, breathing through his nose for a second before he bent slightly, and the next thing I knew, I was in his arms. It was a short walk to the bed, where he put me down gently, and I watched as he took off his vest and shirt . . . everything till he stood before me in only his drawers. When he got on the bed, I swallowed and sat still.

But he smiled, touching my face. "Trust me," he whispered again.

"I do," I repeated. I thought he was about to kiss my lips once more, but instead, his lips were at my neck. I closed my eyes, my mouth parting as I leaned in closer, my hand on his shoulder. Then I found myself on my back as he kissed down the center of my chest, between my breasts, before he kissed each one. And just as I had witnessed that night in the garden, he took my nipple into his mouth, and I gasped at the feeling of not just that but where his hand was—between my legs.

"Evander . . ." I gasped as I felt his fingers stroke me, and I felt the fire spreading throughout my body, the desire pulsating upon my skin and the ache that he once spoke of in the pit of my stomach. "What . . . what is happening?" I finally found the words.

He lifted his head. "Do you remember when I said if you are skilled enough, you can find a release on your own?"

I nodded and then bit my lip as I realized his fingers were inside me.

"This is what I meant," he whispered, watching my body moving against his hands. "You could do this on your own, but I much prefer to give you this pleasure."

That was it, pleasure. It was upon me, blurring all my thoughts and senses, making me tremble. Never in my life had I felt anything like this, and the more I sought to make sense of it, the more lost I became. He kissed me once more, his tongue within my mouth and mine in his. The speed of his hand increased with the sounds coming out of my mouth.

"Forgive me. I cannot hold back any longer," he whispered.

Hold back? How was this holding back? It was a question I easily found the answer to as he removed his hands and knelt before me, undoing his drawers, freeing himself. I saw . . . his manhood. I had been told that it would go inside me, but I did not know how that would fit.

"Aphrodite," he whispered, hunched over me, my eyes shifting to him. "If I could have any wish now, it would be for the words to express how deeply I love you."

I smiled. "And I wish the same for you."

He held my thighs, and my heart ached in excitement and fear. He kissed my face so much that I closed my eyes, greedily accepting them all.

"This will hurt only a moment. I will not move until you feel ready," he said, and I nodded. I threw my arms around his neck and held him, when all of a sudden I felt him enter me and I winced.

"I love you," he whispered into my ear.

I bit my lip, breathing in slowly.

"I thank God you are finally my wife," he said, kissing the side of my face. But besides that, he remained still, waiting for me as I hugged him tightly. I did not know how long we stayed like that until finally, it did not hurt.

So I opened my eyes. "Evander . . ."

It was as if he knew exactly what I wished to say. He moved, and when he did, I gasped, as I was not expecting the sensation. It was even better than the kisses and the fingers, as each time he thrust forward, all the pain melted into pleasure, his gaze meeting mine.

"More?" he questioned.

I nodded.

"Say it," he demanded.

"More." With my hands on his shoulders, I bit my lips as he gave me what I asked for, this time hitting deeper.

"More?"

"Yes . . . all of it," I said.

"As you wish." He held on to my thighs as he thrust himself in once again, harder, and he did not stop.

"Ah . . . ahh . . . oh . . . Evan . . . der . . . ah." I put my hand over my mouth to keep from crying out.

"No, I need to hear you," he said as he filled me in ways that I'd never thought possible. When I did not remove my hand, he leaned over and bit my nipple.

"Evander!" I gasped.

"Yes, just like that." He grinned, licking my skin as I heard the sound of our flesh moving together, the bed shaking with us.

I turned away, seeking even the slightest bit of air, only to see my reflection in the mirror across the room . . . My face, just now, looked like the woman's in the shrubbery, like Miss Edwina Charmant's. I understood why she had looked like this. How could I not when all of me was being taken to such new heights?

The pressure in my stomach rose. This was— this felt— it was heavenly. I wanted more. My chest was on fire, but I wanted more.

He sat up, pulling my hips to him, thrusting harder, faster, shaking, grunting like a beast. Was this what he meant before? I did not know, and I did not care.

I cried out, gripping the sheet, my toes curling as I came undone. His pace slowed for only a moment longer, filling me, before his eyes closed, and he stopped.

When his eyes reopened, his chest was rising and falling quickly. "I am not yet finished with you, wife."

I was not sure what else was to be done, but I felt too good to care. "As you wish, husband."

He laughed, falling onto the bed beside me. "Let me re-claim my wits first."

"Where have they gone?" I teased.

"To you," he said with eyes closed and a smile upon his face. "Always to you."

I smiled, watching him, though my eyes, too, were heavy. "We are married," I whispered and put my hand on his chest.

He took it and kissed my palm.

"That we are," he replied as he kissed my shoulder. "And it is a miracle of the highest order."

"A miracle?" I asked, snuggling closer to him for warmth, only to feel the sheet rise over me. He was on his side, watch-ing me. "Did you not think we would ever be married?"

"After all that occurred, I thought the chance was lost to me forever," he replied, his fingertips on my skin. "I even thought to pray that you would find another more worthy than I, though I also dreaded ever hearing such news. It was why I avoided the ton during the spring."

"I stayed away from society," I replied. "In fear of meeting you and your . . . late wife."

"Is it cruel of me to say I did not consider her my wife? Nor did I take her as one."

"You did not—"

"I did not," he answered.

"Then for the last four years you . . ."

"Took matters into my own hands, as I refused anyone else," he confessed. "I considered it my punishment."

"So, no one else has had you?"

"I fear I am not all that innocent." He chuckled, twisting a curl of my hair.

"So, you were a rake?"

"I was . . . I was . . ." He struggled for the word. "A man."

I made a face, which made him laugh, then leaning over, he kissed my lips.

"Worry not, for you are the only one who shall know me as such."

"You promise?"

He nodded. "With my hand on the *Bible*."

I grinned, wrapping my arms around him and resting my head on his chest.

"I have a confession."

"What?"

"It is an ugly one."

"I am the last person to judge."

"All this time, even when you were with someone else, I

still wanted you. I wished— I cursed your former wife, wanting nothing more than for her to drop dead so that you could come back to me. I knew it was cruel and silly for me to think in such a way, but I could not help it. I told myself I was justified, as you were promised to me first. Then when I heard she had passed, I was . . . part guilt-ridden and part joyous, but sought to temper my expectations, believing you were hurt by the loss and still did not want me."

It felt good to say the truth aloud.

"If you must confess, I shall also, so we may close the book on her," he replied, his hands drawing circles on my back. "In the beginning, I hated Emma. I blamed her and her whole family for my misfortune—the mere sight of her enraged me. I avoided her, spending most of my time elsewhere. In the four years that I was married to her, I spoke to her as little as possible. I thought I had done enough. Part of me still believes that. However, my coldness toward her, the pressures of running an estate she knew nothing about, the weight of her guilt, the stress of motherhood, and the heartbreak Fitzwilliam had given her slowly drove her mad. I returned after she went into a fit. Some days, she was so still that it was as if she were dead. Other days, she tried to run away, to where I did not know. She would run through the forest like a madwoman, resulting in harm to herself, and we would search for her and bring her back. Eventually, I grew so tired of the embarrassment of her actions that I had her confined to the house and under constant watch, but that seemed only to worsen her condition."

"The doctors could not treat her?"

He shook his head. "I sought many, but all they could manage was to calm her. And in that state, she would weep and apologize to me. Beg me for forgiveness. Explain to me how scared she was and how she had known no other way to save herself or her child. It was the first time we truly spoke to each other, and I was able to see her as a victim alongside me. I swore to her I would protect her child always. She confessed her sins on paper when her condition grew to the point where we both knew she would not last till spring. Her death was quiet. On my way to check on her, the maid came and told me she had gone in her sleep. I felt sadness for her loss of life but also some relief."

I thought of all the rumors I had heard of him over the years, about how he was cruel, how he had mistreated his wife, how he was a liar and lacked honor, and how he was just like his father. It amazed me how misconstrued everything had been.

He must have been so very lonely.

I hugged him tighter, now sure that I would never bring up the woman to him again, and that to atone for all my curses, I would treat her child as kindly as I possibly could. "We shall live happily, Evander."

Evander

I was perfectly content to hold her as she slept. I had not expected that conversation to arise so soon. But I was happy to be done with it . . . or, at least, be done with my anger and guilt toward Emma. By the grace of God, I was back to where I wished to be and with the woman I loved. I could allow that pain to fade.

We shall live happily, Evander. How I wished that to be so, and how I would fight to make it so. I still worried about Fitz-william being out there somewhere. The people I had hired still could not locate him, and with Datura back in Everely,

I worried we would not have peace until both were held accountable for their actions. And by accountable, I meant stripped of everything and left bare in the darkest of prisons. Prison would not be the case with Datura, but at the very least, she might be shunned from all society forever.

The only worry I had at striking with such fury was Gabrien. My youngest brother was cut differently from them. How was I to destroy his mother and eldest brother without ruining him and creating another vengeful heart?

My mind was full of worries and fears, but Aphrodite nuzzled into my neck and muttered my name in her sleep. I wrapped my arms around her. I did not know what was to come, so right now, I was going to enjoy this moment to its fullest. I would enjoy *her* to the fullest.

Calm, I thought as I felt myself harden when her breast brushed against my chest.

There will be plenty of nights like this.

Aphrodite

Humming—it was gentle and soft and brought me from the land of dreams to reality. When I opened my eyes, he was beside me, a smile on his face, as his touch was upon my shoulder. I stared in amazement, unable to believe I had woken up to such a sight as him.

"Good morning, wife."

The corner of my lips rose. "Good morning, husband."

He grinned, leaning over and kissing my shoulder. "Forgive me for waking you."

"I am happy to be awake." My dreams were occurring in reality, so why would I need sleep? "Have you been up long?"

"No," he said, shifting to lie so close to me I could feel his body pressed against my own. I had a bad habit of sleeping on my stomach, so I shifted onto my back to look up at him. However, in doing so, a painful ache spread through my body.

"As I feared."

"As you feared?" I repeated when I finally managed to roll over under the sheet.

"I was rougher than I should have been," he replied.

"I am fine." Sore but very fine.

He smiled, bringing my hands to his lips so he could kiss my knuckles. "Did you enjoy it?"

My memory filled with all he had shown and done and how it had made me feel. "Yes, very much."

"I as well," he said as our hands toyed with each other, the smile on his face matching mine.

"We are truly married." I giggled.

"That we are. Lady Aphrodite *Eagleman*, Duchess of Everely."

It was just a name, yet it brought me glee. Holding the sheet, I sat up. "When are we to leave for this dukedom, Your Grace?"

"Never call me Your Grace," he replied sitting up as well. "High society must call me so, strangers must call me so, but as my wife, you address me only as Evander . . . or my love."

"Very well, *Evander*—" I had barely gotten the word out when his lips were upon mine. He filled me with such passion that I was forced back against the pillow, the sheet slipping from my grasp. I inhaled at his cold touch on my breast.

Then he stopped and lifted his head.

"What is the matter?"

"You are still tender, and we must both wash. Come, I will call for them to draw hot water for us," he said as he rose from the bed. Due to his nakedness, now fully on display, I glanced away, only to see the sight of slightly dried blood on the sheet. Embarrassed, I tried to cover it, only for him to chuckle. When I looked at him, he was watching me.

"Are you laughing at me?"

"Yes, as you are precious, especially when you are embarrassed."

I narrowed my eyes at him. "I am not embarrassed."

"Truly? Then come here. Without the sheet."

My mouth dropped open. "I cannot possibly!"

"Why not?"

"Because . . ." I did not have any reason—other than embarrassment. So I was silent, and he chuckled, going to the door.

"Your clothes!" I gasped, holding the sheet tightly.

He stuck his head out the door, and I could not see to whom he spoke, but he reached out the slightly ajar door. He retrieved a pitcher, still naked as the day he was born. He then walked to the table and poured the hot water into the basin already there. He glanced over his shoulder at me, the steam of the water rising beside him. "Come. We shall clean off as they prepare the bath."

"How long have you truly been awake to prepare all of this?" I asked.

"Not much preparation was required. I informed the staff to have water prepared for the morning after," he replied.

"So this is common practice?"

"I would not say that, either. More so a desire of my own," he said.

"A desire of yours?"

"For you to stand before me, in all your glory, as I clean you." He glanced up at me. "Will you allow me?"

Never had I heard of such a thing, but then again, there was much I had not heard of. So I nodded and stepped closer to him.

"Release the sheet," he commanded. I paused for a moment before doing so, now standing before him as naked as he stood before me.

He stared down at my eyes, watching over me hungrily. He so enraptured me that I was startled by the wet cloth upon my skin. Neither of us said a word as he brushed my hair to one side to clean my neck and across my shoulder before reaching my breasts and fondling them. My mouth parted. He leaned forward and kissed them gently before continuing, every so often rewetting the cloth.

"Part your legs," he commanded. I did, biting my lips as he washed me. All the while, he did not look away from my face. "You look aroused, wife."

"Is that not because you are seeking to arouse me?"

"I merely sought an excuse to see and touch your whole body in the light of day, forever engraving the sight in my memory. I have dreamed of doing this many times." He kissed the space between my shoulder and neck, causing me to shiver. "It is even more torturous in reality."

"Torturous?"

"Can you not see?" he asked.

"See what?"

He bit back a smile, tilting his head to the side. "Do you wish to learn something of a man today? I will not tell you should you not wish to know."

"Free me from ignorance," I replied.

He inhaled and said, "Look and see how I rose for you."

I glanced down, seeing his manhood now high. "And what is the lesson in this?"

"Nothing more than a sign that I very much desire you

again," he replied, stepping closer. "When all of me is longing with need, I rise, begging for relief in you. This is painfully aching."

"Should you allow yourself to remain in such agony?" I asked, feeling a burn trembling within me.

"I wish not, but you are—"

I kissed his lips gently. "I desire more of last night. Might I have it?"

Dropping the cloth and lifting me, he took me back to the bed, then hovered above me, kissing the side of my face before bringing his kiss to my ear. "You may have anything you desire in abundance, my love."

I quivered.

Oh, how much better this was than dreams.

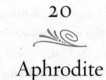

20

Aphrodite

I t was difficult to enjoy the scenery with the pressure of his gaze upon me. "Stop looking at me like that."

"Like what?"

"Like you are . . . thinking of doing something you should not," I replied, shifting in my seat.

"I know not what you mean, as this is how I have always looked at you," he said with a smirk upon his lips and his eyes glancing the length of my figure. "The only difference now must be you."

"Me?"

"Yes, I do believe you have been corrupted, my love." He chuckled. "You have learned a lot the past two weeks, have you not?"

My mouth dropped open. But I could not disagree with him. He had often looked at me like this before, I just had not realized what the gaze meant at the time. Now I was very well aware that when he grew silent and relaxed, and his eyes wandered over me, and there was a slight uptick in the corner of his lips, my clothes would soon be gone. He had said he wished me not to feel as if I had been moved from one estate to another. Therefore, we had taken a great many detours throughout our journey. Sitting under trees, visiting other towns. Never had I felt so free. Finally, we were to reach Everely. Yet still another full two days later than we planned—why? Because we ended up extending our stay several more hours to indulge in each other. Long gone was the pain of the first time. Now I was engulfed in waves of passion to the point where it felt like a sickness, but the most enjoyable kind.

When I snuck a glance at him, he was still staring at me.

"You tell me not to look at you as I am, but then you go and look at me like so," he replied and, with two swift motions, closed the curtains on the windows of our carriage, leaving us in near darkness.

"Evander!" I protested as he took my hand, pulling me to him. "We cannot. It is too dangerous, and we are almost there . . ."

"Then only a kiss," he replied, and I could feel his breath upon my lips. "I beg of you, wife, deprive me not."

When he leaned in, I did as well, closing my eyes, not depriving myself, either, my arms circling his neck as he encircled my body, holding me tight to him. He lied. It was not only a kiss. It was his touch, too.

"Evander, we cannot." I moaned as his lips found my neck, shivering as his tongue licked along my skin. "When we arrive, but not in the . . . the carriage."

"Very well." He bit my earlobe. "When we arrive, I shall have you calling my name out loudly, wantonly, for all the world to hear."

"Evander!" I snapped, and his reply was to cup me between my legs. I stared into his heated gaze.

"Yes?" he asked.

I had learned much, but I was sure, as the sun in the sky, that there was still more he had to teach me.

It excited me—his lack of propriety and civility—for carnal desire was like nothing I had ever experienced.

"I look forward to it," I whispered and kissed his lips once more.

"You shall be my undoing," he muttered to himself.

I giggled, taking a moment to adjust my dress and gloves. He waited for me to finish before he parted the curtains, the brightness of the sun harsh for a moment but then stunning as I saw in the distance his estate, elevated on high land, surrounded by trees on every side.

Everely House was even more significant than our family home in Belclere, and one could get lost in Belclere. Everely House was actually once called Everely Palace. It was gifted to the Eagleman family by Queen Anne and was one of England's largest estates, spanning more than 1,800 acres. The grounds had several gardens and its very own beautiful lake. There were even two great rivers that ran throughout the county, from which some towns fished, though it was not easy due to the rocks. Everything here was green, vast, and beautiful. It all felt far too much for one man and one mistress to be lord and lady over, and yet it was ours. I had once hated all the lessons from Mama, but now, as we approached, I had never been so grateful, as the sight of this place could make one quake in fear.

"Do you like it?" he asked.

"How could anyone not like it?" I was amused, my gaze still glued on the approaching building before us. "It is a sight of splendor."

"Good," he replied.

I took the time to double-check my clothing and adjust my hat. It was much more challenging than I realized to prepare without my normal maid, the ones provided by the inns were never as adequate but I managed. Now I was worried I would not seem fitting. All the house would come to greet us.

"Do I look all right?" I asked sincerely.

His eyebrow rose. "You look perfect, as you always do. Why?"

"I cannot look as I always do, for I am not as I always was. I am now the Duchess of Everely. I must be proper."

He chuckled. "You have nothing to concern yourself with. I fear Everely House has not seen proper in quite some time. You are more than enough."

The carriage came to a stop. In front of the house, I could see the rows—yes, rows, it was double the number I was used to—of people now waiting. I took a deep breath to calm myself, and he snickered.

"Do not laugh at me," I said quickly.

"Forgive me," he said. "You are taking this all very seriously."

"As I am meant to," I reminded him.

He stepped out before outstretching his hand for me. The staff curtsied or bowed their heads.

"Welcome, Your Graces," a tall, white-haired man said to us. I was sure I had seen him at Evander's home in London.

"Aphrodite, this is Mr. Hugh Wallace, my head butler. I sent him on ahead with your maid to prepare for us," Evander explained. And then to Wallace said, "I do hope there were no issues."

"No, Your Grace."

"Thank you, Mr. Wallace, for your care," I said with a smile.

He merely nodded and stepped back. When he did, I was able to see Eleanor waiting among the maids, which gave me solace. I would speak to her later. More pressing, though, was the little girl, just shy of four, dressed in white, with light skin and bronze curls at the heel of an old nanny dressed in black. She stood quietly and far too still for a girl of her age. Had it been Abena, she would have run after the carriage.

Evander led me up the stairs to her. "Aphrodite, I would also like to introduce you to my daughter, Emeline," he said.

"Hello, Your Grace." The girl struggled with her curtsy and nearly fell, but her nanny caught her, holding her carefully.

"Forgive her, Your Grace. We are still practicing," the nanny said quickly.

"This is Mrs. Watson. She is the housekeeper and also Emeline's nanny," Evander said to me. "She has watched over her since she was born."

That is not proper. How can a housekeeper do her duties and watch over a child?

I smiled at the woman and glanced down to the little girl, who looked as though she would have preferred to be behind Mrs. Watson than in front of her. I bent down to her level, as we must have all been giants to her. When I was a child, I'd disliked how big all the world was.

"Hello, Emeline," I said gently. "How are you?"

She clenched Mrs. Watson's skirt and said, "Fine . . . Your Grace."

I wanted to tell her she did not have to call me *Your Grace*, but what could she call me? Mama? That might not feel right after knowing me only a minute.

"I hope you and I will be very good friends," I said and rose. Then to Mrs. Watson, "I can only imagine the amount of effort you have given. I thank you."

"Of course, Your Grace," she said, bowing her head.

"We have had a very long journey. We will rest and shall see you at supper," Evander said, to my surprise, placing his hand on Emeline's head before leading me forward into the house. I glanced back at the little girl and then to Mrs. Watson, now bent down, speaking to her and petting her hair.

I had a feeling it would take me a while before I would be

able to find footing with little Emeline—"Evander!" I gasped when he pulled me to him.

"Where is your mind?" he demanded.

"Here, release me quickly," I said, checking to make sure none of the servants had seen. "Evander—"

"I do believe there was an agreement made between us for when we reached the house . . . lo and behold, we are here, and I shall have my bride!" he replied, taking off with me.

I tried not to laugh, but I could not help it as he took me away.

What would I learn now?

I did not have to wait very long for the answer.

"Evan . . . der . . ." I moaned, as the fire in the pit of my belly grew. I had never known it was possible for a mouth to be used in such a way and feel so good. He gripped my thighs, his tongue going in circular motions one moment and his lips sucking me in the next. I bit my hand to keep from crying out any louder. And to punish me for it, he stopped far too soon.

"What did I tell you about denying me your voice?" he said sternly, crawling up the length of the bed till his face was above me.

"You'd deny me my release," I said, captivated by his eyes.

I could taste myself on his lips as he kissed me. "No, I said you would have to get it yourself."

He had warned me before, but I did not know what he actually meant until he slowly directed my hand between my legs. It was embarrassing and yet, at the same time, thrilling to have him watch me like this.

The only thing was my hands were not as nimble as his and

nowhere as good as his mouth. I grew frustrated to the point where I could only beg. "Please . . ."

"What?" he questioned, brushing my hair from my face.

"I . . . I . . . need you."

"To do what? I am quite enjoying this sight."

Frustrated with need, I sat up, and, pushing him down onto the bed, I climbed on top of him.

"There is another way I can get it myself, correct?" I asked, glaring down at him.

"Is that so?" His eyebrow rose.

"Yes," I replied.

Reaching behind me, I grabbed his manhood, and it was hot in my grasp, jerking from my mere touch. He inhaled through his nose, and I could feel his chest expand under me. His eyes were very serious.

"And what shall you do now?"

I bit my lip, hoping this worked as my brain told me it would, shifting my body up and then slowly back down onto him. I thought it would feel the same, but it was different. My body tingled as he filled me. It was so much at one time that I braced my hands against his chest. When he and I were one again, I found myself unable to stop rocking on top of him. Then he grabbed my waist and suddenly thrust up into me.

"Oh, Evander!" Closing my eyes, I rode on top of him. This was much better than my hands.

It was dark by the time he and I stopped for the day. He said he could request that supper be brought to our room. But, I did not wish for the house to think . . . to think I was doing exactly what I had been doing for hours. Also, I wished not to keep little Emeline waiting on us for dinner. However, when we arrived at the dining table, which was far too long, there were only two chairs at one end. The whole room was also a tad dark, as the candles were not bright, and the décor very . . . old.

"What is it?" he questioned when he saw I did not move to my seat despite the footman who already stood ready to pull out the chair.

"Do you often eat in here?" I asked him.

He paused, thinking. "No, now that I think of it. I mostly have my meals in the study. Verity eats in the drawing room or, when she can, in the garden. Why?"

"I was merely wondering." I smiled, moving to take my seat, but he caught my wrist and spun me back into his arms. "Evander."

"I know you and how you wonder. It shall plague your mind, and then you shall not focus here but on your thoughts. So out with it," he demanded, still holding me despite the fact we were no longer alone.

I leaned in so only he could hear me, but it was so quiet I was sure they heard despite my efforts. "I have not yet been here a full day, so I do not wish to criticize anything."

Maybe it was because I'd always been at the skirt of my mother or because of all of the lessons but, immediately, without much effort, I could see there were things not in order.

"It is your home now, too. If there is anything amiss, merely order it changed to your liking. I care not," he whispered.

"I do not want the servants to believe me too high in the instep," I replied quietly, also not wishing to have this conversation before the servants.

I was the newcomer. I could not just act as though everything required my touch. There needed to be balance. His eyebrow rose and he chuckled.

"We shall have supper on the terrace," Evander instructed them and took my hand to lead me.

"I was fine with the dinner table."

"You were not. And the footmen would have remained there, and you would have been more uncomfortable," he said.

"I would be unnerved almost anywhere, as I have yet to grow accustomed to it," I reminded him.

"You shall not be on the terrace," he assured me, then brought my body to his. "And most definitely not in our bed."

I pushed his face away, and he laughed. "Can we please simply eat without you . . ."

"Without me what?"

"Seeking to seduce me."

"Not at all."

"Evander."

"Aphrodite," he said my name in the same tone.

He opened the door to the terrace, and my breath caught as I looked out into the warm evening. Before us sat a small round table that overlooked the man-made lake. The trees rustled on either side of us, and hanging in the sky like a painting was the moon.

"It is beautiful," I said, walking around the table and to the patio edge. "I could have dinner like this every night."

"The spring rains and heavy winter might change your mind on that. But if you would like, any moment, night or day, as clear as this, we can be out here."

"We will need another chair for Emeline," I replied. "Where is she now?"

"When you were dressing, Mrs. Watson informed me Emeline had eaten earlier and gone to bed. You do not need to exert yourself—"

"As you keep telling me, but I am not," I replied. "When I was younger—actually, that is a lie. Just weeks ago, I desired nothing more than a good book, sweets, hot milk, and a beautiful view. I craved to be left to my own devices and able to soar wherever I wanted to go. I felt very much like a bird in a cage, brought out whenever someone demanded I perform or be on exhibit."

"I know. That is exactly why I wish you to be permitted here to worry of nothing," he replied.

"That is the thing, Evander. I am not worried. And magically, I no longer feel as though I am trapped in that cage. It was quite frustrating that only marriage could give me such freedom. But now that I am married, I feel as though the door has been opened and I have been set free, and instead of flying far away, I have chosen to nest."

"I do not understand."

I took his hand. "I want this place to be a haven for both— for the three of us, I should say, as I seek to be part of her life, too. One day she may even call me Mama."

He simply stared at me, which forced me to calm down.

"Am I being too optimistic?" I whispered. "Forgive me, for as I look to my future days and see they are not so dull, I'm glad. There are true tasks for me now other than sitting pretty at a ball or practicing my needlework."

"You amaze me."

"I have yet to do anything, Evander, so do not be amazed by so little."

He lifted my hand and kissed the knuckles. "You have done more than you even know."

It made me glad to hear, but I did not say it because the

door opened and the footmen set the table and brought out our supper. Evander led me to the table, and under the light of the moon, we ate, laughed, and spoke to each other of nothing significant at all.

It was glorious.

21

Aphrodite

It had been several days since we'd arrived, and I felt as though I had spent almost all of them on my back. The journey *and* Evander had exhausted me. I could not continue this way. I arose from bed early. Evander was still naked and asleep. Part of me wanted to stay in his arms. However, I truly did want to be a good mistress here. It felt ironic, since I had often bemoaned such work, wondering why my future could not be more exciting than the tending of a house. Why could I not go on the adventures I so often read about? There was still part of me that wished to see those wonders. But currently, there was a much larger desire to conquer this battle. My first priority was Everely, and it was essential to the well-being of everyone's lives here.

"My lady—I mean, Your Grace." Eleanor smiled as she appeared in my private room.

I was quite glad Mother had chosen her to be my lady's maid, as she was only a few years older than I, but she had been beside me most of my life. Her mother worked for my mother as well.

"You have had much time to settle? Apologies, I know it is earlier than when you would normally come," I said. I had told her last night to come to me at this time.

"Yes, I am very well familiarized now. Should I bring you breakfast, or are you waiting for the duke?"

"Before that . . ." I stepped closer. "Tell me. What is it like here? What do they say? Whether it be the servants or tenants. The more information I have, the better, and do not think to spare me my feelings."

She nodded. "Yes, I know, Your Grace, and I meant to talk to you when you had adjusted, for it is a lot."

"That bad?" I sat down, motioning for her to sit as well, since I had a feeling this would not be easy to take standing.

"Your Grace, I mean no offense to the duke, but Everely is a mess." She shook her head. "Never have I seen or heard of a great house run such as this."

"How so?"

"Half the staff is not permanent. Apparently, when your husband became the duke, he dismissed almost all those hired by Dowager Duchess Datura, but did not seek to replace many of them because he disliked many people within his house. His former wife seemed to have no care of such things. One would think she did not even live here, as nothing has been upkept for years. The candles are wrong, the place settings are mismatched, and the mistress's accounts are all back-dated. Furthermore, the rooms are not dusted daily. They do so only every other day, as they prioritize the rooms in which the duke and Lady Verity remain. Cleaning is not as it should be because the maids who remain are far too old for such hard work. I discovered that the dowager duchess hired most of them at a later age as she worried . . ." She paused, frowning.

"Do not stop now. It is best to get it all out." I had known it was not going to be good but her frustration told me there was truly cause for concern, for Eleanor was not prone to hysterics.

"The dowager duchess refused to hire anyone young, as she worried they would seduce the former duke. When she left here, Mr. Wallace kept hiring older staff. Now they are even older, and while I do not wish to speak ill of the elderly, it is impractical having them clean and carry throughout this whole house. And they know it, too, spending more time talking in the kitchen than working. As for the kitchen, the cook— you tasted the food last night, so I believe you should judge yourself."

It was not that the food was bad. It just was not good.

I sighed. "What do you recommend?"

"A culling. Gut the whole house and start again with new, properly trained help."

"I cannot," I replied. "It will look cruel of me to dismiss a whole house, especially if they are elderly, upon my first week here."

Especially not after spending half of it in bed.

"I do believe some of them expect it," she replied.

"Why?"

"They have heard of you, Your Grace." She chuckled. "They call you 'the favorite.'"

"The favorite of whom?"

"The queen mostly, and then the duke himself. How that became the talk, I am unsure. But they are under the impression that you might be contemptuous of them."

"This is even more reason that I cannot dismiss them."

"If you keep them here, how will you manage the house? Your Grace, forgive me, but I believe it better to be seen as severe in this case. The reputation of Everely among the town and the tenants is not as it should be."

"Are the tenants unhappy?" That would be even worse than the servants.

"From what I can gather, it seems not an issue of farming or management. I believe the duke's lands and mills are run accordingly. Normally, that would be the first thing anyone would speak on. But I do not know what their true grievance is."

"So, to surmise here, the house is in disarray, the servants are ill-suited, and the tenants are displeased with us for unknown reasons?"

She nodded. "Yes, Your Grace."

"Eleanor, that means *everything* is wrong."

She winced and nodded once more. "Yes, Your Grace."

How was that possible?

Your real work is only just beginning, for the previous holders of this great title left much to be desired, the queen had said to me, and now I understood. There had been a great deal of talk about Everely and about Evander over the years. I had ignored it all, as I could not bear to hear it. The things I did hear were never pleasant, so if *I* had received word even when I actually sought to avoid it, God only knew how much the queen had heard, for she more than anyone enjoyed observing the lives of the nobility as if it were theater. We were many miles away, but her eyes were upon Everely, indeed. Not just hers, but all society's.

"I cannot fail, Eleanor," I said as I stared out the window at the grounds. "I must get everything in order. The only issue is how."

"These issues are clearly long set in, Your Grace. Do not pressure yourself. I am sure over time you may—"

"No." I shook my head, rising from the chair and stepping closer to the window as the sun was now high in the sky. "I feel eyes upon Everely and upon me. If people are watching, I must show them I was not released from my cage to be lost and helpless."

Furthermore, I did not wish for the reputation of Everely, and more importantly Evander, to be further tarnished. It was unfair and unjust what they said about him. They did not know the truth. So, all I could do was show them things were now as they should be. To do that I needed Everely to be the greatest of all estates.

"Your Grace?"

I smiled and turned back to see her standing as well. "Let us focus on the house and servants first. I will meet with all of them to see their ability for myself. Should anyone be lacking, I will keep them in their position but hire a new maid as well."

"So you will leave them be?"

I nodded. "They are not used to having a mistress to impress or having to compete for their work. Instead of dismissing them outright, I will hire hard workers. The harder they work, the more the others will feel as if their position is in danger of being taken from them, and they will either retire of their own free will or work harder themselves."

"What if they simply allow the new workers to do all their duties while they laze off?"

I smiled. "I will gently ask them to retire. By then, many months will have passed, and it shall not seem as if I have dismissed the whole house and established only my own people. It will merely look as though an old maid is going to spend time with her family."

"Very good, Your Grace. I will place an advertisement and keep my ears open," she replied.

"Good. Thank you. That shall be my plan for my house. Then in two days' time, we shall go to the tenants and see for ourselves, as well, as it is customary for a new lady to come with gifts. I shall learn what their complaints are with us then."

"Understood. Would you like to see the servants now or after breakfast?"

"The person I wish to see first this morning is actually Emeline. However, I realize I do not know where the girl's room is. Would you happen to know?"

"Yes," she said, moving to the door. "Because Mrs. Watson is both her nanny and head housekeeper, I have had to go seek her in the young miss's room for any questions, as she is rarely with the other servants."

The tone of her voice told me she also noticed this was improper and was not pleased with the disorder. I followed her out into the hall. I could truly appreciate the grandeur of this house. From the paintings to the sculptures, it was all stunning, yet I noticed there were few of Evander's family. There was, however, a painting of a woman with the lightest of brown skin and curly hair pinned back, beside her a young Evander, and in her arms a bundle of white silk, the tiniest little arm outstretching to her face.

"Lady Luella?" I said as I was unable to remember her face.

"Yes, it was commissioned by the duke. It is the only painting of her here."

"Really?" I repeated. "I would have thought there would be many more than that."

"After Lady Luella passed, the former duke had all the paintings of her removed, and they were then lost, apparently, as no one knows where they are."

"Lost? How does one lose so much art?"

She shook her head. "I am unsure. From what I gather, the duke—your husband—sought to commission new works but was displeased with all the artists except for this one. Sadly, the artist passed and could get only this one done."

"How do you know all of this?"

"Mrs. May-Porter," she replied as though I knew who that was. "The storeroom maid was tasked to give me the lay of the land when I arrived, as Mrs. Watson was tending to the young miss. She loves to talk and does not need a partner to continue the conversation."

"And what else did you learn?" I asked.

"Too much to simply rattle off, Your Grace, and I am not at all sure of the truth behind it."

"Such is the nature of talk." I chuckled. "Falsehood or not, it is good enough that I know what is being said. Eleanor, I am entrusting you to be my eyes and ears. I wish to be apprised of it all, both good and bad."

She glanced at me curiously. "I must say, Your Grace, I do not know if you have changed or if you are merely being yourself without reservation."

I thought about it but could not decide. "I am unsure. I must give myself time to become clear."

"Of course, Your Grace, and here we are," she said, stopping at the door. I had not even realized where we were in the house or how quickly we had gotten there.

Pay attention, Aphrodite, I reprimanded myself. It would not do for me to get lost.

She knocked on the door before opening it, and when she did, there was Mrs. Watson, fixing Emeline's hair.

They both stiffened when they saw me.

"Your Grace." Mrs. Watson curtsied and helped Emeline down quickly, who also tried to curtsy, still finding it difficult. "Good morning. I was not expecting you so early."

"It is fine. I merely wished to see Emeline and ask if she would join me for breakfast," I said, glancing down at the girl.

Emeline looked back up to Mrs. Watson, holding her skirt.

Mrs. Watson spoke, "The little miss has eaten already, Your Grace."

"So early?" I frowned.

"I cannot get her to sit still long enough for me to do her hair if she is not eating. I only just sent the tray back down when you arrived."

I glanced at Emeline, who looked at me as if I were a monster, even more terrified now than when I had first met her. In fact, every day since my arrival that I had seen her she looked more and more afraid. What had happened? Was I that frightening to her?

"Emeline?" I said gently. "I do hope you and I will have lunch then. I wish us to be friends."

She eyed me carefully.

I smiled once more and then addressed Mrs. Watson. "I shall allow you to finish your work, but please see to it that we may have lunch together."

"Yes, Your Grace," she replied.

"I shall see you, Emeline." I waved to her.

Her response was tepid, and I did not wish to force myself upon her, so I quickly left the room.

"I thought children liked me? She looks scared of me, does she not?"

"Do give her time, Your Grace. I doubt it is easy to adjust to a stepmother," she reminded me.

Right, the stepmothers in tales were never kind. "Another thing to add to my list of duties."

"Next, the house staff?" she asked.

I nodded. "Yes, and I would like to see a ledger of all those working here. You should get it from the housekeeper." I stopped, recalling that the housekeeper was tending to Emeline. I did not wish to disturb her again. "I will need to speak to the estate steward directly then."

"Then you ought to wait in the drawing room, Your Grace, and I shall let him know so he may come to see you."

I had a mind to go directly downstairs, but the memory of the last time I had intruded on servants in my own home had stuck with me. If servants who had known me for years felt uncomfortable with my presence downstairs, it would only be worse here, especially as I was no longer a nobleman's daughter but now the duchess.

I could do this. I merely had to take it one step at a time.

Evander

When I awoke to find I was alone, a slight ache of worry spread through me. Only the sight of her things within the room reassured me that she was not a dream. Which then left me to wonder why she had left so early.

The answer to my question arrived with my valet, who informed me that my wife had called an assembly of the house.

I was aware Everely was not in the best state, but I did not believe things were so drastic that she would move with such urgency or severity. I had thought she would give herself a few days to adjust, and even though we had spent more time indulging on our way here, I simply was not yet satisfied. Would I ever be? That was the real question.

"How long have you worked here?" I heard her voice when I came downstairs.

Not wishing to interrupt, I listened from the adjacent room as each person gave her their name, their position within the house, as well as how long they had been employed.

"Should I announce your presence, Your Grace?" Wallace asked from beside me.

I shook my head, glancing through the crack of the door as she sat in her chair while her maid wrote down the information beside her.

"Did we not already have these records?" I asked Wallace.

"The steward looked for them, but apparently most have been lost or mismanaged. He said he would create a new set later, but the duchess preferred to do it this way," he explained.

"How long has she been in here?" I asked.

"Almost two hours, Your Grace."

Two hours? "Has she even eaten this morning?"

"I believe so, Your Grace. However, I would have to ask her lady's maid."

"No need." If Aphrodite was hungry, she would most definitely find food. I did not need to worry about that. "Why are you not in there?"

His shoulders shifted back, and he stood straighter. "I have always maintained my own copies of my paperwork, as well as recommendations. I presented them to her first. Her Grace said she did not require them and, instead, asked that I continue as I am."

Wallace was clearly proud of himself. It was amusing because he rarely ever showed it. Devotion? Steadfastness? Yes, but this look was as though she had patted him on the head.

"Very well, I will not be the one to disturb her." I stepped back from the door to walk to my study. "Where is the steward? I wish to speak to him about the mills. Have there been any letters?" If I knew her family, and I did to a good degree, they most definitely had already written her.

"I have put them on your desk, Your Grace," he said as he opened the door for me. "And I shall call the steward for you."

"Thank you."

Sure enough, there was a group of letters for Aphrodite. One from each of her sisters, her mother, and even her younger brother. The closeness of their family amazed me. Verity and I were close, but it would take at least half a year of my absence before she would think to write. Aphrodite had been with me for only a little more than a week. I carefully put her letters to the side and would inform the footmen to deliver them to her directly from now on.

I sorted through the rest. There were a few from the tenants. It was the last one, unmarked apart from the address, that interested me. I expected it to be another letter addressing a conflict of pigs on the estate or maybe a dispute over farmland. Instead, the first two words sent a rush of rage through me. It took all my strength to stop myself from ripping it in half and throwing it to the wind.

> *Little brother,*
>
> *It has come to my attention that you have wed once again. I bid you congratulations for finally obtaining your beloved and dearest Aphrodite. I have not met the lady, but your determination to acquire her all these years must mean the talk is accurate and that she is a beauty beyond all measure. Such beauty should be seen with one's own eyes, no? How I do miss Everely . . .*
>
> *Sincerely,*
> *Your elder brother*

I crumpled the paper in my fist, as once more I cursed my father for the blight he had put upon this family and me. Was he coming here? Fine. Let him come, so I no longer had to waste funds and men searching the country for him. Let him come so I could rid myself of this bastard once and for all.

"Your Grace."

"What?" I snapped as the door opened.

"The steward?" Wallace replied.

Inhaling through my nose, I nodded. "He may enter, then call for the head guard of the grounds."

I needed to make sure this house was secure, to see that my family was secure. I made an oath to protect them all— Aphrodite, Verity, Emeline. The world was cruel, and I did not wish for any of them to find out just how much.

22

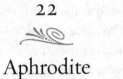

Aphrodite

E veryone was silent.
Evander ate quietly.
Emeline ate quietly.
And so, I also ate quietly.

It had been like this yesterday, as well. I had asked him last night if something was amiss, but he merely kissed me, said no, and went to bed. I had been so busy throughout the day, seeking solutions to the issues here, that we had not talked much, and then, he had been gone for the rest of the evening. I had at least wondered where he had gone. However, he did not say a word as to where he had gone today either.

"Are you well?" I finally asked him.

"Yes, of course," he said, seeming confused as to why I had asked. "Why?"

I thought to tell him but remembered Emeline. She ate exactly as she had yesterday for lunch, slowly and without speaking.

"Just asking," I said, watching Emeline. If I did not know any better, I would have thought that she was trying to make us forget she was here. But she was just a child and could not be that discerning, so maybe it was just her personality. After all, Devana was quiet as well, though not like this. Regardless, that could be due to Devana's older age. Whatever the case, I did not wish to push Emeline. But I also wanted her to know I was not ignoring her. Eating like this with us would help her become more comfortable—I hoped.

"We should have a painting commissioned," I said as I lifted my spoon to my lips. "Of the family. What do you think?"

"That is fine," he muttered and ate.

"Do you have any artist you prefer? I noticed the portrait of you with your mother and sister, which is lovely. He made your mother's radiance shine."

"Yes."

"So, you do not have a person in mind?"

"No, whomever you choose is fine."

He felt very distant and cold and I did not understand why. Did he not want me to talk about the painting? Or maybe he did not want to speak about his mother. Fine. I would focus on Emeline.

"Tomorrow, I will go into town. Emeline, would you like to join me?" I asked as she lifted a carrot to her mouth and paused.

"Into town?" Evander cut in, a grimace on his face. "Whatever for?"

"Tradition," I replied, not sure why he was looking at me like that. "I was taught that a new mistress of the house gives gifts to the tenants and goes to town, so the people may see and get to know her—well, me. Did you not hear me last night? I asked if it was acceptable to give bread."

His continued confounded gaze told me he was not aware of a word I had said, which made me wonder. Had he ignored me the whole night, and I did not realize?

"You wish to give them bread?" he asked.

"Not just bread, it is more like a basket of goods with bread, jams, fruits, and other things. They are preparing them now," I explained.

"If the servants are already preparing the baskets, can they not make the deliveries themselves?" he questioned as he lifted his glass to his lips.

"Does that not defeat the point if I am not there? It is I who am familiarizing myself to them," I asked in return.

"I do not see why that is needed."

I was quickly growing annoyed by this. "I do not see why it is a problem."

He frowned, leaning back in his chair. "It is merely unsafe for you to wander, Aphrodite."

"Wander? Is this not your land? How can I wander?"

He sighed as though I were being difficult. Before I could ask him the actual reason behind his objection, Wallace entered the dining room with a letter, reminding me we were not in private. I glanced at Emeline, who had now stopped eating altogether.

"Have the servants deliver the baskets on your behalf," he said, rising from his chair, his eyes on the letter. "I must go. I will see you later this evening."

He did not wait for either Emeline or me to respond before he walked out, leaving Wallace in the dining room with us.

"Is everything to your liking, Your Grace?" Wallace asked me.

"Yes, everything is fine." It was not. But I could not say that aloud, nor was it fair to take my anger out on him or the staff.

"Your Grace?" Mrs. Watson said as she entered the room, hands clasped in front of her. "If you are finished, I can take the miss for her lessons."

"No," I said, seeing Emeline ready to move. I placed my

hand gently on hers. "How about no lessons today, and we walk through the gardens?"

Emeline stared at me and then glanced at Mrs. Watson, who did not seem to approve.

"Your Grace, it is crucial that the young lady be devoted to her lessons—"

"Yes, I am aware, as I was once a young lady." I rose, the footman stepping behind me to remove my chair, and I walked to where Emeline sat. "Lessons are fundamental, but so is family time. Emeline and I will take only an hour. In the meantime, Mrs. Watson, you can see to your duties as housekeeper. I have left a list of things that I require done. My lady's maid might not be able to accomplish them on her own."

She blinked repeatedly then nodded. "Of course, Your Grace. I shall see to them now and meet you both in an hour in the garden."

"Brilliant, thank you." I waited as she glanced at Emeline, giving her a small smile before finally choosing to go about her work. With her gone, I knelt beside Emeline, who sat as properly as she could, her hands clasped together in her lap, her lips clamped shut.

"Emeline, I want you to know that I really wish to be a good mother to you. I hope you will be a good friend to me also. Will you walk with me?" I offered her my hand.

She hesitated at first but then took my hand, and I led her out of the room with me. From everything I had gathered yesterday from the staff, Mrs. Watson was very protective of Emeline, and Emeline depended on her. I was grateful that Emeline had had someone's attention and care all these years. But at the same time, I had to insert myself now, or I would never get the chance. I wished for Emeline to be able to come to me, not a housekeeper. No matter what the child's circumstance, or the truth of her parentage, to the world, she was the daughter of the duke. Therefore, she was a lady of this house and under my care. And I would see to it that it was the best care.

"Emeline." I glanced down at her. "You are the duke's daughter, and, therefore, I will think of you as my daughter. You may even call me Mama if you wish. I will always help you."

She just stared.

This child stared a lot. I paused, glancing around.

"But first, I think I must help myself to a map." I giggled, frowning, then looking at her. "I am a bit lost. Do you know how to get to the gardens? Or where we are?"

I expected her silence, but when I sought to go back from where we came, she pulled me forward with all her little strength, turning left, then another left, before going right and down the hall. In a few minutes, we stood before the glass doors leading out to the garden.

"Do you know the whole house?" I asked in amazement.

She nodded slowly.

"You are remarkable. When I was your age, I would get lost in my own home numerous times, and my brother would have to come search for me." I chuckled and opened the door, allowing her to go out first. I was not sure what to do, but I figured that maybe like Devana, I should just speak and let her interject whenever she wished. "I was quiet as a child, too. Then my sisters came, and they were very loud, so I learned to find my voice. Even still, I did not talk nearly as much as Hathor, and no one can beat my sister Abena. She is only ten years old. When she comes, I hope you can show her around, too. Actually, before she comes, can you show me? So I do not look foolish in front of her."

I glanced down, and she was just staring at me.

Okay. Maybe less talking. I smiled, walking with her, which was better than nothing . . . for all of ten minutes before she released my hand to try to catch a butterfly. It was a simple action, but it showed me she was at least somewhat comfortable.

"Your Grace?"

I spun around to see Eleanor rushing toward me. "Eleanor, what is it? Are the baskets finished already?"

"No," she exclaimed and tried to catch her breath. "Forgive me, Your Grace, but you are needed right now!"

"Now? Why?"

"The dowager duchess is here and refusing to leave, and the duke is not pleased."

"Oh no!" I moved to hurry back with her but remembered Emeline. Turning to the girl now picking flowers, I rushed to her quickly. "Emeline?"

She looked at me.

"I am sorry. I have work to finish, but we will play again later. Come, we must return," I said, taking her hand.

I did not wish to run, as it was not proper, and her little feet would not allow me to, either. I feared the scene that would be caused between Evander and his stepmother. I waited until we had gotten inside and I knew where I was.

"Eleanor, take her to Mrs. Watson, and then meet me in front," I said and transferred Emeline's hand to Eleanor's before I cupped Emeline's face gently. "We shall have another day all to ourselves, my dear, I promise."

I dusted off the front of my dress before heading to the

foyer, where I could see the back of Evander's broad shoulders, the light of the sun coming in from the door before him. He stood like a lone gatekeeper to the outside hall, his whole body looking as though it were carved from marble.

"I do not know how many times I must tell you that you are not welcome here, Datura." His voice was cold and severe.

"I have a right to—"

"You do not!" he snapped and took a step forward.

Luckily, I had reached them by then, placing my hand upon his shoulder. He paused and glanced over to me.

I smiled, searching his eyes to see only anger. "Dear, I heard we had unexpected company?"

He stepped back. "Datura came to see Emeline, so she says."

"She is family, is she not?" the woman called, not able to even come up the stairs as the men stood guard beside her. "Since my return to Everely, I have heard a great deal of talk, saying that she is being neglected. The duchess prefers her sleep."

It seemed the days I had taken to rest had somehow reached her.

"You have been greatly misinformed, Dowager," I replied politely though angry, walking down the stairs. "Emeline is under the very best of care. In fact, she and I were in the middle of a walk through the gardens when I heard you had arrived."

Holding her cane, a new addition, her blue eyes narrowed on me, and she lifted her head. How she managed with such a massive wig was truly a talent. "Yes, of course, my dear girl. However, one cannot merely take your word for it. Emeline is very important to me, and I wish to know she is well taken care of."

"Naturally, but Dowager, children need to keep to their

schedule. Had you sent word that you wished to see her, I would have arranged a time that was appropriate. I must say, to come to another's home with no notice and demand an audience is highly improper, even if you are the child's relation. Or were you not aware of such etiquette?" I asked.

Everything I had seen of the dowager, from her clothes to her hair to her manner of speech, told me that she wished to be respected despite her low birth. So to insinuate that she did not have common manners was a great insult.

The grip on the cane tightened, and she chuckled bitterly. "Highly improper, you say? May I ask why it is highly improper when I arrive without notice? But when your mother came trampling through here, years ago, she was deemed a heroine."

"I beg your pardon?" I snapped my eyes wide. "My mother has never acted improperly."

"It is past time you leave, Datura." Evander's harsh voice sounded behind me. "And do not return again. My daughter does not need your care. No little girl does, I assure you."

Her glare shifted to him. "Should anything happen to her, I shall not let it go quietly—"

"Oh, I do not doubt that, but it would not be for anyone else's sake except your own. I advise you to be wary of playing games with me, Datura, and to pass this caution to Fitzwilliam."

She huffed and shook her head. "I have not spoken to Fitzwilliam since you so cruelly dismissed us from our home."

"This. Is. Not. Your. Home," he sneered, and I took hold of his arm to calm him.

"Thank you for coming, Dowager. I hope you have a safe trip back from whence you came." I forced a smile and outstretched my arm to her carriage.

"I have returned to Everely, and I will not be forced out once more," she said directly to Evander, then spun around dramatically. We watched as she entered her waiting carriage.

Evander turned to the guards, holding up his finger. "Never allow that woman on the grounds again. I do not care if you must throw yourself in front of her carriage. Am I understood?"

"Yes, Your Grace." The man bowed his head.

Without another word, Evander marched up the stairs. If he thought I was not going to ask, he was mistaken.

"What is going on?" I questioned following after him. "Did she truly come here because she thought Emeline would be treated so poorly? Why—"

"She is lying," he replied. "Pay her no mind."

"That is quite difficult," I said, stepping before him. "Explain what she meant about my mother? Did something happen—"

He cupped the sides of my face and leaned in, kissing my forehead. "Worry not of such things, my dear. It is all in the past. Simply ignore her. She will not come again."

"Whether she comes again does not change the fact that she came *now*. I do not understand. Tell me what she meant about my mother? Also, why—"

"Your Grace," Wallace interrupted at a very convenient time for his master.

Frowning, I turned to see the three large and gruff men, dressed in dark cotton clothes, holding their hats carefully in their hands. They smiled politely at us, and I offered the same. "The tenants you wished to speak to, sir."

"Oh yes!" Evander replied, stepping around me. "Thank you for coming. I have much to talk to you about regarding the next harvest."

All three of them continued to stare at me. Evander glanced at them again.

Wallace moved to speak, but I stepped forward, outstretching my hand.

"Hello, sirs, I am Lady Aphrodite Du— Eagleman." It was the first time I had needed to introduce myself. "Welcome to Everely House."

"Thank you, ma'am—I mean, Your Grace." The first man cleaned his hand on his own shirt before taking my hand.

"Welcome to you, too," the second one replied, also cleaning his hand before shaking mine.

"Thank you. I did not expect tenants today. I planned to come to visit you all tomorrow," I said as the third one took my hand.

"You want to come to the tenants' grounds, Your Grace?" the first one, with reddish-brown hair and a beard, asked, shocked.

"Yes, of course. It is tradition, is it not? Forgive me, what are your names?"

"Right, I am Noah Stevenson," the red-haired man said, then pointed to the man with a crooked nose beside him. "This here is Seth Rowan." He then pointed to the man beside him. "Lastly Homer Toule."

I grinned and looked at the man on the end with dark hair and light eyes. "Homer? Like the *Iliad* and the *Odyssey*?"

He stared, confused. "Odyssey like a journey, Your Grace? I've been nowhere but Everely."

Immediately, I felt very foolish. When would they have had time to read works of ancient Greek literature?

"Oh, never you mind. Your name was merely familiar. Please, do not let me hold you." I glanced at Evander, who shook his head, amused. I ignored him. "I shall have refreshments sent."

Wallace directed them, "This way, if you will."

"Thank you, Your Grace," they said to me before they left.

Evander chuckled. "You are your father's daughter for sure."

I preferred him this way, relaxed, teasing me. Not the Evander who stood before his stepmother enraged. I had questions, but obviously, this was not the time to ask them.

"We will speak later," I said.

His jaw set, but he did not reply, leaving me and walking off on his own.

Truly, nothing was simple here . . . especially not him.

23

Aphrodite

I had acquired a new favorite window. It was in our room, and had a nook allowing one to sit right beside the glass comfortably. I had never seen anything like it, but I loved it immensely. I could imagine reading here . . . if I ever found time to read again. Mama was right. The running of a home was a task that required one's mind all day and night, and I was so tired. It was up to me to adjust every room, down to every detail, from the draperies and the pillows to the type of furniture that would remain or be removed and at what angle it would sit. Every room needed modification, and every change needed my approval. It was up to me to discuss with the cook what type of meals were expected. Not to mention my relationship with Emeline. My head was spinning, and I couldn't ever recall speaking for such lengths as I had over the past few days. I relished having this moment of silence, staring out at the darkness of the trees, as I knew it would not be for long. There was still one more conversation to be had before the day was done.

"You are awake."

I watched as he entered quietly, already pulling at the cravat around his neck. Rising from my place, I crossed the room to him.

"It is fine. I can—"

"I wish to," I interrupted. "Would you prefer I not?"

His brown eyes searched my face before his arms fell to his side. "Continue."

When I had gotten him down to nothing but his breeches and drawers, I brushed my hand over the newly healed scar on his shoulder blade. It was still red and had not returned to the same light, sun-kissed brownish tone of the rest of his body. When he shivered, I leaned forward and kissed it gently. His arm wrapped around my waist.

"Are you not cross with me?" he asked, gently resting his cheek on my head. "You have been glaring at me all day."

"I was not glaring," I muttered, leaning into his embrace. "It is merely the condition of my face."

He chuckled. "I am well versed in your face. I have been its student for many years. I know when you are bored and when you are upset. And you were upset, but I do not know why."

I stepped out of his arms. "Truly, you do not know?"

"So, you were?" His eyebrow rose. "And no, I don't. I thought maybe it was the disturbance of this afternoon, but you were upset before that."

It made me even more upset that he did not see why. I also did not wish to miss this chance to speak calmly.

"What occurred with Datura—"

"As I said," he interrupted, lightly rubbing my arms, "pay her no mind. Datura craves attention. She desires to make herself important. So she arrives unannounced whenever she is given the slightest opportunity and always with some wild excuse. It is better to ignore her than engage further."

"But what is she after? Surely, she knows the crimes of her eldest son. Would she not seek to stay out of your path to avoid further conflict? Should Fitzwilliam—"

"She exists purely on conflict. They both do. They are nothing to worry about."

"What did she mean by Mother—"

"I do not understand that woman, and I truly wish to stop speaking of her," he said.

I fought the urge to press further.

"So, is the matter rectified?"

"No. I also told you I wished to deliver gifts to the tenants, and you nearly *ordered* me not to," I replied, adding a little more space between us, though I should not have removed his clothing because I was fairly unnerved by him.

"I was merely looking to your safety."

"Is it not your land? Your tenants? You may bring them into the house, but I am not free to walk among them?"

"The house and the grounds are full of those who can protect you. You walking through the village is another matter—"

"Then I am to remain in the house?" I questioned.

"There are gardens, the many meadows, along with—"

"I thought you wished not to move me from one cage to another?" I bit my lip to keep from yelling, seeking instead to speak calmly. "Or was the two weeks after our wedding my only reprieve? Now I will be kept inside as I was before, told it is for my safety!"

"I am not seeking to cage you—"

"'When we are married, you will be free to be however it is you wish to be. I swear it.' Were those not your words to me?"

He grinned. "You still recall that?"

"I recall everything you said to me, and I held it as truth."

"If you wish so badly to go see the tenants, fine. Go." He frowned and moved to the water basin.

The matter still felt unsettled, but I did not have the words.

And watching him take the cloth to clean his neck was rather muddling my thoughts. I did not know whether to kick him or kiss him. And so I chose neither. I took off my dressing gown and got into bed, rolling onto my side and closing my eyes tightly.

"You are still upset?"

I did not answer him.

"I shall take that as yes."

I sat up quickly now glaring at him. "You are frustrating me greatly."

"Which type of frustration? As you now know, there are two types." He smirked as he took off his breeches and drawers, but I kept my eyes on his face.

"Not the type you would prefer!"

"Have I not allowed you to see the tenants as you wished?"

"Allowed me." *Calm. I must remain calm.* "Yes, Your Grace, thank you for your magnanimous gesture."

"Is the sarcasm necessary?" He frowned, leaning against the bedpost, still very much naked.

"Good night." I sought to yank the sheet over my face, but he caught it and would not let go. "Release it!"

"No! I will not go to bed with you this way. You wish for freedom, then speak plainly."

"That is not freedom. That is a command," I sneered, trying to hold on with all my might, but he was far stronger than I and was toying with me. "Evander, this is childish! Let go!"

"You let go."

"I am already in the bed. Why must I let go?"

He shrugged and yanked hard, ripping the sheet from me and tossing it to the side. And when the sheet was gone, I could see clearly how erect he had become. The sight sent a slight quake through me. He grabbed my ankle and pulled me down the bed toward him. His eyes were now glazed over with desire.

"I am in need of you, wife," he whispered. "As you see, my condition has become quite grave."

"Yes, I can see," I replied but kept my face serious. "So, what if I refuse you?"

A deep frown came over his face. "I shall be forced to take matters into my own hands."

My eyes narrowed. "How, exactly?"

"Very well. If you wish to be taught, then I shall demonstrate."

Instead of lifting my nightdress, he took hold of himself. I watched as his hand glided up and down the length of his manhood, his chest rising and falling, his breath increasing all while he observed me. I could not look away, and the pressure in the pit of my stomach began to grow, along with the ache between my legs. He had started slow, but soon, his pace quickened, as did my breath. As if I were mesmerized by him or had been taken over by my own desire, I reached out and touched him. He stilled for only a moment before his hand let go, allowing me to feel the full heat of him in my palm.

I continued what I had seen him do, moving my hand down the length of him as well. He licked his lips, his nostrils flaring.

"Faster." That was all he said, and I complied. The more I did, the more I ached, but I was consumed by the look of pleasure on his face, the moaning that came from him, and it was joyous to hear that I could make him sound like this. But it also reminded me of the things he had done to me . . . how he had brought his mouth upon me. And so I moved to do the same when he caught my hand in his.

"What are you doing?"

"Can I not?" I asked.

"It is unbecoming of one such as you."

I stared at him for a moment. "What do you mean?"

"A lady."

"Then those who are not ladies have done this to you?"

He swallowed, rolling his shoulders back before speaking. "Having you like this is more than enough . . . I . . . could not even think—"

I licked the tip of him, and he jumped.

"Aphrodite!"

He tasted salty, strange. I ran my tongue over him. He twitched, and so I kissed, and soon, there was no more protest from him, only a deep gasp of air and a moan.

"Take me into your mouth," he ordered.

"My mouth?" I repeated.

"If you wish to please me so, take me into your mouth . . . to suck . . . unless, if you wish not to—"

I was not exactly sure how to fit all of him, but I did as he asked. His hand brushed away my curls. "Just as you did with your hand, do that with your mouth, take me in—up and down."

I did slowly, and he guided my head. "That's right, but suck harder."

I sucked and felt him throbbing in my mouth. And just as with his hand, it took a few moments before his pace increased slightly.

"Ah . . . yes . . ." I heard him groan above me.

He suddenly pulled away, and I thought I had done something incorrectly. He lay upon the sheet, grunting as he held on to himself.

"Did I do something wrong?" I asked.

He glanced over at me, eyes wide, his chest rising and falling. "Wrong? No. Sinfully perfect? Yes. Absolutely yes."

"Is that good or bad?"

"I shall let you decide." He smiled. He pushed me back down onto the bed, lifting my nightdress and cupping me between my legs. "Look how wet you have gotten. Let me not neglect you, either."

"Evander!" I gasped as his mouth was upon me instantly. The moment his tongue licked me, I could not make sense of myself any longer.

How had this happened? I was furious with him. There were so many things I'd wanted to talk to him about, wished he would explain, yet now I could barely breathe, let alone have a conversation.

He always did this, took over my mind, all my senses and feelings, leaving me trembling.

"Evander!" I cried out, arching up from the bed, and his response was to lift me toward his mouth more.

I swear, he was the king of all my dreams, the lord of all my passions, the captain of all my desires.

I was helpless against him.

Evander

I did not dream, as she had fulfilled all of them. Maybe that was why I woke early, as she was seeking to leave my arms. I watched as she took the top sheet, wrapping it around herself before quietly trying to rise.

"Escaping me?" I whispered to her back.

Startled, she glanced at me. "Forgive me, did I wake you?"

"The lack of you did," I replied, touching her skin. "Where are you going?"

"I must get ready and review the gifts before I go." She was truly dedicated to this task.

"It cannot wait until the sun is fully up?"

"They are working people," she reminded me, and I wondered what she knew of such things. "When the sun is high, they will not be home."

I grinned. "What a thoughtful mistress you are."

"Are you mocking me?" She frowned.

I shook my head. "No, I truly mean it. The tenants do not know how fortunate they are."

"I desire to fulfill my duties."

"You have fully triumphed in your marital ones." I leaned in closer, brushing her hair behind her ear. "I am still enraptured with you from last night—you astonish me."

"Evander, do not speak on it," she whispered, hiding her face from me.

"Now you are shy?" I teased, lifting her chin.

She glared at me as if angry, but it was more from embarrassment. "In the moment, it did not feel . . ."

"What?"

"Unnatural."

"Does it feel unnatural now?" I asked.

She shook her head. "No, it is just . . . I never imagined myself acting like that. Then I go about being a lady again? All the world sees me . . . as proper."

I laughed outright, kissing the sides of her face, then her lips. "No one should ever know what occurs between a husband and wife. Your sinful moments are for me and me alone. Forever."

I kissed down the side of her neck, coming to her breast.

"Evander," she muttered, leaning into my touch. "I cannot be distracted. I must go."

Sighing, I raised my head. "Very well." I kissed her lips once more. "I shall go with you."

"Really?"

"Yes, really. I have not been to town in quite some time."

"Then I should make haste," she said, taking her dressing gown as she moved to her private room.

Rising from the bed, I stretched. I did not wish to go, but I did not want to be away from her, either. More importantly, I worried for her, especially now that I had gotten Fitzwilliam's letter and knew that Datura had settled down not more than ten minutes from this house. They were up to something, I was sure. But when would they attack? And how? I preferred them to strike at my heel *now* so that I could finally be done with them instead of this unknowing that tortured me.

"Evander?"

"Yes?" I turned back to see her head poking around the door.

"Emeline shall be coming with us."

"You wish to bring her?"

She nodded. "It will be good for us all to go together. After all, we are a family now, right?"

Her kindness humbled me. "Of course, but I am not sure she is awake."

"I will send someone—actually, I will get dressed and go myself."

"Whatever you wish." I smiled.

She grinned and went back into her room.

The more dedicated she was, the more I felt a desire to

watch over her, to keep her close. *Oh, dear lord, a lifetime of this?*

Nothing would make me happier, truly.

Aphrodite

"You should be aware of some gossip I heard, Your Grace, from around town," Eleanor whispered as we walked the empty hall to Emeline's room. "I believe it is what brought the dowager here."

"Tell me."

Eleanor frowned heavily, her face severe. "Apparently, the talk is that you are cruel . . . to the young miss."

I gasped. "I beg your pardon?"

"They said that you detest her presence, as she is evidence of the duke's . . . past wife. And you take your anger out on the child."

"That is horrid." Why would I abuse a child because of her mother? Even if it had not all been a tragic set of circumstances, Emeline was still not to blame. "It is very good that she comes with us. Seeing us all together will help kill any such talk. But you must seek out the source." I paused, looking her over. "There has been much said about the dowager, but she would not create such tales herself, correct?"

"Truly, I do not know, Your Grace. Different people tell me different things. I thought to bring this to you since it came from the town."

I understood what she meant. I exhaled as she opened the door for me. Inside, Mrs. Watson was once again doing Emeline's hair, though Emeline was nodding off slightly.

"Your Grace." Mrs. Watson curtsied to me.

Hearing her nanny speak, Emeline's eyes opened and she shifted to see me. I hoped she would be more relaxed, but instead, she looked nervous, quickly rushing off the chair to stand beside Mrs. Watson's skirt just like when I had first met her. Had she heard the talk? Abena often eavesdropped on the staff when she was playing through the house, too.

"Your Grace, she was not feeling well last night. Maybe it is best to leave her to rest this morning," Mrs. Watson said.

I hid a frown and walked right up to Emeline, sinking down in front of her. "Good morning, Emeline."

"Good morning, Your Grace." She barely managed to get the words out before she tried to step away from me.

"Emeline, I promise I shall never hurt you. You are under my protection, and that means I care about you a great deal. There is no need to be afraid. If you wish to stay home today, that is fine. If you want to go into town with us, that is fine, as well." I held my hands out to her. "Whatever you wish to do, we shall do."

She stared at me for a little bit longer before she took my hands. "I want to go."

"Then we shall go." I grinned and stood. "Thank you for preparing her, Mrs. Watson. I shall take over from here."

"Yes, Your Grace."

"Emeline, have you been to town?" I asked as Eleanor opened the door for us. I was hoping to get her to speak more, but she shook her head.

"Neither have I. It shall be good fun. But you must stay close to me at all times, all right?"

She nodded, holding on tight to my hand, which made me glad.

It took us only a few minutes before we were outside, where I could see the baskets already packed on a hay cart.

"Where is the carriage?" Evander asked as he stepped out behind us.

"We shall not need it, as we are walking," I replied.

"Walking?" he repeated. "Why on earth would you wish to do that?"

"It is not far, nor is it a bad day. I am very used to walking, and it would be a bit much to travel such a short distance with the horses and carriage, do you not think?" I replied. He tilted his head, staring at me. "What?"

"Your Grace, your hat." Eleanor handed the purple hat to me.

"Thank you," I said and turned back to Evander. "Are you not coming?"

He exhaled deeply but said nothing, coming down the stairs to stand alongside us. He glanced at Emeline, placing his hand on her head, offering her a smile. "Are you well?" he asked.

Emeline grinned, nodding. "Yes, Papa."

"Well then, if the ladies are not complaining, I surely cannot. Let us walk." He nodded, and spoke to the hands helping to drive the wagon. "Go ahead of us, so you do not need to worry about keeping pace."

"Yes, Your Grace."

I glanced down at Emeline, who beamed at her father happily. When she looked at me, she smiled from ear to ear for the first time.

Yes, this was a good day.

24

Evander

They all lined up to see her as though she were the queen herself, and Aphrodite, who was generally known for being quiet and aloof, was all conversation, speaking to each of them, not at all bothered by appearance or stench, not even allowing it to faze her. Her demeanor seemed to be contagious for even little Emeline—who, to my knowledge, was a quiet and simple child. She now sat with the wagon, happily handing Aphrodite as many of the baskets as she could.

"We did not think you were truly coming, Your Grace." The scruffy red-haired man named Mr. Stevenson chuckled.

"You did not take me for my word?" Aphrodite asked as she passed him a basket. "I am quite wounded, Mr. Stevenson."

His eyes widened, and he took off his hat. "Forgive me, Your Grace. I just meant we hadn't seen any family from the house out and about in . . . in years."

"Years?" Aphrodite repeated, shocked. "Surely, it cannot be that long?"

"No, Your Grace, really. The last time we saw any duchess or sort was about twenty-one years ago," an older woman said, rocking a small child in her arms. "I know because my son, Jimmy, was about the same age as the young miss, and this is his son, my grandson."

"Oh," Aphrodite said, and her eyes shifted to me.

The look in them felt as though she were yelling at me. I said nothing, for I honestly could not remember. Had it truly been that long?

"I don't recall seeing the duke since then, either," the same woman said, smiling at me. "Do you remember my Jimmy? When Lady Luella brought you to town with her, you'd play near the stones with him."

I did not recall knowing a Jimmy, but she seemed so hopeful that I could not bring myself to speak that truth. "Ah yes, Jimmy, how is he?"

Her smile fell, and she just stared at me. "He passed, been four months."

Dear God. "I—"

"Our condolences," Aphrodite said, touching the woman's shoulder before cooing at the child in her arms. "Such a loss and to have such a gift left behind as well. Was he named after him?"

"Yes, Your Grace." The woman showed her the child. "Poor thing, losing his papa working in one of the mines, and then he lost his mama bringing him into this world. He is so young, but I'm going to make sure he grows well enough."

"I trust you will." Aphrodite placed her hand on his head. "Should you need anything, please write to me at the house. If it's an emergency, come to the door."

Now I looked to her, eyes wide. Was she mad? We could not just have them come to our home like that. But she was looking at the crowd not me.

"Thank . . ."—the woman stopped, sucking in the air, and looked as though she wished to cry—"you, Your Grace. You are quite kind. I thought we would never get another like Lady Luella again."

Hearing Mother's name felt as if someone were trying to

open a door within me that I had long since shut and never wished to expose again. I said nothing, nodded to those who addressed me, and allowed Aphrodite to take charge as she wished. The longer we stayed, the more the door cracked. And as Emeline played with the other children I remembered how my mother spent so much time talking with everyone that I ended up playing with the children.

※

"Did you have fun, Emeline?" Aphrodite asked, brushing the girl's hair from her face inside the wagon. I walked beside them as the horse moved slowly.

Emeline nodded.

"Good, we shall come more often, and you can play with the children. You worked very hard today, and I am proud of you." Though Emeline did not respond, Aphrodite seemed unbothered by it. Instead, she shifted her gaze to me, her eyes narrowing.

"Yes?" I questioned.

"Twenty-one years, Evander?"

I knew she would bring that up. "I did not realize so much time had passed."

She sighed, shaking her head. "When Eleanor told me that the tenants were displeased, I was so worried as to what it could be and how to rectify it. I never expected it to be our neglect."

"Neglect?" I scoffed. "All their needs are met, any issues of land or farming or housing are always addressed. They are paid fairly and—"

"You speak merely of work, Evander."

"What else is there to speak of but work?"

"Community," she replied, adjusting Emeline's dress. "It is very good to have a stable estate and lord who seriously cares about those matters. However, it is equally important to maintain a sense of community. We are the duke and duchess here, their master and mistress. We need to show ourselves among them so that we do not become out of touch. Or worse, be deemed uncaring."

I shook my head, not understanding in the least. "I was always taught that as long as they were treated fairly, their basic needs provided for, that was enough."

"Who taught you that?" She laughed at me. "It is a very cold manner of thought."

"My father," I muttered.

She fell silent, and I focused only on the road. We had nearly reached the house when she spoke again.

"Forgive me, I did not mean to laugh. I should remember all estates are different."

"You are not exactly wrong. My father's lessons were always quite cold," I said as I helped Emeline out before extending my hand to Aphrodite.

I truly disliked when she looked at me like that. It felt as though she had found that door and were about to yank it open.

"You never speak about your father. What—"

"Emeline!" We both jumped slightly at the sight of Mrs. Watson rushing down the stairs to where Emeline stood before us. She dropped to her knees, dusting off the child's dress. "Why are you covered in so much dirt?"

"Oh, Mrs. Watson, it's from the walk." Aphrodite giggled, lifting the hem on her own dress, which was covered in dirt as well. "Nothing a good wash cannot cure. Other than that, we are all fine."

"Yes, Your Grace," she replied, standing straight up. "I shall take her in to have her lunch."

Emeline was already holding her hand.

"Thank you, Mrs. Watson." Aphrodite waved to Emeline, who waved back before following her nanny inside. When she was beyond hearing, Aphrodite said, "Emeline is becoming warmer with me. I hope she will come to depend on me more than she does Mrs. Watson one day. Like her own mama. I always had a nanny, but my mama was very involved with us."

"Yes, I recall," I replied, giving her my arm as we walked up the stairs. "All in due time. Emeline smiled more today than I have ever seen. Especially after . . ."

"After?"

"After her mother died," I answered.

"Oh, how was she then?"

"She was . . . I was . . ." I did not know because I sought not to think of that as well. I hung my head. "It was a hard time for her, I am sure."

"Did you speak to her?"

"No, Mrs. Watson—"

"Evander, please tell me you spoke to her after she lost her mother."

"Of course, I did," I said quickly. "I told her what happened, and she said okay. And that was all."

"That she did not cry was not odd to you?"

"She is a quiet child, as you have seen. Not everyone weeps at the loss of a parent. I did not," I muttered, and there it was, another slip, and she pounced upon it.

"What did you do then?"

"I do not remember." I kissed her forehead. "I have work to do. I shall see you later."

I did not wait, as I feared something more would slip. I had done my best not to speak of the past. There was no point since there was no changing any of it. Instead, I sought my future, seeking to create my refuge there. And I was closer now to that life than I ever thought I would be. I did not wish to mar it. However, I'd found myself thinking more about the past over the last few days. And now she had me thinking of Emeline. I truly could not recall her reaction after her mother passed, and I had not focused much on her at the time. Instead, I had left her to Mrs. Watson's care.

I paused as I recalled my father and how he had acted when my mother passed. How he'd barely said a word, either.

Dammit all.

I rubbed the side of my head, sighing.

I am not my father. I am not my father. I repeated the mantra in my mind as I walked near Emeline's room.

"I saw sheep, and then the other girls showed me their dolls. They said their mama made them! The dolls were really dirty, but they said it was because they were hugged so much."

That little voice rambling off was something I had never heard before. In fact, I had to look in and check that it did not belong to some other child instead of Emeline. But sure enough, there she was, running circles as Mrs. Watson looked for a new dress.

"Can I get a doll?" Emeline asked. "I want one that looks like me, too, with curly hair and a pretty dress. Oh, and a hat!"

"Of course, my dear. I will make you one." Mrs. Watson chuckled.

I grinned. Who knew Emeline could say so much and so quickly, other than Mrs. Watson, of course. I was about to leave them be when Emeline spoke again.

"Can Odite do it?"

"Odite?" Mrs. Watson repeated.

"The duchess. The other girls said that it has to be done by your mama. The duchess is my mama now, right?"

I smiled.

"No."

What? I stepped closer to see Mrs. Watson kneeling before her. "The duchess is the duchess. She is not your mama. Did I not explain? It is best for you to be respectful and quiet, not to make her angry. And never call her Odite again. It is Your Grace."

"But she said I could," Emeline whispered. "She is not mean."

"Yet. This is because she is pretending. She wants everyone to like her, and then she will start to bully you. But no one will believe you. When that happens, you will be in grave danger, my dear. She will seek to get rid of you at once. People like her cannot be trusted—"

"Mrs. Watson," I hollered, quaking in horror and rage, as I could not believe my ears. Upon seeing me, she jumped back.

"Your Grace—"

"Pack your things. You are dismissed at once!"

"Sir—"

"How dare you speak so of my wife!" Had she not been elderly and a woman, I would have raised my hand and struck her across her face. "How dare you poison my daughter with your lies!"

"Your Grace, please, I was—"

"I said at once! Never let me see your face upon these grounds again!" I was shaking, rushing to Emeline. I lifted her, holding her away from the snake of a woman. "God only knows what you have done to this child all these years. Get out of my sight. *Now!*"

She jumped and rushed from the room.

"No!" Emeline reached for her, but I held her tightly. *"Papa, no! Mrs. Watson!"*

"Shh." I hugged her tightly as she began to cry, struggling for freedom. "She is not good, Emeline."

"No! Mrs. Watson!" she screamed again, sobbing.

I did not know what to do, so I held her.

Aphrodite

"Your Grace!"

I jumped, nearly spilling my tea upon myself.

"Good Lord! What is it, Eleanor?"

"You must come at once!" She rushed inside my drawing room, still gripping the letters I had asked her to send only moments ago. "The duke has dismissed Mrs. Watson, and he ordered her thrown from the grounds."

"What?" I rose quickly. "When? Why?"

"No one knows, Your Grace. The maids heard yelling and then saw Mrs. Watson crying as she rushed from the young miss's rooms. The duke then gave orders. It was all just moments ago."

"What on earth could have happened in the ten minutes since we last saw her?" I replied as I followed her from the room.

"I am unsure, Your Grace. However, the little miss was irate and sobbing for Mrs. Watson's return."

Just when I had thought the day had gone perfectly, we were faced with this unexplained chaos. It did not take long for us to reach her room, as we were doing what my mama said never to do, running—well, more fast walking but still very unladylike, and I could hear my mama in the back of my head, yelling at me. It was amusing how mothers stuck with you even when they were far, far away—a mama was everything.

That was why, when I entered Emeline's room and saw her lying on her bed, curled into a ball, my heart sank. Mrs. Watson had raised her and was all but her mama, whether that was proper or not. Losing her like this would disturb her greatly, and yet the man who dismissed her stood staring out the window, arms crossed over his chest.

Carefully, I walked to Emeline and placed my hand on her back, but she would not respond to me. She just took deep breaths.

"What happened?" I whispered, looking up at Evander.

"Mrs. Watson is dismissed," he said but did not look at me. "She is . . . she is not as I thought she was. And I will not allow her to harm this family further."

"Harm?" I repeated. "How so? From everything I have gathered, she is very dedicated."

"Lies!" He turned back to me angrily. "That woman is a . . ." He held his tongue when he saw Emeline flinch at his tone.

"Let us speak outside—"

"No need. You remain with her until we find a new nanny. I will go." He was already at the door.

"Evander, you have not explained!" I rushed after him. "Eleanor, stay with her a moment. Evander!"

He kept walking.

"Evander!" I shouted, following after him, and when he still did not stop, I ran, truly ran until I was right before him. "Do you not hear me calling after you?"

"Aphrodite, I do not wish to speak—"

"You never wish to speak!" I hollered in his face, more than tired of this. "That is the problem. You say something, but you do not explain. You do not share your thoughts. You merely state what you want, kiss me, and walk away!"

"Aphrodite—"

"*No!*" I snapped, shaking my head. "I have been trying my best not to push you, not to fight. Not to press upon things you clearly wish to avoid, and it does me no good! Why did you hire more men to watch the grounds? Is it about Fitzwilliam? I do not know, and you do not tell. What did the dowager mean when she brought up my mother? I do not know, and I can ask neither you nor the dowager. Now you dismiss a vital member of the house and you give me no explanation as to why!"

"Aphrodite, I cannot tell you everything you wish to know simply because you wish to know it!" he shouted.

"Then let it not be everything, let it simply be this!"

He inhaled through his nose. "I have already said what—"

"Why are you like this?" I frowned, shaking my head. "Why do you keep pushing me away?"

"I am not pushing you away. I am keeping myself sane!" he shouted. "Has it ever occurred to you that the answers you seek are painful? That we were not all fortunate to live in a loving home, where your mama and papa tease each other and sit by the fire reading together? Has it ever occurred to you that speaking on such things *hurts*?"

I jumped, for never before had he yelled at me so. "I . . ."

"You are fortunate, Aphrodite. You are like fresh air or clean water. I wish to be where you are, not have you join me where I am. So let me be silent and move forward." With that, he stepped around me and I did as he wished—let him go. Alone.

Swallowing the lump in my throat, I did not follow him. Instead, I returned to someone who needed me more at this moment. I found Eleanor trying to get Emeline to take the sheet off her head.

"Your Grace."

"You may go. And later, have things brought from my room. I shall stay with Emeline for the time being," I said, taking off my shoes and lying on the other side of the bed.

"Yes, Your Grace," she said as she exited, closing the door behind her.

I petted Emeline's back gently, not knowing what to say.

25

Aphrodite

It took me three days to piece together the events as they happened, since the only witness to the incident was little Emeline. The day after, she was still very much upset, and I was at a loss for how to take care of her. It seemed I failed in almost every aspect of her morning routine, which only saddened Emeline more, but instead of crying out in frustration, she became withdrawn and barely ate. So, the second day, I asked her to take care of me as Mrs. Watson did for her as a way to both keep her busy and to see if Mrs. Watson had harmed her in any manner. But Emeline took the most care, asking me about my clothes, then making sure breakfast was just right. I realized then the girl could talk as well as Abena. She even sought to do my hair but grew tired rather quickly due to how much hair I had.

Everything she did only showed me how well Mrs. Watson had cared for and tended to her. It was only when Emeline accidentally dropped one of my necklaces, and it broke, that I saw fear enter her eyes, and she asked if I would stop being nice now. It was not until she felt comfortable fully explaining to the best of her abilities that I understood what had happened.

"Mrs. Watson said that one day I would be mean to you?" I asked, genuinely perturbed. I was finishing the doll I had started for her.

"Yes, she said that you were only pretending to be nice so Papa would like you," she replied, her eyes glued to the doll.

"Did she tell you this often?" I pressed, doing my best to keep calm.

She nodded, not at all realizing the fault in this. "Mrs. Watson told me every day. That is why I have to be quiet and mind my manners, so you will not send me off."

I bit my lip in rage, but I pressed it down. "That is silly. You are family. Why would I ever send you off?"

"Mrs. Watson said the dowager is family, but she did not mind her manners, so she was sent off. She showed me from the window how Papa and you made her leave. And Papa did not return with Aunt Ver. Because you had her sent off, too."

The audacity of that lying wench, I thought as I pulled on the thread.

"The dowager and your papa are not very good friends, and he was surprised she came without notice, so she left for the day. But your Aunty Verity wished to spend time in London for the season."

"The season?" she questioned, glancing up at me.

I nodded. "That is when all the ladies in the ton who are old enough go to balls and lunches in the park, so they can dance and sing and meet many good people. It is all very fun."

"May I go?" she asked.

"Of course, but when you are older," I explained, finishing the last loop of the doll's dress. "I shall take you, and you shall have the finest dresses. You are the daughter of a duke. You must look very grand."

She grinned from ear to ear. "So, Aunty Ver will come back?"

"Yes, my dear," I replied, giving her the doll, though it was not very good. I should have focused more on my needlework, but she did not seem to care. She hugged it tightly.

"Thank you, Your Grace."

"Anything for you." I cupped her face. "Because you are important. So very, *very* important. No one can ever send you off or be mean to you. Not even me. And you needn't call me Your Grace. Odite or Mama is fine. Mrs. Watson was mistaken. I shan't be angry."

"But why has Papa become angry?" she whispered, now hanging her head as she poked the doll.

"He heard what Mrs. Watson said to you?"

She nodded. "I think."

He'd dismissed her because she was poisoning Emeline against me. Why she would do such a thing, I was not sure. But I understood his actions. I would have done the same. However, that was not the issue. The issue was his lack of communication and his refusal to explain anything to me. And now, we had not seen or spoken to each other over it. Was I wrong to keep pushing him? He was willing to speak on anything else but his family's past. Surely that was enough.

Knock. Knock.

The door opened to reveal none other than Verity herself, dressed in white.

Emeline rose from the floor and ran toward her. "Aunt Ver!"

"Little squirrel!" Verity exclaimed as she hugged the girl, spinning around. "How I have missed you! Look at how much bigger you have gotten."

Emeline giggled, and Verity tickled her. "You are back from the season?"

"The season. Who told you that?" Verity asked.

"That would be me." I laughed and walked to her. "Welcome home. Forgive me for not being out front when you arrived. I did not know you were returning now."

"Is a month's time still not enough?" She gave me a look.

"Has it been a month?"

"Yes, you did not notice?"

"No." I laughed as time seemed to fly past me.

"Forgive me for not sending word. But I did come with the greatest of escorts."

"Who?"

She grinned. "The Earl and Countess of Montagu!"

"My brother is here?" My heart filled—how I wished to see him.

"He is. Shall we go?"

I nodded gladly, outstretching my hand for Emeline, who took it without question. I was very excited to have some of my family here. I missed them.

When we came to the front of the house, my sister-in-law was at the very bottom of the stairs, staring up at the art upon the wall in utter awe.

"Silva!" I called out.

"Aphrodite!"

When I reached the bottom, we hugged. When I squeezed, she gasped and pulled back. "Careful I am not alone."

I did not know what she meant until I pulled back and saw her place a hand on her stomach. Glancing down at it, then back to her face. She smiled, nodding.

"Welcome and congratulations." I hugged her once more. "Oh my! I am so utterly shocked and yet pleased you are here. Where is Damon?"

"We arrived as the duke was preparing to bring the horse back from his ride, and Damon happily went to join him," she answered, then her eyes drifted down to the girl now holding my dress. "Hello, little miss."

"Emeline, this is the Countess of Montagu. You may call

her Lady Montagu or Aunt Silva," I said, placing my hand gently on Emeline's head.

"Hello, Lady Montagu," she said carefully and curtsied.

"Well, are you not precious?" Silva replied. "I like your doll very much."

Emeline nodded and hugged it. "Her Grace made it for me."

"As you can see, I need practice." I sighed and then looked at her. "Please let us go sit, especially in your condition. How was your journey? I was not expecting any of you."

"Forgive us. Verity wished to return, and Damon wished to leave the hustle and bustle of town, so it worked out well. We could not send word ahead of us."

"Has something happened?" I asked as we entered the drawing room.

"Nothing. As you know, Damon simply does not like the demands of high society, when he knew I was expecting he thought it the prefect time to return." She placed her hand on her stomach as she took her seat.

As it was a tradition in our family, the baby needed to be born on our family estate, though she was clearly months away.

"I am very pleased with this news. I shall become an aunt."

"And a mother one day soon . . . as you have now gotten clarity on certain matters." Her eyebrows rose.

I tried not to laugh but could not help myself. "Yes. A good deal."

"A good deal, you say?" She joined my laughter.

"What are we laughing at?" Verity questioned when she entered the room.

"Nothing, dear," Silva said, and just then, it reminded me of all the times I had caught my mother laughing among friends, only for the conversations to come to a halt when I entered. I thought it had been about me but now I realized that I might have been very much mistaken.

"You have redecorated," Verity said, glancing around the drawing room.

"Oh, yes, I am in the process of it. Do you like it? If not, I can have it removed," I said as a maid brought us cakes and tea.

"No, it's beautiful, very bright." She chuckled. "Like new life in here."

Emeline moved to sit next to her.

"So how have you fared being mistress of . . . all of this?" Silva asked. "It is even more than I imagined. I worry about one day being left to tend Belclere Castle, and this is much larger."

"Ironically enough, I feel even more familiar with Everely. My mother had me focus on this home for years. Arriving here, I felt less overwhelmed and more dedicated to proving my studies correct."

"Your mama thinks of everything."

It was her talent. One day, I wished to do half as well.

Before she could answer, the door opened. "I am searching for a divinely named duchess?"

I rolled my eyes at my brother. "I am here."

"You could not even pretend it was not you of whom I spoke?" he questioned with a grin, walking into the room with Evander. I stood, opening my arms for him.

"Quite difficult when I am the only duchess in the room." I laughed. "Hello, brother. I missed you."

"And I you, though it has not been so long. Nevertheless, I had to be sure that this one was treating you as he swore he would." My eyes glanced to Evander for a moment, but quickly I shifted my gaze away.

"I am perfectly well, thank you. Though I wonder, did you

come to inspect me or get your darling wife back to Belclere Castle?" I teased.

He chuckled and kissed the side of my cheek. "Both. As well as to bring the young Lady Verity back home before she and Hathor came to blows."

"What?" I asked, looking to Verity.

"I know not of what he speaks. Hathor and I are quite good friends now, I like her greatly. We simply hold different views," Verity replied innocently.

"What now?" I asked Damon.

He shook his head tiredly as he stood beside his wife. "So much, sister, so much. Where to begin? The gossip of her desire to marry a duke when there is a lack of available dukes, thus annihilating her plans to marry before the end of this season."

"She is still on that?"

We were halfway through the season. Most weddings would occur within the next few weeks and so there would have needed to be an attachment by now.

"With deep dedication." Silva laughed. "Abena is enjoying teasing her with how many days are left in the season."

I sighed. It was good to know that nothing there had changed, at least.

"Papa, do you like it!" Emeline said, drawing my attention to her as she showed off the horrid doll I had created. "Her Grace made it for me."

Evander knelt before her, looking it over. "It is very well done."

"Liar," Damon muttered, causing Silva to smack him quickly. He merely shrugged. "My sister is known for a great many things but needlework is not one of them."

"It is much better than I could manage. You must keep it well," Evander said to her, and she nodded.

"Papa, are you still mad?"

The room stilled, and I wished to sink into a hole, vanishing from the earth. Immediately, I felt Verity's, Silva's, and my brother's eyes upon me, but I did my best just to watch Emeline.

"I am not mad." He cupped her cheek. "I just have not gotten much sleep, that is all."

"Because you are sleeping alone?"

Kill me.

Hide me.

Dear God, please save me. She was worse than Abena!

Evander

They had come at the very worst possible time.

"What is going on with you and my sister?" Damon questioned now that we were in my study.

I was sure that, after Emeline had thoroughly humiliated me and after a painfully awkward dinner, the situation between Aphrodite and me would be clear enough for him to ask. I knew, and yet I still did not wish to have the conversation.

"It is nothing of concern," I muttered, pouring myself some brandy.

"You are drinking, and she has not been in your rooms in three days?"

I turned to him. "Do you not feel as though you are crossing a rather personal line here?"

"Belclere Castle is only a day's ride away, so if you do not want my sister, I can take her—"

"I would sooner kill you," I snapped, glaring at him. "She

may be your sister, but she is my wife now. The roles are changed. You do not—"

"Relax." Damon chuckled, taking the glass from my hand, "I merely wished to see that you still burned with such a passion for her now that you had finally obtained her."

"I am eternally inflamed." I filled another glass.

"Then what is the issue?"

"Must your family always share?"

"Must your family always withhold?" he shot back. He sat comfortably upon the couch across from me. "Even when people are trying to help you, both you and your sister are withdrawn, though she hides it better than most. We are now family. Why hold back?"

"What does that mean?" I sat up when he brought my sister into this. "Did something happen with Verity?"

He opened his mouth and then closed it once more. "I shall tell you what happened with your sister, should you tell me what occurred with mine."

"Damon, I am not in the mood."

"Very well then." He finished off his brandy. "I am weary from my travels and will make myself comfortable in your home for the night, *brother-in-law*, before my wife and I go home. Should you have questions about Verity, you may ask Verity. But I doubt she shall speak on it, as my sister will be silent on whatever is going on with you. Good night."

Dammit.

"Is it not possible for us to move forward?" I asked him as he reached the door. "Why must everyone keep asking questions about what happened before? I can see it in your sister's eyes. She wishes to know everything about my family's sordid past. All the world knows it was not the best of times, and even still, she persists."

"Has it ever occurred to you that maybe you are the one not moving forward?"

I did not understand. "Of course I am. Can you not see me—"

"We do see," he interrupted, shaking his head. "That is the problem. That is most likely why my sister is seeking answers. You are carrying the burden of it all. It unsettles you and strips the joy from your face. So, of course, she wishes to understand why. Women, I have noticed, are inquisitive creatures, whether it be Pandora's box or Eve in the Garden. They shall seek that knowledge."

"In both of those circumstances, did that not lead to terrible trouble for the rest of mankind?"

"And yet here we all are, surviving this terrible trouble alongside them, so surely we are as mad they." He laughed, as did I, shaking my head.

I would rather answer her questions than suffer from the lack of her.

"Verity," Damon said with seriousness, "had terrors most nights. Once we realized this, we sought to get her care in any way possible, even calling for Dr. Darrington to speak with her. It seemed to be of little help. I believe Verity in the end grew tired of pretending she was well, and she wished to return here."

I knew it. She must have forced herself to stay all this time for my sake. "Thank you for escorting her."

"Of course. As I said, we are family. I hope you *both* shall learn to lean on us from time to time," he replied. All I could do was nod, for he was exactly like his sister, requesting I do something so simple yet utterly antithetical to everything I had been taught.

26

Aphrodite

"Are you in need of anything else?" I asked from the door of the guest bedroom.

"No. You have been a most gracious host," Silva replied. "You are a fine mistress."

I smiled. "Once more, you hold me in too high regard, but I am pleased you feel at ease here. I wish you would extend your stay another day or two."

"We could not possibly. You are still a new bride." She leaned in to whisper that part to me. "Though one may argue that I am fairly new myself."

"When does the novelty wear off?" I asked.

She placed her hand on her stomach. "I am unsure, but I do believe this might be a very good sign."

I giggled and nodded. "Agreed. But if you or my brother wish to stay, it would be no hardship."

She carefully examined me. "Do you mean to use us as a barrier?"

"To what?"

"Forgive me if I am overstepping, but"—she took my hand—"is all well with you and the duke?"

After Emeline had spoken in the drawing room, Silva, my brother, and Verity took to watching Evander very carefully. I had lied and said the reason I had taken to sleeping in Emeline's room was to bond with her, as she had lost her nanny. It was difficult to maintain that lie when Evander and I had barely spoken to each other for the rest of the day.

"It is nothing— That is a lie." I exhaled, holding her hand tightly. "It is not a grand thing. We had a disagreement, though our argument was about more than the issue at hand. I find it frustrating when he does not share his thoughts. I hear so much of Everely from other people, but never from him. He does not speak freely, even when I see something has unsettled him. But now I wonder if I was wrong to push him."

"From my experience, Aphrodite, men are not always adept at speaking their feelings aloud. Even your brother has things he does not wish to share with me."

"Really? Damon has never been able to stop himself from expressing his frustrations, at least to us."

"Yes, very true. He cannot hold that to himself. But you might be surprised that there are times when he grows still and quiet. When possible, he will sit in one place in nature with an apple and watch the sky. What he is looking at, I have no idea. When I ask, he simply tells me he was thinking. Of what? He does not say. At least not at first. And so, I join him and sit and also stare, maybe even read. After some time, he'll share a thought or a memory. All cannot be spilled in a day, but is that bad, since marriage is for a lifetime?"

Was that my problem? I had been so eager to know everything of him all at once. One of the things I enjoyed most about books was getting a full story, beginning, middle, and end. Life so far with Evander felt as though I had gotten most of the beginning, barely any of the middle, and a slice of the end. I wanted more, but that was not very practical to ask of a person, was it?

"Thank you," I said.

Before she could reply, Damon came into the doorway beside me. He glanced between us both. "Oh dear, what are you two plotting?"

"Your sister is merely asking that we stay one more day," Silva answered.

"I have half a mind to do so. But then also do not wish to. I think it shall be the latter."

"How do I convince you otherwise?" I asked.

"You cannot. As you have your home, sister, we have ours, and I would like to get to it. Besides, I will not allow either of us to be used as shields for your little marital disputes." He gently pushed me out of the room. "Solve them without us. Good night!"

Just like that, the door was closed in my face.

"Damon!" Silva exclaimed from the other side of the door.

"What?" I heard him reply in the same tone.

Shaking my head, I walked down the hall, proud I had managed to escort Silva on my own without Eleanor or Emeline. Slowly, day by day, I was finding my path. Such would be the case with Evander. I was ordinarily patient—well, that was a lie. I was not a very patient person. As the second child and first daughter of the Du Bell family, I was not accustomed to waiting. The age distance between my sisters and me gave me priority in most things in our house. When I asked things of my sisters, they heard me. Even my brothers listened to a degree. So I was not used to Evander's hesitation. When it came to Evander, I wished him to tell me everything about everything. I wished for a detailed chronicle of his life, how he felt, what he saw, what he thought at that moment—everything. And for whatever reason, I truly believed that upon marrying him, it would occur instantly.

Which was foolish.

"Please . . . no . . ."

As I passed Verity's room, I paused, hearing the sound of sobbing. I stepped to the door and was preparing to knock when a hand caught my wrist. And there was Evander looking down at me, his expression strained and heavy.

"Waking her will make her feel worse," he whispered gently. "It's best to pretend you do not hear. No matter how hard that may be."

"But is she all right?" The sound of her crying clearly said no.

"It is a nightmare. She shall feel better with the sunlight."

"The sunlight? What do you . . ." I stopped as I felt the question forming once more. "All right."

He stared into my eyes but said nothing.

"Evander, my wrist."

"Forgive me," he muttered and released me.

We both stood there until the sound of Verity's whimpers was too much for him, and he turned to the door. "On second thought, I shall sit with her for a moment."

"Very well, good night."

"Aphrodite," he called before I could leave, and so I turned to him again. "Are you going to Emeline's room?"

"Yes." I nodded and then added, "Just for one more night."

"Should you not be tired, can you wait up for me? It will take only a few moments for Verity to request I leave her be." The corner of his lip turned up, but that smile did not reach his eyes at all.

"I shall wait at my nook."

"Will you be able to find it?" He now smiled.

"Do not underestimate me."

"Never! I shall see you soon."

I nodded. "You shall."

He offered me his lamp. I had been so entranced by his eyes that I had not even realized he had one in his hands.

Taking it, I waited for him to go in before I made my way. I was unsure what he wished to say, and I was now even more concerned about Verity.

"No," I muttered to myself. *No more questioning.* If he did not tell me, then I would not ask. *Could I really do that?* Knowing myself, the answer was a resounding no, but I would at least make some effort.

When I stepped into our bedroom again, it occurred to me how long it had been since I had been here. While three days was a relatively short time in the grand scheme, entering my own space felt . . . pleasant. Setting the lamp upon the side table, I took my seat at the window, where a blanket now rested. I glanced at the bed to see it was made. However, the pillow on his side was gone and was now also in my nook.

He could not have possibly slept in this space, could he?

That question, along with several others, spun in my mind until I heard the door open, and he entered.

"You do not need to stand."

"Force of habit," I muttered, taking a seat again.

He nodded, coming around the table to sit beside me. He adjusted his back against the wall, and he looked out at the dark forest before us.

"I—"

"The—"

We had both spoken at the same time and laughed.

"We are now awkward."

"I do not wish us to be," he replied.

"Neither do I." I wanted us to be as we were. "I will not ask anymore. Anything you wish to tell me or not tell me, it is fine."

He lifted my hand and kissed the back, much longer than necessary, but I did not mind his lips on me.

"Maybe I should open Pandora's box and sort it out with you," he muttered.

"What?" Damn, that was a question. "Whatever it is, you do not have to."

"Thank you for saying so, but that is not what you truly want, is it?" he asked, our hands interlocked. "I have always told myself I would give you the world should you ask, should it mean you would be with me. Now you are, and you ask me about things I do not wish to speak of for so many reasons."

"Then do not."

"That is not what you want," he said again.

"Marriage is not only about me."

"Nor can it be only about me."

I chuckled. "Have we switched roles? I am now seeking to stop you from sharing, and you have begun trying."

"I believe we have." He grinned. "I do not know where to begin because . . . because there is so much to say. So ask. Whatever it is you wish, ask, my love."

I thought to start with something that might not be so heavy.

"Verity, is she all right?"

"Yes and no. She has had nightmares for many years, but come morning, she will act as though nothing has occurred and say she is fine."

"Has she not seen a doctor?"

"It is mental." He hung his head, looking at my hands. "They have given her tonics to relax her, but after some time, they lose effect. Her trauma returns."

"Trauma?"

He inhaled deeply. "When I was sent away for school by my

father, she was a little older then Emeline is now and left under the charge of Datura, as Father couldn't have cared less for his daughter. Datura was cruel."

"She hurt her?"

"She called it reflection time," he sneered, shaking his head. "Whenever she believed Verity had misbehaved, she would lock her away in a wardrobe or cabinet. She would leave her for hours in absolute darkness. No water. No food. This tight, dark hell would be her punishment should Verity even laugh out loud. And if Verity called for help, Datura would leave her in there longer. My father, the bastard, never did a thing to help his daughter. She did this to her over and over again. Verity stopped eating and speaking. Personally, I believed the girl did not even dare to grow taller. And if that were not enough, Datura taunted her and blamed her for being punished."

"Dear God," I whispered, sitting closer to him. "How long did this go on?"

"Years. And it would have continued with no one the wiser had it not been for your mother."

"My mama?"

He nodded. "How she knew was beyond me. I have not the heart to ask. But one day, she arrived, not only with your father but also an old family friend who happened to be the local magistrate, pretending as though they had been invited for lunch. My father, never wishing to look the fool and believing Datura to be at fault for not remembering, agreed to the lunch. Your mother asked for Verity, as she had gifts. Datura had forgotten she'd locked Verity away. When she called for her at your mother's request, Datura lied and said Verity was sleeping. Your mother said she would visit her room. So Datura sought to have her brought, but your mother refused and insisted on walking to Verity's room. When she could not find Verity in her rooms, nor could anyone find her, your mother began to scream and weep, saying that they had killed her."

"Scream and weep?" I repeated, eyebrow raised. "My mama can scream. Weeping, however, is not her forte."

"That day, she did. Everyone's account of it was the same. She even collapsed in grief." A slight smile appeared on his face even as his eyes filled with tears he had not let fall. "And thank God she had, for the entire house was then alarmed. A whole search was mounted to find Verity and prove to your mother that Verity was not dead. After another hour, she was found in the cabinet. My father lied to the magistrate and said she must have locked herself inside while playing. That settled everyone but your mother, who started to wonder why Verity was so thin, and then she remarked about the scratches inside the cabinet. The more attention brought, the more everyone began to wonder, especially the magistrate. He asked to speak with Verity without my father or Datura in the room."

"Did Verity explain what had happened to her?"

"She was young and traumatized, so she could not speak well. Thus, the magistrate could do nothing, as there was not much evidence. Soon after that, there was much talk, regarding my father's anger. To prove it all untrue, he hired several nannies and a governess to take care of Verity and forbade Datura from ever interfering with her. Datura was not even allowed in the same wing of the house as Verity. And your mother showed up unannounced several more times just in case. Verity was never forced to submit to Datura again, and she grew happier and healthier. Still, the ordeal left her mentally scarred, especially when it becomes dark and she is alone."

Verity's pleas replayed in my head. "Datura is a vile creature."

"More than you know." He shook his head. "There are no portraits of my mother because Datura had them burned, by accident she claimed, though how all my mother's portraits ended up in one room that would later catch fire is beyond comprehension or reason. All that remained of my mother was a sketch. With that sketch I had many artists attempt to create new work. But none could truly capture her except Sir Cowles. Sadly, he passed before he could paint more of her. I felt it a sort of curse. Though I am grateful to, at least, have something. For Verity's sake as well."

"Your father allowed all of this to occur?" That was the most perplexing piece of all of this. Was this not his family? His children? Was it not his duty to protect them at the very least?

"My father cared not," he replied bitterly. "The only important thing in his life was himself. He wished to have the butcher's daughter, and so he had her. He wished to marry the very best noble lady of society, thus, he did. He refused moderation or even decency, deceiving my mother into marrying him with no remorse or care. Only exposing the truth to her after he had gotten what he wanted—a legitimate heir. Once he had that, he cared not where she was, what she did, or even if she lived or died. There were days I believed he was pleased she was dead, as he no longer had to keep up with the pretense of their lives together. Do you wish to know what he said the day we returned from a trip to London, after my mother had just passed? Verity not even a week old and brought to him for the first time?"

I did not know that I did, as I was sure my heart would ache more for him. "What?" I asked.

"'So much effort . . . for a girl.'" He clenched his teeth tightly. "Those were his first words to Verity, and then he never paid any mind to her. His attention to me was solely for the running of the estate, maintaining our good name—the name he'd dragged through the mud, dumped in my lap, and wished me to maintain. He cared for no one, Aphrodite. There was no love in this house. It was cold and cruel and harsh till the day he died. Sometimes, even to this day, I feel a chill here. I cannot explain it any more than this. And I feel mortified speaking of it."

I kissed his knuckles, holding on tightly. "I do not mean to force you to relive such agonizing memories. I was merely seeking to understand you better, and now I do. You need not say any more. Forgive me for pushing you so. You are right. I am ignorant of such hardships."

"Do not apologize for that ignorance, it is one of my favorite qualities in you." He chuckled, resting his forehead on mine. "I fell in love with you, but I also love your family. I wish for the same for myself—for us."

"So, six children then?"

"I prefer eight," he replied.

"That is far too many!"

"The more, the merrier. I wish Everely to be louder than Belclere Castle, with siblings who laugh, tease, and fight but deep down truly love one another."

"I promise you that it is not advisable. My mama made it look simple, but I am not her, and such a litter would drive you mad."

"You have whipped the house into order, and I believe you will do the same with our children. However, if you insist, we may settle—you'll have six."

"With Emeline, that is seven, which is barely a concession!"

He laughed. "Yes, but barely a concession is better than no concession at all, so shall we begin?"

He kissed my lips, and it felt as though ages had gone by since I had kissed him. I wrapped my arm around his shoulder. Soon I found myself drawn into his lap.

"Wait," I said as I felt him lift my skirt. "I cannot stay the night."

"Why ever not? Have we not reconciled?"

"We have. But I promised Emeline I would read to her."

"It is late. She may very well be asleep," he replied, kissing my neck.

"She will still be awake. I have noticed she does not sleep well until she hears a story. Mrs. Watson used to do it for her."

He paused at the mention of Mrs. Watson's name, then lifted his head. "I dismissed her because—"

"I know," I replied, cupping his face. "Emeline told me."

"She . . . she did not harm Emeline in any other way, correct?" A deep frown hung upon his lips. "Please tell me I did not also ignore any further insult to or abuse of her?"

With the context of what had occurred to Verity and how his father had done nothing, I understood what he meant by *not also*. He wished not to be like his father.

"No, not that I can see," I said, brushing his face. "Mrs. Watson took good care of her, all other things considered."

He exhaled a breath of relief and rested his head on me. He said nothing more, and I would not push. This was fine. Holding him, being near him, was perfect.

"I love you, Evander," I whispered.

"And I you."

"Thus, now there is true love in Everely. We brought it."

"That we very much did." He smiled, and my heart shook.

27

Aphrodite

"You know," Verity suddenly said as we walked into town with Emeline and Eleanor.

"I know what?" I asked.

"About my nightmares," she said, holding my arm. "I was sure your brother would have said something before he left, or you might have heard me over the last two days."

"It was the latter. My brother said nothing to me, nor did Silva," I replied softly.

Her face bunched bitterly. "Your family is kind. That is why remaining in your home any longer was not possible. I could see how concerned they were for me, how much effort they made on my behalf. It grew to be . . . too much."

She was pained. I could see it in her eyes; she looked as though she were fighting back tears.

"I shall not ask you about anything you do not wish to speak of," I replied, nodding to the tenants in town as we walked by.

Her grip on my arm tightened. "Thank you."

"Not at all." I had learned my lesson. I should have learned it before, when he had told me the truth of his brother's misdeeds. I would not force either of them. Instead, I would wait for them to share whenever they were ready.

"Good mornin', Your Grace," Mrs. Stoneshire, the keeper of the Three Boar Bar & Inn, called to me as she swept over the front door.

"Good morning, Rosemary." I waved to her. "Fully booked?"

"Not quite, just a load of mornin' drinkers." She nodded back inside. "Hopin' for more people to come through."

"They shall. I am sure of it."

"Good mornin', Your Grace. Can I offer you any treats today?" Mr. Lupton, the oldest baker in town, said from outside his shop as we walked by.

"Please, do not tempt me, Mr. Lupton. I ate far too many last time!"

"That is exactly why I am asking again!" He roared with laughter.

I grinned, shaking my head. "I shall refrain until I have walked off the rest."

"Nonsense, Your Grace. You are beautiful as always. The duke is a very lucky man."

"I shall let him know you said so!" I smiled and waved.

"How is it you know so many people?" Verity asked. "I have lived here all my life, and I have never spoken to the baker or innkeeper."

"That might be the reason you do not know them." I giggled, looking at her. "After all, an introduction is necessary to be familiar."

"I am in no need of lodging, as my home is here, nor treats, as there is a baker at home. Since you now live in that home, neither should you need such things, so how is it that you know them?"

"When I was a child, my papa made it a point of duty to take my brother with him to walk the local town, as he would one day be the landlord and wished the people to know him and think well of him. I did not understand why until my mother brought me along, and I saw how everyone treated us—like we were family."

"That is most unconventional, especially for the marchioness. I always believed her to be a lady of the strictest order."

"She is." I laughed, as I could very well attest to it. "And many years prior, she may have believed that. However, that changed with the French."

"The French?"

I leaned closer, whispering in her ear. "Their revolt."

Her eyes widened. "Their revolution?"

I nodded, making sure no one could hear us. "My governess told me that there was great fear amongst all the nobles during that time. People felt the discontent would arise here. While, of course, nothing did, the fear impacted my parents. My father had been known throughout the county already. He began to exert himself more, listen more, speak to them as though they were all of the greatest importance. And years of that yielded fruitful results. My sisters and I had more freedom at Belclere Castle. We could walk the streets and talk amongst our neighbors. And they felt very attached to us Du Bell ladies. Of course, my mama made sure to remind us of who we are and our station in life. But we enjoyed it, though we were never without chaperones."

"So, in part, it is a safety measure and also a way to allow us ladies greater freedom?"

"Yes, but—"

"Little miss!"

My head snapped up to Eleanor, who stood beside Emeline, who had fallen into the dirt. I rushed to her.

"Emeline, sweetheart, are you all right?" I asked, lifting her as her lip quivered. "Are you hurt?"

She shook her head no, but her face still turned red as she tried to clean her hands. I bent down and cleaned off her dress.

"It is all right, my dear, so long as you are uninjured," I said.

"And all together," said a voice from behind me.

I had never seen this man with light-brown hair and squared shoulders, who was quite handsome and tall. In his hand was Emeline's hat. He held it out to me.

"Pardon me, Your Grace. She dropped this."

"Thank you." I nodded as Eleanor took the hat from him. "Mr. . . ."

"Topwells."

He was not the one to answer, but when I glanced back to Verity, she was glaring with an intensity that would put Evander to shame.

Topwells? Where had I heard that surname?

"Verity. You are lovely as always. How is Evander? He has not answered any of my many letters. I am hurt."

My eyes widened as I saw the carriage of the dowager farther behind him and heard Datura calling out to him. My heart began to race.

He smiled. "Your Grace, it is a shame that we meet like this. I have heard much of you from my mother. You are truly as beautiful as everyone says. Quite surprising, as gossip is never completely honest."

"Fitzwilliam?" I said.

"Ah, then Evander has spoken of me to you? How grand. I did not think he would do so, as he is known to be taciturn."

"I beg your pardon, Mr. Topwells. My husband is the kindest of men, truly the best among them." I smiled and carefully put my hand on top of Emeline's head, bringing her closer to me. But I should not have, as his eyes shifted down to the girl.

"I see. Well, pardon me then, and you be careful, little miss.

You are very precious." He smiled down at her, but she held on to my dress. He waved to Emeline before turning to walk freely, as if Evander were not seeking to hunt him down.

"Fitzwilliam?"

The soft bell-like voice belonged to a beautiful young woman dressed in the finest blue silk, her brunette hair in a single side braid underneath her hat, her face white, and her lips bright pink. She wore a set of pearls around her neck, and in her arms carried a small pug dog.

"My dear, are you finished?" Fitzwilliam smiled at the woman.

She sighed heavily. "Yes, I could not find much, but I am very pleasantly surprised at the standard of the town shops. It is better than I assumed."

From the corner of my eye, I noticed her purchases being taken to the dowager's carriage.

"Did I not tell you Everely was unmatched, my dear? Look, even the duchess is found here." Fitzwilliam snickered and brought her forward. "Your Grace, allow me to introduce my wife, Miss Marcella Wildingham—pardon me, I am not yet used to it, I mean Mrs. Marcella Topwells now."

"Your Grace?" the girl gasped and then curtsied before me. "Forgive me, for I did not expect to see you, nor did I see a carriage."

The girl was a little young to be a wife, younger than Hathor, and dare I say, perhaps even closer to Devana's age.

"I thought it better to walk," I finally managed.

"A walk? You jest, but what of your clothing?" She laughed and looked down at my hem, but she contained herself. "No matter, I am sure you have plenty. It is truly an honor to meet you. We never crossed paths while you were in London for the season."

I tried to contain my shock. "You were out this season as well?"

"I . . ."

"Verity, you are awfully quiet," Fitzwilliam interrupted, shifting our attention to Verity, who stood still just beside me. "Marcella, this is Lady Verity, the duke's younger sister."

"Hello, my lady." Marcella happily curtsied once more.

"Hello, Mrs. Topwells. We ought not to keep you, as I see the dowager is waiting for you, Fitzwilliam." Verity spoke softly next to me. "One cannot keep the dowager waiting."

"You are correct. I shall see you, Lady Everely, Lady Verity." He tilted his head to us both before leading his wife away.

"How did this happen?" Verity whispered as we watched him go. "The Wildingham family is one of the wealthiest in the land. Mr. Wildingham has only one daughter, Marcella, and she is not yet sixteen."

Immediately, the words of the great Roman Stoic philosopher Seneca the Younger came to mind. *The tempest threatens before it comes; houses creak before they fall.*

Evander

"I should have known!"

The signs were there. What had brought Fitzwilliam to London at the same time as me when he knew I searched for him? How had his mother been able to so finely decorate herself in jewels and the like? The allowance I provided her was only to keep her from utter destitution, not enough for diamond-encrusted canes or strings of pearls. The purchase of a home should also have been out of the question, yet she had managed it. I assumed it had been from funds she'd succeeded in stealing away from my father over their years together. The greatest sign of all should have been her confidence in returning to Everely. I dismissed it because Datura had always been brazen.

Now I was torn between screaming and falling silent. For how could one man and his mother be so difficult to bring to justice?

"I do not know this Wildingham family. I do not wish to press, but is it so severe? Obviously, beyond the poor girl's age, though it is not all that uncommon." Aphrodite asked quietly as I paced before her in the drawing room.

Verity and Emeline had gone to change while Aphrodite explained what had occurred in town. I could tell she was trying to be patient because she was sitting awfully still, the way she had whenever her mama and papa were discussing something and she was forced to be a good young lady.

I was not her mama or papa.

"Mr. Unwin Wildingham is a powerful and very wealthy landowner in the county, part of the gentry. Once hailed to be the very best of marksmen in all the county. He had two children, but his son died young along with his wife, leaving only him and his daughter, Marcella. She is to inherit his home, along with a substantial dowry. That is not the worst of it. The rest of the estate and fortunes will go to Mr. Wildingham's cousin, who happens to be Sir Zachary Dennison-Whit."

"Is that not . . ."

"The county's MP, who is also the rumored right hand of the prime minister? Yes, my love, it is. Fitzwilliam disappeared and has turned up with a very powerful backer. I doubt I will be able to simply capture him and throw him in prison now, even with the evidence I have collected. The local magistrate is also friends with the Wildinghams."

"But you are the duke. Surely, you are of greater importance?"

"Yes, surely. Even still, it will take much stronger evidence than what I have to bring him down as his fate is now intertwined with the Wildinghams', and they will fight before allowing such embarrassment to their name."

"That very well may be true, but you must not be silent. My papa told me that an evildoer who does not repent only continues to do more evil. You must show the magistrate everything you have, your witness also."

I frowned, not sure. "I put so much effort into gathering everything to crush Fitzwilliam with a single blow, especially after his letter. Knowing that I have been chasing what I believed to be a shadow, only to learn now that he was sipping tea with the Wildinghams on their estate, is maddening."

"Letter?"

"He wrote to me, telling me he was returning, but it felt like a threat. Thus, I increased the checks and guards around the estate. That is also why I wished you not to go into town. I believed him brutish and determined to strike like a beast in the night. This, however, is much different, as he has come pretending to be a gentleman. The disgrace of it all."

"What shall you do now?" she asked softly.

"All my methods to capture him have been disasters, botched one way or another. I am at a total loss. I believe I shall take my wife's advice," I replied, going over to her, kissing her cheek. "I will go to the magistrate, though I do not know what good it will do."

She smiled, glancing up at me. "Let us believe justice will come of it."

Fitzwilliam had returned to Everely. I was sure there was to be no good in this. None at all.

Knock. Knock.

"Enter," I said. The door opened to reveal her lady's maid.

"Your Grace, you have a letter."

"From whom?" Aphrodite asked.

"Mrs. Marcella Topwells," she answered before quickly excusing herself.

I scoffed, shaking my head. Everely was not big enough for both them and us.

"What does she say?" I asked, seeking to control my anger.

Aphrodite handed me the letter so I might read it for myself.

> *To Her Grace, the Duchess of Everely,*
>
> *I beg your forgiveness for our introduction this morning. I was quite shocked to see you in town. I had hoped to meet you, but thought it would be over a cup of tea, not at the side of the road. Whatever I said arose from pure nerves. I write this letter in a pleading request of another audience with you, should you find me acceptable. I shall wait eagerly for your reply. I pray this letter finds you in as good health as I am at present.*
>
> *Yours sincerely,*
> *Mrs. Marcella Topwells*

"I shall invite her tomorrow," Aphrodite said.

"I do not wish them here."

"Then she shall come alone."

"Aphrodite—"

"I am quite aware you wish me to stay out of this. But, Evander, if you saw me struggling, would you allow me to handle it alone? We are to depend on each other, are we not?

Let me invite the girl—the young woman—to see what I can learn from her so we may discern, at least, whether she knows the truth of her husband and how she became married to Fitz-william. You said you have lost time and time again using brute force to keep them away. Let us try another strategy. Let me help you."

Depending on another was not a strength of mine. For so long, it had been only me fighting this battle. All my life, it was me against them all, and it had made me weary.

"Evander," she said, rising and holding the side of my face to bring it closer to hers. "It is not just you any longer. It is *us*. Your glory is my glory. Your harm is my harm. If you are in a fight, I am in a fight. There is no way to spare me from it."

I knew that. Which is why her father had wished for me to handle this before she married me. But I was so glad she had fought for me anyway.

"I do not deserve you," I said, placing my hands upon her waist. "Truly, you are a miracle to me."

"So, it is a yes to tea with Mrs. Topwells?"

I sighed. "Fine, invite her."

Dear God, let it not be a mistake.

28

Aphrodite

I'd believed myself to be wise, or at the very least mature enough, to be a wife at sixteen. I was greatly displeased my mama refused to allow me to marry when I was that age. Her reasoning was she did not believe a girl of sixteen was fit to wed yet. The difference between sixteen and eighteen seemed illogical to me. If I had a suitor already, why wait? She had refused to humor my questions and said I would not understand until later. Thus, I was forced to wait silently.

But now later had come. As I sat across from the young Mrs. Marcella Topwells, I was aghast at how childish she seemed. I did not wish to believe I had looked so immature at the same age, but the way she giggled, kicked her feet slightly, ate her cake with a twirl of her spoon, and, most importantly, the way she spoke was all evidence to me why Mama believed no girl was fit to marry at fifteen, nor sixteen for that matter.

She was a child.

"All my cousins shall be most jealous that I was given an audience with you, Your Grace." She giggled once again. "We have all heard the Du Bell ladies are the finest and most amiable of the ton. And how even the queen holds you all to such high esteem. Gwendolyn and Minerva sought desperately to be invited to your mama's ball earlier this season. But the invitations were of the greatest difficulty to secure. They even begged Mr. Winchester."

"Prime Minister Winchester?" I asked, stirring my tea.

She nodded eagerly. "Yes. He and my uncle were discussing something or other around the same time, so all my cousins tried, not just Gwendolyn and Minerva, though they waited at the door."

"How many cousins do you have?" I asked.

"Seven—six girls and one boy. My uncle obviously seeks another boy for good measure. But my aunt is quite advanced in age for that and always tells him he must learn to accept what is before him." She giggled once more.

She spoke of her family and personal matters so openly that I was quite shocked.

"So you spend much time with your uncle Sir Zachary Dennison-Whit, I understand?"

She nodded, sitting up in her seat. "Yes, Your Grace. As I am now an only child, and my father is more advanced in age. My father thought it best for me to be amongst female company. It was much more female company than I expected, as the house is quite full. I am most pleased to be married now and a mistress of my own."

Now we had reached the conversation I truly desired to have.

"And how did such a thing occur?" I asked, gently lifting my teacup to my lips.

"It was destiny." She beamed, grinning from ear to ear. "I was going to London after visiting my father when my carriage got caught in a rut. It was only my maid and me and, of course, the driver. The sunlight was fading, and it began to pour. I feared we might have to send the driver up ahead or, worse, walk. That was when suddenly the dowager's carriage arrived and there was Fitzwilliam. He dashed to my rescue, removed his coat, and held it over my head, bringing me to shelter within theirs. During the ride, I was able to speak with him."

Damn the roads and the weather this season.

"The very next day, he arrived with my carriage and inquired as to the condition of my health. All my cousins were quite jealous, as he is most handsome, is he not?" she asked.

I smiled and nodded.

"My aunt sought to push Gwendolyn on him, but he had no interest in her. I found him to be smiling at me. My heart all but leapt from my chest."

There was something amiss in this tale, not that I believed her to be deceitful. I was confused as to why the dowager would have been returning to London when she lived there? From what I had heard of her, she never left London, ever, as she had no other place to go.

"He wrote me a letter, seeking forgiveness, as he felt quite transfixed by my beauty and believed there was no chance for him in my eyes, since he was older. It was the sweetest of letters."

"What did your aunt say?"

"She was displeased, as my cousins had not received suitors." She giggled and took another bite. "She worries they never will."

"Yes, all mothers worry so. But what did she say to you upon receiving such a letter? Did she not read it?"

She tilted her head to the side. "Read it? It is my letter. Why would she read it?"

"Did you not have your letters read by a chaperone or one with you when you were in the company of men?"

"No. I do have my maid, though." She paused then added,

"And Fitzwilliam is a true gentleman, always seeking to take care of me."

"Quite well, then. And now you are married to him."

"At first, my papa would not accept, believing me to be too young. It nearly broke my heart, and Fitzwilliam did not wish to disrupt our family. He even said we should part for the sake of peace. But I believe love needs to be fought for, so I wrote to my papa and my uncle and left with him."

I coughed, nearly choking upon my tea. "You left with him? As in eloped?"

Again, she giggled. "Almost, but my uncle retrieved us. By then I had already given myself to him so uncle sought for it to be done. It feels very much like a dream. It happened so quickly, and I am now the first married of my cousins. They are all jealous—"

"And you are pleased?"

She nodded. "Quite so."

"How much do you know of Fitzwilliam?" I asked.

Her demeanor changed. She looked around the room quickly and then back to me. Leaning forward, she whispered, "I know the truth."

"The truth?" I repeated.

"Many believe him to be the dowager's first son from a previous marriage, but the truth is he is the former duke's son. And his mother was the true love of the former duke, but they could not be together. Thus, he and his mother were banished by the new duke." She sighed heavily, glancing down at her cake.

"You believe my husband to be so petty and cruel?" I asked angrily.

Her eyes widened. "Forgive me, for I know this is now your

family as well, and I do not want to upset the current duke with such information. I simply wish to end the rift between the two of them so that we could be one family."

Naïve.

It was the kindest word I could use for her. The more I looked upon her, the angrier I became. The girl seemed to have been left to the winds and rains of heaven with no guidance from anyone! Fed lies as truth and tricks as love. This was all horrid, and she did not realize any of it. Instead, she saw herself as quite clever.

Was I to tell her the truth and shatter this fantasy that was in her mind? Or was I to pretend and smile, not revealing to her that the worst type of fiend had derailed her life? I tried to imagine it, saying, *He does not love you; he is using you.* I was sure of it, even without the history of Evander or Emeline's mother. Fitzwilliam was a despicable bastard!

"Your Grace?" she asked as I had not spoken in some time. "What do you think of it?"

"Think of what?"

"Mending the bond between our husbands."

I thought it impossible. "Let us first focus on our bond. My mama says where women go, men follow."

"A friendship with you, Your Grace? Gwendolyn and Minerva will never believe it. I must write to them. It is such an honor. Can I ask if you have thought about having a ball? I sought to have one myself, but I do not know much of anyone. And obviously, Everely is much grander. I have heard you are not yet acquainted with much of the local gentry and have only been to town and met the lower folk."

"Yes, as is customary, I thought to wait until the London season was over," I replied.

"Your Grace, it is quite unfair for the locals who cannot manage such a trip to London. The town balls are never as magnificent, and many are left with only stories of how delightful the season is elsewhere. You could very well make Everely the new center of social society."

"I shall think on it."

I offered more sweets, which she happily accepted. I hoped Evander was having greater luck exposing Fitzwilliam for who he truly was.

Evander

I knew visiting the magistrate's office would be of little use, but I had not believed it would be so obviously discouraging and enraging. The moment I entered, I was met not by the magistrate but by the bastard swine himself, sitting upon a chair, tea in hand as if he were not a criminal of the highest of order.

"If it is not the duke in all his glory," the devil said, smiling from ear to ear.

In anger, I stood still, unable to move or speak for fear I would strike him. I glanced around the office to see he was the only person in the rooms.

"If you are seeking the magistrate, he will return momentarily. We were having a grand conversation before he stepped out. Between you and me, I believe he has greater aspirations in life."

I clenched my fist and turned from him.

"Well, little brother—"

"You have no brother in me," I sneered, nearly spitting. "And you may think you have fashioned for yourself a very good safety net, but believe me, I will not rest until you are held accountable for your misdeeds."

"Misdeeds?" He dared laugh at me. "I know of no such thing!"

With the mocking look on his face, I could not stop myself from grabbing his coat, wishing to throw him across the room. "That girl . . . Emma, even as you tricked and abandoned her to misery, even as she was dying, her last thoughts and desires were of you. She wept for you. You proved to be nothing but a monster, and still, that poor one wished to hold on to the lies you fed her in any way possible till the end."

"Poor one? Lies? I told her she would be a duchess and live in a grand estate. Was she not? Any misery was by her own foolish—"

My fist collided with his face once and then a second time, sending him to the ground. "You and your mother are exactly the same! Vile, gluttonous pigs, using whomever you please as if they were mere ladders for your lives!"

He wiped the blood from his nose. "Us, gluttonous? As if you do not know your own disgusting greed! You took everything, threw us to the wolves, and now you lament the way in which we survive?"

"I took what was mine *by right!*"

"I am the first—"

"*You are a bastard!* The son of a butcher's daughter! You have no right to Everely. You have no right to the nobility! We will not have you. The lot you were given was better than you deserved!"

"Be damned!" he hollered, throwing his fist toward me.

I caught the punch. "Do not mistake me for the younger and smaller one now, Fitzwilliam."

He replied by grabbing the teapot and throwing it at my

head. When his hand reached around my neck, I took a shard of the broken teapot and slashed it across his cheek, throwing him off me.

The door burst open and the magistrate yelled, "What in God's name!" He saw our fists raised and our clothes bloodied. "Lord Everely?"

"Forgive me, sir, for intruding. I came to divulge information of the highest importance. But I was greatly put off by your guest. I must go. Please feel free to send me the bill for any and all damage," I grumbled as I pushed past Fitzwilliam toward the door.

"Everything you took from me, I shall see it returned," Fitzwilliam snapped.

"Then you shall have nothing as I remind you once more that you were given nothing," I said and walked into the hall in which three men, two of them witnesses of the scuffle, stood waiting with eyes wide. The third, however, was an unexpected face, coming down the stairs with a bag in hand—Dr. Darrington.

"You will need to wrap that hand, Your Grace," he said, eyeing my excruciating red knuckles.

I hid it behind my back and looked at the two men, the first, Mr. Danvers, the witness to the duel I'd had with Emma's father, and the second, Mr. Lyndon, a lawyer who could attest to seeing Fitzwilliam claim to be me. "I believe it best we come another time. I thank you for your patience, gentlemen."

"It is best to have all this put to rest, once and for all, Your Grace," Mr. Danvers said as he placed his hand on my shoulder.

"Should you need us again, we shall be here. You need not worry. We stand with you, Your Grace," Mr. Lyndon said.

"Thank you. Good day to you all," I said. They followed the

butler toward the door, leaving me with the doctor, who still stood waiting. "Yes?"

"You are in need of treatment. Where else were you struck?"

"I am quite fine, thank you," I said.

"Doctor!" a maid at the door called for him. "Mr. Topwells is in need of your help once you have seen to the duke."

"I am fine. Good day," I snapped, showing myself out.

I did not dare look at anyone as I stepped into my carriage, grateful I'd thought to bring it instead of a horse.

"To the house," I spat out. Inside, I reached under my coat to feel the wound at my side on my rib.

Inhaling through my nose, I closed my eyes, wishing to calm myself. I knew Fitzwilliam was not capable of remorse, but now that I had seen him, it was even clearer that he had not returned only to provoke me, he still truly believed himself to be the rightful owner of Everely and my title. The man had secured himself a rich wife, and still . . . *still*, he desired more. He desired what was mine.

Curse him.

Damn him.

To eternal fire with him.

29

Aphrodite

I had been waiting for his return, and when he did, tattered and bruised, I found myself in shock. Had he gone for a boxing match or had he gone to see a magistrate? He glanced at me, defeated, and said not a word as he walked up the stairs.

"Eleanor, have a maid fetch water, cloth, and brandy while you call for the doctor," I said, grabbing my skirt as I went up the stairs behind him.

I did not rush him. I merely followed until we had reached the safety and privacy of our rooms. Still, he said nothing, but walked to the chair by the fireplace, sat down, and closed his eyes. I placed my hand gently on his face, and he winced.

"What on earth happened to you?"

"Fitzwilliam was there and . . . and we reacted as we often have when we are in the same room—in violence. There can be no other way. He is my enemy, and I am his."

Knock. Knock.

"Enter," I said. The maid had brought what I had asked. "Set it beside me." I waited for her to leave before I handed him a glass of brandy.

"How do you know I seek brandy?"

"You and Damon are alike in that regard," I replied.

"If only he were my blood instead of Fitzwilliam."

"If that were the case, you would be my brother and not my

husband, and that would be a great loss to me," I said, gently cleaning off his face.

He laughed but then stopped, wincing and grabbing his side.

"What is it?"

"Nothing," he lied.

"Fine, if you choose not to let me see, then you must be truthful with the doctor."

"You called for a doctor?" he asked.

"You are injured!"

"Barely."

"Evander, there is blood on your clothes. Your hand is now swollen, and you are wincing at a mere touch. That is not barely. That is serious."

"My love, it is—"

"No." I held my hand up to him. "When I was fifteen, I saw a man get beaten on the side of the road. Then later heard he had jested about how he was made of 'strong stuff' and would not seek treatment, that he was fine. The next day, he died."

He laughed once more. "I truly do not believe it to be that severe, my love."

"You are not a doctor, and I trust only the advice of medical professionals for health. The doctor will see you, and you will allow yourself to be seen. In fact, was it not refusing to get treatment before that led to you getting a fever? Why must you refuse to learn from your mistakes—"

"I yield!" He raised his hand and then winced.

"Good."

"For a moment there, you sounded like your mama."

I turned my eyes on him in horror, and he chuckled at me. "Do not tease me!"

"I was not teasing. You truly did."

I reached to take the glass from him, and he held it from me, laughing despite his pain. "You have clearly had too much."

He kissed the side of my cheek. "Not at all."

We locked eyes. "Are we still speaking of the brandy?"

He shook his head. "No."

He leaned forward to kiss me when there was another knock at the door. "Damn," he muttered.

"Enter," I said, standing taller as Eleanor came in.

"Your Graces, the doctor is here."

"Already?" I was amazed.

"Yes, Your Grace, he was already on his way. Mr. Wallace said he has treated His Grace before."

"Who?" Evander asked. "Dr. Cunningham?"

"No, Your Grace, a Dr. Darrington?"

Evander made a face but nodded. "Bring him in."

I was quite stunned by the youth of the man who entered our rooms. He glanced at me and tipped his head. "Your Grace."

"You've treated him before?" I asked.

"I told you I am fine," Evander said. "Yet you followed me here?"

"You said the same thing in London, and I figured someone would call tonight if not in the morning," he replied.

"I do have another doctor—"

"Please check him carefully, Dr. Darrington." I smiled and left the room.

Once outside, I saw Verity farther down the hall, checking around the corner as though she were spying.

"Verity? What are you doing?"

"Are my eyes deceiving me, or is Dr. Darrington here?" she asked.

"Yes, he is."

"Truly, he is here?"

"Yes," I repeated, not sure why she seemed so interested.

She exhaled, then turned around and left, muttering to herself.

Strange.

"Your Grace?"

"Yes." I turned to Eleanor.

"Nanny Phillipa shall be here by nightfall."

"Oh, finally."

Phillipa had been my sister's nanny. I had written to my mother, asking for her help in securing her services, as I could not bring myself to trust anyone else with Emeline, nor did I want anyone who would threaten what I was building with her.

"Is Emeline napping?" I asked.

"Yes, Your Grace, I checked in on her earlier."

"Thank you. I will go sit with her and explain about Nanny Phillipa." I didn't want her to think I had passed her off. "How are we with the additions to the staff?"

"So far, all is well, but it will take more time, Your Grace."

"Of course," I replied as we walked. I was pleased to realize I was finally getting more familiar with where I was going in the house. "How is the talk of late?"

"Much improved, Your Grace."

"Well, we should be prepared for more."

I did not know the details of Evander's actions, but I was sure the town would be abuzz when they heard that their duke had fought a local man like a ruffian. Part of me had wished to lecture him on his behavior, as I was working so hard to improve our reputation, but upon seeing how dejected he looked, I could not bring myself to do so.

"That is all for now," I said to Eleanor before entering Emeline's room.

Once inside, I leaned against the door. It was always one thing or another now. Nothing was simple, despite all my efforts. Though I was not sinking from the weight of it, the burden of Evander's house and this family was heavy. Which made me think of Marcella and what it would have been like had I been placed in this role at sixteen. Surely, it would have broken me. I worried about her.

"Your Grace?"

Opening my eyes, I looked to see Emeline sitting up in bed, rubbing her head. Going to her, I placed my hand on her face. "Did I wake you?"

She shook her head.

"Well, I am glad you are awake. I wished to tell you of your new nanny."

She froze, looking at me.

"Do not worry, she is very nice. Well, she is nice *and* a bit strict. My sister Abena loved her greatly. And she is only to help when I am not able to spend time with you. But I will be with you as much as I can."

"What about Mrs. Watson?" she asked.

"Your papa is unhappy with her. And you do not wish him to be unhappy, right?"

She pouted but shook her head.

"If you dislike your new nanny, I will find a new one."

"Yes, Your Grace."

"Good, then let us prepare for her and have time in the garden. We'll eat whatever you like for dinner."

She nodded, and I lifted her from the bed, hugging her tightly, and when she hugged me back, my heart skipped.

I had become very much attached to this one.

It surprised me.

Evander

It had been one nightmare of a day, and I simply wished for it to be over. Which I thought had been the case when Aphrodite and I had gone to bed, but when I awoke she was not beside me any longer. I waited in bed, but when she did not return after ten minutes, I arose, wearing my nightshirt to search for her. She was not in Emeline's room, the drawing room, or the kitchen. Panic began to rise until I saw the light by the patio.

Gravitating to it as if I were a moth, I found her, sitting at the table with a bottle of port beside her and a piece of cake on a plate in her hand. With her curly hair down and wearing her dressing gown, she sat in the garden.

"At times like this you make me wish I were an artist."

Her head spun around to me, and seeing the spoon in her mouth and how . . . shocked she was at being caught, I could not help but laugh.

"You are awake?" she asked.

"As are you," I said and took a seat beside her. "What keeps you from my bed tonight? Port and cake?"

"Forgive me. It is very good."

"I must judge for myself," I replied, parting my mouth for her to feed me.

She gave me a look, but I remained, waiting. So, she lifted the cake, taking a small portion of it with her spoon before feeding it to me.

I chewed slowly, observing the beauty that was she. How could such a fine woman exist—and not only exist, but be mine and mine alone?

"You were truly and aptly named," I whispered.

"Oh, please do not," she begged as she took another bite.

"I have never understood why it displeases you to be called what you are—a true beauty. Is that not what a woman desires to be?"

"It is, and I am not displeased with it. More . . ." She paused to think. "Fearful."

"Fearful of being beautiful?"

"Fearful that it is *all* that I am," she replied. "If my only claim to glory be my beauty, what am I when it fades? I am no goddess and will not remain young forever."

"I am certain you shall be divine at any age, and I the luckiest of all men."

She giggled, glancing at me, eyebrow raised. "Are you not biased?"

"Very much so, but my opinion as your husband ought to be worth the most, correct?"

She was silent and ate another bite of cake. She was teasing me, and so I leaned closer to her, my nose nearly touching her cheek.

"Correct?"

She did her best not to laugh and shrugged. So I took her cake.

"Hey!"

"What is the point of filling your mouth with sweetness if you will not speak sweetly?" I asked. She glared, and I glowered back. "If you wish, we may remain like this till sunup."

She laughed. "Fine. Yes, as my husband, your opinion matters the most."

"I am no longer satisfied, as now I believe you said it for the cake."

She rolled her eyes and leaned over to place her lips on mine. Indeed, heaven was here.

"Truly, you matter the most, my love. The very most," she whispered. No other woman on earth could make my heart skip as she did. But for her, I would commit blasphemy and erect statues in her honor to give praise.

"Explain why we are on the patio instead of in our rooms so I may have you there?" I asked, my forehead on hers.

"I needed to think, so it is good we are on the patio, as you have a tendency to distract me."

"I shall take that as a compliment and remind you later. For now, share with me your thoughts."

She took her cake and set it to the side. "There is so much to take in. Every day there is something to do, which is quite odd to me, for I never thought this life, tending to house and family, would be so taxing."

"If it is too much, we may—"

"It is not," she replied quickly, holding my hand. "It is not too much for me. Nevertheless, at this moment, I wished to breathe and reflect. Do not think I am unhappy, for I am greatly pleased with Everely and you—though you try me. Especially when you cannot control your anger and fight within the magistrate's office, leaving everyone with enough gossip for the next few days if not weeks."

I sheepishly smiled. I was a duke. I ought to have been better. My smile faded the more I thought of it. "Forgive me. I lose myself when I see Datura or Fitzwilliam, which is strange because I quite like my youngest brother."

"Gabrien, right?"

I nodded. "Yes. He avoids conflict like the plague and comes here only when he must. Even now he is seeking to go on tour after he finishes at Eton."

"I am glad you at least have one brother you like," she said, glancing up at the stars. "I am trying to think of a way this can end with Fitzwilliam, but I see no solutions, only more conflict. And the more conflict, the worse your name will be attacked."

"And the worse my name, the worse yours?"

"It is *our* name."

"Very true."

"I have come up with one possibility," she said as she handed me her port. If she was giving me a drink, I was most likely going to need it.

"What is it?"

"A ball."

I chuckled. "A ball?"

"Yes. Currently, everyone is no doubt talking of you attacking a member of society like a madman—"

"He attacked me as well."

"He is not a duke. Your actions are automatically judged more harshly because you are *supposed* to be better."

"I feel as though I am being lectured."

"You are, but you sought me out, remember?"

"So, had I not come, you would not have said anything?"

"I would have told you we were having a ball but not the reason why," she replied. She took the bottle of port from me and drank straight from it, which was quite a sight. "I am a bit foxed now, so I shall simply admit it."

I grinned. "Very well, to your ball then."

"Mr. and Mrs. Topwells must be invited."

"Aphrodite! I do not want him here."

"We will have the festivities outside and men throughout the house to keep watch."

"It is not the point. Everely—"

"Is yours," she said sternly. "And he is in the wrong, but he is also being welcomed into the gentry by others. Should you keep him away, it will cast you in a bad light. His wife believes you to be the villain. Half the town believes you are getting vengeance on behalf of your mother, and that is why you keep Datura at bay—truth or not. We must be seen as better, not worse than they are."

How did she gather so much information so quickly? Her plotting seemed a greater skill than her beauty, whether or not she knew it. Still, I never wanted that man or his mother here.

"Evander, I know how this pains you. But I seek to repair the reputation of Everely because I cannot bear to see you branded as cruel. You have suffered and yet it is you who is blamed. It is unfair. So please allow me to do what I can." She nearly begged.

And just like that, I was powerless to deny her.

It was not fair to make a mortal man fight against a goddess.

30

Aphrodite

"Never has Everely seen anything such as this," Evander said, astounded. We were both on horseback as he gazed at the house. "It seems that everyone is abuzz with this ball of yours, desiring to secure an invitation. Even my banker asked if he and his family were on the list. And he did not seem to believe me when I told him I knew nothing of any list."

I grinned and nodded. "Mr. Marworth's invitation shall reach him this afternoon. He should at least see why there is such a large hole in the accounts this month."

"So you are aware of the excitement you've caused then?" he mused as our horses passed groundskeepers planting decorations.

"It is my first ball. It must be a tad excessive," I answered. Then as if to prove my point, *or his*, the animal keeper walked by, nodding to us. In his arms were the peacocks I wished to have wandering the grounds.

"A tad excessive?" He laughed at me. "Aphrodite, I have never seen such decorations, not even at the palace!"

"You are exaggerating. This is nowhere near as fantastical as the palace—well, maybe close," I said the last part quickly.

"Good morning, Your Graces," additional decorators said, their arms full of silk ribbons.

I nodded down to them. "Good morning."

"Pray tell, men, what on earth are you carrying?" Evander asked.

If we had not been on horseback, I would be tempted to kick him!

"Silk, Your Grace, for the trees," one answered.

"For the trees?" he exclaimed.

"Carry on. I shall explain!" I waited for them to go before glaring at Evander, who was still grinning at me. "Leave my decorations be."

"Very well, wife, but what will you do if it should rain?" he asked, speaking my greatest fear aloud, as I had no remedy for nature.

"Do not use your mouth to curse us!"

"I think I foresee at least drizzle."

"Evander!"

He laughed, then rode ahead of me, and I followed after him.

"If it rains, I shall lay the blame at your feet."

"Surely you cannot think to blame me for poor weather."

"I can, and I shall, for it has been beautiful the last several days."

I had announced this ball a few days ago and put most of my effort into securing all that needed to be done. I was grateful that Nanny Phillipa was here for Emeline as I worked. Emeline was wary of her, but not hostile.

"I heard Mrs. Topwells tried to visit yesterday," he said as we entered the forest.

"She did, but I rejected her, as I was far too busy. I did respond, though, and of course, sent her an invitation."

"You have written back and forth quite a bit. Why have you taken to this girl?" he questioned.

"I feel something is amiss with her," I said, trying to think of the best way to explain it. "Maybe I just see myself in her."

"I have not spoken to the girl, but I am very confident there is no comparison. You are the daughter of—"

"Yes, yes, I know the difference in our status, despite her wealth. It is not that." I frowned as I looked at him. "I know what it is like to be enraptured by a man. And sometimes, when I look at her giggling and smiling, it reminds me of how I was at that age with you. So young, so in love, so . . . blind."

"Blind to me?" he asked, looking me over seriously. "You believe I deceived you?"

"No, blinded to the fact that I was most likely not ready to be a wife then," I replied. "I loved you so much that I wished to marry you as quickly as possible with no regard to whether I was ready to manage an estate. There was so much I did not see because you took up all my vision. If not for my mama, I would not be as prepared as I am now. She protected me from myself. Marcella does not have that. Part of me believes she married only to best her cousins."

"Or maybe she has seen all she needs to see and accepts it is part of the bargain," he pressed, unfailing and cold.

"You truly have little faith in people."

"I have never hidden that from you." He shrugged. "I do not see how anyone could fall for a man like Fitzwilliam. Is it not obvious his words are laced with poison meant to trick and seduce?"

"It may be obvious to you, but to a girl who has never seen anything beyond a drawing room, with limited exposure to any men, it all seems very sincere."

It was unfair, really. How were women to know the difference between roses and snakes when they blinded us from birth and threw us into the bush after a set number of years?

"This world sees us—women—as lambs, and our survival depends upon our shepherds."

"And yet you all buck at the shepherds," he teased. "For you and Verity both hate chaperones and the like."

"No, we hate being the sheep," I replied.

He laughed deeply from his chest.

"What?"

He shook his head.

"You cannot laugh at me and not explain why." I frowned.

"I had the image of a herd of sheep rising in revolt and found it funny!"

"You believe us not possible of revolting?" I asked.

"It would be very cute of you."

I glared and then lifted my leg over to the other side of the horse, no longer riding like a lady.

"Long live the sheep!" I snapped at him before I kicked into the horse and bolted forward with all my might.

"Aphrodite!" he hollered after me.

I rode through the forest with ease, having done so many times with my father when it was just the two of us. It felt nice, seeing the blur of the trees and feeling the pounding of my chest. I had not realized it had been so long. I went on and on until I thought I saw a figure in the woods. I pulled on the reins, but when my horse came to a stop, I couldn't see anyone.

"Where in God's name did you learn to ride like that?" Evander asked, beside me again. "I dare say you may be better than your brother."

"Oh, please do not tell him that. You know how competitive Damon is," I said, as I peered through the trees. "Did you see someone?"

"You believe I was able to look beyond you? You nearly gave my heart a shock."

I tried not to laugh. "Now you are dramatic."

"Yes, very, but I am amazed to find that there is something about you that I did not know already." He smirked, bringing his horse beside me. "I am tempted to encourage this, for I wish to see how fast you go on clear land."

"Are you challenging me to a race, sir? That is most inappropriate."

"I am merely trying to catch a runaway sheep!" He laughed and then looked me over. "Or are you a caged bird? I must make a list of all your analogies. Though I wonder why they are always animals."

Because animals, like women, could be owned by men. Just then, I heard a rustle through the bushes. Evander heard it as well.

"Who is there?" he called out.

There was no response. A moment later, she revealed herself.

"Marcella?" I gasped, staring down at the dirt-covered, terrified, and shaking young girl as she picked herself up off the ground. "Are you all right?"

Evander hopped off his horse to help her, but she held out her hands to stop him.

"I am fine!" she said, quickly dusting herself off, but she kept her eyes down. "Merely startled and lost my footing is all."

"What are you doing—"

"Marcella!" the booming sound of his voice echoed through the trees with such force and rage that birds scattered.

Fitzwilliam.

Immediately, Evander's fist clenched as Fitzwilliam walked over to Marcella, his eyes wide and crazed.

"Are you all right, my dear?" he asked, brushing the leaves off her hair gently. She seemed to tremble slightly.

"What are you doing on my land?" Evander snapped.

"You're mistaken, Duke. You and your wife have just crossed over to my property. Ponsonby is mine now," Fitzwilliam shot back, lifting his chin proudly.

It was hard to know without a map where Everely House ended and the estate of Ponsonby began, but that had never been an issue before. At least, not to my knowledge. The owners—well, former owners—of that estate had been a relatively old and unbothered couple.

"You have bought Ponsonby from the Allen family?" Evander flexed his fist.

"Yes. Am I supposed to seek your permission before purchasing land?" Fitzwilliam mocked, his head tilted.

I looked again at Marcella, who stood silently.

"Marcella?" I leaned forward on my horse. "Are you sure you are well?"

She seemed to be stuck in thought, but even so, the manner of his grip on her was worrying. She winced for a brief moment before glancing up at me with a smile. "I am fine."

I did not believe that. There was a smile on her face, but her eyes looked like she was begging me for something.

"Yes, she's perfectly fine, though clumsy at times. I tell her she must be careful in these forests. There is quite a deep river up ahead by the rocks. It's very dangerous, my dear," Fitzwilliam said, brushing the side of her head.

I glanced at Fitzwilliam, who smiled at me. "I do hope you both shall still attend my ball this evening, Mr. Topwells."

"Of course, Your Grace, it is my honor, though I must admit I was surprised to receive an invitation after my last interaction with the duke." He shifted his gaze to Evander, who was already back on his horse.

"Of course you are invited, Mr. Topwells, as your wife and I have formed quite an attachment. Marcella, should you need anything of me, do not hesitate to call on me."

"Of course, Your Grace," she said softly. That was not her usual tone of voice, either.

I wished to understand what was wrong. But she seemed ill-suited to explain, if the grip Fitzwilliam had on her arm was any indication.

Something was not right.

I sought to move closer, but Evander's horse blocked my path. "We must head back, as there is still much to prepare," he said with all humor and joy removed from his voice.

What was I to say? "Right." I looked once more at Marcella. "See you both tonight."

"Yes, you shall," Fitzwilliam replied. They stood there as Evander turned his horse around.

I followed but glanced back once more at the pair. Fitzwilliam was still giving me a chilling smile.

"Aphrodite," Evander called, and I refocused. It was only when we were a good distance away that he turned to me angrily. "Let me restate how deeply I desire for him not to be there."

"That would defeat the purpose," I replied. "I thought I explained."

"You did, but then I saw him and remembered how little I trust him."

"We must get through the night at least. Did you notice anything wrong with Marcella?" I asked.

"Marcella?" he said her name as though he did not recall her even being there.

"Never mind." I would speak to her later that evening, for I was sure something was not right.

Evander

She had banished me.

Not far but a banishment, nonetheless, as she could not take my so-called "brooding" while they finished preparations for the night. I placed men throughout the house and had warned the staff to exercise the highest level of vigilance. My last check was on Emeline, who had all but kept to her rooms.

When I entered, her nanny was sitting beside her on the actual floor, could one imagine, reading to her. Why not on the bed or the settee? Truthfully, the nanny was quite an odd one, long-necked and round-faced. I was surprised my godmother would hire such a woman, but then I knew little of what made a good caretaker, as evidenced by my history.

"Papa!" Emeline exclaimed.

I placed my hand on her head. "How are you?"

"Fine," she said. "Can I go to the ball? Please?"

I grinned, kneeling before her. "What do you know of balls?"

"There is dancing, food, and more dancing."

"Can you dance?"

"Nanny Phillipa has taught me some." To prove it, she stood up and slowly began to do the steps . . . like a little lady.

I clapped for her. "Very well done."

"Then I can go?"

"Unfortunately not," I replied and she pouted.

Ever since Aphrodite came, Emeline seemed to be getting bolder and more expressive. I wondered if it was simply the effect of having a woman, a *real* mother figure, especially one like Aphrodite, present in her life, or if it was a matter of age. Verity had also changed over time, though it did not feel the same. Either way I was pleased.

"Please, Papa."

"How about a compromise?" I said. "You and I may dance in our own ball, but you remain here."

"You will dance with me?" she exclaimed.

"I shall."

She quickly turned to her nanny. "Miss Phillipa, we need music!"

"Emeline, the piano is downstairs. We can dance without music."

"Miss Phillipa has a box!" she said.

"A box?" I repeated, glancing at the woman who now held a music box in her hand. Where it had come from, I was not sure. Emeline pulled me farther into the room. "Emeline, remain calm. I am here."

"Papa, we have never danced before," she said. The amusement fell from me as I realized that she recognized such a thing.

I never sought to ignore her, but I could not say I had been very attentive either. It was hard for me, but what excuse did I have when Aphrodite had taken to her so? Despite everything that had happened, despite what the girl's mother had done, Aphrodite already cared for the child greatly.

"Are you ready?" the nanny asked.

Emeline nodded excitedly. When the music started, I stepped to the side of her and beamed. Yes, I would have to make sure this happened more often.

31

Aphrodite

E verything had come together quite nicely, but I could not bring myself to enjoy it. The silks hanging from the trees were stunning, the peacocks that meandered through the grounds fantastical, the dance floor was outstanding, the entertainment nearly as dazzling as any I had seen in London. I had done well, and I knew it from all the smiles as our guests drank and danced. Still, I felt anxious, as there was one person I had yet to see.

"Am I rewarded when it does not rain?" Evander asked from beside me.

I glanced up at him, confused. "What do you mean?"

"Did you not say you would hold me accountable should it rain on all your hard work?"

"Oh, right." I nodded and looked up at the clear sky. It was not yet dark, but it would be soon. Where was she?

"Is something the matter?" he asked.

"I am well . . ." My voice drifted off as I saw the footman present Marcella, at last. She was dressed in white, with a white feather in her hair.

"Damn him for actually coming," Evander muttered as not only Fitzwilliam but Datura also appeared, on either side of Marcella.

"Remember, do not show your anger," I whispered.

"It would be easier for me not to breathe," he grumbled. I linked arms with him, trying to walk toward them, but he stood unmovable. "What are you doing?"

"Going to welcome them."

"You are the hostess, not to mention the duchess. You need not do such a thing," he reminded me.

He was not wrong, as it was customary for a duchess to greet the guests but once at the very beginning, and I had done so. The next time I was to address them all would be at the closing of the night. However, I truly wished to get rid of whatever this feeling was that persisted to nag at me. I watched closely as they entered the grounds. Fitzwilliam held one of her arms and Datura the other. It almost looked as though they were pulling her forward. On her face now was a large smile, and she giggled as she went.

"Your Grace, how wondrous Everely has become since your arrival," said one of a gaggle of local women who soon surrounded me.

"Thank you." I smiled at them, feeling Evander slip from my side as quickly as possible.

"And your gown. It is the finest I have ever seen. Is it from London?" another asked.

"Yes. I am pleased you like it, for I was unsure of the color." I laughed for them, but my eyes followed Marcella.

"It is so splendid to be able to speak with Your Grace. Many of us were wondering if you only preferred the company of the townsfolk." The shortest of the women snickered.

"My company is quite varied, but I do hope to know all of you ladies, too."

"Oh yes, we must spend more time together. I would love to invite you and the duke to my home for dinner next week."

"I—"

"If you are having dinner with her, you must have one with me."

"I shall see to my schedule," I replied. They all kept speaking around me quickly, joyfully, drunkenly.

I smiled, nodded, and laughed along with them. I was so occupied with the conversation that I barely heard a short gasp, followed by the breaking of glass. When I looked to my right, Marcella stood with a stain upon her dress from the champagne she had spilled. Using this chance, I rushed to her side.

"No need to worry," I said, linking arms with her. "We can have it cleaned quickly."

"Thank you. I do not know what has come over me." She giggled, petting her dress. Before I could move, another hand was on her as well.

"My dear, it is not so bad that you must trouble the duchess," Fitzwilliam said to her, holding her arm. Once more, she was rigid.

"You men never know the importance of a dress. If it is not cleaned, it shall surely set," I replied, trying to take her with me. "Worry not, I shall bring her back in one piece."

"I will accompany you both," Datura said, coming up beside me.

Was Marcella his wife or a prisoner? Not wishing to fight, I smiled and nodded. It was only then that he saw fit to let go of her arm. I was unsure of what to do, but I glanced around and met the eyes of Verity, who was observing us curiously. I did not know what look I gave her, but I hoped it was as desperate as I felt. We'd nearly reached the stairs into the estate, and I was losing faith that I would be able to rid myself of Datura when suddenly, Verity's voice rose loudly.

"Dowager, we have not spoken in some time," she said. "I feel as though you are ignoring me, I hope I am mistaken?"

"I beg your pardon?" Datura looked at her as if she were insane.

"I have written to you several times, and you seem never to reply," she said even louder, causing some guests to turn to her.

"I have gotten no such letters."

"How is that so?" Verity frowned.

"We shall leave you both to speak," I said quickly and took Marcella inside with me.

Datura called out, but I pretended not to hear her.

The footmen had barely closed the doors after we entered the drawing room when she collapsed in my arms.

"Marcella!"

She broke down crying, gripping me tightly. "Please . . . please help me!"

"Breathe. All right. Breathe," I said, trying to lift her to her feet, but she was still shaking and trembling, sobbing on me. "Marcella, you must walk. We cannot be here like this."

"I cannot."

"What do you mean you cannot?"

She only sobbed more.

"Marcella!"

"My . . . legs."

I did not understand, so I lifted the hem of her dress. Her legs were purple and bruised. "What . . . what in God's name?"

"I should not have run," she sobbed.

"You were running," I whispered. I knew it, had felt it but had not wished to believe it. "You were running from him?"

She cried, holding on to me tightly.

"Did he do this to you?" I asked as I looked at her legs.

"He . . . it is my . . . fault. I was mad at him . . . I am to blame . . ."

"Shh," I said, hugging her and patting her back, trying to contain my rage.

Oh . . . oh . . . that no-good pugilistic-bully, slug-a-bed-faced, death's head upon a mopstick, white-livered, vile creature of man!

"We need to get you away from him—"

"He is my husband—"

"He is a monster," I snapped. I did not realize my eyes were wet until this very moment.

"He was not like this in the beginning," she tried to tell me. "It's me . . . I made him angry—"

"Listen to me." I held her face. "It was never you. Never. Come. I have you. I will fix this. I will help you."

"You cannot. Forgive me. I must go back," she muttered, trying to get up.

"You can barely stand, and you wish to return to him? Marcella, you cannot. He is hurting you."

"What will you have me do?" she cried out. "He is my husband. My family will not speak to me. They are too angry about what I have done. I have no one else! I must go back!"

It was madness. She was trembling in fear.

I had no idea how on earth to save her, but every part of me wished to do so. I wished to lock her away in the house and keep her safe, but I could not, for that was kidnapping. But what could be done? How could I protect her? He was her husband. He had every right to her and could do as he pleased.

How could you stop a monster?

How could a woman fight against such a monster?

I did not know, but I knew I would no longer dare lecture Evander on why he'd fought that villain.

Evander

They had been gone far too long for a single spill, and watching Fitzwilliam eyeing the house made me wary. Datura had sought to make her way inside, but the men at the doors barred her entrance.

"What in the heavens is going on?" Verity whispered beside me.

"I know not," I whispered back. "How did you know to help keep Datura away?"

"Odite was staring at me so intently that I felt compelled. And for me to speak to Datura willingly? You must know it is grave," she said. "Should I go in? I fear Datura will try to follow—"

"Your Grace," Fitzwilliam's voice rang out like the cries of hell before me. "When do you believe I shall have my wife returned to me?"

All eyes were now upon us. Verity placed her hand on my arm. "When I see my wife, you shall see yours."

"And when will that be?"

"Whenever they please." I bit the inside of my cheek. "Do you always keep your wife so close?"

"Only upon hostile grounds."

There was muttering as those with long ears shifted to hear in even greater detail. Before I could reply, the doors opened, and our wives returned, causing us both to rush to them. Once I reached Aphrodite, I could see that the expression in her eyes was darker than I had ever witnessed. I had seen her angry. I had seen her weary or uninterested, but this was different. This was similar to what I felt—unadulterated hate.

"My wife looks ill, Your Grace. I think it best if we retired for the evening," Fitzwilliam said. He had clearly noticed the expression upon my wife's face. "Marcella, shall we?"

When the girl took his hand, Aphrodite reached out to stop her.

"I shall check on you to see how you are faring, especially the condition of your legs." She spoke to Marcella, but she did not avert her gaze from Fitzwilliam, whose jaw was set in annoyance.

"Thank you, Your Grace," the girl said as Fitzwilliam took her away.

One would have hoped Datura had the good sense to leave with them, but she still thought herself the mistress here and went about the grounds, drinking and giggling.

"How can people be so vile?" Aphrodite whispered under her breath. Her glare was now upon Datura as she drifted from one place to the next.

"What happened?" I asked. She did not get a chance to answer as, once more, a group of women sought her out.

Not wishing to be gathered into their conversation, I tried to leave, but she held me firm, squeezing my hand. I was sure she shook with rage.

⟡

It was nearly dawn by the time we had seen the last carriage off, which belonged to none other than Datura. The first thing I did, despite my exhaustion, was unlock and check my office then once more look in on Emeline. Maybe they were greater villains in my mind than in reality. Either way, erring on the side of caution brought me comfort. I expected Aphrodite to be asleep since she, herself, had worked incessantly. Instead, she was staring out the window, hands clenched.

"You are still—"

"How do we stop him?" she asked. "Have you gone back to the magistrate and told him of his misdeeds?"

"I told you it was useless. He brushed it off."

"Even with your witnesses?"

I had told her this. "It was long ago. It might have succeeded when Fitzwilliam was only a bastard, but now, it is different. The magistrate all but told me to let the past remain so and move on for the good of everyone."

"It is not good for anyone!"

"Aphrodite, what is wrong?" I asked, placing my hands upon her shoulder. "What occurred between you and Mrs. Top-wells—"

"Do not call her that," she bit out, her arms crossed. "She deserves better than to be called by the name . . . the name of he who beats her."

Must that man inherit all of our father's worst traits? I exhaled slowly. "You saw proof of this?"

"He hits her in places no one will see, Evander! Her family has all but abandoned her. She has no control over her own home or dowry. She is a prisoner brought out like a doll to smile and then locked back away. God only knows what is happening to her. We must help her. We must bring that . . . that devil to justice!"

"A task I have worked toward all my life to no avail. If I could simply throw the man into a cage and leave him to rot, I would. But I cannot."

"Then what are we to do!" She was on the verge of tears. "We are the duke and duchess. Surely we can do something."

We could not. Marcella was his wife, and it was none of our or the law's business. All I could do was hug Aphrodite, for I understood her frustration. For all the wealth, titles, and land we held, we were powerless against one man.

"I will speak to the magistrate again tomorrow." It would be of little use. Nevertheless, I would try.

In truth, I had no means of bringing him down and feared his impact on this family. I reached down and lifted her, bringing her to the bed and laying her down.

"I know you to be a person of great character," I said, cupping her cheek. "But you must accept, as I have learned, that not all the world is full of the same integrity, and sometimes the immoral are not punished for their actions. We must simply protect ourselves from them."

"So, we sit by and do nothing?"

"Let us be grateful our own lives are not as such."

The frown upon her face remained even as I kissed her.

Aphrodite

I watched as he slept soundly beside me, his arm over the top of my body. In his arms, I felt better but only slightly. I could not help but wonder what was happening with Marcella. I had tried with all my might to convince her to stay here, but she was too afraid. I now understood what Evander had explained. There was nothing that could be done.

It was horrifying.

Fitzwilliam's victims were forced into silence. Marcella, Evander . . . Emeline's mother. I could not take the injustice of it.

Rising from the bed, I donned my dressing gown and went

to my drawing room. There, upon the dresser, were letters from my mother and sisters, along with a pen and paper for the replies I had yet to send.

Sitting down, I stared at the blank page for the longest time before I lifted the pen and dipped it in the ink. The moment I began to write, I could not stop.

32

Evander

"I write to tell you of a tale most ghastly in nature, one deprived of all morality and sickening to both the hearts and minds of decent people everywhere. The truth behind the brute of a man, born of the former Duke of Everely, who stalks among us now under the name of Fitzwilliam Topwells." I read the paper aloud in horror.

When I had awoken that morning I was met with, in both the local paper and the gossip sheets, the story of my private life, and my father's, alongside Fitzwilliam's. Listed there were all of his crimes against me—with the exception of the truth of Emeline's birth, though I am sure others would guess given the timing of her birth. Emma's life was written of in detail that was known by only one person besides myself. Which was why I stood before Aphrodite, reading aloud, waiting for a look of surprise or shock, but she merely sat quietly in her chair, her hands folded in her lap.

"You did this," I snapped. Yesterday, I thought she had spent her day replying to letters and was still melancholy over her discovery about Marcella. Instead, she was exposing my family shame to the world. "Aphrodite, what have you done!"

"I have told the truth."

"You have told the world, and they did not ask."

"Because they did not know to ask!"

"No, because it is disgraceful. Not only have you made my life public without my permission, but you have also all but accused the magistrate of covering up Fitzwilliam's misdeeds—"

"Did he not do so?" she asked. "You went to him twice! You told him of Marcella, and still he did nothing!"

"You gave him no time! I told him of Marcella only yesterday, while you were publishing this!"

"Had he done something the first time you went, we would not be in this position now!" She had gone mad. Truly, there was no other explanation for it, and I was at a loss for what to say.

"With these papers, you have left us all open to ridicule and danger. You believe your arrow was fired at Fitzwilliam to shame him from society, but, Aphrodite, his whole life has been like this, and he cares not. You have grazed an already vicious animal. What do you believe he will do now? He shall deny it all and then retaliate!"

"Is that not what you already fear he will do? You have men walking the grounds at all hours of the day and night fearful of this vicious animal, leaving many to wonder why. Now, at the very least, everyone's eyes shall be on him. Let them be wary. Let them watch him as you do. If he cannot be jailed, then let his life feel as though it is a prison. I do not care! Someone needed to speak, for it is wrong for the innocent to suffer in silence!"

"And what shall this get us?" I asked, seeking to reason with her. "Marcella is still in that home with him. The past is still the past. Nothing has changed, except now we have become entertainment for further talk. Now all the world will know that my father was a fiend who spawned a villain. Will that not reflect on me? On Verity and Gabrien? Are we not your family and, thus, more important than the justice you seek to gain for some girl? You have exploited our family and dishonored us to the world."

"I just—"

"If it was the deeds of your father, your blood, would you feel compelled to act so rashly?" I asked, shaking my head. "This was selfish and cruel of you. You have ripped us open and have given us no place or time to hide our faces."

"Evander—"

I held up my hand, begging her to keep her distance. "I have nothing more to say to you," I said and turned from her, slamming the door behind me.

I hated my father, but at the same time, he was still my father. And while he had failed to show my siblings or me the love a father ought, he had instilled in me at least one good thing—the importance of honoring our name. It was ironic to me that while I thought him to be a shameful example, I nevertheless wanted to mend the name of the Duke of Everely. I knew it would take time, but with Aphrodite beside me, I had been certain that day would come. Now, once more, I found myself engulfed by the wretched stench of the past.

"Evander!"

It was a shout that seemed to echo through the whole house. As I glanced out the window, I saw him—Fitzwilliam—out front, yelling as my men fought to hold him back.

"Evander!" he screamed once more.

Oh, bloody hell!

I knew he would come. It was only a matter of when, and he apparently had chosen immediately . . . just like a wounded bear. Previously, he had at least the thinnest desire to be respected in the eyes of society, offering fake smiles and pleasantries on demand. Now with the curtain lifted to reveal his true nature, he would not hold back. I was sure of it.

"*Evander—*"

"How many times must I remind you and your mother that you are not welcome here?" I asked as I stepped out the front door.

"You no-good bastard!" he screamed. The guards held him back against his thrashing. "Now you dare not even face me as a man?"

"Make way for him."

"Your Grace—"

"Make way," I repeated. When they did, Fitzwilliam wasted no time rushing toward me.

"It is not enough that you have everything!" he sneered grabbing me. "That you were left everything that ought to have been mine! Even my daughter is in your godforsaken hands!"

"This is your doing, not mine. The fact that you still believe anything ought to be yours is the problem. Now release me at once!" I snapped.

"*Why?* Why is it not mine? Because my mother was unwed. For that mere fact alone, I was thrown to the side for an arrogant, condescending man such as yourself? By a mere technicality, all my life, I was thrown to the winds. Not one thing was left to me. All I had was this name and even that you seek to destroy!" He all but spat in my face.

"Why is it you always think yourself the wretched one?"

"Because I am!" he screamed. "I am the most misfortunate one, and you are the villain you so clearly wish to make me out to be!"

He was mad, truly and deeply. "You see no fault in yourself? You sincerely believe the world to be your enemy? Fitzwilliam, do you not see the ruin you have left in your wake! And now you dare call me the villain! *Me!*"

"You are—"

"Evander!" Aphrodite rushed up behind me.

"Get back inside."

"But—"

"Go!" I snapped. She did as I ordered.

"You suffered one setback in your life." Fitzwilliam laughed bitterly, his whole body shaking. "Only one, Evander, and yet you grieved and sought to chase me to the end of the world. Now look at yourself. In the end, did you not still get what you desired? In the end, is not all the world at your feet? Why must you seek to poison my life?"

"It is you who poisons yourself!" I hollered back. "It is your greed! It is your desire, your viciousness, and your cruelty that has brought us to this point! You had other paths before you and chose not to accept them. You and your damned mother. Had she known her place, your life would not have been so! Blame her if you seek someone to admit fault!"

"You—you, curse you!" He spat in my face. "I shall sue you and proclaim it is all a lie, and I am sure the magistrate shall hear my plea! You have slandered me. And you shall pay!"

"I know nothing of what you speak," I lied, dusting off my clothes. "Once more, I must tell you to get off my property, Fitzwilliam, for you are a mad fool, and I shall not tolerate you a second longer."

"And you are the bigger one, little brother. The greatest and cruelest of them all!" He cursed before marching down the stairs and then was upon his horse with ease.

"Fetch me my horse," I ordered.

I needed a plan.

"Where are you going?" Aphrodite asked from behind me.

I did not have an answer for her. When my horse arrived, I was upon it and took to the forest myself. My mind reeled as I sought a way to prevent this from going even further out of control. For if Fitzwilliam could trace the papers back to Aphrodite, he very well could press libel charges against her, and the magistrate would most surely refuse to look the other way. I could prove the truthful parts of her words, but what I needed now more than anything was another witness. Proof of my claim. And my only chance to acquire it very well might have been gone now, for Fitzwilliam seemed more likely to be returning to town than his home.

I was just about to come upon Ponsonby when I saw her from the corner of my eye, standing over a rocky bank above the rushing river below.

No! No! No!

"Marcella!" I called out to the girl, riding faster toward her.

She turned to me, her eyes swollen red and tears falling down her cheeks. Jumping off the horse, I sought to get closer. "Marcella, it is all right. Come back this way."

"It is not all right," she cried out, grabbing her head. "I do not know when it went wrong. How it all went so wrong."

"You surely will not find out like this," I explained. "Come, let us talk . . ."

"He is so angry. I cannot go back," she sobbed, shaking and taking another step back.

"Then you do not have to. Come, let us talk. This is dangerous. Take my hand."

She shook her head. "He is my husband. I have to go back . . . I do not want to."

"Marcella! Please, do not let him do this to you. There has to be another way, we—"

"There is no other way." She wiped her face and inhaled.

"Marcella—"

"Tell the duchess thank you for being kind to me," she said. With all my might, I ran toward her.

"No!"

Aphrodite

When I had been alone thinking of sending the letter it had felt as though it were the only logical thing to do, but now I was not as sure.

"Was it really you?" Verity asked from behind me.

I turned to her. "Verity, I—"

"Do you understand how embarrassing it is to have a father like that or to have a family like this?" she asked with tears in her eyes. "I know you do not; you come from such a kind family. So I will tell you it is a very deep wound. One that we do our best to hide even though we know all the world is laughing. Do you know how mortifying it was to come out to the queen? I had practiced over and over again. Prepared and begged Datura not to come, but we knew she would anyway. How could she miss such a chance? I had to prepare myself for that. Prepare to walk out, on a day that was to be for my own glory, only to be the subject of mockery. And I was. For that is what this family has been all my life—the subject of talk and mockery."

"I wanted to help and get the truth out," I replied.

"The truth is out, but whether it helps anyone, I truly doubt. Did you even pause to think of me? Or Emeline?" she asked, looking at me. "For even I have questions. I did not know much of Emma. Nor did I understand how it was possible for my brother to stray from you when he loved you so.

You have put doubt in my head of Emeline, and if I, who care for her, have it, then others shall as well. What will become of her when new twisted talk reaches her ears? How will you explain all this then?"

I had no words, for I had not thought that far.

She shook her head. "Excuse me."

I watched as she ran up the stairs. When she was gone, I placed my hand on my face, not sure of what to do or say. I had not sought to hurt them. But I had, and now I was unsure of what I had unleashed.

All I could do was sit back down, shamefully, to reflect on my actions and wait for Evander to return. The longer I watched for his horse, the more anxious I felt, to the point where I felt sick as minutes turned to hours. By evening, he still was not home. Nor had I gotten any word. The whole house felt empty without him. I worried, knowing he was upset with me. So worried, in fact, I gave up watching the world outside and sought needlework to make Emeline another doll.

Knock. Knock.

"Come in," I muttered as I fixed a knot. Eleanor entered with a tray of food. "I am not hungry."

"Your Grace, you have not eaten."

"Yes, as I am not hungry," I replied as I threaded my needle into the back of the doll. "Has there been word of the duke?"

When she did not answer, I glanced up at her. But she was looking at me, her eyes transfixed, gripping the tray tightly.

"Eleanor, what is it?"

"Nothing. I shall return this to the kitchen then," she stammered, as she was known to do when she lied, which was why she did her best not to.

"It surely does not seem like nothing," I said and then

quickly rose from my chair. "Has something happened to the duke?"

"No, of course not! I mean, I do not know anything of him."

"Then why is your expression so? Are you all right?"

"Yes. Pardon me." She curtsied and turned to leave but then paused and turned back to me.

"Now you have exposed yourself and must tell me," I said, placing the doll down. "What is it?"

"There is talk," she whispered.

"Of the papers?" I sighed. "Of course, I expected that."

"No, Your Grace, of Mrs. Topwells."

I stilled as nerves filled me, from my ankles and upward. "What of her?"

"They . . . they are saying she threw herself into the river."

Oh . . . *oh* . . .

"Your Grace!" Eleanor rushed to me as I collapsed into a pile on the floor, my throat heavy and chest burning.

I shook. This was . . . this was because of me.

I was wrong. I had done a grave wrong.

And I had helped no one.

All of me felt weak, so much so that Eleanor and a footman had to pick me up from the floor and move me to a chair. I sat there, seeking to understand, seeking to go back just one more day and stop myself from sending those papers.

Dropping my face into my hands, I sought breath to calm myself, but with each passing minute, my heart burned in the worst way. I wished it to all be a lie, but when Eleanor came into the room once more with a forlorn look upon her face, I knew it was true.

"Is that fire?" I rose from my chair and rushed to the window, staring in horror at the orange glow in the distance and the smoke that rose into the sky.

"The townsfolk have set the Topwells' home on fire, Your Grace," Eleanor said, coming to bring me from the window. "You ought not to stay close to the windows now."

"They have set a fire? Upon his home?"

"They are incensed and wish to hunt Mr. Topwells down," she said.

"A mob," I whispered.

They were enraged from the words I had written and Marcella's fate, and as such, had taken to action themselves.

"Where is Evander?" I turned back to her. "Has he returned?"

"No, Your Grace. I believe many are still at the river searching for her body before darkness falls. The duke is said to be among them."

All of Everely had turned on its head, and regret spread through me as a fire spread through that home.

I watched into the night as orange illuminated the sky in a hellish blaze, and by daybreak, I had not yet slept. Although the fire was now gone, smoke still rose in the distance in the light of the early morning.

"Your Grace, please, you must rest," Eleanor said, seeking once more to draw me from the windows, but I could not be moved. If these were the consequences of my actions, at the very least, I needed to see it with open eyes. I, more than anyone, should be the greatest witness of the events unraveling before me.

"Has the duke returned yet?" I asked as I hugged the shawl around me tighter.

"No, Your Grace," she replied.

He had sent word the evening prior for the house to be guarded, and that he had gone to see Mr. Wildingham. I could only believe it was to return her body to that poor, *poor* man.

Evander had spoken of how he had faded with the death of his wife and son. Now he would have to grieve the tragic loss of his daughter. What could be said to him? Who could console such grief? Evander alone?

"Have them prepare my carriage."

"Where do you seek to go, Your Grace?"

"The home of Mr. Wildingham," I said, removing the shawl from my shoulders and immediately taking my gloves and hat before stepping into the hall.

"Your Grace, is that wise? Should you not wait here for the duke?" she asked, following after me.

"I do not know what is wise anymore, or if I ever did. All I know now is that I must see with my own two eyes."

And I must ask for forgiveness as well.

33

Aphrodite

I thought of all I would say, the condition in which I might find the man upon arriving, or Evander's reaction to me being there. My greatest fear was seeing the broken body of Marcella. I could not bear it. Nevertheless, I soon arrived before a small manor covered in vines. The morning air was stale and heavy, my heart beating faster as we waited for the door to be opened.

"I cannot imagine a house such as this not having a butler," Eleanor whispered once more as she knocked.

I knew Evander, at least, was here, as I could see his horse. Just as I was about to try the doors myself, they were opened, not by a butler but by . . . a doctor.

"Dr. Darrington?" I wanted to ask him what he was doing here of all places, but the stain of blood on his clothes stole all further questions from me.

"Inside quickly, Your Grace." He made way for us before shutting the door.

"My husband?" I asked him.

"Asleep," he said. "He suffered a further injury."

"Injury?" I panicked, looking at Eleanor, who shook her head. "What has happened? Why was I not informed, why was he not brought home? Where is he? Take me to him!"

"Your Grace, forgive me. He sought to keep these events secret. I did not think it wise, but . . ." The doctor sighed heavily as he cleaned his hands.

"What events?"

"The ones pertaining to me."

At her voice, I spun so quickly I nearly fell back. But I had to make sure my ears were not mistaken, and my eyes confirmed Marcella was not dead, but standing before me, albeit bandaged and bruised. I stared at her, fearing she was some apparition or figment of my mind. When she stumbled, causing the doctor to rush to her side, I knew she truly was real.

"How?" I questioned in confusion. "All of the town . . . did you not throw yourself into the river?"

She hung her head. "I tried to, Your Grace, but the duke saved me. Even though his arm was cut upon the ledge, he would not let me go, and pulled me from death. It was he who brought me home."

I felt . . . I felt far too many things, the greatest being relief, followed by exhaustion, and then anger.

"If that is so, why does the world believe you lost, Marcella? The town is enraged." I had even heard their rumbling as we crossed roads to arrive here.

"The duke said that if I am lost, I cannot be found and returned to my owner," she responded. I could think of nothing else to say, other than to walk to her and hug her.

"We shall speak more later." I nodded to her and then looked at the doctor. "My husband?"

"This way," he said before addressing Marcella. "Did I not tell you to remain in bed? You are not to be walking."

"Forgive me, I . . ." Her stomach growled, and I smiled, for it was the type of innocence I expected of her, and it reminded me of myself once more. She quickly grabbed her stomach.

"Are there no maids for the kitchen?" I asked. Looking around, I saw no one but the four of us.

"My father has few attending to him, and they were dismissed," she said.

"I shall see to it, Your Grace," Eleanor said, already looking around the house.

When there was a knock once more, I noticed Marcella rush to hide, and the doctor motioned for me to be quiet before going to the door.

"May I help you?" the doctor said as he opened the door partially.

"I am in Mr. Wildingham's service. I seek to check on him," said the maid.

"There are to be no guests. Should your services be required, the gentleman will call," the doctor said to her. I listened to them speak back and forth, a little unsure as to why we were all hiding. But finally, when they did leave, the doctor motioned for me to follow him up the stairs.

None of this was what I had expected. I had prepared myself to see Marcella in a bed or within a casket upon arrival, yet when I got here, it was Evander who was injured and who looked as if he had seen the end of days.

"Evander?" I gasped, rushing to his side. "Why does he look so poorly?" I asked the doctor.

"The medication I gave him last night must be waning. He has dislocated his shoulder," the doctor replied as he moved to his bag that was set in the far corner of the room, "as well as managed to obtain a few lacerations on his arm. Other than that, he should be fine. Though at the rate he puts himself at risk . . ." He muttered the last part under his breath, so I was unable to hear, but I was sure it was not a compliment.

"Thank you," I said. "Whatever your price, we shall surely pay it."

"I have no doubt. I shall go check on Mr. Wildingham to give you both a moment," he said, collecting his bag and exiting the room quietly.

When he was gone, I laid my head upon Evander's chest to listen to his heartbeat, as only that could soothe my nerves and mind at this moment.

"How is it possible for one man to be able to drive me as mad as you?" I whispered.

"I believe it is possible by the same manner in which you vex me."

My head snapped up.

Tiredly, he smiled. "Good morning, wife."

It might have been out of relief or exhaustion or anger, but I found my eyes filled with tears. With his good arm, Evander reached up and cupped my face.

"Why are you crying as if I am in real danger? It is but a flesh wound." He grinned, and if he had not been injured, I would have sought to smack him with the pillow.

"I am not crying. I am merely tired," I managed to lie, blinking the tears from my eyes. He caught my arm and pulled me on top of him. "Evander!"

"If you are tired, rest."

"I cannot possibly rest in another person's home. I must—"

"You must what?" He took my hat off my head, tossing it aside without a care. "It is still early. We are guests here, so nothing remains to do but rest. Now come, lie next to me."

"But . . ."

"Listen to me at least this once."

I frowned. "I have listened to you more than once."

"And when ever has that been? For since we met, you have been rather formidable." He chuckled.

"Did you not ask me to forgive you and offer a second chance? Here I am," I said with my head raised.

"I do believe I had to ask a great many times before you did so, my love. Is that not formidable of you?"

I made a face but lay down in his arms. "Forgive me for being rather troublesome, then. Forgive me for—"

"Should you even burn all of Everely to the ground, I would forgive without question," he whispered as he rubbed my back gently. "But promise me, Aphrodite, that you will never do such a thing again. No matter how important you believe it to be."

I hung my head for a moment and nodded. "I promise. I did not think it through and have caused even greater chaos."

"Let us not dwell on it any longer," he said gently. "Though I must say how it vexes me that I cannot even be cross with you for longer than an hour."

"Good." I grinned, hugging him tightly. Finally, I closed my eyes to rest, making a note to apologize to Verity as well.

Evander

When I awoke again, she was still sleeping soundly. I knew that she would be pained upon hearing the lie I had spread of the demise of Marcella, but I did not think she would forgo sleep or even food. This whole ordeal had taught me something I had not realized about her: My wife, the Duchess of Everely, was a crusader, a person who held overzealous campaigns on behalf of those she considered weak or downtrodden. So much of her vision became narrowed, and even if it meant exposing herself or our family to harm, she would go to any levels afforded to her.

But I should have known. How could she not be so with the mother who raised her to be all that was good and the father who fed her a diet of Greek philosophy and literature's greatest heroes?

I had to admit that her morality and steadfast dedication to justice made me feel somewhat unworthy. Had Marcella not been Fitzwilliam's wife, and therefore a useful witness, I do not believe I would have put myself at risk or even sought to be here, conspiring for her sake.

"Will this be enough?" Marcella asked as she gave me her letters. The poor girl was still bruised and tired.

"Yes," I said as I read over them. "They shall do nicely."

"Then what should become of me now?" she asked.

"I have spoken to your father, and we shall act as though you are truly gone. There shall be a funeral for you, and at such time, you will be taken to a distant relative of yours in France. There you shall start again," I explained. It had come to me once I managed to lift her up from the edge of that cliff.

There was nothing to prevent her from returning to Fitzwilliam except death, so we would use death as a means to free her. In return, Fitzwilliam would lose the protection he had derived from her name, and with all the county now knowing of his misdeeds, I would once more use everything I had collected against him to have him thrown into prison for the rest of his days. I was sure the snake of a man had gone into hiding, but now, with the town on the hunt for him, he would be found sooner rather than later.

"Of all the patients I have had, Your Grace, you are the

most exhausting. And now you seek to be a poor influence upon her."

Standing in the doorway of the drawing room was the rather slumped and weary doctor.

"Did I not prescribe you both rest?"

"That you did," I replied. "But I believe you may need rest more than the both of us. Have you not slept?"

"How can one rest in such chaos?" He muttered something else I could not hear before taking a seat in the corner, leaning back on the chair. "When you sent for me, I thought I had only Mr. Wildingham to tend to, not three patients in total."

"How is my father?" Marcella asked as she unsteadily pushed herself to stand. "I believe the truth of all this has greatly affected his heart."

"He's ill. All that can be done for him is to rest so what little of his strength remains and to make him comfortable," Dr. Darrington replied, looking to her.

"Is it not possible for us to wait?" she asked, looking at me. "I do not believe my father has much time left. I would not wish him to be—"

"The longer you stay, the greater chance of discovery. And should that happen, I shall not be able to help you, nor will as many people believe your plight," I explained. "Go sit with him now while you can."

She nodded and slowly managed to remove herself from the room, leaving only the doctor and me, who looked at me disapprovingly.

"If there is something you wish to say, say it," I said as I took a seat, careful of my battered arm.

"Are you not just using her as well?" the doctor asked. "Seeking to help her so you can clearly take aim at her husband?"

"Do you believe her to be better off returned to him?"

The frown upon his lips deepened. "She is not. But such a deceit has come at a great cost already. A mob burned a home to the ground last night. The hearts of people enraged are not easily tamed."

"Justice shall bring forth the taming. And when Fitzwilliam is arrested, they will have it," I replied. I had not foreseen the mob, but there had been no choice. Still aching, I rose to prepare. "She must leave tonight."

"Your Grace!" The door nearly burst open as Aphrodite's maid rushed into the room.

"What is it?"

"Mr. Topwells . . . he is coming here with the magistrate."

Fuck!

I looked out the window to see the magistrate's carriage, and the man now coming off his horse was none other than Fitzwilliam. I had no time to prepare. Damn him. How had he known I would be here? He would not have come even if it was to collect Marcella's body, let alone atone to her father. He sought to preserve himself by any means necessary. "What cause does he have to come here? Has anyone else been here?"

"A maid arrived early this morning after your wife. I sent her on her way, but she looked rather suspicious of me," Dr. Darrington said. "I thought her worried about her master. I did not think anything strange of it."

What was stranger than a duke, a duchess, and a doctor all within a gentleman's home in the early hours of the morning? I had sent Aphrodite's carriage, as well as my horse, back in the hopes of not drawing further attention to the house. But this was only hours later. Surely she must have said something to arouse suspicions.

"Eleanor, go find Marcella and hide her."

I had no other choice here. I glanced to the doctor. "You know it is better for her to leave than suffer greater abuse by his hands."

"You know I do."

"Then I shall lie, and you shall cover it." I did not give him a chance to disagree before I went to the door.

Taking a deep breath, and standing firm, I opened the door just as they both entered into the front garden.

"Lord Everely?" the magistrate said as he looked over in confusion. "What are you doing here?"

"Mr. Wildingham was rather distraught upon hearing the news of his dearly departed daughter, and I sought to help here. What brings you, sir?"

"So distraught you've stayed here overnight, and now your wife is here as well?" Fitzwilliam questioned. "I did not know you cared so much for Mr. Wildingham."

"My wife and his daughter shared a bond of sisterhood and I was injured in trying to save your wife," I explained. "If only one could have saved her earlier. My doctor was summoned to tend to my wounds."

"Has the body been recovered from the river?" the magistrate asked solemnly.

"No, sir. All our efforts were of little use before darkness fell, then the mob set upon the streets." I glanced once more at Fitzwilliam. "I am told they are looking for you, Mr. Topwells. I am surprised to see you out and about."

"I am free of guilt and believe you a liar," he sneered. "What reason do you have to send your carriage home without either you or your wife inside it."

He had been watching the house.

"It is not I who must explain myself to you. But you to the rest of us. And fear not, for that time has come. I thank you for coming," I declared before lifting my hand to give the magistrate the letters. "Before Mrs. Topwells took her life, she penned these letters and had them sent to her father so he might know the truth. Are these, along with my witnesses attesting to Fitzwilliam's offenses against me, not enough to rid us of such a devious character?"

"He lies!" Fitzwilliam yelled and then looked upon the house. "This is all some deceitful trick. *Marcella!* Whatever he has told you are lies. *Marcella!*"

"If you will not believe it from my lips, then let it be from another," I said, making way to Dr. Darrington, who was rigid and his face stern as he stepped out of the house.

"Sir, I must beg of you, for the health of Mr. Wildingham, please refrain from yelling," he said sharply.

"I want my wife!"

"That is no longer possible!" he said.

Fitzwilliam glanced between us both and shook his head. However, he was cut off by a cough from the magistrate.

"You, sir," he snapped at Fitzwilliam, "shall report yourself to my court by evening. And should you not, I shall send soldiers to bring you in, you wretch!"

"It is a lie!" Fitzwilliam grabbed on to him as the magistrate marched back to his carriage. Seeking to appeal his case, he continued, "Do you not see the games they play? Do you not see the holes in this story? Should Sir Dennison-Whit hear of his niece like this, he shall also blame you—"

"Unhand me, you madman!" the magistrate shouted, pulling his arm away and nearly kicking Fitzwilliam as he rushed to enter his own carriage. "You shall be judged for your crimes. Driver!"

The yell that stemmed from Fitzwilliam's frustrations was like a wounded wolf. He turned back to me, his teeth bared and his eyes blazing. He said not a word as he got up onto his horse and left.

"Should you not go after him?" Dr. Darrington asked me.

I shook my head. "Our biggest priority now is to get Marcella from here quickly."

The moment there was even the slightest darkness, she had to go.

Aphrodite

She was to be dressed in my clothes and her hair hidden under a hood. Evander had explained the plan, and all of us were now eager as the sun set. I had never been involved with such a plot before. My heart raced as we waited for her to say good-bye to her father upstairs. Evander nervously checked the windows every so often, and unlike the night before, the air was still.

"It is time," he said.

I nodded, going to leave the room, but Dr. Darrington came in. "She is in the garden."

"Did I not say to remain in the house?" Evander demanded angrily.

"She is with her father. There is a commemorative for her mother and brother there."

Evander sighed and turned to go, and all I could do was follow suit. Luckily, we saw the small, white-haired, slightly hunched, almost breath-deprived older man who was Mr. Wildingham reentering the house with Marcella. Quickly, I moved to help him back in.

"Did I not tell you to remain inside?" Evander said to Marcella. "We must go—now."

"My father."

"Go . . ." The old man coughed as I held him. "My . . . dear, go."

She rushed to hug the man once more before Evander gave her his arm. Under the darkness of night, she was to pretend she was me, with none of her skin or hair showing and wearing my clothes. People would believe it, as who else would be on Evander's arm? From there, she would switch carriages with whomever Evander had arranged to take her.

"Remain here," he whispered to me. "I shall fetch you the moment it is done."

I nodded quickly. "Go."

I helped Mr. Wildingham as they walked toward the front door to our waiting carriage.

Never had I been so nervous, watching them prepare to depart, when all of a sudden, I heard what sounded like thunder crack outside.

But it was not thunder.

I watched the horses in front buck in fear and Evander, by the door, fall to the ground!

"Evander," I screamed, rushing to the door.

Across from him, with a pistol in his hand, was Fitzwilliam.

"I knew it," the wretch said as he rushed to Evander.

"Evander?" I called and rolled him onto his side, blood escaping the corner of his mouth. *"Evander!"*

"Ummm." He groaned, and I gasped out. "What happened?"

The answer to his question came as we heard screaming.

"Let go!"

I glanced up to see Marcella now being pulled by the hair away from us.

Fitzwilliam shook her violently. "Shut up! Do you not know the trouble you have caused me?"

"Stop—" My voice cut off as he held the pistol on us once more.

"You're still alive, Evander? Exactly how many lives do you have?" he hollered as Evander tried to sit up. "I should end you right here, right now, and be done with this for good."

"And then no one will let you off for murder," Evander sneered.

"Then our war continues, little brother. But now, when I bring her before all the town and expose you to be a liar, who shall believe you?" He pulled tighter on Marcella's hair. "I will tell them you sought to steal her from me. That this was all a wicked plot to ruin me, and they shall believe it!"

"*Let go!*" Marcella cried again.

"*I said, shut up!*" He nearly brought her to her knees as he pulled her to his horse. "Or would you rather be the reason your benefactors met such a horrid fate? You dare lie about me? Your husband—"

Once more, that sound, like the crack of a whip and thunder in the sky, echoed through the night. Evander covered me, throwing us back down onto the ground.

"Are you all right?" he asked, checking me over even though blood was upon his face, not mine. "Aphrodite, are you all right!"

"Yes," I said quickly. "Are you?"

He nodded, but then where had the bullet landed? I sat up, worried Fitzwilliam had in his anger shot Marcella, but she sat on the ground in stunned silence and beside her was Fitzwilliam. Both of us confused, we rose to see a stunned Dr. Darrington standing at the door, not looking at us, but at the window. There stood the feeble Mr. Wildingham with a gun pointed directly at where Fitzwilliam had stood.

"What have you done?" Dr. Darrington was now running toward where the man bled upon the ground.

"Fitzwilliam?" Evander whispered, eyes wide, slowly walking forward. I grabbed him as he made his way to him.

I saw blood everywhere. Dr. Darrington knelt over him, seeking to save him, but even I knew such a thing was not possible. Fitzwilliam looked up at Evander, and Evander back down at him.

"Little . . . brother . . . why?" Fitzwilliam spat out with the last of his breath and blood.

Trembling, my hand covered my mouth.

34

Aphrodite

At the funeral of Mr. Fitzwilliam Topwells were six people—the clergyman, Datura, Evander, and me, along with two drivers, one for each of our carriages. No one else dared come. The town was overjoyed to see the villain I had exposed slain, and even more that it had been done by the father of the young heroine they thought lost but was now close to freedom in France. Verity had refused to come. Evander had sent word to his youngest brother, but he would not arrive back in time. The war between Evander and Fitzwilliam had come to an end the same way all wars did—in blood and death. And Evander did not celebrate. He did not smile. He had long sought to bring Fitzwilliam to justice but was not pleased, and I could finally understand why. Despite how much he hated the man and how much Fitzwilliam had wronged him, he was still Evander's elder brother, a person also cursed by their father's actions.

"What more of a price must I pay?" Datura whispered, looking truly low. It was the first I had ever seen her not in jewels or silks. Nor was her face covered in powders or hair styled with curls and wigs. She looked common and meager. She glanced at us tiredly. "Was seeking better for myself so wrong? From beginning to end, you have done all one could to remind me of my place in this world, and when I refused, you take my son? Who is the villain here? It is you. All of you."

Evander inhaled once and then looked at her. I thought he would fight her on those remarks. But instead, he bowed his head once to her. "May God be with you during this difficult time."

With that, he took my hand and led me to the carriage. He did not look at her again, and neither did I. Her cries and her sobs filled the air, and any sight of her would have been heartbreaking.

"Drive on," Evander called out, gripping my hand tightly. I lifted it to my lips and kissed the back of his hand. "This was not how I wished it to end."

"I know."

"Your father was right. I ought to have settled things before marrying you, as I have only shown you the horrors of the world," he said bitterly, shaking his head.

"You have not," I replied. "I promise, you have not."

"From now on, it shall be just you and me," he said, gently placing his other hand upon my own. "Evander and Aphrodite."

"Aphrodite and Evander," I said with a smile to tease him, to get his mind off darker thoughts.

"Why would your name be first? That is not how tales go."

"Alphabetical order? Do you prefer Aphrodite and the duke?"

He chuckled and then hugged me. "I see, just as your father seeks to tease your mother, you seek to tease me."

I could not wait for a quieter future with him. Closing my eyes, I felt I could rest for days. He kissed the top of my head gently.

"My love, we are here," he said.

When I opened my eyes, we were already home. "That was quick."

"It was not so far. Shall they see you holding me like this?" he teased. I glared and released him to adjust myself, but he leaned in and kissed the side of my cheek, whispering in my ear, "I am also glad we did not listen to your father and wait to be married, for having you beside me has been the greatest solace."

I smiled but said nothing as the doors opened for us. He helped me out first, and when I looked upon Everely, I was reminded that though our days were to be less dramatic, I still had so much to do here. This was just the closing of a chapter.

"Welcome back, Your Graces," Mr. Wallace said as we entered.

"Thank you. Where is Emeline? I should go to her."

"With her nanny, Your Grace."

I turned to Evander, and he merely nodded.

Evander

Little brother, why? Fitzwilliam had asked me. Those were his last words to me, and now, days later, I looked up at the answer to his question.

My father's portrait, painted to be fierce and wise, surrounded by books and draped in finery. He was puffed and proud, severe in his brutality, but wise, he was not. What would all of our lives have been like had he been a man of greater honor? I wondered if Fitzwilliam and I could have been as true brothers had we not been pitted against each

other, had he been the firstborn of my mother and not his.
Had I ever even called him brother? Whenever he had called
me *his* little brother, I thought he attempted to mock me, to
remind me that he was the one who should have inherited
this damned title. But at that moment, when he stared up at
me, he had not appeared to be mocking. He had looked as sor-
rowful as I was, as though he were wondering all these same
things as well.

Why?

I had wished him gone, punished, but never did I wish him
dead. I'd never believed this would be the end, and it felt . . .
gutting, not relieving. The pain had not been removed, and I
could not bear to look upon this portrait any longer.

"Take it down," I muttered as I lifted my brandy to my lips.

"Your Grace?" Wallace looked confused.

"My father's portrait, take it down. Then have it burned," I
ordered.

"Your Grace—"

"Do it!"

"Yes, Your Grace. I will see to it," he said before excusing
himself.

I would have all of his paintings burned. His whole legacy,
I would see it forgotten, for he did not deserve to be remembered. This misery he wrought should never be passed to another generation. Let the curse end here, with Fitzwilliam's
death and my sorrow.

"Evander?"

Verity stood in the doorway, exhaustion on her face. I was
sure the events of the past few days would cause more nightmares.

"You have not gone to bed?" I asked. She shook her head.

"I am going to now, but I wish to tell you . . . I am sorry I could not go to the funeral with you." Verity hung her head. "Part of me wanted to. A great part of me did not."

"I felt the same. Had Aphrodite not spoken to me this morning I very well would not have either," I confessed.

"Are we . . . cruel, brother?" she asked with a deep frown upon her face. "Despite his actions he was kin to us. And his life, the earlier half at least, was inequitable. He did not choose the circumstances of his birth. He did not choose to be born illegitimate."

I did not know how to answer her, as I had just been reflecting on the same injustice.

"Society must have order and even if we dislike it or find it cumbersome we must adhere to it and do our best to be honorable nevertheless. That is where Fitzwilliam failed, not in his birth."

After all, the world was filled with bastards but they did not all cause chaos and misery in their wake.

"I understand," she said but did not look satisfied with my response.

But what else could I say? We were not cruel, society was?

"Will you be all right, or will you remain here, drinking?" she questioned.

"If my wife is not complaining, I do not see why you should," I said. "You need not worry about me so, Verity. I am well. Truly. You may focus on your own happiness now. Do you still think ill of marriage?"

"No," she replied. "But I shall leave before you start on this. Good night."

She hurried from the room as if she feared the topic. Did she not plan on marrying? Then again, I'd rather not have her rush, either. I glanced once more at the portrait before leaving the room. I would not fault myself for this. As tragic as this whole ordeal was, I was finally free of the shackles of my father and brother. There was no point lamenting now.

I was not sure where to go, but found myself wandering, and upon doing so, I found Aphrodite with Emeline in her arms as she sat out upon the patio, fanning the little girl now asleep.

"It seems no one can sleep but her," I whispered as I stepped out.

She glanced at me and smiled slightly. "Yes, but that is a good thing, is it not?"

It was, for it meant none of this had affected her, that she was still ignorant to the truth. "I hope this is always kept from her so she may be innocent of it."

"I fear I have ruined that," she whispered as I sat down opposite them. "I fear the talk of the town has become even more twisted and some question—"

"As long as I treat her as my daughter, she is my daughter," I said, placing my hand upon Emeline's head. "And I shall do so all my life. No matter what anyone says, she has me, and now you, I see. I doubt you shall allow such attacks upon her person. You went so far for a girl you barely knew. I fear you will be worse than your mother."

"I will not be worse." She huffed but did not declare she would be better. It was amusing. Leaning in to her, I rested my head against hers. "You were drinking."

"I was."

"Are you all right?"

"I shall be," I whispered, closing my eyes and inhaling the scent of her. "As long as you are here, I shall be."

"Then I shall be here," she replied. "'One word frees us of all the weight and pain in life. That word is love.'"

I lifted my head. "Have you become a poet, or have you stolen from a philosopher again?"

"I do not steal, merely borrow."

"And from whom did you borrow that?"

"Sophocles."

I shook my head. "To think you know all of this, and you did not know what the word *aroused* meant."

Her face contorted as she fought between her desire to yell at me and to hide her embarrassment. I could not help but laugh.

"It is not my fault! My papa obstructed words and definitions he deemed inappropriate for a lady."

"And now you know far more than I bet he would wish." I grinned, enjoying teasing her as much.

She smacked my shoulder, but when I winced, she gasped. "Sorry!"

"It is fine."

She checked just to make sure, allowing me to admire her face and to appreciate this moment—her here with me.

"This spring has been one like I never thought possible," she said.

It felt like years had come to pass, not mere weeks. My life had changed so drastically that I found it hard to believe.

"This spring, no, this moment, here with you, is what I always dreamed," I replied and she turned to look at me. Leaning over, I kissed her forehead. "My duchess, my wife, my Aphrodite."

"My Duke, my husband, my Evander."

EPILOGUE

～◎

Aphrodite

My Dearest Papa and Mama,

Forgive me for not writing sooner, as I meant to upon receiving all of your letters at once. However, as you have often said, Mama, I did not find the time, despite many attempts. I know not where to begin to tell of the events that have taken place since I arrived at Everely. But I am sure I need not explain it all as some word must have already reached you both. Whatever you have heard, worry not, for Evander and I have weathered the storm. We are much stronger and better for it—

"Evander!" I giggled as he kissed the side of my face. "You are going to make me mess up my letter."

"Forget the letter," he muttered into my ear.

"I must finish and send them. I have been quite neglectful of my family. I am certain the only reason they have not found a reason to visit is Hathor's desire to remain in London." I looked over my words, but was still greatly distracted by Evander's arms around me.

"Very well." He sighed dramatically and released me as he stood straighter. Instantly, I missed the warmth of his embrace.

"If only to prevent your father from throwing his books at me when we see them."

I grinned, glancing up at him. "My father greatly reveres books. He would never throw those. If anything, he would most likely throw stones."

"And you smile at this for what reason?" he questioned, cupping my face. "My dear, sweet wife, if stones were to fly, it would fall on you to defend me."

I huffed. "From where did such a rule come?"

"Nature." He kissed my forehead. "Husband trumps father. Thus, I am your greatest priority."

I fought the urge to roll my eyes and opened my mouth to speak, when there was a knock at the door.

"Enter," I said. I expected to see Eleanor; instead it was Emeline's head that poked inside and she looked directly at her father.

"Now?" she asked.

Evander's face was hard to read as he quickly moved over to her.

"Did we not say lunch?" he asked her.

"That is now," she replied.

"I meant while at lunch. When we eat."

"What is it?" I asked, not liking how I was utterly at a loss to their conversation. They both turned their heads to me.

"We can wait till after you finish your letter," Evander said.

"Later. What is going on?" I asked. "Have you been plotting something without me?"

Emeline nodded and Evander shook his head.

"I see. Well, no good plot is ever done without me," I said, rising from my chair.

"Since when?" Evander's eyebrow rose.

"Now. Emeline, will you tell me?" I stretched out my hand

to her and she came quickly. I noticed the box in her hands. "What is this?"

"Papa and I bought it for you." She lifted it up for me to see.

"Me?" I looked to Evander, but he just smiled and nodded for me to open it. Doing so revealed a pair of silk gloves embroidered with roses. "They are beautiful, thank you."

"Papa gave me the same ones." Emeline stared up at me for a moment before adding, "So . . . now we will look the same in town, *Mama*."

My heart stopped. That word echoed in my mind. Slowly, I glanced up at Evander, but I could not see him clearly on account of the blurriness of my vision. Though I did notice him nodding at me. Swallowing the lump in my throat, I bent down before Emeline, brushing her curls gently.

"How marvelous, sweetheart," I tried not to cry as I looked over her face. "I love them dearly, and we must wear them at once for all to see."

"Right now?" she asked with a grin.

"Of course. My daughter gave me gloves; everyone must see them!"

"Let me get mine, Mama!" she said and rushed to the door. I'd teach her not to run later; today she could do whatever she pleased.

"She wanted to say it for a while now, but was a bit nervous," Evander said. "I thought we'd agreed to do it over a picnic, but as you see, she could not wait a second longer."

It was one word.

"Are you that happy?" he asked as a tear fell from my eye.

It was one little word but it meant more to me than any philosopher or writer in the world.

"Madly so."

ACKNOWLEDGMENTS

This is the part where I thank the amazing people who helped bring this book to light. My editor, Shauna Summers, as well as Mae Martinez and the entire wonderful team at Random House, my agent, Natanya Wheeler, and my parents, thank you. To the teams of people behind my beautiful book cover, and to those who helped share this story everywhere, thank you. I truly could not have done this without any of you.

That said I believe my deepest gratitude is owed to romance. Yes, the whole genre of romance because without it I am sure I would be a miserable and lonely person.

So Dear Romance,

Thank you for making me smile on days I thought I would cry. Thank you for giving me hope when everything felt hopeless. Thank you for allowing me to dream while still awake. Thank you for the book boyfriends I wish were real. Thank you for existing and thus allowing the characters in my soul to exist as well. I am eternally grateful.

Your biggest fan,
J.J.

COURTESY OF THE AUTHOR

J. J. MCAVOY has written numerous independently published novels. Her books have been translated into six languages and are bestsellers in Turkey, Israel, and France. She is active and delightful on social media.

jjmcavoy.com
Twitter: @JJMcAvoy
Instagram: @jjmcavoy